LILIAN'S SPELL BOOK

TOBY LITT

Printed in the United Kingdom by Alphabetical

First Publication as an Ebook, 2017

www.tobylitt.com

ISBN 978-1-9998021-0-3

About the Author

Toby Litt was born in Bedford, England, and grew up in Ampthill, Bedfordshire. He is the author of numerous novels including *Corpsing*, *deadkidsongs* and *Ghost Story*. He is a *Granta* Best of Young British Novelist.

Toby won the Manchester Fiction Prize and was shortlisted for the Sunday Times EFG Private Bank Short Story Award.

His book, *Free Country: The Children's Crusade,* co-written with Neil Gaiman, was a *New York Times* Bestselling Graphic Novel.

Praise for Toby Litt:

'Toby Litt is awfully good—he gives something new every time he writes.' - Muriel Spark

Adventures in Capitalism – 'the most exciting young talent on the literary scene' – *Independent*

Beatniks – 'A great book' – *Literary Review*

Corpsing – 'a first-rate thriller' – Muriel Spark

deadkidsongs – 'Should put Toby Litt firmly and deservedly in the big league' – *Daily Telegraph*

Exhibitionism – 'Serious entertainment of the highest order' – *Guardian*

Finding Myself – 'Entertaining, inventive and original – *Literary Review*

Ghost Story – 'Agonising, innovative and very moving' – *Esquire*

Hospital – 'Litt has created an extraordinarily vivid comic nightmare, an apocalyptic vision for our own weird times' – *Guardian*

I play the drums in a band called okay – 'It's like he's been hiding under the bed in hotel rooms, in the corner of rehearsal rooms, in the toilets in bars, in the darkest corners of our minds, listening all the time. Spooky!' – Peter Hook, New Order

Journey into Space – 'One of the most inventive and original writers around' – *Sunday Mirror*

King Death – 'Litt has honed a storytelling formula that laces plots with sinister tensions' – *Time Out*

Life-Like – 'quite an important addition to the unimportant world of short stories' – *Guardian*

Mutants: Selected Essays – This is a collection you should read if you are interested in literature, in reading it or writing it' – *BRSBKBLOG*

About the Book

Lilian's Spell Book is a thrilling and intimate paranormal adventure novel about an ordinary English family – mother, father, pre-teen son, baby daughter – who inherit an extraordinary house. They move to this vast Elizabethan mansion in rural Sussex from their small South London maisonette. Very soon, they all find out their new home is haunted. But it is the mother of the family, Jeane Jonson, who begins to suspect that the secret to the house lies in the Elizabethan portrait that hangs in a gallery just off the vast entrance hall – a glittering, gorgeous oil painting showing the proud, red-haired Lilian holding in her hand a small leather-bound book. But the real wonders start when the narrator discovers the book itself, in the secret library of the mansion. Lilian's father was an alchemist…

In the very heart of the fire

I could see it clearly – there stood a figure. I thought for one mad moment that it must be my husband, and that he must be burning to death. But the figure stood there, quite calm, quite still, completely unaffected by the furnace-like blaze surrounding them. I could see them through the open doorway that, for some reason, wasn't burning. The fire did not come that far.

Perhaps I should be clearer. This was not a figure made of flames. This was the outline of a figure where the bright flames left a darker gap. And the gap went all the way to the bricks of the far wall. It was almost as if there were a person-shaped tunnel running through the whole infernal room, from front to back. And there was nothing there to burn, I was sure. This room of our house was totally empty. It was the air itself that seemed to be on fire.

The light from the burning room scorched into the backs of my eyes. How long before the fire spread? How long before our beautiful old wooden dreamhouse was razed to the ground? But still I didn't turn and run. Still I stared into the light.

I knew this figure. With every passing second, I was surer of that.

I knew her, and I knew she had a message for me.

As I watched, she put her left hand out and beckoned me towards her. Of course she was left-handed! – I'd known that all along.

It was madness but I felt certain that she wouldn't let me come to harm. It was a while since I had started to trust her. But did I trust her enough to trust her with my life?

Of course I hesitated. Nobody wants want to die like this. Nobody wants to be burnt alive. What I was about to do was against all reason.

Reason, though, was something I had given up on or which had given up on me quite some time before.

I nodded to her.

The figure beckoned me again.

I moved forwards, to the edge of the flames.

I could see her better now. My eyes seemed to be getting used to the bright light. Was that a smile I could make out among the flames?

With a final thought for my husband, my children, I stepped over the threshold – into the heart of the burning room.

PART ONE

Chapter 1.

It's the sort of thing that only happens in books – a relative you haven't thought about for years dies, their solicitors track you down, you're called to a small, incredibly old-fashioned office and told you own a house you never even knew existed.

If it hadn't happened to us, I really wouldn't have believed it. But the solicitors were called Gibbons & Jump, and their old-fashioned office was at 17 Winchester Road, Worthing, and Peter and I went there for ten thirty on a Tuesday morning in May – taking baby Mary with us and leaving my parents to entertain six year-old Jack.

I breastfed Mary in the car before we went upstairs. She slept in my arms for most of the meeting, which lasted just under an hour. That was how long it took to change our lives completely.

The dead relative, Michael Francis Jonson, was a great uncle of Peter's on his father's side. That part of Peter's family seemed to enjoy falling out over things, especially religious things. Michael Francis had been Catholic, and had taken it all extremely seriously. So much so that he refused to leave his house to anyone who wasn't of the old faith. But most of his family was either wishy-washy Protestants or nothing much at all. (Michael Francis never got round to having children himself.) Even though Peter hadn't been a practicing Catholic for years, he had gone through the rigmarole of conversion while at university. He said it was because he found the whole thing very glamorous, silly idiot. So, when Michael Francis Jonson decided he needed an heir, he had ordered his solicitors to search out one who was a proper Catholic, and Peter, I suppose, was the best they could come up with.

'You don't have a photograph?' asked Peter, after Mr. Gibbon broke the news. Mr. Gibbon didn't look like a gibbon. He looked like a grizzled chimpanzee.

'I think you should go and see it for yourself,' said Mr. Gibbon. 'Then you can make up your mind about taking on the responsibilities, etcetera. It's about half an hour from here. You could be back by teatime.'

I could tell this was the kind of office where teatime was still held sacred. Four o'clock, and not a minute after.

There was a silence.

'Who gets it if we don't take it?' I asked.

'The taxman,' replied Mr. Gibbon, as if Peter and not me had asked the question. 'Mr. Jonson would die intestate.'

If we took the house, he said, we would have to sign some papers, and agree to bring up any children of our own as Catholics – otherwise they'd be disinherited and lose the house, or any money from the sale of it. Also, we couldn't just auction off the whole kit and caboodle.

The solicitor explained, very carefully, that this last bit was binding. 'You will not be able take *anything* out of the house for the purpose of selling it – the furniture, paintings, even the crockery. It is all part of the estate, and must be maintained by you. Paintings can be loaned for exhibition, if they are properly insured. The building itself, of course, cannot be sold. Nor the land it is build upon. Nor any of the surrounding acreage. Either you own it, as the heirs of Mr. Jonson, or it passes to the state. The same conditions will apply to your children. However, there are outbuildings, some garages, a garden shed, and the same strictures do not apply to these properties and their contents as to the main house.'

'Oh good,' said Peter, 'so we can sell the lawnmower.'

'I am merely relating the terms of the will,' said Mr. Gibbon.

'I am merely saying that we can sell the lawnmower,' said Peter. He was never able to take official people all that seriously. That was one of the reasons I loved him like I did.

'I believe there is a lawnmower,' said Mr. Gibbon. 'And it would of course be yours to sell – though that might leave the gardener in some difficulties.'

'Could we rent the house out, and live somewhere else?' I asked.

'No,' said Mr. Gibbon. 'That is explicitly forbidden.'

Then he handed Peter the keys and a piece of paper with the address.

'You'll find an inventory of the contents in the middle drawer of the desk in Mr. Jonson's study, rear room, left hand side.'

'There's no alarm?' Peter asked.

'No,' said Mr. Gibbon. 'It's all rather old-fashioned.' Which was rich, coming from him.

As soon as we were out on the street, Peter said, 'I don't like the bit about Mary and Jack having to be Catholic.' It was a sunny morning. People whose lives were still the same walked past us with shopping bags in their hands.

The key was nothing special – just a dull brass Yale attached by a steel ring to a fob of new leather.

Peter held it up next to his ear and shook it like a bell.

'I'm trying to hear money,' he said.

I looked at him properly for the first time in a while. Blue eyes. Stubble. He was a bit of a scamp – could never get his dark hair to sit down properly. When we'd started going out I'd thought he was very attractive, but that I was the only person to see it. It wasn't that Peter was the greatest looker; it was the energy he had inside him. Turns out, I wasn't the *only* person to see it. At least one other did.

'This is fun,' I said, trying to clear those sad thoughts out of my head.

Chapter 2.

My name is Jeane Jonson.

I'm an ordinary woman and I have an ordinary family, at least that's what I thought. We lived ordinary, happy, suburban lives – in Tulse Hill, South London. Peter had his own business, creating and maintaining financial software for small companies. As for me, before I had the children, I'd been a schoolteacher at a primary school. I intended to go back part-time as soon as Mary was in nursery. We couldn't afford for me not to work. We weren't rich. We were as normal as normal gets. This inherited house was the first extraordinary thing that had even happened to us. Even Peter's affair had been perfectly normal.

With the traffic, the drive took more than twice the half hour Mr. Gibbon had promised. Almost as soon as we started, Peter had to pull over so I could get in the back. Mary had woken up, and wouldn't stop crying. She calmed down when she felt me beside her, and we set off again. Luckily, Peter had recently put Sat Nav in our car, so finding the village was easy. We had the postcode, and the solicitor had told us to follow the road down past the church. This went on for about a mile, only wide enough for one car, and with tall beech trees on either side. Here was where Mary decided to fall asleep again. She's a very good baby – typical second child. Or at least the kind of second child everyone hopes for.

The road ended at a pair of tall black metal gates, beyond which was a gravel track curving round to the left. The gates were open.

Peter stopped the car and turned off the engine.

'What are you waiting for?' I said.

'I need a moment or two,' he said.

'Don't be so melodramatic.'

'I'm just preparing myself for the full horror. It probably doesn't even have a roof.'

'Then we'll get a roof put on. Anyway, Mr. Gibbon said there were paintings – and they wouldn't just leave paintings open to the rain.'

Peter was silent for a moment. 'I don't want to force the children into anything that's not good for them, Jeane. Not just for the sake of money.'

'Of course,' I said. 'If we don't like it, we don't take it. Now, drive.'

He started the engine.

The track curved round to the left, then to the right, then left again. A thick wood surrounded us. Trees high over our heads made the inside of the car quite dark.

And then, without warning, the house was on top of us. Peter had to do an emergency stop, and the tyres skidded on the gravel. He pulled up a few inches short of a green garage door.

In front of the house there were only a couple of parking spaces, nothing more. No grand drive down an arcade of trees. The trees were growing very close, all around the tall two-storey building.

The jolt had woken Mary, who started to do her worst kind of cry. I picked her out of her backwards-facing car seat and cuddled her. She was three months old but chubbing up nicely. I was pleased about that. Jack had been just the same. They took after me, that was for certain.

'Oh my God,' I said.

'Wow,' said Peter.

'Look at it,' I said. 'It's a stately home.'

'It is a bit over-the-top,' said Peter. He was looking up at the black beams and white plaster of the building, and the diamond patterning in the glass of all the tall, narrow windows. This house *definitely* had a roof – with bells on. Three bells.

'No decisions yet,' I said. 'Let's go inside.'

To the sound of Mary's screams, Peter put the key in the lock and turned it.

Even with a hard shove, the door wouldn't open.

'There's another lock,' said Peter.

He pushed the door at top and bottom.

'Down there,' he said, pointing. 'I can't see anything on the outside.' Peter stepped back. 'There isn't even a deadlock.'

'Perhaps there's another door,' I said.

'But this is the *front* door, and Mr. Gibbon said the *front* door. And this key was the right one.'

'Well, maybe someone's in there.'

'Who?' asked Peter.

'Let's find out,' I said.

If the house key wasn't impressive, the doorknocker certainly was. It was shaped like the beak of a brass griffin, and when I let it slam home Mary – who had just quieted down a little – started screaming again.

'Let me,' said Peter, and banged on the door for a deafening minute.

Then we spent another minute stepping back from the house and squinting towards the upper windows. They were all of them closed, and it was only in my imagination that I saw anything moving behind them.

'I'll have a look round,' said Peter. 'See if there is another way in.'

He took the key from the door and started off round the right-hand side of the house.

I cradled Mary gently on my shoulder, stroking her back and telling her everything was all right. If she kept on crying, it meant I couldn't try knocking on the door again – which I was going to, even though Peter wasn't with me anymore.

It had been sunny on the road but the air around the house was very cold. The tall trees put it in a deep wind-shadow. The place had the still, secluded atmosphere of a pond waiting for its surface to be broken. Nowhere in London ever felt like this, and nothing in my life did, either.

I turned to go back to the car, and just then the front door cracked open.

'That was quick,' I said. But when I turned round, I didn't see Peter.

The door was ajar by only an inch or so, a long line of darkness down its right-hand side.

'Yes,' said a female voice.

'We've come to see the house,' I said.

'Well, you can't see the house,' said the voice.

'Yes, we can,' I said. 'We're the new owners.'

The door slammed shut. I heard a chain rattle and tap against the wood. The door opened wide.

'Hello,' said a woman of around fifty-five, stepping out into the dim light. 'I'm Mrs. Forster. I do the housekeeping. I'm sorry, I wasn't expecting you.'

'We've come straight from the solicitors,' I said.

Mrs. Forster stepped closer. 'And who is this little darling?'

'Mary,' I said.

'And how old?'

'Thirteen weeks,' I said. 'And a half.'

'Oh, so young. What a sweetie.'

It's hard not to be disarmed when people are nice about your children. Mrs. Forster had short, wavy brown hair that managed to shine even without sunlight to strike it. She was wearing what I'd call country clothes – a green cardigan over a cream shirt, tweedy skirt, green stockings and slippers.

'I heard you knock the first time – I have very good hearing. But I was quite a long way away. Are you on your own?'

'No,' I said. 'My husband is looking for another way in.'

'Oh, he won't find one,' said Mrs. Forster. 'The house is quite secure.'

'There's no back door, then?'

'There are several other doors but none of them are used.'

Mrs. Forster was trying to intimidate me, by speaking very properly.

'He'll come back,' I said. 'Once he's gone the whole way round.'

'Oh, no. He can't do that. There's a path one way but the woods come right up to the wall on the other side.'

Mrs. Forster pointed towards the trees behind the garages. They were certainly dense.

'We'll go through the house,' she said, 'and try to catch him in the garden.'

I was reluctant to cross the threshold without Peter beside me. Not that I'm particularly superstitious. I'm not funny about ladders or broken mirrors or black cats. But, if this was going to be our new home, I wanted to enter it together. I was slightly annoyed that Jack wasn't there, too. We did almost everything as a whole family.

'Follow me,' said Mrs. Forster, and went into the dark hallway.

After a moment more of hesitation, I obeyed – entering that strangest of places for the very first time.

My first impressions weren't unpleasant. The hall was vast, with a double staircase zigzagging up at the far end. It smelt powerfully of wood and wood polish. The walls were done in tight, oblong panels, right up to the high ceiling where there hung, yes, a real chandelier. Not a crystal one. It, too, was made of wood.

Mrs. Forster switched on the lights and I was dazzled. Everything shone back at me. Jack would love this, sliding around in socks on the parquet. And I would spend my life expecting to fall over and crack a hip. Mrs. Forster certainly knew how to polish.

'I don't waste the electricity when I'm just by myself,' she said. 'This way.'

There were two wooden doors directly in front of us. They went underneath the stairways, which zagged out and then back in again to meet in the middle. Mrs. Forster turned the gleaming brass handle on the left-hand door and passed through. Over her shoulders, I could see daylight. It took us a little while to reach it, though. First there was a longish hallway, also wood-paneled, and with paintings in the dark on either side. Then there was a small cloakroom. Beyond that was a huge sitting room. I only had time to take in a very large and ornate fireplace to my right and, to my left, a grand piano. Heavy tapestry curtains hid the far wall – a bit moth-eaten, perhaps. There were some holes where beams of light shone through. Mrs. Forster was about to pull them back when a furious rattling started behind them.

'That must be him,' said Mrs. Forster, completely unfazed. I couldn't say the same for myself.

She pushed aside the left-hand curtain. As it started to catch the light, I saw that it was a tapestry inlaid with golden thread. I recognized from the crab, the scorpion and the pair of little boys that it must be the signs of the zodiac.

Peter's face moved back from the window, but not before I'd seen his mouth give a little gasp of surprise, or perhaps fear.

Mrs. Forster had now moved this curtain as far as it could go, and was walking across to push the other.

I carried Mary towards the brighter light. Beyond the glass was a beautiful walled garden with an ornamental fountain in the middle and rosebushes around the far edges. This was the moment I decided we should definitely move in.

'Look,' I said to Mary, and turned her round to see. 'Daddy.'

He came up close to the glass and made a funny face at Mary, then caught sight of Mrs. Forster beside me.

'Hello,' he shouted.

'Come in the front way,' I shouted, pointing with my finger.

As Peter walked away from the window, I saw that the elbows of his best suit were bright green and the soles of his best shoes were spattered with mud.

We went back through the house to meet him. It took him longer than I expected for him to arrive – but, finally, there he was.

'This is Mrs. Forster,' I said, as he came into view. 'The housekeeper.'

'Not really,' she started to say. 'I live in the village – '

But Peter had stepped into the house and, without meaning to, had made two muddy footprints on the spotless floor.

Mrs. Forster looked down in dismay.

'Never mind,' she said.

Peter apologized, and took off his shoes. The two footprints he left behind were very clear – like footprints in a cartoon.

'Would you like me to show you around?'

'Yes,' said Peter, at the same moment as I said, 'No.' It wasn't that I disliked Mrs. Forster, or found her creepy, it was just that I thought it would be fun exploring the house, rather than being given a guided tour.

Peter looked at me, then said, 'I think we'll find our own way round.'

'It is quite big,' said Mrs. Forster. 'And there's lots of nooks and crannies you'd never find without someone pointing them out.'

'Next time,' said Peter. 'Do you come every week?'

'I come every day of the week. You wouldn't believe the amount of work there is.'

'Well, it looks spotless,' said Peter.

Mrs. Forster couldn't help but glance at the muddy footprints.

'When are you thinking of moving in?' said Mrs. Forster.

'We're not sure that we will,' I said.

'What?' Mrs. Forster said. 'And leave this place empty? You can't do that. It's such a beautiful house. And such a good home for a family. There's the countryside…' She seemed baffled we were even considering living elsewhere.

'We probably will,' said Peter, not wanting to upset her.

'Let's have a look around first,' I said. 'Come on – I'll show you the living room.'

Peter smiled at Mrs. Forster then followed me through the left-hand door beneath the stairs. Once we were out of earshot, he said, 'Why didn't you want the old dear to show us around? She can probably tell us a load of the history.'

I explained about wanting us to explore, together, and Peter seemed to understand. The more nice things we did together, the better.

He stood in the middle of the room, which was about as big as a tennis court. 'Can you imagine us living here?' he asked.

I looked around. 'We'll have to get some Irish wolfhounds,' I said. 'And, when we've finished feasting on mutton, we can throw them the bones over our shoulders.'

'I've always wanted to do that,' said Peter. 'No, really. I have.'

'It's such a big fireplace,' I said.

We went over to look at it. Mary was dozing on my shoulder. There was a large coat of arms front and centre. It contained lions, gryffins, dragons and stars, all intricately carved in bright stone.

'No,' I said, 'I can't imagine us living here. I think it would change us. Not straight away. To begin with, we'd probably camp out like intruders. But, if we ever got used to it, we'd be very different people.'

Peter took a last look around. 'That we would.'

A whooshing sound suddenly came from directly above our heads. It took me a moment to realize that it was Mrs. Forster doing the hoovering.

Off to the left of the sitting room was a study with a big desk, a Windsor chair and several filing cabinets that I guessed were full of Michael Francis Jonson's papers. One wall was covered with trophy heads of animals: deers, wild boar, even a zebra; the other was dominated by a large map of the house and grounds.

'We're going to take it, though,' said Peter. 'Aren't we?'

I didn't reply, but walked back across the living room and through the opposite doorway. This was the library. It didn't contain any paperbacks, that's for certain.

'These must be worth something,' said Peter. 'We'll have to have everything valued.'

'But the solicitors said we can't sell anything from inside the house.'

'If we're going to afford to do anything to the place, we'll have to find a way round that. Where else is the money going to come from?'

It was true. Since buying our house, we'd been able to keep up the mortgage payments but hadn't been able to take anything off the balance. If we sold it, we'd be left with only a few thousand pounds cash.

Back in the hallway, we found another couple of doors opposite one another. The first (on the left as you came through the front door) led to a kitchen and a small dining room. The other went directly into a more formal dining room, with another large fireplace and plenty of painted portraits.

'You must be related to some of these,' I said.

'All of them, probably.'

Most of those upon the walls were men. But there was a very striking woman with red-golden hair above the mantelpiece. I was drawn to go and look at her more closely. In the bottom corner of the canvas was a date, 1585. Her pose was rather stiff, and her clothes looked very ceremonial, but her face was full of life, full of passion. Her long slender fingers held a small leather-covered book – a red silk ribbon dangling down from between the pages.

'I wonder who she is,' I said.

'A Jonson,' said Peter. 'She has the Jonson nose.'

I looked, and it was true. Peter has what most people would call a Roman nose. It's not something you can miss. I always found it attractive, and thought it showed strength of character.

Looking up at the young woman, in all her spangly glory, I felt terribly frumpy. Not that I thought she'd looked like that in real life. I didn't have a portrait painter to flatter me, and iron out all the little imperfections. Jack would have told you that I was perfect, but then your children have to, don't they? I felt like I was starting to get back to my old self, physically, after having Mary. I'm quite petite, and I prefer to have my dark hair short and out of the way. My eyes are probably my best feature – chestnut brown. Not that I'm vain about them. I wish my legs were slightly longer, and my upper arms a little firmer. Overall, though, I haven't done too badly in the genetic lottery.

'Upstairs?' I said.

We could leave all this for later.

'Upstairs,' said Peter.

And already I was starting to think about how soon that later might be.

Chapter 3.

The two zigzag staircases brought you out on the same long landing. Directly beyond this was where Mrs. Forster was hoovering – a vast sitting room just as intimidating as the one downstairs. We didn't go in, just hovered in the doorway.

'That can be the playroom,' said Peter, which made me laugh.

Mrs. Forster looked up and tried to smile. It didn't really work, coming out as more of a grimace. She had turned against us when we'd decided not to take the guided tour.

Along to the right was a large bedroom with a four-poster bed.

'Imagine it,' I said.

Mary was now fast asleep, so I laid her down in the middle of the counterpane. She looked so incredibly small and vulnerable, even though I knew she hadn't started to roll yet, and so couldn't possibly make it to the edge.

Through a door on the left-hand wall was a bathroom and off that another what I suppose you'd call parlour. I don't know what they'd used it for when the house was built, but it looked as though Michael Francis Jonson more recently had it as his dressing room. There were two large wooden wardrobes and a chest of drawers. Peter opened them up, expecting to find them full of clothes. But they were totally empty. That was something to ask Mrs. Forster about, before we went.

'This could do for Jack's bedroom. And Mary's, when she moves out of ours.'

That wouldn't be for another three months, at least. For now, she slept in a cot at the foot of our very modest double bed in our very modest magnolia-painted bedroom. To tell the truth, I really didn't want to let go of her. Not because I feared cot death or anything like that, although I did think of it every evening as I did up the poppers on her babygrow, but because we were definitely stopping at two children, and when she moved out of our room, she'd stop being a real baby and start being a little girl. I wanted to postpone that change, just a while. I'd loved having babies so much.

Anxious, I went back into the master bedroom, where Mary slept blissfully on.

'*She* likes it here, anyway,' said Peter.

'Do you?' I asked.

'I think so,' he said. 'We haven't found any dark secrets yet, have we? Hold on.'

He disappeared back into the bathroom. I heard him turn the taps on in the sink and then the bathtub. Then the toilet flushed.

'All seems to be in working order,' he said when he came out.

'As if that would make a difference,' I said.

He smiled. 'Good plumbing is very important.'

'Now for the West Wing,' I said.

Here was another bedroom, not quite so grand and perhaps a little more cosy. There was another small bathroom and a room that was completely empty. Like the hallway downstairs, and like most of the other rooms, it was brightly wood-paneled.

The only unusual thing about it was a spiral staircase in the far corner, leading up to a door in the roof.

'Attic, I suppose,' said Peter. 'Want me to go and take a look?'

'You mean you want to take a look,' I said. 'Go on, then.'

He climbed up and around, but when he reached the top he discovered the door was locked. Something else to ask Mrs. Forster.

When Peter rejoined me, I asked him, 'Have we made a decision yet?'

Just then, the Hoover was switched off.

'Let's go into the garden,' he said. 'I want you to see it from there.'

We walked out onto the landing.

'Why?' I asked. 'Does it look as if it's about to fall down.'

'Not at all. That's the strange thing. It looks practically new.'

Finally, Peter had put his finger on it – the thing that had been troubling me all along. I knew this was a very old house, dating way back to Tudor times, but somehow it didn't feel old. And this despite having all the props familiar from TV dramas about Henry the Eighth and his poor, ill-fated wives – all the props except the suit of armour.

'Mmmm,' I said, which is what I say when I feel Peter has said it all. This doesn't happen more than once or twice a month.

We were just at the top of the stairs when Mrs. Forster came out of the upstairs sitting room, carrying a large cream-coloured Hoover of the sort I remembered my mother using. It looked more ancient than the carpet it had been cleaning – though still in very good condition.

'I'm going to start on the candlesticks now,' said Mrs. Forster. 'I usually gather them together in the kitchen. Will that be acceptable to you? There's food in, if you were thinking of lunch.'

'No,' I said. 'We'll be heading back, after we've had a look round the garden. I do have a couple of questions, though.'

'Yes,' said Mrs. Forster.

'Mr. Jonson's clothes,' I said. 'Where are they all?'

'He took them with him when he went,' said Mrs. Forster.

'Where did he go?'

'To the North Pole,' she said. 'Although he didn't make it. He died in Lapland.'

'But there's nothing left,' said Peter. 'Not even a sock.'

'No. He took every last scrap. It was very peculiar. As if he'd ever need spats in the Arctic Circle. Galoshes, maybe.'

This made me laugh a lot, although Mrs. Forster hadn't meant it as a joke. She was clearly upset at thinking of her old master.

'I'm sorry,' I said.

'You never met Mr. Jonson?' asked Mrs. Forster.

'Perhaps,' said Peter. 'When I was very small. I can't really remember it. I think I may have come here once before.'

'What?' I said, a little angry. 'You never mentioned that.'

'I didn't think I had,' he replied. 'But there's something in the garden. I'll show you.'

'Was there anything else?' asked Mrs. Forster.

'The key to the attic,' I said. 'Do you know where it is?'

Mrs. Forster pulled a large bunch of keys round from behind her back. 'They're all labelled,' she said. 'Mr. Jonson put labels on them before he went away.' She sobbed. 'He knew, you see. He knew he wasn't coming back. It was suicide.'

I didn't know Mrs. Forster well enough to hug her, and couldn't really manage it holding Mary, but I rubbed her upper arm and gave her a sad smile.

'He was fit and well, was he?' I asked.

'Perfectly,' she said, when she had recovered a little. 'Not a health problem at all. Not until he left. He shouldn't have left. It was just, he'd taken it into his head to see the wildlife of the Arctic.'

'Was he a kind man?' asked Peter.

'Very kind,' said Mrs. Forster. 'I never had a hard word out of him. Apart from on the subject of religion. He was very definite about that.'

It didn't seem the right time to press for details.

'Such a gentleman,' said Mrs. Forster, 'if you know what I mean.'

'Yes,' said Peter, awkwardly. That she had to ask him if he knew must suggest that *he* wasn't a gentleman.

I gave Mrs. Forster's arm one more squeeze and turned for the stairs.

'Such a dear little thing,' she said, touching Mary's hair. 'I hope she's happy here.'

'We have a son, too,' I said. 'Jack. He's six.'

'Wonderful,' said Mrs. Forster. 'Then the house will be safe for a long time.'

'We'll pop in before we leave,' said Peter.

'I think I may finish early today,' said Mrs. Forster. 'It's been a bit of a shock, if you don't mind me saying.'

'Of course not,' I said.

'I always leave the keys hanging on the brass hook in the kitchen,' said Mrs. Forster. 'You can't miss them.'

'Thank you,' said Peter.

We didn't say a word until we were out the front door. Midday beneath the tree cover seemed darker than the brightly illuminated hall.

'Put your foot in it there, didn't you?' said Peter.

'A hundred and four,' I said.

We started around the house. Because we now knew there was a path, we found our way quite easily, although it took us on a slightly winding route through the woods.

The garden was in full sunlight, and reminded me that it was still a gorgeous early summer day.

'What's the thing?' I asked.

'This,' said Peter, and pointed to a stone carving of a phoenix above the doors at the back of the house. It was brightly painted, red feathers, yellow eyes with black pupils, and was rising from a heap of ashes, which were grey. 'I remember it from when I was little. I think I used to have nightmares about it. It used to chase me. It was burning hot.'

'You might have seen another one, somewhere else.'

'Perhaps,' said Peter. 'But that one wouldn't've had my name written across the bottom of it.'

He pointed out the old-fashioned lettering, weaving in and out of the flames around the phoenix's feet.

'Could you read?' I ask.

'No,' said Peter. 'But I remember someone telling me.'

'Who?' I asked.

'An old man,' he said. 'A very old man.'

Mary was waking up. I knew I would have to feed her again, so we made our way over the twenty or so paces to a bench covered in green lichen. Ivy was growing up all four of its legs. It faced towards the house, and gave us a chance to sit back and assess the place.

'We'd be fools not to,' said Peter. 'I mean, look at it. It's unbelievable.'

The patterning of the black wood and white plaster up the rear of the house included shapes like the diamonds and clubs in a pack of cards. The roof, which wasn't thatched but tiled with wooden tiles, looked just as well preserved as the rest.

'Maybe that's my problem,' I said. 'I still can't really believe it. But, yes, before you ask again – I do want to live here.'

'You're sure?' Peter asked.

I looked around the walled garden. It was the most beautiful place I'd ever been or seen.

'Absolutely,' I said.

Chapter 4.

I drove on the way home, and Peter called the solicitors when we hit the motorway.

He spoke to them for a while, explaining that we wouldn't be returning the keys that afternoon. Then his voice started to rise. It almost seemed as if they were trying to persuade him – us – not to take the house.

'But we'd like to move in as soon as possible,' he said. 'During the summer holidays.'

He listened.

'Middle of June would be fine.'

Then he listened some more.

'No, we've met her already. She can stay on, just as before. And the gardener, and Uncle Tom Cobbley and all. You don't have to worry about that.'

He listened for even longer.

'I know it's historic. I know it's a big responsibility. But it is my family home, isn't it? Now, is there anything we need to do?'

When he finally finished, he clicked the phone shut and said, 'I think Mr. Gibbon secretly wants it for himself.'

'But we're okay, aren't we?'

'We're fine,' he said, and put his hand on top of mine, on top of the gear-stick.

Returning to our little maisonette in Tulse Hill was a very strange experience. In some ways, it felt even less real than the Elizabethan mansion. Did we really live *here*? – in this tiny little box that would fit a dozen times inside the entrance hall of the house down in West Sussex? It was hard to believe it, although we'd moved here over six years ago – just before Jack was born.

And now, we were going to be leaving. Everything seemed to be working out for the best.

Since Peter's affair, I'd wanted us to move – it just didn't seem likely we'd get the chance. The woman he'd started seeing lived only about a mile away. That was one of the reasons the two of them had been able to meet up without me finding out. Her name was Jennifer Leyton, and she owned – get this – a carpet-cleaning business. At first, she called Peter to help sort out her cash flow, then – I later learned – she called Peter to chat, then to invite him round to her flat and finally to say she had fallen in love with him. All of this was on his mobile phone, of course – his second, secret mobile phone.

I found out about them because of the foxes on our street. One night they ripped open a bag of rubbish that we hadn't been able to fit inside the wheelie. The next day, whilst rebagging burnt toast and gone-hard baked beans, I spotted an envelope from a phone company we didn't use. Peter's was the name in the clear window. The address was for a post box. As it had been opened already, I felt fine about looking inside. The bill showed that Peter had only used that account to call one number, but that he'd called it every day for the past month.

I'm not stupid. I knew what it meant – knew even before I dialled the number and heard her say, 'Hello, Carpet Superheroes.'

I didn't scream at her. I just put the phone down. I didn't call Peter. I waited until that evening, waited until Jack was in bed. Then I told him I knew.

I've never seen him so upset. Not even when his parents died. I think he thought I was going to leave him and take Jack. (Mary hadn't been born or even conceived then). But I'm tougher than that. I asked him about the bill. He said he had brought it home by mistake, and then tried to get rid of it, badly.

'I think I wanted to get caught,' he said. This made me angrier.

'Do you love her?' I asked.

'I don't know.'

'Do you love me?'

'Yes,' he said. 'But – '

Things had been difficult since Jack was born. Sex had been difficult. Staying awake had been difficult. Not sniping at each other had been difficult. It wasn't an excuse but I suppose it was a reason.

'Tell me you love me,' I said. 'Look at me when you say it – really look at me.'

He did look, and he did love me – that's what I saw in his eyes.

I told him straight, he'd had his silly fling, nothing could be done about it, but if he promised he would never see her again, and this would never happen again, I would give him a second chance. It's old fashioned, I know, but that's how I am.

'One second chance,' I said. 'I'm not the doormat type.'

I made him call her straight away, on the secret mobile, then – when he'd finished – plopped the handset in a glass of water, and that was the end of her.

The morning after our first visit to the house, Peter spoke to the solicitors again, and they confirmed there was nothing to stand in our way. We could move whenever we were ready – tomorrow, if we felt like it.

'We'll let you know,' said Peter.

And now I started to get properly excited. It was amazing. We were heading towards a completely new life, in a good way. Most people never get that chance – to start again. Of course, I knew we'd be taking a whole heap of our old problems with us. But it looked as if worrying about our son and daughter sharing a bedroom was going to be a thing of the past.

I had a sudden panic, and went online to check that there was a decent school nearby for Jack and later on for Mary. I needn't have worried – the local primary got top marks for everything, and the nearest secondary was clearly a step up from anything Lambeth had to offer.

After this, I couldn't really think of any more obstacles to us moving. I would miss London, but it wasn't as if I'd been able to make much use of it since Mary had been born. I liked the idea of my children growing up in the country. I'd been a country girl myself. They could run around outside, climb trees, walk on frosty grass, and I wouldn't have to spend all my time worrying about dog poo, broken glass, and syringes. Or about Carpet Superheroes.

Chapter 5.

Moving house was the usual nightmare.

I had visions of us arriving to find Mrs. Forster standing there behind locked iron gates, not even allowing us pikeys onto the grounds.

I also had visions of the removal men making off with all our worldly possessions, or smashing my grandmother's china teapot, or losing one of Jack's most heavily-armed Transformers.

In the end, the worst they did was put a long scrape down the paint on the stairway, from one of the corners of Jack's bed.

With nothing in it, the maisonette suddenly looked quite spacious. Light and airy, which was what people wanted.

After deciding to move, we'd had three lots of estate agents round to give us a valuation and to tell us what we'd get as rent. Together, Peter and me decided to keep the maisonette and let it out, rather than sell it. That way, we could always move back if things didn't work out. After engaging the least sleazy estate agent, we found their promises of a quick let to be true. We had viewing after viewing, all in one afternoon. Light and airy did it for several of the couples we met. Our new tenants – we were landlords! – were going to be moving in two hours after we moved out.

On a Saturday morning in mid-June, I stood in our front room, holding Mary, and thought about our new-old house. That couldn't be called light and airy, could it?

I'm quite a sentimental person, deep down, and I would have liked to have taken a little longer to look around our first proper home – to store up my memories: the bathroom, where Jack screamed like a banshee the first time I tried to co-bathe with him; the bedroom, where Mary was born on the floor beside the bed. (I could still make out a slight stain on the pale carpet, though Peter swore it was just my imagination.) But there was a toot-toot from the removals van, and we had to be off.

'Let's go! Let's go!' said Jack, standing on the pavement with his dad.

He was buzzing. As soon as we'd told him we were moving to an old house, he'd started to talk about ghosts. He was at that stage. He loved anything spooky or weird. Not that he got properly scared. We'd been quite protective, and so Jack had never really had his bravery tested. Still, he seemed to think he'd be fighting an army of wailing apparitions from the moment we arrived at our new home. I was worried he'd work himself into such a frenzy that he wouldn't be able to sleep – or not unless he came into bed with us. And, to be quite honest, I didn't want his ghost-obsession to rub off on me. I've always found old places a bit disconcerting. They often give me that being-watched feeling.

‘Will it be a headless man with his head under his arm?’ Jack asked, when we got in the car. ‘Or a nun who floats over the ground?’

‘Who knows,’ said Peter, who tended to encourage these sorts of ideas – he said it was good for Jack’s imagination. ‘It’s a very, very old house.’

‘But I’m sure all the ghosts there are very friendly ghosts,’ I said.

Peter started the engine.

‘Even the ones without heads?’ asked Jack.

‘Especially the ones without heads,’ I said, as we drove away from our old life.

It rained all the way down but the sun finally came out just as we were passing through the village near the house. Almost immediately, though, we were into the lane and beneath the shade of the tall trees. I thought about having to drive miles and miles every time we ran out of bread or milk. But maybe I could buy flour and yeast and do lots more baking. And perhaps there would be a farm with cows nearby. Jack would love that. (He’d probably hate the fresh bread. Cheese straws were his favourite food.)

Even though we were expecting it, the house appeared just as suddenly as before – almost as if had crept ten metres nearer to the gate.

‘Wow,’ said Jack, as we scrunched to a stop. He’s quite a hard lad to impress, and I’d have been really disappointed if he’d thought the house was nothing special. ‘Creamy!’ he said, to show just how amazed he was. Creamy was one of our family words for the best things of all – Jack used to stir his ice cream round and round with his spoon until it went soft and creamy. We didn’t use it very often. A trip to Pizza Express, for example, was creamy – but not much short of that.

Mary was asleep.

The removals men, all three of them, stood beside their van, staring up at the black and white frontage. Then they looked at us, and our battered P-reg Ford Fiesta. They were probably trying to work out what sort of tip they could expect.

‘Moving up in the world,’ said the gaffer, a man who, as far as I could see, was entirely pink – all except the pupils of his eyes.

‘If you get started,’ I said, ‘we’ll put the kettle on.’

‘Now you’re talking,’ he said.

Peter used the brass Yale key to open the door. He shouted for Mrs. Forster but she didn’t appear. The smell of wood polish was so overpowering it was hard to know if she’d already been and gone or was still to come.

Mary needed feeding, so I asked Peter to deal with the teas. I carried her little body through into the downstairs sitting room, and sat on one of the vast sofas. It took me a while to get comfortable, the thing was so lumpy. Then I sat there as Mary suckled, looking out the window and trying not to feel like some weird kind of burglar.

‘This is your new home,’ I said to Mary who replied with some gentle slurping noises.

Jack, I could hear, had already taken off his shoes and started setting records for long-distance sliding in the hall – and was already being told off for it.

‘Why don’t you go and have a look round?’ his father said.

‘Whoooo-whoooo!’ said Jack, being a ghost.

The floorboards directly above my head started to creak as Jack looked around the upstairs sitting room.

Peter brought in two mugs of tea. They were our cosy-time mugs, one read ‘World’s Best Mum’ and the other ‘Live Long and Prosper’. That morning, last thing, I’d wrapped them in newspaper and stowed them in a cardboard box beside the fridge – the box with MOST IMPORTANT BOX scrawled on the lid. Strangers had already moved into our London kitchen. They were maybe having a cup of tea or coffee there right now. And we were off and away in our new lives. It was funny seeing the mugs sitting on the antique side tables, but they made me feel more at home.

‘I’m shattered already,’ Peter said.

‘Just imagine if you were moving out of here,’ I said.

‘That’s why the aristocracy’s so messed up,’ he said. ‘They get stuck in places like this. Ancestral piles.’ He gave a wince and pretended to shift his bottom.

‘We won’t get stuck,’ I said.

‘Oh no. If we don’t like it, we’ll be out in three months.’

I could feel that Mary was finished. I sat her up and began to burp her. She took one look round the room and began to giggle uncontrollably.

Peter and I couldn’t help joining in. When she goes for it, Mary has a really dirty laugh, just like that baby on YouTube.

The pink gaffer came in carrying a digital camera.

As part of the service, his company did change of address cards with a photo of you in your new home.

‘Shall I do it now while you’re all happy?’ he asked. He’d obviously worked with little babies before.

‘Good idea,’ I said. ‘Peter, can you go and fetch Jack?’

He knocked back the last of his tea then set off.

When he wasn’t back in five minutes, I began to worry. I’d already heard him calling out to Jack, telling him that now wasn’t the time to be playing hide and seek.

‘Can you go and help?’ I asked.

The gaffer went off, too.

Peter’s shouts became more anxious.

He came down to see me.

‘He’s not got up into the attic?’ I asked.

‘It’s still locked.’

'What about the cellar?'

'Is there a cellar?'

'There must be.'

Peter went to find out.

A couple of minutes later, the gaffer ran into the room. 'I can hear him,' he said, out of breath and even pinker. 'But I can't see where he is.'

'You mean Jack?' I said, standing up.

'It sounds as if he's got under the floor.'

'What do you mean?'

We were walking towards the hall.

'His voice is low down, like this.' The gaffer's hand went to knee level.

'He's probably just hiding under the bed,' I said, pretending not to be worried.

'Peter!' I shouted, when we reached the hall. 'Peter!'

The second doorway beneath the zigzag staircase was wide open. I could see steps leading down.

'Coming!' Peter shouted, out of the darkness. It sounded echoey.

The other two removals men, carrying Jack's bed through into the hall, put that down and came to see whether they could be any help.

I carried Mary up the stairs, her head nodding against my shoulder.

'Which room?' I asked.

'Bedroom on the right,' puffed the gaffer.

I went in as quickly as I could.

'Jack, where are you? Jack?'

I thought I heard something, but the squeaky trainers of the removals men covered it up.

'Shhh,' I said to them, a little too aggressively.

The gaffer stood to attention, as if I were a sergeant major. I hadn't realized he was so scared of me. The others backed out through the door on tiptoe.

'Jack?' I shouted.

'Mum! Mum!'

His voice was down, definitely down.

'Keep shouting! I need to find out where you are!'

But Peter's footsteps crashing up the stairs, taking them two at a time, covered over any reply.

'Where is he?' Peter gasped, when he reached my side.

'Under the floor, I think,' said the gaffer.

'I'm here!' shouted Jack. 'I'm in the wall.'

Nothing up until now had spooked me. But the idea of Jack disappearing into a wall was just too much. Mary was starting to wail, what with all the shouting. She must have thought we were terribly angry at one another.

Peter got down on his hands and knees.

'Jack,' he said, 'listen to me. I'm going to knock on the wood. Can you just shout "Louder" when it gets louder and closer to you, and "Quieter" when it goes away?'

'Okay, I will,' replied Jack, then coughed hard.

Peter started to knock. He began in the middle of the floor, and moved towards the doorway.

'Quieter! Quieter!'

So Peter reversed his direction, and moved towards the wall. It was the interior wall, facing towards the hallway.

'Louder!'

Peter reached the wall.

'Louder!'

As Peter moved, Jack's location became clearer and clearer. I felt I could almost see Jack through the floor.

Peter reached the wall and began to rap with his knuckles on the panelling. He hadn't gone far up before Jack started to shout 'Quieter!'

Peter pointed to where the floor met the wall.

'He's in there,' he said. 'Somehow.'

'I found a hatch,' said Jack. 'It was open.'

Clearly, he wasn't having any difficulty hearing us.

'I fell down. It shut behind me. It's dark in here. I can't breathe. It's so…' He coughed again. 'It's all dust and dust!'

'Don't worry,' said Peter. 'We're going to get you out.'

His hands began to feel their way over the oblong grid of the panelling, trying to discover a catch or handle.

Jack's coughing got worse.

'I can't breathe,' he said. 'Mum, I can't breathe.'

'Cover your mouth!' Peter shouted. 'Cover your mouth with your sleeve, and spit on it to make it wet!'

But Jack's cough got worse and worse, turning into a kind of wheeze.

All this time, Peter was scrabbling at the wall to try to find the opening.

'Mummy!' Jack cried. 'Help me, Mummy!'

Just then, a voice from downstairs shouted out, 'Yoo-hoo! Hell-ooo!'

It was Mrs. Forster.

I went out onto the landing. 'Up here,' I shouted. 'Jack's suffocating. He says he's found a hatch.'

'Oh,' said Mrs. Forster. 'Has he, indeed?'

'Can you get him out?'

'Oh yes,' she said, and began to climb the stairs, still wearing her coat. 'There's a bit of a trick to it. You just have to turn… Well, it's easier if I just show you.'

I stood aside to let her pass. Then Peter did the same.

She approached the wall, went straight for one of the horizontal stripes of wood, pushed it downwards and, almost miraculously, a small doorway appeared – just big enough for an adult to clamber through, and easily big enough for Jack.

Mrs. Forster stepped away. Her hand gesture was a bit like that of a magician – ta-*dah*!

Fingers appeared in the doorway – the pale fingers of Jack's right hand.

The gaffer came forwards to help Peter, and together they heaved Jack out of the gap in the wall.

'The priest's hole, they used to call it,' said Mrs. Forster. 'I'm surprised he found it.'

I wasn't really listening to what she was saying. I was staring at Jack – he looked like Stig of the Dump. I've never seen anyone quite so covered in dust and cobwebs. He looked as if he'd just stepped out of a crypt.

'Panic over,' said the gaffer to his men. Like they couldn't see for themselves.

'I'm afraid I don't go in there to clean,' said Mrs. Forster. 'It's not used for anything.'

Peter gave Jack a huge hug, and Mary and me joined in. I was aware of the four strangers watching, but I really didn't care. We've always been a huggy kind of family.

'You silly fool,' Peter said to Jack. 'You haven't been here five minutes, and you're already getting yourself into scrapes.'

'Sorry, Dad,' said Jack, but I could tell he wasn't, not now he was safe again. Priest's holes were much more exciting than computer games.

'Did you see any ghosts?' I asked.

'No,' he said. The whites of his eyes looked very white, against the grey of his skin.

'I think you better have a bath,' I said.

Mrs. Forster moved over to the wall. 'I'll just close this up,' she said.

We all watched as the hole disappeared.

'Show me,' said Jack. Then, remembering his manners, 'Please.'

'You're not going in there again,' said Peter.

'I just want to know,' he said.

Mrs. Forster looked to me, which I appreciated.

'Only if you promise never to go in there when we're not around.'

With pretend-weariness, Jack said, 'I promise.' We had made him make a whole heap of promises in the previous couple of days: not to rush around the house breaking things, not to scare his little sister with ghostie-wails. We knew it might be hard for him, moving away from his school and his friends. But we assured him that one of them, Jameel, could come and stay very soon.

I gave Mrs. Forster the nod, and she demonstrated how the secret catch worked. Jack wasn't the only one watching closely – even the removals men looked on with amazement.

'Marvellous craftsmanship,' said the gaffer. He turned to walk down the stairs. 'I've been doing removals for twenty-five years, and – I have to say – that's the first time anything like *that's* ever happened. But, then, you don't get many houses like this one. Not in South London. Not anywhere.'

Peter suggested cups of tea all round, and orange juice for Jack – and then that bath.

'I think we'll just be getting on with it,' said the gaffer. 'If you don't mind.'

He went towards the removals van with his two men. I could hear them talking about what had happened. It was a good story, for their girlfriends, for the pub. Myself, I was concerned that it might add up to something more. Your first day in a new home is so important. If bad things happen, it can sour the place forever. This wasn't really a bad thing, more a comic thing as it turned out, but it made me anxious that the house might be full of hidden dangers. The sooner I could talk to Mrs. Forster about these, the better. Today wasn't the day, though. She was a little flustered, and might forget something important. But I knew I should try to befriend her as soon as possible. She had gone into the kitchen and was fetching the cleaning stuff. I went in after her. Already, she had put on her pinnie. Immediately, she seemed more relaxed. It was her uniform, I suppose.

'Thank you for that,' I said. 'He was getting really scared.'

'Was not,' said Jack.

'Don't mention it,' Mrs. Forster replied. 'Boys get into all kinds of scrapes, don't they?'

Peter and Jack sat down at the table and began to drink their orange juice. Both of them were doing their best not to look like they were listening.

'Oh, I don't know,' I said. 'I seemed to get into plenty of trouble when I was a kid.'

'Ah, you were a tomboy, were you?'

'No,' I said, 'just a normal, healthy girl.'

I knew I shouldn't have challenged her. People in the country say these sorts of old-fashioned things – you just have to let them. They're not going to learn.

There was an awkward silence while Mrs. Forster waited to see what I'd say next.

'They're just going to make a mess today,' I said. 'Perhaps you can find something to do that you don't normally do.'

'You mean keep out of their way,' said Mrs. Forster. 'It's quite all right. I was planning on dusting the books in the library. They won't be going in there, will they?'

I thought of all our dog-eared paperbacks. We'd certainly have to find somewhere else to put them. It would be ridiculous to have them leaning up against all those leather-bound volumes.

'No,' I said. 'I don't think so.'

Mrs. Forster gave a nod. If I'd been someone who impressed her more, I think she'd have done a curtsey. She picked up her wicker basket full of dusters and polishes then left the room.

Peter waited until she was out of earshot.

'Trouble with the domestics?' he said.

'What's a "domestic"?' Jack asked.

I tried to explain without using the word 'servant'.

'Does that mean I don't have to tidy my bedroom?' said Jack. 'Great.'

'Mrs. Forster will not be picking up your stinky socks,' I said.

'I don't want her to,' said Jack. 'She's creepy.'

'You think anyone over fifty's creepy,' said Peter.

'Not like her,' said Jack. 'She's supercreepy. She's a ghost-helper.'

'Thank you for pointing that out,' I said. 'You must be polite to her.'

'I will.'

'Promise?'

'I promise,' he said.

Mary was ready for a proper sleep. We'd brought the travel cot in our car. I asked Peter if he could go and fetch it, then put it up in our bedroom.

'Okay,' he said. Because he'd been drinking juice, his top lip was a crescent of orange.

'Come here,' I said.

He approached, a little wary.

I wiped the juice off with the muslin I always carry for Mary.

'Thanks,' said Peter, then gave me a kiss on the lips. The orange smelt very strong, very chemical. For a moment, but only a moment, I couldn't smell wood polish.

'Stop!' shouted Jack, who, despite us being a huggy family, hated parental PDAs.

But Peter took the opportunity of whispering in my ear. 'I've got something to show you, later.'

I stepped back to give him a questioning look.

He leaned towards me again. 'In the cellar,' he whispered. 'Very odd.'

'What? What?' shouted Jack.

'Nothing,' Peter said.

Mary went down without much of a struggle, despite the occasional bangs and clatters from the removals men.

Back in the hall, I asked the gaffer to keep everyone away from the main bedroom until Mary woke up.

It's a strange thing, being moved. You know it's all being done for you, for your benefit, but, at the same time, you yourself are surplus to requirements. The removals company had done most of our packing for us – and each box now had a label on it, to say where it should go. The sum total of our possessions wouldn't take up more than a tiny fraction of the hall. I knew that, over the coming weeks, our things would spread out, until we had colonized the house completely. Then, perhaps, it would really feel like our home. I wasn't going to be sticking up any of Jack's drawings of spaceships and Transformers on the wooden panelling, though.

Thinking that I could probably risk it, I went out of the front of the house and round to the garden. The afternoon was still very sunny. I sat at the far end, on the bench I'd shared last time with Peter, and I looked up at the house, our house.

This little moment was the happiest, least troubled one I was going to have – until the whole thing was over.

Chapter 6.

Our first night in the house began quietly enough. The removals men left around five thirty, after both Peter and me had checked inside their van to make sure we hadn't lost anything. We gave the pink gaffer an even more generous tip than we'd planned, to thank him for finding Jack. He said he would share it with the lads.

It wasn't until I had closed the door behind them, and heard their van start up and drive away, that I began to realize what living in such a big old house really meant. The feeling was similar to when you pass your driving test – that first time out in a car on your own, when no one is there to grab your hands and stop you ploughing into the opposite lane. All this, I thought, and we are responsible for every last bit of it. Perhaps the solicitors had been wise in trying to put Peter off. They were coming to see us first thing Monday morning, to deal with the last of the formalities. There was the rest of the day and the whole of Sunday to get through before then, though. It felt like a vast amount of time.

We had brought enough food with us for the first couple of days. Earlier, though, I'd looked around the kitchen and discovered that Michael Francis had made do without either a fridge or a freezer. This was perhaps because there was a large larder, off through a side door.

When I went inside the larder for the first time, and switched the light on, I was quite astonished. It was stocked with food – cheese, eggs, some glass bottles of milk. And there were two shelves full of bright, shiny apples. I'd given one to Jack straight away, because he'd been doing between-meal whining. This must all be down to Mrs. Forster.

But when I'd tried to thank her, she seemed surprised, then awkward. Finally she said, 'Oh, well… Mr. Jonson always liked to keep it well stocked.'

Later on, when I was starting to make us all a big omelette, I noticed something very strange. Mary was in her relaxer chair, up on the kitchen table. She was gurgling away in her own little language. I went into the larder, and fetched out everything we needed. In the light of the kitchen, I saw that the eggs had dates stamped on them, like eggs do these days – digital-type lettering, in pink ink – and, if what I saw was right, they were from the week before Michael Francis died, which was over two months previously.

I cracked the first egg into the white china bowl, expecting it to explode or slide out as a horrible green mess. But it was perfectly fine. I picked up the bowl and gave the yolk and white a very suspicious sniff. It didn't smell of anything much.

I had been intending to make a cheese omelette, because that was Jack's favourite. The cheddar from the larder was a proper truckle, with cloth-like texture around its edge. Alongside this was a selection of other cheeses bought from the supermarket. And these, I saw, had a use-by date that was only a week after Michael Francis's death. They looked fine, though. No mould on them.

Because I wasn't sure about the larder eggs, I decided to use those we'd brought with us from London. But I cut a large chunk out of the larder cheddar, and grated it on top of the bubbling omelette.

I shouted for Peter and Jack, my voice sounding huge in the echoey hall. They had been exploring the ground floor rooms. Peter had found the inventory that the solicitors had mentioned – it was in Michael Francis's desk, just as they'd said.

'Mum,' said Jack, 'we've got a gains-brew.' Or that's what I heard him say.

'What?' I asked.

'A painting of a field. It's a bit boring.'

'Jack means,' said Peter, 'that we have a Gainsborough. And a Constable. And two Canalettos.'

'Those ones are of canals in an old city,' said Jack. 'And the other is just of clouds in blue sky.'

I put my hand to my mouth and stopped thinking about eggs and cheese. For a moment, I was speechless.

Peter, who seemed very calm, said to Jack, 'Go on. Sit down.'

'Are you happy, Mum?' asked Jack. 'Dad said you'd be very happy.'

'They're worth lots of money, aren't they?' I said to Peter. 'I mean, millions.'

'We're rich,' he said.

'Yippee!' shouted Jack.

'Go on, eat your omelette,' I said. 'Before it gets cold.'

'We're rich,' said Peter. 'But we can't really sell them.'

'No,' I said. 'But…'

'Plus,' said Peter. 'I quite like them.'

'Oh, in that case,' I said, 'we *definitely* can't sell them.'

Difficult as it was, with all the excitement, we sat there and ate our dinner. But we finished it really fast, and then went through to have a closer look at the paintings. Jack pointed out which was of clouds and which of canals. Peter held the inventory, reading the proper historical details. They were certainly lovely. It was something new to feel that we owned them. I'd never owned a painting before, apart from the beautiful browny-orange ones Jack had brought home from nursery.

'Do you like them, Jack?' I asked.

'They're all right,' he said, pretend-grumpily.

'Yours are better,' I said, which seemed to cheer him up.

It was his bedtime. What with his adventure in the priest's hole, he'd had an exhausting day. Some questions were better left until the morning.

When Jack wasn't looking, I gave Peter our secret wink – which he understood.

'Come on, then,' he said, and led Jack upstairs to get ready for bed.

Mary was quite perky. I laid her on one of the sofas in the downstairs living room, on top of a blanket, and she kicked and gurgled very happily.

After the boys had gone upstairs, I was able to have a good look through the inventory. Once I had it in front of me, I realized that I was looking for something in particular: the identity of the beautiful young woman in the portrait. The inventory dealt with each room separately, and as all the other pictures in the dining room were of men, it wasn't hard to find out who she was. This is what the entry for that painting said:

Full-length portrait of Lady Elizabeth Jonson (1562-15??), dated 1585, once attributed to Nicholas Hilliard, now thought to be by a follower (Isaac Oliver?) with, perhaps, the face and hands done by the master himself. 50 1/8" x 31 ¼"

When I next looked at her, I saw that Mary had fallen asleep – so I carried the inventory through into the dining room.

'Hello, Elizabeth,' I said, looking up into her strong-nosed face.

I half expected her golden brown eyes to move or disappear, as they do in very corny horror movies when the villain is looking out from behind a painting. They didn't move, but they did do that thing of seeming to follow you around the room. I felt a little awkward. There was something I wanted to say as well as hello. 'I hope you don't mind us moving in to your lovely house. We will try to take good care of it.'

Just then, there was a screaming from the drawing room. When I ran through, I found Mary had been a little sick on herself – in her eyes. She was fine, really. It happened quite often. The posse had all gone on her neck, and she didn't even need a new bodysuit. I carried her into the kitchen and cleaned her up.

Peter, who was able to tell which of our children's cries were trivial and which meant something, appeared at the top of the stairs and shouted, 'Everything okay?'

'Yes,' I called back.

'Jack's ready for you to come and say goodnight.'

I handed Mary to Peter, halfway up the stairs.

'Pukely-puke,' I said.

'Great,' said Peter.

Sitting up in bed, Jack was very tired but also very excited. I told him to lie down and he did.

Jack always tries to delay going to sleep by starting a very involved conversation. I call it Question Time.

'Will I see a ghost?' he asked.

'I don't think so,' I said. 'Do you want to see a ghost?'

'Not really,' he said. 'Not unless it is a friendly ghost.'

'I'm sure all the ghosts in this house are friendly.'

I realized I'd already said this to him once. If you repeat things to children, they know it's something you're worried about.

'How do you know?'

I couldn't give him an answer straight away. 'Well, it's just an instinct. The place feels friendly. It's not some spooky old castle, is it? It's our new home.'

Saying it, I really did believe it

'I suppose so,' said Jack.

He was fighting hard to stay awake, but his eyelids were flickering and the whites were appearing behind them. I sang him Rockabye Baby, which he still likes.

'Sweet dreams,' I said, and kissed his forehead.

When I was sure he'd gone off, I rejoined Peter downstairs in the living room.

'Okay?' he said.

'Fine,' I said. 'Just worried about ghosts.'

'Me, too,' said Peter.

I checked to see if he was serious.

'Well,' he said, 'you never know.'

We sat for a moment in exhausted silence.

'You got the energy?' he asked.

'Oh, the cellar,' I said, remembering his whispered words of the afternoon. 'Yes, I think so. As long as we go to bed straight afterwards.'

I forced myself off the sofa. Peter, carrying Mary, led the way into the hall.

The door to the cellar wasn't concealed like that to the priest's hole, but it was another very neat piece of carpentry. I turned the iron door handle and saw a couple of steps heading down into pitch black.

'Light switch is to the right,' Peter said.

I stepped back. I was worried about spiders' webs.

'You do it,' I said.

With Mary on his shoulder, Peter reached around, fumbled for a moment, and then flicked it on.

The steps, as I now saw them, went down a long way, walls on either side. Later, when I counted, I found there were thirteen of them.

I started to descend then stopped.

'What is it *exactly* that I'm going to see?' I asked.

'I don't want to explain,' Peter said.

After a deep breath, I continued down. The place smelt very strongly of earth, of being underground. The walls were plaster that looked freshly whitewashed. In a few places there were pencil drawings. Although I didn't look at them closely they looked like rough architectural plans of buildings.

The floor of the cellar, when we reached it, was made of smooth grey flagstones. This wasn't the first thing you noticed, though – that was the doors. We were in the middle of a square-ish room, and in the middle of each wall was a door.

'What's behind them?' I asked.

'Three of them are locked,' said Peter. 'But not this one.'

He indicated the one directly in front of the bottom of the stairs.

'Go on, open it,' he said, after I had hesitated for a few moments.

'No,' I said. 'I want to know what's behind it.'

'Nothing scary. Just something very weird.'

The door looked extremely old. It was made of dark brown wood and the handle was twisted iron. I glanced round at the three other doors. Each of them was unique, completely unlike the others.

'You're not playing games, are you?' I asked.

'Just open it,' said Peter. 'Mary's getting cold.'

It was very chilly down there – as if it were icy winter outside, not summer.

I turned the handle and tried to push open the door.

'Other way,' said Peter, so I pulled it towards me, stepping back.

What I saw took a moment to understand. At first, I thought I was looking at a painting of lightning. Then I realized that the zaggy white diagonals were forked roots and that the black background wasn't the sky but rich, dark, tightly packed earth.

'It's – what?' I said.

'It's not a room,' he said. 'It's just underground.'

I touched the black earth. It was moist and the texture of it was like the most expensive compost.

'Very weird,' I said, turning to look at Peter.

Almost immediately, something touched the back of my head. It felt like the light stroke of a child's finger. But I could also feel a featheriness to it.

Quickly, I lurched forwards, turned round and saw what I'd been expecting to see – one of the roots, without the door there to hold it in place, had flopped out of the earth. It was still quivering with the energy of my twist away. The main part of the root was a ghostly white. The smaller side-roots coming out of it, fringed with something like old lady hair, were nicotine yellow. Even though I wasn't really afraid of it, I didn't want to touch it to put it back in place – into the long groove in the earth it had fallen out of. But for some reason, I *did* want it to be put back just as it had been. I didn't want us to have moved anything around.

One of the reasons I love Peter is that he understands me even when I don't understand myself. First, he put Mary in my arms, then he replaced the long root – pushing it in all the way to the tip – and, lastly, he closed the door. It made a sound I'd never heard before – a low whistle as the air behind it, with nowhere else to go, came out through the keyhole.

'Do you want to try the other doors?' Peter asked.

'No,' I said, a little breathless. 'Not right now.'

I started back up the staircase, and was about halfway up when a small, high voice asked, 'What are you doing?'

It was an eerie moment before I realized that it was Jack, standing at the top of the stairs.

'We just went down to check on something,' I said. 'Nothing to worry about. Nothing at all.'

Then I realized that this was exactly the sort of thing you *shouldn't* say to a boy of six.

'Was it a ghost?'

'Of course not,' I said, reaching the top of the stairs. 'Can you let us through?'

'What if I shut you in?' Jack asked. His hand was braced against the door.

'Then you wouldn't get a new bike,' said Peter from behind me.

'It wouldn't be a very nice thing to do,' I said. Preferring to concentrate Jack's mind on the idea of being good rather than torment him with images of lost-forever treats.

Jack stepped back to let us pass. Peter switched off the light with a loud click, closed the door and then turned towards Jack. 'The cellar is completely off-limits. Do you understand?'

'Yes,' said Jack. 'But what's down there?'

'I will show you another time,' said Peter. 'We will go down together, but you must promise not to go down on your own.'

'I promise,' said Jack, so quickly that it was hard to believe him.

I could tell that Peter was thinking of making Jack repeat his promise. Then he changed his mind, and decided to trust him.

'How about a glass of hot milk?' I asked.

'Sounds good,' said Peter.

'Hot chocolate,' chanted Jack. 'Hot chocolate!'

'Well,' I said, 'it's still packed up in one of the boxes. I don't want to search for it now.'

Jack looked disappointed, but didn't protest. He was glad we were letting him stay up.

We all went into the kitchen. I put Mary in the relaxer chair, fetched some milk from the larder and started to pour it out into a large saucepan.

'You, too?' I asked Peter.

'Yes, please,' he said.

I let the whole bottle flow out, then turned on the gas.

Of course, going into the larder had reminded me of the eggs and their sell-by date. It wouldn't be wise to say anything to Peter whilst Jack was there to hear.

At the far end of the larder was a long shelf of condiments – I'd seen it earlier, and again whilst getting the milk. I thought it might be worth checking to see if there was any chocolate or cocoa powder. There were at least a hundred different jars and pots. Some of them were for brands I'd never seen before – probably the sort of thing you get in hampers from Fortnum & Mason. From what I could tell, Michael Francis had been especially keen on honey and powdered English mustard.

I was about to give up when, behind a glass jar full of demerara sugar, I saw the right kind of label – brown, cosy-looking. It was a tin of old-fashioned cocoa powder, made by Bourneville. I picked it up, and the sugar, and carried them triumphantly through into the kitchen.

'We're in luck,' I said.

'Great,' said Jack.

I put the tin and the jar down, then fetched a wooden spoon. I was already getting the hang of what lurked in which drawer. It was only when I was about to scoop the cocoa out into the bubbling milk that I noticed the jar had a price label on the side: 4d, it said. I couldn't remember exactly when the currency had gone decimal, but I knew it was years before I'd started to use money, and I was almost thirty-six.

Cocoa powder doesn't go off, I thought. Maybe Michael Francis bought new stuff and just kept it in this old tin.

The strange thing was, the tin didn't look old at all – brightly shiny on the top, it might have been bought yesterday.

Rather than disappoint Jack, I decided to go ahead and make the hot chocolate. But I would taste it myself before I gave it to anyone else.

As it turned out, the rich sweet drink was utterly delicious – much tastier than the light brown stuff we usually bought.

'Mmmm,' said Jack, after his first sip. He was enjoying being up past his bedtime, and I could tell he was trying to stretch it out as long as possible.

'Delicious,' said Peter. Then he turned to Jack. 'Well, what do you think of it so far?'

'Rubbish!' shouted Jack.

It was one of our family jokes, borrowed from Morecambe & Wise.

All three of us laughed, with top lips stained dark brown. Mary, asleep, tossed her head from side to side.

Later, when Jack was safely back in bed, I sat talking to Peter and feeding Mary at the same time. We were up in our room – Peter, looking out the window into the black of the woods, and me, propped up in bed with four plump pillows. The linen didn't smell at all musty, which was surprising given how long it had lain unused.

Our bed, a four-poster, was so vast and ornate that I felt I should be delivering lines from Shakespeare, rather than asking Peter if he could remember where Jack's football was.

Peter undressed, put on his stripey pyjamas, turned off the overhead light and joined me in the four-poster. The room was quite dark. Both of the bedside tables had a lamp, but only Peter's was on. The shade on it was thick, and most of the light went downwards.

Even though Peter had put up the travel cot, I easily persuaded him to let Mary come into our bed. She had slept quite a lot during the day, but still seemed very tired. I hoped we were going to have a good night. Mary might even sleep through. If she woke up, I could feed her easily enough by just turning towards her.

I knew I could drop off in moments, but I needed to tell Peter about the out-of-date eggs and the ancient cocoa powder first.

'It tasted fine to me,' he said, after I'd explained.

'I know,' I said. 'And I'm sure the eggs would have been fine, too. That one didn't smell.'

'Why didn't you use them?'

'You're not meant to, are you?'

'Sell-by dates are a load of rubbish,' he said. 'Everyone knows that.'

'But the cocoa was probably older than me.'

'You're not that old.'

He wasn't taking it seriously. I knew he wanted to get to sleep.

'Anyway,' he said, 'we're going shopping tomorrow.'

He was right. Even though it was a Sunday, we planned to drive to the nearest big supermarket and stock up on everything we'd discovered we needed.

I snuggled down with Mary beside me.

Although I was shattered, it took me a long time to get to sleep – because the house was so quiet. I couldn't remember going to bed anywhere where I couldn't hear traffic or airplanes coming in to land. I was lying there, waiting for something to make a noise. But we were a long way away from any roads, and between the nearest house and us was a thick cloak of woods.

It would be exaggerating to say 'I felt the dark gathering in around us', or anything spooky like that. But I was very aware we didn't have any upstairs or downstairs or left and right neighbours. We could make as much noise as we wanted, scream our heads off, and no one would ever complain. The downside of this, though, was that if anything bad happened, we would have to deal with it all by ourselves. There was nobody to borrow a cup of sugar from, or to call 999 if they saw smoke coming from a window.

After a while, I realized that I could pick out the ticking of Peter's wristwatch, on his side of the bed. It was a high, needy sound. I don't think I'd ever realized that his watch ticked before – and I was the one who'd bought it for him, as a thirty-third birthday present.

In London, I had often dropped off to the sound of police sirens. I missed them, now. Although they meant bad things happening, somewhere, they also meant someone going to try and sort them out.

The house itself wasn't completely silent. There were creakings and crackings from the wood. And the bed made the odd settling noise. But, in the gaps, the silence was enough for me to hear the blood in my head.

I ruffled my hair against the pillow, trying to get rid of the idea of my own heart. Knowing it was there, beating away, and had been since before I was born – that always made me feel panicky.

All of these thoughts must have ended up exhausting me. Peter started snoring, and to the see-saw of that, I fell asleep.

Chapter 7.

Mary woke up for a comfort feed at one a.m. and then again at three thirty. The second time, she wouldn't go straight back down. Something seemed to have upset her and she was wailing pitifully. Peter could sleep through an atomic bomb, but I didn't want her to disturb Jack, so I picked up the changing bag and carried her downstairs.

'It's all right, little Boo,' I said, as I'd said so many times before, to Jack and to her. 'It's all all right.'

As we went down the wooden steps, I could smell the ripe fruity smell of a poo. The easiest place to change her was a table. I thought I might as well use the one in the dining room. It would give me another chance to get to know Elizabeth Jonson, after our interrupted conversation.

There were two light switches beside the door. One of them did the overhead lights, the other made the lights above the paintings come on. I flicked both, then got the changing mat out of the bag and unrolled it on the table. Mary, distracted by having something to look at, wasn't wailing quite so much. I undid the zip on her sleepbag and then the poppers on her bodysuit. We'd used both of these night-clothes for Jack, and repeated washing had made them very soft and cosy. Mary looked so small without anything on, her little arms only just starting to get some strength – unlike her little mouth, which could suck like mad.

I pulled back the tabs on her nappy and had a peek inside. It was a big one, and wet. My expert eye decided that I needed six wet-wipes. This was a little game I played with myself, to keep changing amusing. I needed something – Mary often had to be done seven or eight times a day.

Gently, I wiped her clean, pressing the dirty wipes into the old nappy. Mary had gone quiet. Her roving eyes had focussed on a point to her right. A quick glance confirmed what I'd thought. She was looking towards Elizabeth Jonson. This wasn't surprising – with her red-golden hair and fantastic outfit, Elizabeth was the brightest and sparkliest creature in the room.

Mary's bottom was a bit sore, so I rubbed healy cream into it and then put on the new nappy. Before I put her back in her night-clothes, I sat down for a cuddle. Even though you're exhausted to the point of tears, these are some of the best moments – when you have your baby all to yourself, and the rest of the world is asleep. I smelled her downy head, the sweetest smell of a tiny person, milky but with a little edge to it. I knew from Jack that she wouldn't be this way very long, and I wanted to indulge myself in it so that I had lots of good memories.

To hold Mary close, I'd turned her away from Elizabeth. Mary didn't like this. Almost immediately, she started to make grumbly noises. So, I stood up and carried her over to the foot of the painting. We both looked up at it, shining golden in its light.

‘What do you make of her?’ I asked. ‘Isn’t she lovely?’

Then I turned to Elizabeth and, almost without thinking of it, as if she were a friend of a friend, asked her, ‘Do you have children?’

Of course, there was no reply. Things didn’t work like that, in this house. But as I looked more closely at her face, I saw a definite sadness there. She was only young when this painting was done. There had been years afterwards, in which she could have had a family. Perhaps she was a direct ancestor of Peter. That would be weird.

‘I’ll find out,’ I said.

The next thing I thought was how difficult it must have been, having a baby before wipes, disposable nappies, Sudocrem and Calpol. They had servants, of course, those that were rich enough. But infant mortality was so high. From school, I remembered Henry VIII’s desperate attempts to have children, and the early deaths of so many of those he did have. And then there was Elizabeth, the Virgin Queen. I knew a bit about her from the recent films. What an awful life!

These thoughts made me want to snuggle up in bed with my arms around Mary. One-handed, I packed up the changing bag. Then I carried it and Mary towards the door.

‘Goodnight,’ I said to Elizabeth, before I switched off the lights.

The nappy bag full of stink, I dumped by the front door. I could deal with it in the morning. All this, I was sure, was quite a long way from how old Michael Francis used to live. A snifter of brandy in the library and then an early night. Or maybe not.

In the middle of the hall, nothing but dark around me, I stopped for a moment, just to see how the whole house felt. Was it spooky? Did I think a restless ghost haunted it?

No.

How wrong can you be?

Chapter 8.

We were woken very early on Sunday morning by the sound of a sharp rap-rap-rap.

At first, we had no idea what it was. I said it might be something to do with the plumbing. Peter said it was a neighbour doing some hammering.

The rapping started and stopped, started and stopped.

In our old flat, we'd had a doorbell. Perhaps that was why it took us a few minutes to realize that it might be the gryffin-shaped knocker on the front door.

Peter managed to get downstairs before the racket woke Jack.

He returned about five minutes later.

'It's a priest,' he said. 'No, let me rephrase that. It's *our* priest. He's called Father Giuseppe Trovato. It seems that we have a chapel in our garden. A private chapel.'

'What?' I said. Not that I didn't believe him. We now owned several hundred acres, and hadn't done anything to explore them. We hadn't even looked at a plan of the grounds.

'Michael Francis Jonson always had a private mass said, at this time.'

'Every week?' I asked.

'Every Sunday. Without fail. Before the priest goes off to his regular. So, he's going to hurry us through today.'

'But I've never been to mass.'

Peter was already getting his clothes on.

'I asked him if he'd come back later.'

'And what did he say?'

'Basically, he knows. He knows that we can only inherit this house if we're practicing Catholics. And this is how we practice – attending Sunday Mass.'

It all seemed a bit mad to me. But I remembered what the solicitor had said. We didn't seem to have any choice.

'All my smart clothes are still in the suitcases.'

'Just put anything on,' said Peter. 'We can dress up next week.'

He pulled a sweater with a shirt inside it over his head.

'I'll get Jack. Mary can go as she is. You can carry her.'

About five minutes later, we were ready. Jack was not best pleased.

'We're going to see a special chapel,' I said.

My son had certainly never been woken up early for architecture appreciation before.

Father Trovato was waiting for us in the front porch.

I don't know what I was expecting. I hadn't had much time to picture him. For the first moment, I thought Father Trovato was a man dressed up as a priest rather than an actual real-life priest. When you separated him from his costume, he looked a bit like a smaller version of Pavarotti, complete with the dyed black combed over hair.

'Mrs. Jonson,' he greeted me. 'It is very nice to meet you, at last. And these are your beautiful children?' Despite his name, he didn't sound very Italian.

'Jack, six, and Mary, three months, Father,' said Peter. He was obviously more used to speaking to priests than I was – though a little out of practice. I felt as if I were meeting a member of the Royal Family. I didn't really respect his position all that much, but I was still overawed.

'Beautiful,' said Father Trovato. Then he asked, 'You really don't know where the chapel is?'

'No,' I said. 'Father.'

'Then you can follow me.'

He had parked his car, a very old, very small orangey-red Fiat, right up against the front door. When I looked in the back, as I squeezed past, I saw that it was full of cardboard boxes some of which were open. Inside the boxes were pictures of smiling black faces. I didn't have time to see any more. But I thought they must be pamphlets about good works in Africa. The Catholic Church is all about converting the heathen, isn't it? I wondered whether that was how Father Trovato saw us.

The round black figure led us down the path around the house that Peter and then Peter and me had taken on our first visit.

'It was extremely sad about your great uncle,' he said to Peter. 'He was a very fine man. Very devout. Very principled.'

'Yes,' said Peter. 'I didn't know him very well. Hardly at all.'

'And now…' said Father Trovato, and he gestured around him. And now, he meant, you have all this. If you behave.

The path continued straight for about fifteen feet, then came to a fork. I hadn't really noticed it before. I'd known I had to bear left to find the garden. Father Trovato took the right-hand path, and we followed him down a slight incline.

I suppose we must have gone another ten yards when Father Trovato said, 'It is a very unusual chapel. For many years, in times of persecution, it had to be completely secret.'

We looked around.

'Where is it?' asked Jack. 'I don't think it's here at all.'

'It is here,' said Father Trovato, and pointed to his feet.

He was standing on a pair of wooden doors.

'In previous times, the path didn't lead straight here, of course. And the entrance was hidden under a pile of timber.'

He produced a large keychain from his pocket. I was surprised when he selected one of the largest keys and handed it to Jack. 'Why don't you open it?' he said.

Jack liked this idea a lot.

He got down on hands and knees, and began to jiggle the key into the keyhole.

Father Trovato said, as an aside, 'If I can avoid bending down, I do.' I could see he wasn't a man for rolling around on the floor. 'It turns to the right,' the priest said.

'I can do it by my own,' said Jack, as the key scraped around clockwise.

'Bravo,' said Father Trovato, when the job was done. 'And now, we enter. Please, as we do so, take some water from the bowl on the right and make the sign of the cross.' He demonstrated.

'Well,…' said Peter.

Father Trovato faced us squarely, very squarely. 'I know everything,' he said. 'Peter, you used to a practice the faith a long time ago. But your wife and children, they don't know anything. So, I am going to teach them. That isn't a problem, is it?'

Peter hesitated before saying, 'No. I don't think so.' He turned to look at me. Perhaps he was expecting me to say what a load of nonsense I thought religion was. I wonder what would have happened, if I'd said that. The terms of our inheritance were clear enough. We all had to be practicing Catholics – not just Peter, but me and the kids, too. I hadn't given much thought to what this would mean. Perhaps I had hoped it just meant we had to say we were Catholic, if anybody asked.

'It isn't a problem?' Father Trovato asked me.

'No,' I said. I suppose this was true. I had no desire to find God, or anything like that. I was curious, though – curious about what Peter had once been like, and curious about what Father Trovato had to teach us.

'All right,' said the priest. 'If you could open the doors. Please be careful. The drop is rather steep.'

Chapter 9.

The underground space was deeper than I'd expected, and bigger. It was all properly laid out, with an aisle, pews, an altar, everything. Of course there were no windows. But the place was brightly lit. It smelt a little earthy.

The chapel looked to me like the same person had built it as had the hall of the house. Or, at least, following orders from the same person. Almost everything that I could see was made of wood – although it was much less shiny than the stuff Mrs. Forster got her yellow duster on. There were four rows of pews, leading up to an altar with a table. Hanging up behind that was a crucifix, which looked like it was carved from ivory.

We sat in the front row of the pews. To put ourselves anywhere else would have been silly.

I felt quite embarrassed, as if we were on a beach, and a Punch and Judy show was about to happen just for us, no one else in view.

Father Trovato had gone to a cabinet off to the side, and produced from it a bottle of wine and a white paper packet. He also brought out a brass cup with some fake-looking jewels on it, which I guessed were probably real.

Before he began the formal part of the service, Father Trovato explained that only Peter could receive the sacraments. Until Jack and I had been received into the church, we weren't allowed to.

'Everything will be taken care of,' he said.

The whole thing didn't take that long. Father Trovato didn't rush through it – that would have been rude to God – but he had obviously done the whole thing so many times that he knew where you could cut a few corners. For me, the best bit came when he asked Peter to go off with him so that he could hear Peter's confession.

'Don't forget about Mother's Day,' I whispered to Peter – the year before, he'd failed to take me out to dinner, or even buy me a present or a card.

I was glad when they returned after only a few minutes. If Peter had still been seeing Carpet Superheroes woman, and he was being honest, it would surely have taken longer than that. So, I'd learned something today. Maybe there were a few little advantages to being Catholic.

At the correct point, Peter went up and had the wine and the bread. Jack was intrigued by this, and wondered why he couldn't have any. Mary chose this moment to start doing her hungry whining. I decided to risk Father Trovato's annoyance, and started to breastfeed Mary there and then. If he minded, he didn't say. I gave her just enough to keep her quiet. When the service stopped, I did, too.

Father Trovato made the sign of the cross over us. He told us to go in peace. Then Peter got up and led us out into the light of morning.

After a few minutes tidying up, Father Trovato followed us. He turned out the lights then he locked the doors in the earth.

'You may keep the key, now,' he said to Peter. 'It is your place. For you to visit, if you need to gain strength.'

'I'll be back after breakfast, then,' said Peter. 'I need all the strength I can get, with this lot.'

Father Trovato pretended to be amused, but I could tell he had been trying to make a serious point. I couldn't guess why he thought Peter would feel the need for strength. Father Trovato handed over the key, which was actually a bunch of keys.

'This one,' he said, holding up an ornate iron L-shape. 'I don't know what the other ones are for.'

When we got back to the house, Peter invited Father Trovato in for a cup of coffee.

'No, thank you,' said the priest. 'I must get to my other church.'

'Another time,' said Peter.

Father Trovato hesitated. 'I will see you next week.' He turned to me. 'We can discuss when to begin your instruction, Mrs. Jonson,' He ruffled Jack's hair – something Jack usually hates. 'And yours, too.'

'Okay,' said Jack. I was surprised. He seemed to like the priest. I think because he reminded him of something out of a fairy tale. Or Obi Wan-Kenobi.

Inside the house, the shoom of a Hoover started up.

Peter looked startled. 'Not today as well,' he said. 'It's bloody Sunday.'

Father Trovato gave him a look. Already something to be covered in their confession-session next week. Then he said, 'Mrs. Forster likes to spend as much time cleaning as she can.' It seemed an odd thing to say – and the way he said it made me suspect that he and Mrs. Forster didn't get on very well.

Before I'd had a chance to ask a question that might tell me more, Father Trovato was walking towards his beaten-up Fiat.

'God be with you,' he said, turning round to smile. It might have been my imagination, but I thought I saw him glance at the house with something like fear. The way I understood it, he'd been wishing that God be with us *inside* the house.

'That wasn't too bad,' I said to Peter, when the Fiat had disappeared from sight.

'Maybe,' said Peter. He was thoughtful.

'I thought it was fun,' said Jack. Children are so weird. You can take them to Disneyland and, on the wrong day, it'll be the dullest thing ever. And then, you make them get up early and go to Mass, and they can't get enough.

'Well,' said Peter. 'We can do it all again next week.'

'And what did you confess?' I asked, flirtatiously.

'I can't tell you that,' he said. 'I'm meant to be a man of mystery, aren't I?'

We stood for a moment, listening to the hoovering.

'I think we're going to have to sort this out, once and for all,' said Peter. 'I'm not having my weekends ruined by her and her racket.'

'Let's go and have breakfast,' I said to Jack.

We went inside, us into the kitchen and Peter upstairs to find Mrs. Forster.

I had just finished dishing out Jack's cornflakes when Mrs. Forster came in with the cleaning materials.

'Good morning, Mrs. Forster,' I said.

'No, it's not,' she said, putting the bucket away. 'It's awful.'

Her cheeks were wet with tears.

'What's wrong?'

She pulled her pinnie off over her head and folded it angrily.

'Your husband, Mrs. Jonson – your husband can be a very cruel man.'

'Excuse me?' I said, but she didn't reply. Not immediately. When she had put her coat on and buttoned it up, she said, 'Some people just don't know what they're doing.' After which, she burst into tears again, rushed through the hall and out of the house.

Peter, who I think had been avoiding her, came into the kitchen a few minutes later.

'Handled that well,' I said.

'I was very gentle,' he replied, helping himself to muesli. 'I really was.'

'What did you say?'

'Just that I thought that, for the moment, she didn't have to come on Saturdays or Sundays. And that we would see in a month's time whether the house needed more cleaning. I'm sure it won't.'

'And what did she say?'

'At first she insisted that it needed every moment she could give it.' He sat down with a full bowl but didn't start eating.

'And then?' I asked.

'Then she started to beg me.'

'She what?'

'She said, "Please let me come. I'll be very quiet. I'll just polish. You won't even know that I'm here. Please, Mr. Jonson."'

'Please, please, please!' mimicked Jack.

'Was that when she started crying?'

'No, she started weeping as soon as I mentioned we didn't want her cleaning all day long, seven days a week.'

'Please!' cried Jack. 'Please! Please!'

'Stop that now,' I said. 'The woman's obviously upset about something more than the cleaning. Perhaps it's the money. Do you think she's in debt.'

'Not at all,' Peter said. 'The last thing was, she offered to come in for nothing.'

I couldn't believe this. Why would she want to work so hard, and not get paid?

'She agreed, though – in the end?'

'She had to. I told her that if she didn't, we would give her her notice and advertise for another housekeeper.'

'Ah,' I said. 'That was the being cruel bit.'

'You don't want her here any more than I do.'

'But I don't want to spend my life polishing this place to a shine, either.'

'Please!' said Jack.

I'm sorry to say I shouted at him. I think I was feeling more guilty than Peter. Mrs. Forster obviously loved the house. Being here probably brightened her days. Wherever she lived, this place was going to be nicer, wasn't it?

After breakfast, we piled into the car and set off for the supermarket. The drive took about twenty five minutes, though Peter reckoned he could have done it in fifteen if he'd been on his own. We had the radio on. Steve Wright playing the same soppy records he'd played the week before, for happy people sending the same messages to one another. That's why I like it so much – hearing about people who've been married longer than you've been alive. It gives you hope, shows it can be done.

I didn't have a shopping list, so we bought everything we could think of. It was annoying not to be able to stock a freezer. I wasn't yet prepared to trust the larder with fishfingers and ice cream.

Peter said he would go out and buy electrical goods on Tuesday or Wednesday.

'The village shop probably has the basics,' he said.

'I hope so,' I said. 'Jack can't survive without fishfingers.'

'And ketchup,' Jack said. 'And Daddy's sauce.'

We drove back and spent the whole of Sunday settling in. I unpacked the rest of the kitchen stuff, and all the clothes I had – not so many. The grand house made me feel I needed a whole new wardrobe. I didn't want to dress country, like Mrs. Forster, but I really couldn't slop around in sweatshirt and maternity trousers any longer. What if I had to answer the door? People would think I was a squatter. I shoved my grey knickers and nursing bras into the drawer, feeling ashamed of them, too. Jack was amazingly helpful – putting his own clothes away in his old covered-in-stickers chest of drawers. Mary was more difficult. She was used to a lot more attention from me than she was getting that day, and by the middle of the afternoon she had started to become distressed.

I took her with me and went to find Peter. He was in the living room, trying to get our television to work.

'There's no signal,' he said. 'I need to put an aerial on the roof.'

I told him I thought Mary needed a walk. She was letting him know this too, in her own loud way.

'We're nearly done,' he said. 'Just a couple of boxes of books. I'll put them in the study for now.'

We were still working out what to call everything. The *study* was Michael Francis' old office, the one full of animal heads and filing cabinets. The *dining room* was where Elizabeth was. The *living room* was the one downstairs, the one upstairs we called the *other living room* or the *playroom*.

'I'll see if Jack wants to come,' I said.

But he was quite happy playing with his unboxed toys in his new bedroom.

I got Mary into the buggy, stuffed a muslin under the hood, had a quick look at myself in a mirror – ugh! – and then went out the front door.

It wasn't until then that I'd thought about where we were heading. The path to the back garden had too many roots growing across it to be a comfortable ride for either Mary or me. And I wanted to go further than that. The only alternative seemed to be down the drive, and then left or right at the end.

When we got there, Mary already a lot calmer, I decided to turn left. Right was the village, and I knew I'd be going there tomorrow.

Once we were away from the dark trees surrounding the house, I found that it was quite a hot day. The road was smooth grey Tarmac and felt sticky under the soles of my flip-flops. I wished I'd brought some sun cream for Mary. The best I could do was drape the muslin over the hood of the buggy to keep the sun out of her face.

After about a quarter of a mile, the Tarmac ran out and the road turned into a pair of parallel gravel tracks. Off to either side, behind tall hedges, were fields of wheat and of rape.

We were just coming to a turn in the road, to the left and quite sharp, when I heard the chug of a large engine. This sounded too deep to belong to a car. It was coming from the direction I was heading in.

The track was too narrow and the hedges too close together for me to be sure I could squeeze out of the way. So, I pushed Mary's buggy up against the verge and ran round the corner to slow down whatever it was.

The tractor – that's what it turned out to be – was coming even faster than I'd feared. It was only about ten metres away when I rounded the corner. And the driver, I could see, had a newspaper propped up on the steering wheel.

I shouted, but the engine was chugging too loud for him to hear me. He would probably glance up before reaching the corner, but I couldn't take that chance. There were a few clods of mud to the side of the road – ones that had probably fallen out of tractor tracks earlier in the year. I picked up a couple and chucked them towards the windscreen as he drove past. The first flew wide. The second overshot, but hit the roof.

As the tractor went past me, I saw the driver look up, spot me, panic, drop the newspaper. The wheels locked and the tractor began to skid. It had been going at least twenty miles an hour.

I turned and ran along behind it.

The tractor, still skidding, disappeared round the corner. It was slowing down but was it slowing down fast enough? My poor little baby.

When I came into sight of the buggy, I saw that the tractor had stopped only a few inches from where Mary lay.

The driver immediately got down out of the cab. He was a man of around thirty four or five, bald but with a very neat dark brown beard. He was dressed in blue dungarees over a blue gingham shirt, but his wellies were bright green.

'I'm so sorry,' he said. 'I know I shouldn't have been doing that. It's just – Well, I've been driving back and forth along this road for five years, now, and you're the first person I've ever come across.'

'People,' I said, indicating Mary.

'Of course,' he said. 'I always stop looking at it just before the turn. Up until that point it's just a long, straight, boring road. It's the *Telegraph* crossword. I usually get two or three clues.'

'You're the farmer, then,' I said.

'If you mean, I own the farm. Yes, I do.'

'I'm the – We're…' I didn't know how to say it. 'We've just moved in to the Jonson house. I'm Jeane Jonson. This is Mary.'

'Lovely,' he said, coming forward and offering his hand. 'Matthew Maddox. Great. I mean, we'd heard you were in.' He was very posh-sounding for a farmer. His teeth were perfect, not country teeth.

'You've been here five years?' I asked.

'I bought the farm after I retired from the firm.'

'Aren't you very young to retire?'

'Well, I could, so I did. Corporate bankruptcies. Not very interesting. But lots of money. And I always wanted a farm, from this high.'

He touched the side of his stomach with his hand.

'I have another one, about that size. Jack, he's called.'

'I look forward to meeting Jack. If he's interested in animals at all, we have plenty. Horses. He could have a ride. Can he ride?'

'No,' I said. 'Not yet.' I thought about his guided pony rides at the city farm. 'Do you have children?'

'No,' he said. 'Sadly not.'

I felt we'd got onto awkward territory, and very quickly.

'Did you know Michael Francis Jonson very well?'

I'd hoped this would move things to safer ground. But if anything, Matthew Maddox seemed even more unsettled.

'No. Not very well. He kept himself to himself. I know that's the cliché they use about serial killers, isn't it? Not that he was a serial killer. Oh dear. This isn't going very well. I think I'm still a bit flustered about the crossword.'

Matthew Maddox was the most un-farmerlike farmer I'd ever come across. Not that I'd come across many farmers.

'We don't really know much about him,' I said. 'He was a distant relative. I think my husband only met him once. When he was very young.'

'It's a lovely house. I hope you'll be very happy there. If you need anything, just ask. We do a bit of everything. We're not really a proper farm. I mean, last year we even made a profit.'

I was starting to like Matthew Maddox. We talked for a while longer. I told him about how different everything was, us having come from the city. He assured me that the village shop was very good for everyday items. If we wanted eggs, milk, butter, bacon, he'd be happy to sort us out. I asked what his wife's name was.

'Gracie,' he said. 'Gracie Dearie. She kept her maiden name. Did you want to carry on down the road? I can reverse…'

'No, I think we'll head back.'

'I'll reverse anyway. Goodbye.'

Matthew drove the tractor a little way onto the opposite verge, allowing us to squeeze past him. Then, with a wave, he chugged off.

I waited a while, until his diesel fumes had dispersed, then pushed Mary back to the house.

'I've just met our next-door-neighbour,' I said, when I eventually tracked Peter down to the living room.

'Well,' he said, 'I've just met our M.P.'

'What? Was he canvassing?'

'Not exactly,' Peter said. 'Tea?'

'Oh, yes, please,' I said. 'Where's Jack?'

'Out there,' said Peter. I looked through the French windows, and saw Jack throwing a model airplane down the exact middle of the lawn. 'And look…' He stepped up to the garden door, turned the handle, pushed it open. 'I found a bunch of keys in the kitchen.'

I immediately wondered if any of them would open the three mysterious doors in the cellar. Peter, reading my thoughts, shrugged and said, 'I haven't tried them anywhere yet. How's Mary?'

'Asleep in the buggy.'

Peter went off and made tea while I sat on the sofa and watched Jack. He seemed incredibly happy. It was a shame Matthew and Gracie had no children of the right age. Jack needed to find someone nearby to play with, preferably without having to wait until school began. Mary probably wouldn't ever be all that much interest to him – the gap between them was too big. Not that we'd intended to wait so long. Not that we'd waited, in fact. After Jack, I'd had two miscarriages. The second was quite late on. Which was one of the reasons why I made such a fuss over Mary, when she arrived.

'Tell me about the M.P.'

'He's a Tory, of course. And a mason.'

'How do you know that?'

Peter held out his right hand, took hold of it with his left and shook it up and down.

'I thought that was a joke,' I said.

'No,' said Peter. 'I made that mistake, too.'

'What do you mean? You're awful. Tell me properly. From the beginning.'

'There was knock on the door. I answered. The Right Honourable Douglas Longbone was standing there, all tweeded up, his Jaguar XJS behind him. "Jonson," he said. "Good to see someone in the old place, at last." And he grabbed my hand, before I'd had a chance to offer it. And he gave it a proper squeeze, all the time pressing his thumb down between my knuckles. I can still feel it.'

'And that was the funny handshake?'

'Don't interrupt. He looked disappointed. Gave my knuckles one last go. "So you're not…?" he said. "No," I said. "I'm not." "Ah, well," he said, "If you're interested…" "I'm not," I said.'

'Thank God for that,' I said. 'Mason as well as Catholic. All in one day.'

'Anyway, he was really disappointed. He tried to hide it, but I could tell. In fact, he started giving me the old sales pitch. How it was useful, living out here. Contacts. Support. Blah-blah.'

'I hope you kept a straight face.'

'I did my best. When he saw he wasn't getting anywhere, he began to point out all these Masonic symbols in the hall. Triangles, squares, compasses, dragons, eyes, the letter G, whatnot. Some of them are hidden. The number of wood panels is significant, somehow or other. And he told me the dimensions of the hall, length and width, obey the Golden Mean.'

'It's an old house, isn't it?' I said, not exactly sure what he meant by Golden Mean.

'What he eventually said was that, before Michael Francis, the Lodge used to be here, in our hall. But, being strict Catholic, when he took possession Michael Francis turfed the Masons out. And they've been slumming it in the village hall ever since.'

'What's the village hall like?'

'Not like here. That was sixty five years ago.'

'God, so it was a big day for him, coming here.' Another thought struck me. 'How old was Michael Francis when he died?'

'I don't know, really. Have to find out.'

'There was something else,' I said. With the M.P. There was more, wasn't there?'

'Well, yes. He didn't exactly *threaten* me. But he did say how *extremely well appreciated* it would be if I would reconsider.'

'And you…?'

'I said we'd think about it.'

'We're not going to say yes, though, are we?'

'No, we're not. But it's not a good idea to piss off your local M.P. on day one. Not if you can help it.'

Then I told Peter about Michael Maddox, the crossword, Gracie and free horse-riding.

Jack came inside just in time to hear the last bit.

'Would you like to learn to ride?' asked Peter.

'Maybe,' he said. He seemed a lot less keen on this than on going back to the chapel. It was understandable – he was a city boy. He hadn't been around big animals all that much. But he wasn't going to tell us directly that he was frightened.

We had one final visitor that day. It was Gracie Dearie, she came at teatime, and she was carrying a large wicker basket full of farm produce.

'Jeane?' she said. 'Matthew told me what happened. I'm really sorry. You are all right, aren't you?'

'I'm fine,' I said.

'And Mary, too?'

I'm always well-disposed towards people who know the names of my kids without ever having met them.

'She slept through the whole thing.' Mary was asleep, again – in the recliner, in the living room.

Gracie smiled and handed me the basket. Even younger than her husband, she was – I guessed – around thirty. Her hair was bright yellow, done in Heidi plaits, and you could easily tell it was dyed. (The woman from Carpet Superheroes had had dyed blonde hair, too. It was one of the things I felt most angry about. How could Peter fall for something so obvious?) Gracie's cheeks had lovely freckles on that made her look very healthy. She was wearing a short sleeve shirt, jeans and trainers. The weird thing was, the shirt was made from just the same gingham material as her husband's. They probably bought cloth and had their clothes made for them. Her voice wasn't as posh as her husband's – I could detect more London in it, which made me feel a little homesick.

Just then, Peter came through from the kitchen.

'Hello,' he said. 'You must be Gracie.'

She blushed and said that she was.

'Please come in,' Peter said.

'I'm afraid I have to get back,' Gracie said. 'But I'd like to another time, if that's okay.'

'That would be lovely,' I said. 'I'll write down our number.'

'Oh, I'm sure we have it already. Well, goodbye.'

I waved her off, then carried the wicker basket through to the kitchen. It was a beautiful spread. Radishes, carrots, sweetcorn. And all arranged as if for a country show.

'I'll put it in the larder,' I said.

'Should keep,' joked Peter.

We were both exhausted and were planning on an early night. But once Jack was in bed, Peter decided that he wanted to find out a little more about Michael Francis.

I couldn't stay awake. I knew I'd have to be up with Mary a couple of times in the night.

'What about trying the keys?' Peter asked.

'Not tonight,' I said. 'And you're not doing it on your own.'

He smiled.

When Peter eventually came to bed, he tried to get in without disturbing me. But I'm a light sleeper. My alarm-clock told me it was two a.m. I knew Peter must have found something pretty interesting, to keep him from his kip. I wasn't going to start a conversation, though.

Chapter 10.

On this second night in the house Mary only woke up once, at three thirty a.m. And all she wanted was a little feed to send her back off. I wasn't so lucky myself. I started to wonder about Michael Francis. What had Peter been looking at, for three whole hours? My mind began to race through possibilities. Michael Francis had died bankrupt? Or he'd had a huge stash of hardcore pornography? Or he'd been gay? If it had been something really serious, Peter would have woken me up with the bad news, surely?

When I couldn't sleep in our old flat, I'd always made myself some hot milk. I thought I'd do that now. But the kitchen there was only ten carpeted steps from our bedroom. Here, it was quite a hike, and not a warm one.

I didn't want to wake up completely, so I didn't turn the overhead light on, just the one above the hob. Then I went into the larder to fetch some milk.

The carton, when I picked it up, felt gritty – and when I brought it into the light, I saw that it was covered in dirt. It was almost as if it had been buried and dug up again. I ran my finger down the side. Yes, that was definitely dirt and not dust.

Going back into the larder, I switched on the light. I could hardly believe it. Everything was dirty. Everything that, only a few hours before, had been so pristine.

I looked up. The ceiling was made of wooden boards. It was just possible, I thought, us moving about upstairs had dislodged something. Jack had been banging around rather a lot. But not really in the rooms directly above the kitchen, and not for very long. Certainly not after we'd had our evening meal. And I'd been into the larder since then.

It was a total mystery.

I washed the dirt off the milk carton and went ahead with pouring it into a saucepan and heating it. Even with my best efforts, my fingertips left darker marks on the waxy white cardboard.

I sat down and drank from the steamy hot mug, knowing that if I took it upstairs with me the smell would wake Peter. Then I washed it up and headed back to bed, but not until I'd checked in on Elizabeth. I'm a proper one for routines. They're how I cope with stress. Elizabeth looked as beautiful as ever, though perhaps a little sadder.

Even though the appearance of the earth had been so odd, the milk did its work, and I managed to fall asleep.

In the morning – Monday – I had that feeling, the one you get when you know you've had a really powerful dream but you can't for the life of you remember what it was.

Only when I entered the kitchen, carrying Mary with me, did I remember the fallen dirt and the ruined food. I was sure the cereal and milk would be okay, so there was no problem with breakfast. We'd probably need to go shopping again, later.

But when I put Mary down in her relaxer, and turned the light on in the larder, everything had changed. All the dirt was gone.

'Peter,' I called. 'Come here.'

He had just been coaxing Jack – still in stripey pyjamas – down the stairs. Jack isn't very good in the mornings, although as a toddler he regularly used to wake us at ten to five.

'Yes,' said Peter.

'Last night,' I said, 'when I came down – ' Then I stopped. I realized that Jack was listening, too – and I didn't want him getting spooked about the house. Spooked was definitely how I was feeling. 'I didn't think we had enough milk,' I said, making up some nonsense to cover myself. 'But we do.'

Peter gave me a quizzical look. 'I thought you said we had too much.'

'L.A.T.E.R.,' I said, speak-spelling.

Unfortunately, Jack knows his alphabet now. 'What letter?' he asked. Well, he almost knows his alphabet.

'Porridge?' I asked.

'Yes,' he said, then added 'Please' when he saw my Say Please face.

I managed to speak to Peter while Jack was off getting dressed. He can do himself now, all apart from if he has laces on his shoes. I explained to Peter about not being able to sleep.

'When I went for the milk, the food in the larder was all dirty. And now, it's clean again.'

'What do you mean, dirty?'

'Like someone had sprinkled dirt on it. From the garden.'

'Let me have a look.'

'But it's gone now,' I said. 'That's what I'm saying.'

He still went into the larder – where, of course, everything was perfectly pristine.

When he came out, he said, 'You're sure it wasn't a dream?'

'Absolutely.'

I knew that if I'd brought the mug upstairs with me, I would have some proof of what had happened. But because I was so neat and tidy, there was nothing – not even to give me proof for myself. Because once Peter started to question me, I found that I wasn't as sure as I had been before. They say that when you move to a new place, your dreams are often more vivid. Perhaps I had been asleep all the time. Perhaps I had never really made that mug of hot milk. There seemed no other explanation for the appearance and disappearance of dirt.

'We can ask Mrs. Forster to clean in there,' said Peter. 'She should be here soon. Unless she's topped herself.'

'Peter,' I said. 'Don't.'

Mrs. Forster arrived at ten minutes to nine. Luckily, we were all ready by then.

'Good morning, Mrs. Jonson,' she said, very formally.

'Hello,' I said. 'Did you have a good weekend?'

Rather than say no, she just gave me a hard stare. She looked in a bit of a state, as if she hadn't slept. Her face was greyer, and her hair seemed frizzier and less under control. There was a slight tremor in her hands, which I put that down to suppressed emotion. I really didn't want to think about what feelings Mrs. Forster had towards us. They would only make it difficult to speak to her politely.

'Morning, Mrs. Forster,' shouted Peter from the top of the stairs. 'How are you?'

'I'm fine,' she replied, too quietly for him to hear. I could tell she thought shouting in a house, unless there was an emergency, was something only ill-bred people did.

'Could you start by dusting in the larder?' I asked.

'Yes, Mrs. Jonson.'

I turned away. I was planning on letting Mary have a roll around on the exercise mat, to tire her out before the solicitors arrived. They had said they would get to us around ten. If I fed Mary just before then, she might give us the peace we needed. Solicitors don't work very well, unless they have peace.

'Excuse me,' said Mrs. Forster. 'But I may have to stay a little later today. To catch up.'

'Well,' I said, 'we'll see. Please don't do any unnecessary hoovering. It makes too much noise.'

'Yes, Mrs. Jonson.'

I felt ashamed of myself. Two days in, and I was already talking like the lady of the manor. But now that we'd started the battle with Mrs. Forster, we had to see it through. I would get Peter to tell her she had to leave on time. With her there, the house didn't really feel like our own.

At half past nine, I heard the whining engine of a car arriving outside. I thought it was the solicitors, but when I opened the door the man standing in the porch, just about to knock, looked more like a homeless person. There was a lot of brown hair and beard on display, and very little face. His clothes were dark and ragged.

'I am Robert Mew,' he said, very clearly, in a high voice full of emotion. 'I am the gardener. Do I still have my old job?'

He smelled of compost, like people who burn patchouli or smoke lots of pot. I realized he was standing to attention. I felt I should tell him to be 'at ease'.

'What do you normally do?'

'I keep the garden just as it is, in the old style. And I do the forestry, though I could use another hand with that.'

I wanted Peter to come. He was upstairs, playing with Jack. I could hear Jack shrieking, which probably meant the Tickling Monster had just leapt out at him. Either that, or they were playing ghosts.

I looked at Robert Mew. His face looked polished to a brown shine, like banisters get because so many hands touch them. Robert Mew, I suddenly decided, looked just like a gardener should.

'You can carry on as before,' I said. 'What days do you come?'

'Monday to Thursday. The ivy on the trees is the main problem. It is too much to keep up with.'

'You want an assistant?'

'My nephew could help. That would be enough.'

'Just do what you'd normally do, to start with. We can talk about anything else later.'

'Thank you,' he said, and turned around. He hadn't smiled. He hadn't made eye-contact.

His car, a Volkswagen Beetle, made our car look brand new. One of the triangular windows in the back had been replaced with a piece of wood. I knew it hadn't come from a hardware shop because it still had bark on. There was a curved line of moss behind where the windscreen wipers sat.

After he'd gone out of sight, I realized that I hadn't properly introduced myself. At least he hadn't called me Mrs. Jonson all the time.

Peter came into the living room a few minutes later.

'We have a gardener,' I said. 'He's outside.'

Peter unlocked the French windows and went out to say hello. I soon heard wheezy chuckling from Robert Mew. Sometimes Peter just hits it off with people.

When Peter came back in, I asked, 'So, what kept you up so late last night?'

'Well,' he said. 'It's very interesting. I found some photographs of –'

That was when the solicitors knocked. Their car – a blue Mercedes –was so quiet that I hadn't heard it draw up.

Today, we had Mr. Gibbon *and* Mr. Jump, both in dark blue suits. Mr. Jump was fat enough to be Mr. Bounce. They both seemed quite familiar with the house, and wanted to do business in Michael Francis Jonson's office, rather than the living room – even though the office didn't have enough chairs.

I was allowing Jack to play computer games – as a special treat – while we did our business. Mary was asleep in a BabyBjorn around my chest. Neither of the solicitors mentioned or even looked at her.

'Right,' said Mr. Gibbon, who was in charge. 'There are just a few more things. As owners of the house, you are responsible for its upkeep. That includes insurance. Details of the current policy are here.' He passed it to Peter. 'These things don't come cheap any more.'

Peter flicked through to the last page. 'Wow,' he said. 'Where does that come from?'

'You have some world-famous pieces of art here. Placing them on long-term loan with galleries could minimize costs. But, to answer your question, income from Mr. Jonson's investments will cover most of your basic costs. Maintenance on the building has traditionally been extremely low, although we cannot guarantee that state-of-affairs will continue.'

'Can I just ask,' I said. 'How old was Michael Francis when he died?'

'He was one hundred and seven,' said Mr. Jump. 'He had been dealing with our firm for almost ninety years. He was our oldest customer.'

'Ever,' said Mr. Gibbon. 'A remarkable man.'

'And he decided to go to the North Pole, aged a hundred and seven?' I asked.

'A *very* remarkable man,' said Mr. Gibbon. 'But to return to the matter in hand…'

He talked for a while longer. What became clear was that while, on paper, we had lots of valuable assets, and a large income, most of that income went on insuring those assets. And paying the staff to maintain the house. The only way to make any real money would be to open the house to the public – something Michael Francis had always resisted. In other words, we were rich but we weren't rich. And if anything disastrous happened, like a fire or the roof falling in, we would have to pay for the repairs out of our own funds – out of Peter's earnings. By the end, it seemed to me like we might actually be worse off than when we'd been living in the maisonette. No holidays in the Caribbean, then.

'Thank you,' said Peter.

'If there's anything else we can do for you,' said Mr. Jump, 'please don't hesitate to be in touch.'

Peter showed them to the door, then returned.

'I thought they might give us a big surprise, this time,' he said. 'A nice surprise.'

'They have done that once already,' I said, recalling how we'd felt after our first meeting with them.

'I'm going to have to get back to work sooner than I thought. I was planning on hanging around the house, getting under your feet, getting on your nerves.'

He came across and gave me a kiss.

'It's not so bad, is it?' I asked. 'I mean, we get to live here.'

'But if we can't do anything, it's like we're living in a museum.'

'I always liked museums,' I said, which was true.

We had a cuddle, Mary cosy between us.

'Hey, come and look at this,' said Peter.

'Let me just check on Jack,' I said. He was fine. He would have bounced Mario around on platforms for the rest of the day, if we'd let him. 'Ten more minutes,' I said, 'and that's it.'

'But Mum – ' said Jack.

When I returned, Peter had a photo album out on Michael Francis's desk. It was an old-fashioned one, with black glue-down corners holding the photographs in place. The pages were black, too, and written on in white pencil. The handwriting, which I recognized, belonged to Michael Francis – he was very neat, with spiky tops to his letters, even the round ones.

'Look at the date,' said Peter.

It was 1999. The photograph showed Michael Francis in the garden of the house.

'Does that look like a ninety-nine year-old man?' Peter asked.

Michael Francis was standing square, feet apart, arms crossed. It was a gloomy day, a few streaks of light showed that it was raining, and Michael Francis's stance seemed to defy the elements. He was wearing neatly cut country tweeds – just like I'd imagined the M.P. in.

'He looks about sixty to me,' I said.

'More like fifty five,' said Peter. 'And what about this?'

He turned a few pages on. The date now was 2006. The photograph looked almost identical. Michael Francis was wearing the same tweedy clothes, standing in the same aggressive stance. It didn't look as if he'd aged at all.

'And then he went hunting for polar bears,' said Peter.

'I don't think he wanted to kill them,' I said.

'Well, it looks like he could have done – with his bare hands.'

'Very funny.'

'You want funny?' said Peter. 'Here's funny. He turned back to before the 1999 image of Michael Francis. What he showed me was a formal photograph of his great uncle in the walled garden, his staff around him. The date was 1985. There was the gardener, Robert Mew, looking very fresh-faced without a beard. There was Father Trovato, about half the size he was now – quite handsome, in fact. And there, just above Peter's index finger, was Mrs. Forster, absolutely exactly the same as she was now. Mrs. Forster was the thing that was funny. Or maybe not. Maybe she was something else completely.

'Some people are just born old, aren't they?'

'And here's more funny,' said Peter.

He turned back another couple of pages and another decade. Michael Francis obviously wasn't one for taking lots of photographs. The date was now 1977. A second caption added 'Her Majesty's Silver Jubilee'. It was another formal shot of the household. Michael Francis, defiant as ever, a different priest, a different gardener, and the unchanging Mrs. Forster.

If you asked me, there'd been more alteration in her appearance between Saturday and Monday morning than between 1977 and 2006.

Just then, as if deliberately, Mrs. Forster came through the door. 'I beg your pardon,' she said. 'I thought I would start in here, now.'

'Don't worry,' said Peter. 'We're finished.'

Mrs. Forster caught sight of the album. She came forwards to get a better look. 'Where did you find this?' she asked.

'It was in the safe,' said Peter.

'Doesn't Mr. Jonson look well?' she said, awkwardly.

'And you, too,' said Peter.

'Oh, I wore such horrible clothes,' said Mrs. Forster. It was all I could do not to laugh. Apart from the width of the collars, her clothes had been just the same then as they were now.

'It was the Seventies,' said Peter. 'No one looked their best.'

'I suppose so,' said Mrs. Forster. 'Still, I don't like to look at myself.' And it seemed she didn't like us looking at her, either.

Chapter 11.

Jack had had quite enough computer games for the day. I made some cheese on toast – his favourite – and then called him in for lunch. Afterwards, he went off to play, up in his room. I had kept his Gameboy, just to make sure he did something physical.

Peter and I were eating big doorsteppy peanut butter sandwiches and drinking milk. We called it our American lunch. Mary was sitting in the relaxer chair, gazing at us. She'd been a bit grizzly, but had settled down when I gave her a dummy. Mrs. Forster was still dusting in Michael Francis's office. Now and again, we could hear her as she moved a chair or closed a drawer.

'She wasn't too pleased about the safe,' said Peter.

'Do you think it's weird?' I asked.

'What? Her being so nosy?'

'No, her never aging.'

'She does age,' said Peter. 'Just, more slowly than it seems she should. It's probably the fact that she keeps fit, shoving that Hoover around.'

'You're the one that was pointing it out to me as strange.'

'It is strange. I can't explain it. And I certainly can't explain Michael Francis looking so sprightly at a hundred. He should at least have lost a bit of weight.'

Just then, the phone rang. Peter answered it, then came to fetch me. When I said hello, a woman introduced herself as the Health Visitor. She wanted to come round the following morning, to check up on Mary. I had told our Health Visitor in London we were moving. The two branches must have been in touch.

'You're being very efficient,' I said.

'We don't get so many babies as we used to,' she replied.

I suggested she come at nine o'clock. Might as well get it over with first thing.

I had to shout goodbye. Jack seemed to be thumping around unusually loudly in his room.

Next thing, there was a sharp scream and Jack was standing at the top of the stairs, crying like I hadn't heard him cry for ages.

'Mum!' he shouted. 'There are stones! There are stones!'

I didn't have any idea what he meant. But when I rushed up to him, he grabbed my hand and dragged me along. When I got to his bedroom, I saw that the floor was covered in exactly that – stones.

'What have you been doing?' I asked, perhaps more angrily than I should've.

'Nothing,' Jack wailed. 'Nothing.' Sometimes it's easy to forget just how young he is.

I hugged him and spoke more gently. 'How did the stones get up here?'

The huge heaves of his chest stopped him speaking for a little while. Then he managed to say, 'Falling down. They were falling down.'

'You mean you were dropping them?'

At this, he shook his head – and pointed upwards.

'The ceiling. They came from there.'

'They fell down from the ceiling?'

He nodded his head.

'So, you promise you didn't bring them in for them garden, to play with?'

He shook his head, then buried it into my shoulder. I couldn't remember Jack being like this for a couple of years. He certainly seemed genuinely upset.

Peter arrived, carrying Mary.

Jack told him the same story, with all the essential details in place.

'None of them hit you?' asked Peter.

'No,' said Jack. 'But they came very close.'

Peter picked up one of the stones and carefully examined it. Then he tried to hand it to me. 'It's very round,' he said. 'Like a marble.' For some reason, I was horrified by the idea of touching it. 'I think he probably found a stash of them somewhere.'

'I did not,' Jack said, very defiantly. 'They fell.'

'Let's pick them all up,' said Peter to Jack, trying to turn it into a game. Peter glanced into Jack's Transformers wastepaper basket. As usual, it was empty.

'This'll do,' Peter said, and handed Mary to me.

Jack, however, was even less keen on touching the stones than I was.

'Okay,' said Peter. 'I'll do it.'

By the time he was finished, the wastepaper basket was almost full. I could tell by the way Peter held it, tucked under his arm, that the stones weighed quite a lot.

'They're all the same size,' he said.

'Take them out!' shouted Jack, getting upset again. 'Take them out!'

I left Peter to deal with them.

Jack and me were just having a cosy cuddle, with Mary in between us, when there was a sharp rap on the floor.

I turned round to see another of the stones rolling along.

'It must have fallen off the chest of drawers, or something,' I said. But I didn't really believe that.

I led Jack by the hand into the bedroom with the four-poster. At least nothing would fall on our heads while we were sitting on that. Mary was wriggling about, so I started to feed her. Jack usually pretends to be disgusted by this. He says my nipples look yuck and asks why I can't feed Mary from a bottle, like normal mums. This time, however, he seemed comforted by her little sucking sounds. He lay down beside us on the bed.

'Does this mean I've seen a ghost?' he asked.

'I don't think so,' I said, then tried to make up for sounding so hard. 'But it's definitely something very strange.'

'This is a haunted house,' Jack said.

I didn't want to agree, although it was hard to think otherwise. Part of me still thought he'd been playing around with the stones himself. But what about them being identical? Jack would never have the patience to dig through the garden, looking for marble-sized stones. And, even if he'd done that, they'd all still be covered in wet earth, not as pristine as if they'd been washed with soap and water.

'It's a very old house,' I said. 'And sometimes odd things happen in very old houses.'

There were footfalls up the stairs. Peter came through the door.

'Mrs. Forster,' he said, 'tells me that's happened before. More than once. And always in that room.'

'What happened?' asked Jack.

'A materialization, she says.'

I gave Peter a look. Jack was mad keen enough on ghosts as it was. I didn't want Mrs. Forster's confirmation to really set him off.

'Why don't you play downstairs?' I suggested to Jack. 'If Mrs. Forster thinks the living room is safe.'

'And if she doesn't hoover you to death,' Peter said, and began making monster-sucking sounds. Jack gave a delighted shriek. He didn't seem to have been deeply affected by the materialization, or whatever it was.

We all went downstairs. Jack took a couple of books with him. He had darted into his bedroom to fetch them himself. I was glad he wasn't too terrified to go back in. If he wanted to, we could move him to the spare bedroom – but then he'd be further from us. He'd never slept more than a few feet away. He'd never even been on a sleepover.

Perhaps it was this that made me think about our flat. The new couple would be properly settled in, by now. Although they'd been perfectly nice, I didn't like to think of them living in our house. I'd always been on the tenant rather than the landlord side of the equation – the minus side. Now, I'd crossed an invisible line. I had become one of the people I used to complain about. But, more than this, I felt sensitive to the new couple's presence in our old rooms. What would happen to them there? Would they be happy? Would they argue? Would they be haunted by the lives of the people who'd been there before? Would they see the stain in the carpet?

Jack went and sat in the living room, and I began making tea for Peter. He told me that he didn't want tea. He said he was going out to buy the electronic goods we needed – *he* needed.

'Can't you go tomorrow?' I asked.

'You're not worried about the house, are you?' he asked.

'No,' I said, realising immediately that I did feel more than a bit nervous. 'Not really. Not as long as you're back by dark.'

This just made him laugh.

'We can try the keys out this evening,' he said.

'You're joking,' I said.

'Don't you want to know what's behind those doors?'

'Of course,' I said. 'But maybe we can wait until we've had a day where nothing weird has happened.'

'I want to know,' he said. 'I think it could be full of Michael Francis's secret diaries, or something like that. What I've found, apart from the photo album, hasn't been personal at all. It's as if all that stuff has been removed.'

While Peter had been speaking, I had poured out some orange juice. Now I went to take it through to Jack. Mrs. Forster was dusting in the hall. As I came out through the kitchen door, she made a kind of flinching-away movement – and that was enough to tell me she'd been eavesdropping. I decided to be direct.

'I don't take kindly to being spied upon,' I said. 'If I catch you doing that again, you'll be dismissed.'

'You should be careful of the doors,' she said, nodding towards the cellar. 'Best to leave them alone. Stick with what you've got.'

'So, you're not exactly denying that you were listening?'

Peter came out of the kitchen, having heard raised voices.

'I can help you,' said Mrs. Forster. 'I can help you understand this place.'

'What, exactly?' he asked. I thought he was talking to me.

'Mrs. Forster was listening to our conversation,' I replied.

'I heard that,' Peter said. 'What can you help us understand?'

'How to survive here,' said Mrs. Forster. 'It's not as simple as it seems.'

'If you knew about the stones, why didn't you tell us?' I asked.

'I don't know what's going to happen next.'

'Is there anything dangerous here?' I said. 'Anything that threatens us – that threatens my children.'

Mrs. Forster didn't answer.

'Tell us,' I said, 'or you can walk out of here now, and not come back.'

'This is a lovely place,' said Mrs. Forster. 'It's a perfect home. But there are things I can't tell you about it. You have to find them out for yourself. I can't promise that it'll never hurt you. Anything can happen, depending on how you react.'

'That's not much of an answer,' I said. 'Peter?'

'You're not making a particularly good impression, Mrs. Forster. To be honest, you're coming across as creepy and interfering. Now, would you like to be a bit more direct?'

'I would,' said Mrs. Forster, then burst out crying. I felt bad that she was upset, but she shouldn't go round trying to frighten us out of our house like that.

'We'll talk about this another day,' Peter told her. 'When you've more calm.'

She nodded, then went back across the hall and into the study.

'You let her off pretty lightly,' I said.

'She's been working here for years. It must be difficult, seeing new people around the place.'

'If she wanted, she could quit. Doesn't look like she needs the money.'

'Perhaps she needs the company.'

'So she spies on us?'

'Let's see what she says.'

I made Peter the tea, anyway, and he stayed to drink it. But then he went off in the car. Jack, always keen on things that go beep and buzz, was happy to go with him.

Chapter 12.

As I'd planned, I took Mary along to discover the village and find out the shop. This also gave me an excuse to get away from Mrs. Forster for a while. To be honest, I was having difficulty coming to terms with everything that had happened. If stones really *had* fallen from the roof of Jack's room, out of nowhere, then the world was a much weirder place than I'd ever believed. Shouldn't I be calling the police? Or running down the road shouting my head off? Instead we were all of us carrying on just as normal. I was going shopping. Did that make me mad? Looking back, I sometimes think so.

Mary and me encountered no tractors on the road, which was wider than the track to Matthew Maddox and Gracie Dearie's farm. Most of it I was familiar with – flowery hedgerows behind ditches and fields of rape and corn only visible when you went past a gate. But then came a new turn, a short row of thatched cottages, a small church, a pub called The Green Man, and then an open marketplace where the village shop was obvious because it was the only house without net curtains. Everything was picture postcard.

I paused outside the door of the shop. This was an important moment, I knew. I needed to make a good impression on whoever was behind the counter. Making sure I was wearing my brightest smile, I gave the door a push. It didn't open. Only then did I see the notice: 'Back in ten minutes.'

It was a long time since I'd seen anything like that. In Tulse Hill, a sign like that would mean 'Please burgle me now'.

There was a wooden bench on the other side of the marketplace. I pushed Mary across to it, then got her out and sat down to wait. Five minutes passed. Not a soul went by – not even in a car.

I'd fed Mary before we came out, but she was starting to wriggle around. A little drool came out of the corner of her mouth. She opened it wide, and I saw her gummy little cave. I decided I'd better give her a top-up. Better that than have her scream down the shop, and making a bad impression.

I was wearing a loose linen top, a smocky-type thing, and I was able to slip Mary's head almost completely under it. That was before I undid the flap of the nursing bra. Nothing could be more modest, I swear. But, of course, as soon as I started breastfeeding, the market square turned into Piccadilly Circus.

First of all, a couple of boys came along. The older one was about ten, but it was the younger one who interested me. He looked exactly Jack's age, with bright yellow hair and freckled cheeks. Both of them dressed in t-shirts, shorts and leather sandals. They wore socks. When they saw what I was doing, they blushed and began to snigger. 'Did you see her titties?' I heard the older one say. 'Yes,' said the younger. 'Did not!' 'Did!' When they saw the shop was closed, they sat down on the pavement to wait. Now and again, they looked at me, and the sniggering started again. I smiled at them, but this only made them snigger even more.

Next was an elderly man in a stripey jacket and dark blue trousers with sharp creases. He wore brown brogues. He was very bent over and walked with two sticks. On his head was a straw hat of the sort cricket umpires wear. This, he politely raised when he caught sight of me, after slowly transferring one of the walking sticks to the other hand. It was only then that he caught sight of the baby. 'Bloody hell,' he said, and quickly turned away. I could tell he was massively embarrassed. Probably his eyes weren't good enough to see exactly what was, and wasn't, on display.

Then three teenage girls swished past, all wearing tight t-shirts, pedal pusher jeans and trainers. 'Oo-oooh,' said the prettiest of them. 'Tits out,' said the tallest. 'What a slag,' said the podgiest. They giggled, and kept going.

Finally, an old lady came along. She was tiny, with a grey perm. She wasn't wearing a coat or pulling a wheelie, so I guessed she might be the shopkeeper.

I was right. When she reached the door, she pulled a key out of her pocket and turned it in the lock. Only then did she say hello to the old man and the young boys – greeting each of them by name, Andrew, Archie and Harold. She also glanced quickly in my direction. Not long enough for me to know whether she approved or disapproved of public breastfeeding.

Mary was still sucking quite hard, so I let her keep going. With any luck, she'd fall asleep on the nipple and – after I'd wiped her mouth – would look perfect when I went into the shop. Also, this would give the embarrassed man a chance to get clear.

He was gone in a couple of minutes, a packet of pipe tobacco in one pocket and something else, probably a bottle of washing-up liquid, in the other. I guessed that he'd hurried his purchases, in hopes of avoiding me. There was no raising of the hat as he hobbled off.

Mary slowed down and stopped. I knew I was only going to be feeding her like this for a few months more, and then I'd never do it again, ever. When I let myself think about it like this, every little tug was a pull at my heart. I felt particularly emotional when other people were negative about what I was doing. It was as if they were criticizing every other choice I made – as a mother. If I'd let myself, I would have started crying then and there.

Instead, I extremely carefully hooked my bra back into place, brought Mary out from under the smock, put the muslin over my shoulder and began to burp her.

All of this was so much less pressured, back in the house, with only Elizabeth to watch us. I had adopted her room as the place where I breastfed, even though the sofa in the living room was more comfortable than the high-backed chairs. I liked to have something interesting to look at, while Mary went about her gluggy business.

I wanted to ask Peter if he could find out something more about who Elizabeth had been, and what she'd done. Part of me, though, was quite keen to discover this for myself. It might take a little longer, but not involving him would bring me closer to the mysterious woman in the picture. What was between us was only between us – that was important.

Right on cue, Mary let out a satisfying little pop of a burp. She'd never been a windy baby. Not like Jack, who would save it all up till he was back in his buggy, then turn himself into a fountain of posset.

The boys came out of the shop, each carrying a paper bag of sweets. They looked like something out of Just William.

I put Mary down in the buggy, tucked her in, and wheeled her across the road. This time, I smiled even harder.

What a feeling it was – to step into that village shop, and to feel you'd gone back in time to a time you'd never really known! The place smelled of sugar and of fresh white bread. Even though a lot of the packaging was up-to-date – upside-down squeezy bottles for pickle and tubes for mustard – it still seemed as if nothing had changed here since the 1960s. It felt a little bit like your granny's front room, and a little bit like the storybook sweetshop you dreamed of when you were five. There was a row of painted plates up above the old-fashioned counter. I saw a picture of our house in very detailed dark brown, but I didn't have much time to look at it.

'You must be Mrs. Jonson,' said the shopkeeper, the tiny old lady. To serve people, she'd put a pinnie on over her baby blue woolen twin set.

'Yes,' I said.

'I'm Mrs. Willows,' she said. 'Welcome to the village.'

'Thank you,' I said. 'How did you know it was me?'

'We've known you were coming for weeks. Mrs. Dearie does me some vegetables, so she was in this morning. She told me about your little encounter with Mr. Maddox. And this is Mary, is it?'

Even better than people who remember your children's names are those who make sure they know them in advance.

'Yes. She's three months,' I said.

'And you breastfeed her?'

'I do,' I said.

'Just as it should be,' said Mrs. Willows. 'I did all my three. Of course, they've children of their own now.'

I felt immensely relieved. Mrs. Willows was just the sort of old lady you want to run your village shop. 'Is there anything you would like?' she asked.

I realized that, what with worrying about making a good impression, I hadn't thought of anything to buy.

'Milk,' I said, as it was the first thing I thought of.

'One pint or two?' said Mrs. Willows.

I bought a few things, not that we really needed them. Already I felt guilty for having gone to the supermarket. In future, I decided, I would do as much of my shopping here as possible.

Mrs. Willows loaded everything carefully into my bag, tins at the bottom, breakables and squashables on top. It was exactly as if she was packing her own shopping.

'Thank you,' I said, and paid.

The till rang up with an old-fashioned ker-ching!

'I look forward to meeting Mr. Jonson,' said Mrs. Willows.

'Did you know the other Mr. Jonson well? Who used to live in the house.'

'Not really,' said Mrs. Willows. 'Mrs. Forster did all his marketing for him. And he wasn't one for walks.'

'Not until he went to the North Pole,' I said.

'No,' said Mrs. Willows. 'Indeed.' Some of her warmth was gone. Perhaps my joke had been in bad taste.

'Mrs. Forster is very efficient,' I said.

'She was always like that,' said Mrs. Willows. 'I went to school with her, you see.'

It was hard to disguise my shock. Mrs. Willows seemed so unmistakably an old lady. And Mrs. Forster was… Mrs. Forster was Mrs. Forster.

'Really?' I asked. 'Were you in the same year?'

'No, she was in the year below. It was a very small classroom. We were all in together, really.'

I didn't know what else to say.

'We're glad you let Robert Mew stay on,' said Mrs. Willows. I guessed that by 'we' she meant the village in general. The word was another step towards coldness.

I wanted to ask her about the house. She must have heard about strange goings-on. But now wasn't the time.

I said thank you and left, perhaps too obviously in a hurry.

Chapter 13.

When I got back home, I stowed the food in the larder then took a blanket out into the garden and lay down with Mary on a shady part of the lawn. It was very quiet. Robert Mew was nowhere to be seen or heard. I guessed he was working in some far-off part of the grounds, doing battle with the ivy. The sound of hoovering started up, inside the house. I wished Mrs. Forster would just give it a rest. No house needed that much cleaning – not even one where dirt and stones mysteriously appeared and disappeared.

Sitting outside in the fresh air, it was impossible to believe those things had really happened. They certainly didn't seem dangerous or threatening. Looking back, I'm surprised I was able to dismiss them so easily. Perhaps I am more adaptable than I give myself credit for. I'm certainly not any braver than the average person.

I smiled at Mary, and she smiled right back. Three months is a lovely age. Babies start to come out of themselves. Until they give you some response, it can be a hard grind. You feel like you're a slave to something that does nothing more than cry, sleep, and make a mess. But those first few smiles are a whole new world of possibility. 'I like being here,' they seem to say. 'I could be happy here.' And that's what you want for your children, isn't it? For them not to blame you for bringing them into the world – a world which, for the first years, you create and dominate. Even at three and a half, Jack had started to give us flashforwards to his teen years. Three and a half was the first time he said, 'Oh, what*ever*,' when I asked him what he wanted for tea.

The hoovering stopped, and I looked up at the house. Would Jack and Mary be happy here? Wasn't I already starting to feel trapped myself? I hated the way I was thinking about Mrs. Forster. She was a person too, with feelings that were obviously quite hurt. If I'd been a servant, I knew I'd have tried to listen in to conversations. You needed to know what your employer was thinking. It was her manner that really annoyed me, though – both subservient and superior. Like she didn't think we had the right to live there. Like she wanted us to know that's what she thought.

Mrs. Forster was in the doorway.

It took me a moment to realize that this was actually her and not just my thoughts of her.

She walked out of the house, looked around, saw where I was and started coming towards me.

'I'm sorry, Mrs. Jonson,' she said. 'I shouldn't have been listening.'

I stayed where I was, sitting on the blanket. But I felt awkward, with her so far above me.

'I do want to tell you everything I can about the house. I'm not trying to be unnecessarily mysterious.'

'Is it haunted?'

‘Not exactly. You won’t see ghosts floating around. Not traditional ones.’

I motioned for her to join me. Awkwardly, she sat sideways on the bench – as if she were a member of the Royal Family trying to look relaxed in an official photograph.

‘What will we see?’

‘Strange things. Like the falling stones.’

‘We already know about that,’ I said. ‘You haven’t told us anything we don’t know.’

‘The house isn’t exactly alive,’ she said, ‘but it does *react*. It has moods. Sometimes it’s angry, but mostly it’s a happy house.’

I had a sudden feeling of distance – like I was myself from a week ago, listening to the same words. They were nonsense, weren’t they? Some lines from an old song came into my head, ‘This is a happy house, we’re happy here in the happy house.’ I smiled, and I could see Mrs. Forster’s dismay. She thought I didn’t believe her. But already I’d seen and felt enough to know that something far beyond the ordinary was going on. I straightened my face. Siouxsie and the Banshees, that was it. And then the words went, ‘We’re all quite sane.’

‘Was the house angry with Jack?’

‘I don’t know. Perhaps. Maybe it was just saying hello.’

‘It’s a funny way to do it.’

‘Boys are often quite rough with one another,’ she said.

‘Well, the house hasn’t greeted me yet,’ I said.

‘Hasn’t it?’ asked Mrs. Forster.

And then I realized that of course it had.

‘We are safe here, though?’

‘Perfectly safe,’ said Mrs. Forster. ‘Safer than anywhere else in the world.’

‘Thank you,’ I said. Although I was sure she could tell me more than she had. Better to leave it until after we’d made up properly. This little scene was just about keeping the lines of communication open.

Mrs. Forster looked at Mary. ‘She’s such a lovely baby,’ she said. ‘And so quiet.’

‘Second child,’ I said.

‘That’s what they say,’ Mrs. Forster said, ‘isn’t it?’

‘Sometimes,’ I said, ‘you wish they could stay like this.’

Mrs. Forster didn’t say anything. But she looked at me in an extremely intense way.

After Mrs. Forster had gone, I sat for a while longer on the lawn – until it began to get a little chilly. Mary had a feed, then we went inside. I thought I’d have a look around the library, to see what I could find out about the house, and perhaps about Elizabeth.

There were so many books, several thousand at least, that it was difficult to know where to start. Many of them had leather spines with gold lettering. A few of them were very tall and were an ivory colour. I looked in one of these, and found that it was written in what I guessed was old Latin.

Hunting around, I discovered some cabinets where all the more modern hardbacks were kept. Michael Francis was obviously a systematic kind of man. The books had been arranged into categories. A couple of shelves were architectural. On one of these was a black guide to the architecture of West Sussex by Nikolaus Pevsner. I'd seen one of these guides before. My grandfather had the one covering Lancashire, where he grew up.

I was almost certain that Nikolaus Pevsner would have written something about our house. It was so old and big that it must be important.

After pulling the book from the shelf, I sat down in one of the leather club chairs. It wasn't hard to find the entry – someone, probably Michael Francis, had ringed the page number in the index. Dark black ink, not faded.

This is what the entry said:

'THE NEW HOUSE. 1 ¼ m. NW. Which fails to live up to its name, yet still is one of the best preserved surviving examples of Elizabethan domestic architecture. Originally a larger dwelling, the house was destroyed circa 1580 and rebuilt over the ensuing years, though on a diminished scale. The timber-framed frontage, with four gables upon either side of a neat porch, is not the most impressive part of the building. That honour is reserved for the magnificent entry hall, about which a whole volume might be written. This is a masterpiece of carved wooden panelling. Notable features include the family crest of the Jonsons, certain symbols that many interpret as Masonic in origin and some wonderfully vivid animals. Particularly exquisite is a serpent to upper l. of the door by which one enters.'

I couldn't resist going to have a look. It was hard to see how I'd missed the serpent before. The carpenter had made it crawl from one panel to the next, in three very lifelike dimensions. The only thing wrong with it was that it had teeth, like one of Jack's dinosaurs.

How bizarre it was – to read something in black and white and then look up to see it right in front of you! I'd only ever done that on holiday in France, when the wonderful B&B turned out to have closed for refurbishment or the great restaurant was full of people with the same guidebook.

I went back to my cosy seat and continued reading. Perhaps, I thought, there might be something in here about the four doors in the cellar.

'The large room to the rear of the building, downstairs, boasts an ornate fireplace c. 1582. The preservation of this, and all the period features of this house, is quite remarkable. A very fine double-sided staircase leads from the hall to a long gallery that serves to communicate between the rooms of the upper floor. It is rumoured that one of the bedrooms contains a priest's hole, although I was unable to discover it. As the Jonsons were recusants, such a feature would be in keeping.

'One reason for the exquisite preservation of the house is that, following the death of her father in 1587, Elizabeth Jonson refused to allow any alterations whatsoever to the house. She died without heir, in mysterious circumstances, but, by then, an almost religious veneration towards the original condition of the property was established, which has thankfully been maintained ever since. (Apart from the execrable addition of some French windows to the back of the house, some time in the 1930s.)

'The New House is not open for public viewing.'

I wondered why Mr. Pevsner hadn't been shown the priest's hole. A sudden image of Mrs. Forster, leading him primly from room to room, came into my mind. I checked the date of the book, which was 1965. She would certainly have been here, back then.

I turned the page, and saw that another nearby house was being described. Mr. Pevsner had also failed to see the underground chapel, or perhaps he had been allowed to see it on condition that he didn't mention it. Even after all those years, it was possible that Michael Francis wanted to keep the secrets of his ancestors. He might even have expected the return of religious persecution, one day.

Of course, the main thing that excited me was the mention of Elizabeth's death in 'mysterious circumstances'. That might explain the question marks in her dates, 1585-15??.

What I needed was something specifically about the family. Perhaps a biography, or a local history book.

I had just put the Pevsner guide back on the shelf, after saying thank you to it, when Mary started to whimper. I thought I might be able to feed her and then return to my search, but while I was sitting in the dining room, gazing over Mary's head at the now even more fascinating Elizabeth, I heard Peter and Jack come through the front door.

'We got it,' said Jack.

'What did you get?' I asked.

'Everything,' he said. 'And I got this.'

He showed me a new game for his Nintendo. It was called Danny Phantom: The Ultimate Enemy and seemed to feature ghosts quite heavily.

Peter stood in the doorway. I gave him a questioning look. He nodded in response. Trust me, he was saying.

'Can I play it?' Jack asked.

'Not that you haven't been playing it in the car,' I said.

Jack looked at his father.

'I didn't get a word out of him, the whole way back.'

'But you said I could,' said Jack. 'There's this ghost called Clockwork and he says – '

'You can play until dinner time,' I said. 'But not afterwards.'

'Thanks,' said Jack, and went off to the living room.

I told Peter about my afternoon – the village shop, the talk with Mrs. Forster. However, I didn't mention my researches into Elizabeth. I thought I'd wait until I had something more impressive to reveal. A mysterious death was all very well, but a mysterious death with a brilliant new solution was much better.

'Well, we ordered a fridge-freezer,' Peter said. 'They're going to deliver it tomorrow morning. I brought the rest of the stuff back with me, including the new television. I'd like to see if I can get that and the computer going as soon as I can.'

The way I was feeling, I couldn't imagine myself just sitting down to watch the gogglebox. I was having too much fun with my historical investigations. The library seemed much more exciting than another weepy talent show.

Jack wasn't able to kill ghosts for too long. I made pasta with peas, ham and cream for dinner. We were just sitting down to eat when Mrs. Forster came in and said she was finished for the day, unless there was anything else we wanted her for.

'I don't think so,' I said. 'Thank you.'

'See you tomorrow,' she said.

'Yes,' I said. Although I could tell that she wanted some more reassurance than that.

Mrs. Forster stowed her cleaning clothes and left.

'She knows all the secrets,' said Jack.

'What do you mean?' Peter asked.

'She knew about the pee-hole.' This was what he had decided to call the priest's hole. 'I'm sure she knows loads of other things.'

'I'm sure she does,' said Peter, and gave me a look.

'Some people just take a bit of getting used to,' I said. 'I'm sure that's how she feels about us.'

'But we're normal,' said Jack. 'And she's a freak.'

'Jack, that's really rude. Mrs. Forster is not a freak.' I said it, but I didn't believe it. I thought of old Mrs. Willows in the village shop, Mrs. Forster's schoolmate, and I knew I was lying.

I glanced at Peter. He knew it, too.

As Jack and Mary hadn't had more than a flannel wash for several days, we made this bath night. It was time for us to get into some proper routines, and that didn't just mean having cocoa at bedtime.

The water was steaming hot – too hot for Jack to get into, not until I'd run some more cold. That was one thing about this house, even though it was old, everything seemed to work efficiently – the water, the electricity, the heating.

Because he was worried that the stones would start falling again, and also because he'd become whizzy playing so much Nintendo, it took Jack a long while to calm down and go to sleep. When he's nervous like this, he asks even more questions than normal. Tonight, he wanted to know all about Father Trovato. Where he was from? What did he do all day? What did he believe? 'Like, does he believe in ghosts?'

'I don't know, Jack. Probably not.'

'Catholics believe in the Holy Ghost,' said Peter.

'Don't confuse him,' I said. 'That's different.'

'What does the Holy Ghost look like?' asked Jack. 'Is he white?'

'No one really knows,' said Peter. 'Sometimes he's shown in paintings as a dove flying over people's heads.'

'But he's really a ghost,' said Jack.

'He's really completely made-up,' I said.

'Don't let Father Trovato hear you say that,' said Peter, 'or we'll be evicted.' I could tell he was uneasy about me dismissing the Holy Ghost just like that.

'What's a vict?' Jack asked.

'Close your eyes,' I said. 'Question Time is over.'

'Am I a vict?' Jack asked.

Eventually, after about five lullabies, and lots of reassurances that the stones weren't coming back, Jack began to nod.

Luckily, Mary went off around the same time. I laid her down in the middle of the four-poster bed.

'Come on,' said Peter. He meant, Let's explore the cellar.

I was reluctant to go down again. Not that I was scared of it, although I didn't like the idea of meeting a rat. What really put me off was fear of what we might find behind the other doors. I didn't want to find some nasty presence in the house – something that would affect how I felt about the whole thing.

Peter gathered together all the keys he had collected – the ones from Father Trovato, those from Michael Francis's office, and Mrs. Forster's, too.

We descended the cellar staircase quite breezily, as if going underground was no different than going into any other room.

'What do you think we'll find?' Peter asked, his words sounding echoey off the walls. He led the way down.

'A secret passage,' I said.

'It wouldn't be very secret if it was just behind a door,' he said. I could tell he was incredibly excited – trembling with it.

The bottom of the staircase was against the right-hand wall. A little further along was the first of the unopened doors. Let's call that the East door. The next door round, anticlockwise, was the North door, then the West and South. Each stood in the middle of a long, featureless wall of grey plaster. The one with the tree roots and earth behind it was the South door. Peter now began with the East door. It took him five minutes to try all the keys. None of them fit.

We moved on to the North door. Our breathing went quiet as we calmed down. I was listening out very hard, in case I heard Mary crying. And so it was that I heard what I thought was something behind the North door. At first it sounded like static on the radio. But there couldn't be anything electronic in there, could there? Some receiver from the 1940s, still working. That would be too weird. I really hoped that Peter would find a key for this door. I didn't like the idea of going to bed not knowing what was making that noise. I'd keep thinking I was hearing it.

One of the keys on Father Trovato's chain went snugly into the lock, and Peter turned it once, twice. A loud and satisfying click rang out.

'I'll just check they're okay,' I said, about to head for the staircase.

'They're fine,' said Peter. 'This won't take long.'

I closed my eyes and took a deep, deep breath. I knew what we were about to discover might change everything.

'Okay,' I said.

Peter turned the handle and pulled open the door.

PART TWO

Chapter 14.

At first, I thought something had gone funny with my eyesight. The room looked distorted, wobbly. Then I realized that I was seeing it through a sheet of falling water.

Peter put his hand out and touched it before I had time to say, 'Careful!'

I don't know what I was thinking. That it might be very hot, or be something that wasn't water – acid, perhaps.

Below where Peter put his hand in, a ragged strip of air appeared in the glassy drop of the water. He opened his fingers, and the single strip divided into five. Then he drew his hand back, leaving the water to heal itself back to a smooth vertical sheet.

'Wow,' he said.

The water didn't splash at the bottom because, as we could clearly see, the floor level in this new room was a couple of feet lower than that of the room we were in. It looked very pale – almost white. And when Peter put both his hands into the water, to create a bigger gap to peer through, we saw that the whole room, floor, walls and ceiling, was covered in large white tiles. This was not the most noticeable thing, however. That was a large jet of water shooting horizontally out of the wall on the left side. It was coming from a white pipe that glistened as though it was made of china. The whole of the floor seemed to be moving in a circle. After a moment, we realized that this was where the water was escaping – through a hole in the floor, in a huge clockwise whirlpool.

I swore, using a word reserved for very special occasions.

Peter repeated the word.

There really wasn't much else you could say, even if you weren't ill-bred like what we were.

The water was quite chilly. Peter pulled his hands out. The sleeves of his shirt were damp at the cuffs. We stared one another in the face. I was glad he was so familiar, even though he looked so completely freaked out.

'What is it?' he asked.

'A spring,' I said. 'Or an underground river, perhaps.'

'It's not Jack's bathwater,' said Peter, 'that's for sure.'

Jack's bathwater, whilst it had started sparkling had ended up the colour of very weak tea. Bless him.

Peter cupped his hand under the flow then sipped up a tentative mouthful.

'That's delicious,' he said. 'Better than tap.'

Not wanting to seem a scaredy cat, I tried some too. It was delicious – very refreshing and diamond pure. The flow of it was icy around my fingers.

'This is a very weird house,' I said.

'I think we already knew that,' Peter replied. 'Weird and sometimes wonderful.'

Dirt in one room and some kind of antiseptic drain in another.

Peter left the whirlpool room open whilst moving on to the next door.

This door, the East, had a very different kind of lock. It wasn't old-looking at all – just a modern Yale, and quite shiny.

Peter found the key for it almost straight away, on Mrs. Forster's bunch.

'Hang on,' I said, and put my ear to the door.

Peter did the same.

'Hear anything?' he asked.

'No,' I said.

I stepped back. All my instincts demanded that we find out what new oddity was hidden away behind this door. But I also didn't feel like taking everything too quickly. Peter, though, had already turned the key twice, anticlockwise, and was pulling the door wide open.

Behind the East door was another door.

This one looked much older. Underneath all the cobwebs, it was painted a dull black.

I felt a chill as I looked at it. The water room had been quite funny, but this one, for some reason, I didn't like at all.

'Be careful,' I said, instinctively. It was something I said dozens of times a day to Jack. I was worried that 'Be careful' would turn out to be Mary's first words.

Peter started to try the bigger keys one by one. This lock was very large. It looked to me as if none of them would fit, but the third one on Mrs. Forsters' key-chain did.

At first, it wouldn't turn at all. Peter had to put another key into the oval eyehole bit and use that as a lever to add some force to his twist.

'Don't break it,' I said.

'It's shifting,' he grunted. With another moment's strain, the key began to turn. At least we could be fairly certain that no one had been in here for a long while. Peter turned the thing as far as it would go, then stepped back and pulled at the door.

Slowly, with a very corny creak, it opened to reveal – yet another door.

This one was covered in pale papery leather.

'Let's leave it,' I said.

'What? After we've opened the other two doors?'

'I think something horrible is behind it,' I said, and I really did.

Peter put his ear to it.

'No monster,' he said. 'Not that I can hear.'

'Don't joke,' I said.

He was already trying the remaining keys. But one after the other they failed to fit into the lock. The hole of this one was very squarish, and it looked as though the key to open it would be square rather than round.

'No,' said Peter, after he'd gone through all three bunches. 'How frustrating is that?'

He knew I was more relieved than anything.

'Let's shut up the other ones and go,' I said.

'Wait a minute,' he said, and put his ear once again to the door.

'What?' I asked.

'Just thought I heard something.'

'If you're trying to scare me, it's working.'

'No, I did. I thought I heard…'

'What?' I said. 'What?!'

'Something moving,' he said.

'Like an animal? A rat?' I gave an involuntary shudder.

'No,' he said. 'It was more like something slipping down. Maybe it was cobwebs falling off the door.'

Peter locked up the black door and the first door. I immediately felt better.

'Still,' he said, 'we opened one of them. And we've still got this one to try.'

'Oh, come on, Peter,' I said. I wanted to check on Jack and Mary. As if our opening the doors had put them in danger. But Peter was determined to have a go. It didn't take him long to realize it was pointless – the keys didn't even go into the keyhole. 'Hold up,' he said, going down on his knees and peering into the hole. 'This lock's been filled with something. Might be plaster or cement.'

'Good,' I said, taking what he said on trust. 'Come upstairs, now, or I will lock you in here for the night.'

The very thought made me shiver. And it seemed to work on hurrying Peter up. Perhaps he really believed me.

Upstairs again, in the kitchen, Peter made us both a cup of tea.

'What do we make of that, then?' he said.

'The water?' I replied. 'I think it's something Michael Francis put in. To make sure the damp didn't get into the floorboards. It's an underground river.'

'I wonder if he ever went in there.'

'It's not the sort of place you take your bath,' I said. 'Too chilly.'

'I might try it,' Peter said.

'You will *not*,' I said. 'You might drown. Get sucked in. Who knows where that hole in the floor goes to, or how big it is.'

'Okay,' he said.

'Promise me you won't go exploring down there on your own.'

'I'm not Jack,' he said.

'Promise,' I said.
He promised.

Chapter 15.

You can't keep Peter away from technology for long. He was soon in the living room, trying to get the TV working.

I went to check on the children. Mary was fine, although she had a very wet nappy, and needed to be changed. She must have been like that for a while because it had gone cold. Her wee was very pale, hardly any colour at all – though it was only later that I took any notice of this. Before I left her, I turned the radiator in our bedroom up. It gave a couple of gurgling glugs and I assumed it was about to start warming up.

Jack, strangely, seemed to be too hot. There was perspiration on his forehead and his pyjamas were damp under the arms. I opened the diamond-paned window by a crack. All the windows upstairs had funny metal catches that seemed to be as old as the building. It worried me that Jack might be able to push through and fall out. But he'd never sleepwalked before.

Just to be sure, I took the shoelaces off a pair of my old running shoes and tied them across the gap. Peter would have to sort out something more permanent in the next few days. Another job to be done.

'There's no coaxial socket,' said Peter. He seemed annoyed by this.

'That's for the telly, is it?' I asked.

'It looks like they've never had a TV here before. We'll have to put an aerial up on the roof. Until we get cable. I think that's the simplest thing. It'll sort the computer, too.'

'And until then I suppose we'll just have to talk to each other.'

'I'll phone an electrician tomorrow, about the aerial. Jack can watch DVDs till we get something set up. I feel sort of cut off. There might be important emails waiting for me.'

'I don't miss it at all,' I said. 'I wish they'd never been invented.'

'Don't you want to know what's on the news?'

'Not really. It's never going to make you happy, is it?'

'The football results,' he said. 'Sometimes.'

'I thought they weren't playing at the moment.'

'They're not.'

'Anyway,' I said, 'I think there may be other, more serious issues about this house – such as stones falling from the roof.'

'You know, I think he probably found a bucket of them somewhere. Old marbles. He didn't want us to be angry with him for spilling them.'

'What about the dirt in the pantry?'

'That I can't explain. Unless you were dreaming. That would be an explanation.'

'I was awake,' I said, although I was no longer certain.

'Well, the tenants have moved into our house. If you want us to leave, we'll have to go to a hotel.'

‘I don’t want to leave. I just want to know what’s going on.’

‘I’m sure we’ll find out,’ he said, infuriatingly straightforward. ‘It’s probably just your common or garden poltergeist.’

‘You just told me you thought there was a rational explanation for everything.’

‘There is,’ said Peter.

I told him about the architecture guide and what it said about the house being destroyed. But I didn’t mention Elizabeth’s death in mysterious circumstances.

‘I’m going to the library,’ I said. ‘I want to find out more.’

‘There were some history books in the study,’ he said. ‘You might want to start there, instead.’

Because I was annoyed with Peter, I stuck to the library – to begin with, at least. I found a couple of books about the Tudors, and one about Elizabeth I, but Elizabeth Jonson wasn’t mentioned in any of the indexes.

After about half an hour, I gave up. As I went through the hall, I saw that Peter was now in the kitchen. He was clearing space for the fridge-freezer. I snuck past, so he wouldn't see me.

There were two whole shelves in Michael Francis’ bookcase dedicated to Catholicism, and another one and a half to the North Pole. This was obviously where he kept the books on the things that were dearest to him. Down at the bottom, I found half a dozen volumes on local history.

They were in very good condition even though, when I checked, I saw that some had been printed in the mid-seventies. One in particular caught my eye. Called *A Kindly Place*, it was all about the history of the village.

There was no index. But an entire chapter was devoted to our house, with the titled ‘A Dwelling Unlike Any Other’. Andrew Gatward, the author of the book, has very kindly given me permission to quote from it.

The part that caught my eye was about Elizabeth’s father.

‘William Jonson was a most remarkable man, whether considered in his time or out of it. With the building of what was known as ‘The Great House’, he, for a while at least, brought considerable prosperity to the village. What had, before, been a cultural backwater, was now opened to the full flood of contemporary European thought, both religious and scientific. The local farmers were astonished to see the number of books being brought to the house. For a short time, it was jokingly referred to as ‘the University’. (We are lucky that William’s diary is still in existence, to recall a few of these details.) It is clear, however, that from the first there was considerable hostility towards the new family. Particularly, it seems, when rumours started to go round that they were of a Catholic disposition. This news, I would speculate, did not take very long to percolate through the community. The fact that William did not attend Sunday service at St Edith’s would have been noticed within a month, if not a week.

‘On first being completed, the house was more extensive than it is in the present day. A vast hall stood at the rear of the property, covering the area now occupied by the knot garden. This was burnt to the ground, along with the whole of the original house, in 1580. William’s diary is strangely silent on the cause of the conflagration. The most likely explanation is that there was an accident in the kitchen, or that one of the many chimneys caught fire. However, more colourful local legend has it that William was engaging in necromancy, and that, at the height of the blaze, the devil himself was seen dancing with delight along the guttering.

Whatever the truth might be, it is certain that the villagers always regarded William with great suspicion if not outright loathing. This is hardly surprising. They had none of them met a man of his calibre before. Educated at Balliol College, Oxford, William had for four years been present in the court of Mary I, first as a page and later as a courtier. He took part in several important ambassadorial expeditions, mainly to the Low Countries, and was rumoured to have been present, as a young man, at the marriage of Mary I to Philip of Spain, later Philip II. William’s reasons for retiring to the country around 1560 are not definitively known, although it seems unlikely that he was as comfortable with the new Queen as with the old. His deep devotion to Rome was almost certainly a prime motivation for his removing himself from court. One of the rooms in William’s rebuilt abode – known thereafter as the New House – contains a priest hole that I myself, in my boyhood, was once permitted to inspect, inside and out. I shall not reveal its exact location, although it seems highly unlikely it will ever be seriously required again.

In 1562, the first of William's three surviving children was born – although there had been a stillborn son, not named, the previous year. Christened Elizabeth, she turned out to be one of the most remarkable products of her age – quite worthy of comparison with her royal namesake. Her name seems to have been chosen in tribute to the young queen, perhaps as an attempt to appear loyal. Her younger brothers, Emanuell (1564-1579), a well-liked young man who died whilst out hunting, and Peter (1567-1641), a devoted gardener who eventually inherited the house, were no match for the brilliant Elizabeth.

Privately tutored from an early age, Lilian, as the family knew her, spoke Latin, Greek, Spanish, Italian and High Church German. Among her other accomplishments were dancing, playing the lute, writing sonnets (all unfortunately lost), and, most remarkably of all, sword-fighting. Besides his religion, William had very advanced ideas, for his time, and believed young women equally as capable of achievement as young men. However, Elizabeth's principle love was not for the arts but the sciences. The New House was the first in West Sussex to possess a telescope. It is easy to imagine the delight with which this amazing young woman, standing upon the midnight lawn, examined the moon, planets and stars. The universe was beginning to reveal its mysteries to her.

Another pursuit of William's was chemistry. He had a room of the house, believed to be the cellar, dedicated to experiments of this sort. Perhaps Elizabeth showed a desire to join her father at an early age. Where were all those curious smells coming from? What had made that extremely loud bang? Children hate to be excluded from anything that seems exciting. It is to William's credit that he did not exclude his enthusiastic young daughter from his arcane pursuits.

'More books arrived at the New House. And, no doubt, Elizabeth read all of them for soon William was recording that she had outstripped him "in al materes chymicall and beyond". This entry of his diary continues: "She if a wonder, and beftowed upon myfelf by God to mitigate solitude". How a man with a wife and two other children could complain of solitude might, at first, be hard to understand. But of his wife the best that can be said is that she was companionable, when not suffering from one ailment or another. Margerye Jonson had been known as a great beauty. It must have been for this that William married her, for she was to provide him with no intellectual stimulation.

Between 1582 and 1584, Elizabeth is believed to have travelled widely on the continent. Cities we know her to have visited include Paris, Cologne, Madrid, and of course Rome. It should be noted that her father, after coming down from Elizabeth's court, never left the country or, so far as we know, the county again.

Upon her return, Elizabeth resumed her usual life in the New House. There seems to have been no pressure put upon her to attend court, or to find herself a suitable husband. By this time, her younger brother Peter was attending the court of Queen Elizabeth, in its fullest imperial pomp. A few of his letters survive. Unfortunately, they are remarkably dull. Peter's main concern was for the health of his four horses, about which we knew a great deal more than we need. The only mention of Elizabeth is the cryptic sentence "Bid my fifter to ftop her night-speeking; none good will come of it." Although it is possible that this reading is wrong, and that the crucial word is "night-seeking".'

After this there were a couple of pages about Peter's progress through the Elizabethan civil service. He sounded a bit of a creep, and I was sure that Andrew Gatward didn't like him at all. Finally, he got back to Elizabeth, who I think he was totally in love with. I certainly was.

'Sadly, we know very little more of the life of sweet Lilian. After 1590, no record exists of her at all. Her father died the following year, of causes not recorded. His grave can be seen in the churchyard of St Edith's, backing on to the nave midway along the side nearest the main road. Emanuell and Margerye are interred there, too. Peter's grave, which is separate, is located in the far corner, beneath the oak trees. There is no record of Elizabeth's death or burial.

'Rumours explaining her disappearance are legion. Some of them are extremely wild and unreliable. The charge of necromancy returns, along with the suggestion that the devil came one night in a thunderstorm and stole her away. One legend has it that she blew herself up whilst trying to create gunpowder. Another, more gruesome yet, that she deliberately threw herself upon one of the large open fires in the house. It is just possible that she committed suicide, perhaps in some less grotesque manner, and was therefore not allowed to be buried on hallowed ground. In this case, a private internment within the grounds of the house would seem likely.

'And so, in sad mystery, passes from record quite the most fascinating character in the history of our village. Yet the papers of the Jonson family are vastly extensive; and it is to be hoped that, if historians were once again permitted access to them, more might be discovered of the wonderful Elizabeth Jonson, her life and death.'

My first thought was to wonder whether Andrew Gatward was still alive. I turned to the start of the book, where I found a small note about the author.

‘Born in Lambeth in 1931, Andrew Gatward moved to the village at the age of two and a half. He early on in life developed a fascination for St Edith’s church, and served there as a choirboy. Fifty years later, he wrote the definitive history of the church, *St Edith’s, Early and Late*. In 1950, Andrew Gatward went to Jesus College, Oxford. He read Divinity, but later decided against ordination. Instead, he pursued his fascination with local history, authoring, as well as the present volume, *A Small Sussex Village at War*, *Hidden Histories* and the illustrated children’s book *Local Ghost Makes Good.*’

I decided then and there to find him and talk to him. It didn’t seem possible that he would have moved away from the place he loved so much. Not unless he’d been forced into a nursing home.

It was now close to ten o’clock. Mary would be wanting a feed. I checked in on Peter, who was still fiddling with something or other, then went upstairs.

Jack and Mary were fine. She was still dry and he had cooled down a bit.

In the bathroom, I turned the tap to put some water on my toothbrush, but nothing came out. I tried the hot tap, but the story was the same. The shower too didn’t work.

As I couldn’t be bothered going downstairs to test the taps in the kitchen, I started brushing with just the toothpaste. There’s something icky about this – I don’t know what. You need that little bit of water on the bristles, otherwise it’s just all your spit.

Mary fed without waking up. I think the fresh air of our walk had tired her out. Tomorrow, I decided, I would go into the village again – look at the Jonson graves in the churchyard, and try to track down Andrew Gatward.

Half an hour later, Peter came up.

‘Water’s not working,’ I said, as he went into the bathroom.

I heard a creak and then a gush.

‘Seems fine now,’ he said.

I hate it when that happens, when you can’t do something and your husband can. I’ll strain and strain before I let Peter open a jar of pickles or bottle of juice.

I think I was asleep before Peter got into bed.

Mary stirred twice in the night, but only to feed. Without really waking up myself, I sat on the side of the bed and let her take what she wanted. From outside, I could hear the sound of rain. It sounded quite heavy. But the shutters were closed, so I couldn’t see much of anything.

Chapter 16.

The Health Visitor came first thing, as we'd arranged. She was called Miriam Shoulder and she was, let's say, a large lady.

'What a fascinating pile,' she said. 'I didn't even know it was here.'

When Miriam arrived, Mary was having a nap upstairs. That's always the way – when someone needs to prod your baby, they're fast asleep. Rather than force Miriam up the stairs, I brought Mary down.

'Lovely,' said Miriam, when I handed Mary over to her.

She asked me the usual questions. I told her that everything was fine. All the while, Mary was waking up and starting to grizzle.

Jack came in and tried to turn the television on. The screen came to grey life but there was no picture.

'It's not working,' I said, 'and even if it was, you wouldn't be watching it at this time.'

Luckily, Jack wasn't still in his pyjamas. Peter had got him dressed. I didn't want Miriam thinking we were a bunch of slackers.

'Dad said I could go with him to the electric shop again.'

'Well, that's all right,' I said.

'I'd just like to weigh her, now,' said Miriam. She had a little hammock-type-thing that she dangled from a hook with a round dial. Mary absolutely hated being swung round in the air. She kicked and wailed. The needle didn't stay still at all.

'Fine,' said Miriam.

She lowered Mary to the sofa, and I picked her up. I could tell she wouldn't settle until I'd given her some more milk.

Miriam noted down the weight in Mary's baby book with the red plastic cover. The proper name is 'Personal Child Health Record'. Then Miriam plotted the week and weight on a growth chart.

'Wow, she was shooting up,' she said.

'She's a hungry girl,' I said, 'Aren't you, love?'

I began to feed her.

'It's a little less in the past fortnight. But that's nothing to worry about. I'd like to see you in a week's time, if that's okay with you. Just to check you're all settling in.'

I knew there was no need for it. She was just being careful. Sussing us out.

'That would be fine,' I said. 'Same time?'

We agreed she would come back on Tuesday morning.

'I'll show myself out,' Miriam said. 'Leave you to it.'

She stroked the back of Mary's head and then walked off into the hall. Peter came out of the kitchen to say goodbye. He was holding a drying cloth because he'd been doing the washing up.

'Nice woman,' he said, as he came to join me. 'Everything okay?'

'Nothing wrong with our Mary,' I said, although I was slightly worried she might have stopped putting on weight. She'd been such a great grower, so far.

'I'll take Jack off as soon as we're ready.'

It didn't take them long. Jack always hurries when he knows there's a chance someone might buy him something. He was also carrying his Gameboy, so I knew he was expecting to be slaying ghosts in the car – all the way there and all the way back. I still wasn't quite sure what Peter needed so urgently.

'Don't forget the fridge-freezer's coming,' he said, just before they left.

That was annoying. It meant I had to stay in and wait for the delivery men.

Mrs. Forster arrived, bang on nine o'clock, and started cleaning. She was mopping the floor in the hall, which turned it even more treacherous.

I decided to make a cup of tea and take it, and Mary, out into the garden. It was a very sunny day. Looking through the windows, I couldn't see any trace of last night's heavy rain.

When I got to the kitchen, though, I found that the taps here didn't work either. But, then, how had Mrs. Forster filled her bucket? I didn't want to start a conversation with her, so I thought I'd go without. Luckily, though, there was enough for one mug still left in the kettle – although I found the thought of reboiled water a bit yucky.

I don't know why I didn't realize the significance of the water not working – not working for me. Looking back, it seems so obvious. And that it hadn't rained in the night.

I was halfway across the hall when there was a knock on the door. Mrs. Forster opened it – to be faced by a tall white oblong. It looked for a second like some futuristic robot. Then a man appeared to one side of it – it, which was our fridge-freezer.

They carried everything in to the kitchen and left it there, still in the bubblewrap. Jack would have fun with that. I thought about offering them tea, but was worried that if the taps still refused to work I wouldn't be able to make them any. They left a little slowly, taking the chance to examine the hall. Probably, because we lived in such a big house, they were expecting a big tip.

It was a relief to know I could now escape. I got Mary ready as quickly as I could, shouted goodbye to Mrs. Forster – not really caring if she heard – and pushed the buggy through the door.

Once we were out from the cover of the trees, it was a scorchingly hot morning. I stopped to put sun-cream on Mary's face and arms. We didn't meet any tractors or cars on our way to the village.

The shop was open, so I went straight in and said hello to Mrs. Willows. She didn't seem as warm as she had the day before – not as interested in Mary or as keen to chat to me. I bought a few things, then said, 'I was reading a local history book last night.'

'One of Mr. Gatward's?'

'Yes. It was very interesting.' This was the big moment – alive or dead? I tried to make my voice sound as casual as possible, but it still came out a bit flutey. 'Is he still around?'

'He's in and out all the time. He smokes too much. Wasn't he here yesterday, when you first came in?'

'The man with the hat,' I said.

'Cricket,' said Mrs. Willows. 'Apart from history, that's his great passion.'

'I'd quite like to speak to him. It's about the house.'

'He hasn't been in today. He lives down the road. Number six on the green. But he's a late riser. You'd best give him another half an hour, just to be certain. He'll be at home, unless there's a match on at the Oval or Lords or Hove County.'

We chatted for a little while longer before I thought to ask. 'Do you have any of his books on sale?'

Mrs. Willows smiled. 'Of course. Which one do you want?'

'Could I have a look at them?'

She went into a back room, rustled around for a while, then came back with a small pile. On top was *A Kindly Place*, with a different cover to the one back home. Then was *A Small Sussex Village at War*, which I flicked through quickly. It started in 1913, so wasn't any use to me. Next came *St Edith's, Early and Late.* This, too, didn't seem to mention our house. It was possible it might have something about the Jonson's graves, though. I put it to one side. The bottom book was *Local Ghost Makes Good.* It was very old-fashioned, but the illustrations looked quite fun. And because Jack was going through a ghost phase, I thought I'd buy it anyway. Only as I was closing it did I recognize that the windows in one of the pictures looked just like those in our bedroom. I didn't turn back – I'd have plenty of time to look at it.

'You don't have *Hidden Histories*?' I asked.

'Well, you do know your stuff,' said Mrs. Willows. 'No, that went out of print quite a few years ago. Mr. Gatward always talks about reprinting it. It was probably his bestseller.' She looked around the small shop. 'Relatively speaking.'

I decided to buy *St Edith's* as well as *Local Ghost.* At worst, I could ask Mr. Gatward to sign them both. He couldn't object to that. The copy of *A Kindly Place* in the library hadn't been signed. But it sounded as if Michael Francis and Mr. Gatward hadn't got on. That was one of the things I wanted to ask about.

Mrs. Willows rang the sales up with great pleasure.

'He will be pleased,' she said.

'I don't need a bag,' I said, and slid the books into the hood of the buggy.

'Mr. Gatward's a bit deaf,' said Mrs. Willows, as I was halfway out the door. 'You'll have to make sure you speak up.'

'Thank you,' I said.

I went back to yesterday's park bench, and tried to feed Mary. But she was too sleepy to take the nipple. Then I went through *St Edith's* page by page. There was no index, but the book was divided into sections for different parts of the church – altar, nave, pews, etc – and then a long chapter about the graveyard. I skim read this, until I came to a paragraph containing the familiar names.

'It is perhaps surprising that William Jonson, a well-known recusant, desired his mortal remains and those of his family to be buried in the grounds of a then-Protestant church. However, with the less intense religious climate of the years leading up to his death, it is possible that his views moderated. It is also possible that he was in some way compelled to submit to convention. Records show that the plot was purchased around the time that William purchased the land on which he built the first Great House. So economy might also have been a reason for using what he could not, once paid for, sell back.

'The carvings of the headstones show some unusual, not to say unorthodox features. These, perhaps, were William's revenge. It has been suggested that the very unusual shape of the stones is that of a Bishop's mitre. Arranged around the frontage of William's headstone are four large keys, one of which is surmounted by a crown. This may be intended to signify that although there are many authorities that claim to possess the means of entering heaven, there is only one true church. St Peter received the keys from Jesus, and they have been passed from Pope to Pope ever since. This lineage is what Catholics believe gives unique legitimacy to their faith. At the bottom of the stone is a large and rather fierce-looking cock. This surely represents the cock which crowed thrice upon our saviour's death, before which Peter – as prophesied – had thrice denied Jesus. Perhaps this should be taken as a check to all human vanities of orthodoxy and belief. It would be nice to think so.'

I went through the rest of the book, but only found one more mention of William, to do with tithes or taxes to the church – and nothing at all about Elizabeth or Lilian.

Half an hour had passed. Mary was completely zonko. I decided to look through *Local Ghost* before knocking on Mr. Gatward's door.

I'd only just opened the first page, though, before I saw a familiar straw hat and, beneath it, a familiar body – one shaped just like a question mark.

Chapter 17.

Mr. Gatward was just where I'd seen him yesterday. This time, I saw him glance across, but he didn't raise his hat. Perhaps, as a breastfeeding woman, I was beyond the pale. He went inside the shop. I thought it would probably be best if I waited until he came out, then I could go and introduce myself. There was no doubt that, even with a buggy, I'd be able to catch up with him.

A couple of minutes later, Mr. Gatward came out of the shop, the door tinkling as it shut behind him. I was just about to get up and follow him when, instead of turning hard right, he crossed the road and made straight towards me.

'Mrs. Jonson,' he cooed. 'It's a very great pleasure to make your acquaintance.'

He held out his hand to shake mine. I realized that I was still holding his children's book. Authors must like that sort of thing, though – I know I would.

'A little old for that one, aren't you?' Mr. Gatward said.

'It's for my son. Jack.'

'And this is Mary who is three months. Is that right?'

'Yes,' I said.

'Mrs. Willows told me. She also told me just now that you were interested in speaking to me.'

'Yes,' I said. 'I am.' Although I was finding it quite difficult. His spine was so curved that in order to look at me, he had to turn sideways on and twist his head round at what looked like a painful angle.

'Please, then,' he said. 'Come to my house.'

He looked both ways before setting off across the road. I followed, with Mary still fast asleep in the buggy.

Until we reached his front garden, we chatted politely about the weather and my children. Mr. Gatward had none of his own, he said, although he liked them very much.

The cottage was one of those I'd noticed before, right after the turn into the village. It had a thatched roof that came down very low. Even I had to stoop to go through the front door, and I'm certainly not six foot.

'Please, make yourself comfortable. We can sit on the patio,' said Mr. Gatward. 'Tea will be up shortly.'

The front room was full of books – and, when I say this, I really mean that it was full of books from floor to ceiling. A narrow path (luckily wide enough for the buggy) led through this towards a glass door. Beyond that was a conservatory, also full of books. And, beyond this, was a charmingly overgrown garden.

Living in the maisonette, I'd never had the chance to have a garden. But, when I'd imagined one for myself, I'd always had something like this in mind – the cosy sort of space where all the flowers and bushes seem to be reaching in towards you.

There were a couple of wicker chairs, so I parked Mary and took the one without the cushion. Mr. Gatward, carrying a metal tray that also just fitted through the book-alley, joined me five very relaxing minutes later. I'd been watching bees going in and out of flower-heads, and thinking how magic it was they turned pollen into honey.

'It really is wonderful to meet you, at last,' he said. 'I had been meaning to visit you at the house. You must have had quite a few visitors.'

'Yes,' I said, 'I suppose we have.' And I mentioned Father Trovato and the local M.P.

'Well,' said Mr. Gatward, 'that's interesting. Church *and* state. I'm hardly surprised, though. Everyone's been speculating madly about you ever since we knew you were coming. In a village like this, there's not a lot else to do. You're big news.'

'You would have been very welcome,' I said, though it was a little difficult to see when we could have fitted him in.

'Unfortunately my Alvis is out of action, and it's too far to walk in my present condition.' This made me wonder whether he was expecting his condition to improve. 'Also, I must admit, I was wary of antagonizing you. Relations between myself and the previous owner were…'

'There was something in your book,' I said. 'You say that Michael Francis wouldn't let you examine the family papers.'

'He wouldn't even let me on the grounds,' said Mr. Gatward. 'I was *persona* totally *non grata*.'

'We'll let you look at whatever you want,' I said. 'Don't worry about that.'

'Really?' he asked. 'Just – Just like that. Without proviso?'

'You can come whenever you like. Only, give us a little notice.'

'Excuse me,' said Mr. Gatward.

He tucked his head into his chest, which gave a heave and then a shudder. I saw a couple of teardrops fall onto his silk tie.

'This is wonderful,' he said, after a couple of minutes. 'Bless you, Mrs. Jonson. It's been such a very long time.'

He needed a few moments more before he was composed enough to ask, 'So, you're interested in history, are you?'

'Oh yes,' I said. 'But why didn't Michael Francis want you near the house?'

'Perhaps I should give you a little background information,' the local historian said. 'The previous Mr. Jonson, as you probably know, was an obsessively private man. He took over the house at the age of fifty-six. I had been quite friendly with his uncle, and had even played in the house when I was a child.'

'That's when you went in the priest's hole.'

'Indeed. You are an attentive reader. Well, like any family, I suppose, the Jonsons have their secrets. And when Michael Francis came into possession, he soon became quite cranky. For example, the milkman always used to leave the bottles on the doorstep. But Michael Francis now insisted they be left halfway down the drive. He had a special little hut constructed out of bricks, so that the sparrows didn't get at the tops. The only person allowed into the house, apart from himself, was Mrs. Forster – who I'm sure you already know better than I do, although we were schoolmates a long time ago. Of course, the masons weren't very happy about this. They had been using the hall for centuries. Some of them practically wanted to storm the place with guns. But Michael Francis could not be pressured. He didn't care what the village thought of him, because he never visited the village. Everything he wanted came to him. Including a priest to say mass in his private chapel.'

'You know about that?' I asked, a little disappointed I hadn't been able to surprise him with it.

'I have never seen it. But I believe I know where it is.'

'We could give you the guided tour.'

'Wonderful woman.'

Mr. Gatward looked at me with glistening eyes – I swear, he was a little in love with me.

'So, what is it about the house that you want to know, most of all?'

'It is a puzzle,' he said, after a moment's thought. 'It is a very old house, but it doesn't seem to have very much history. Not in the conventional sense. The Jonsons are an extremely long-lived family. And one has succeeded the other, as owner, quite smoothly.'

'I'm interested in Elizabeth Jonson,' I said.

'Ah,' replied Mr. Gatward, 'beautiful and brilliant Lilian. Yes, we'd all like to know more about her.' He finished his tea and put his cup and saucer down.

'You wrote quite a lot about her in your book.'

'Which book?'

'*A Kindly Place*.'

'There's a tiny bit more in *Hidden Histories*. But that, alas, is all the information I have upon her.'

'So you don't know why she disappeared?'

'I have theories,' he said, then quickly added. 'Completely unsubstantiated.'

'Do you think you might be able to find out something for definite, if you could look through the archives?'

'I *might*,' he said, sitting up straighter. 'There are no certainties. But… Who knows?'

'You can start whenever you like,' I said. 'This afternoon.'

'I would love to. Things aren't quite that simple, however. I could probably come… tomorrow, Wednesday, in the morning?'

‘Whenever you like,’ I said.

Mary woke up quite suddenly, and began to cry. I knew Mr. Gatward, however well-disposed he was towards me, and however much he said he liked children, wouldn’t be comfortable with what I needed to do. So, I said a hurried goodbye and rushed back to the bench on the green. It was only when I’d sat down and had Mary on my lap that I realized I’d completely forgotten to ask him to sign the books.

On our way back to the house, after Mary had been satisfied, we stopped off in St Edith’s churchyard.

Now that I knew where they were, the Jonson gravestones weren’t hard to find. Mr. Gatward’s description of them was very accurate – there were the four keys, and there was the cock. The only thing I wasn’t sure about was the crown on the last key. It did have three triangular points, like a child’s drawing of something a king or queen might wear, but also like a child’s drawing, the lines were rather wavy – and the points weren’t all in a neat row. To me, they looked more like flickering flames than a crown made of metal.

Then I realized something about the doors in the cellar. I couldn’t wait to tell Peter, so I rushed home. Of course, he wasn’t there.

Chapter 18.

I was thirsty when I got back to the house, and wanted a glass of water. But the kitchen tap still wasn't working. I poured some orange juice out, from one of the cartons in the pantry. Jack practically lives on juice, so we always have plenty.

Although I wasn't very hungry, I made a sort of picnic lunch and took it out to the garden. Mary lolled around on the blanket beside me, kicking at things only she could see.

I left her there while I took the plate back in. Mrs. Forster was at the sink, filling a bucket with hot water.

I didn't say anything, just waited until she'd finished.

'Oh, I'm sorry,' she said when she saw me. 'Did you want something?'

'It's fine,' I said.

After she'd gone, I tried the cold tap. As I'd expected, it didn't work. Air came out but not a drip of water. Then I tried the hot tap Mrs. Forster had just been using. Still nothing. This was weird.

I hurried back out to Mary, anxious that something might have happened to her in the few minutes I'd been away. And something had happened, Robert Mew was sitting with her on his lap.

'Afternoon,' he said. 'I wondered where you were.'

'Just inside,' I said.

'There are foxes about,' he said. 'And a couple of fairly wild cats. I'd be careful about leaving the baby just lying around outside.'

'Thank you,' I said. Then I asked, 'Have you ever had problems with the water supply in the house?'

Robert Mew looked a little embarrassed. 'There's a standpipe behind the garage, and one further out in the woods. I've never had a problem with either of those.'

'Could you come into the kitchen for me, and just try one of the taps.'

Robert Mew handed Mary to me. At first I thought he was going to refuse. I could see thoughts passing behind his clear eyes, but they went too fast for me to guess what they were.

'All right,' he said. It was hard to tell what his expression was, underneath all that beard. His voice seemed slightly shaky, though.

We walked up the lawn together. He stood to one side to let me go in. I thought he was just being polite. But when I glanced back, I noticed that he crossed himself before he passed over the threshold – crossed himself just like Father Trovato had made us do, before entering the chapel. I wanted to ask why. He strode ahead, though – I think because he'd seen me looking, and seen my surprise.

'Which one?' he asked.

I pointed to the cold tap.

He turned it, and a thick column of water came out.

'No problem there,' he said.

I thanked him. Then, feeling slightly shaky, I tried the tap myself. It worked, thank God.

'Anything else?' he asked.

'No,' I said. 'Thank you.'

He wandered off through the hall. I waited until I could no longer hear his footfalls.

Again, I tried the tap.

This time nothing came out, just a hiss.

'Oh, come on,' I said.

Suddenly, water started to gush out.

'Yes?' said Mrs. Forster, who'd done her old trick of sneaking up on me.

'Just talking to myself,' I said.

But later, as I was upstairs changing Mary, I realized that I hadn't been talking to myself. I had been talking to the house. I had been telling it to stop misbehaving.

This scared me a little, and I hurried outside again and waited in the garden with Mary. My mind was going very fast, all this time – making connections. The dirt. The water. The carved phoenix.

Mary was very happy, making her little noises and kicking her legs. She got a dimple in her left cheek whenever she smiled. I wondered whether this would still appear when she lost her chub.

But my thoughts couldn't stay on simple things. I realized I needed to check something.

Carrying Mary on my hip, I reentered the house and went through to the study. On my last visit here, I'd seen a battered dictionary on Michael Francis's desk. I opened it and looked up the word I needed.

I was just reading the entry when I heard the grrr of our car's engine and the crunch of its wheels on the gravel.

Peter and Jack came into the hall, carrying brightly coloured cardboard boxes. Peter also had a plastic bag dangling from his fingers. As I approached, I saw it was full of DVDs.

Although I didn't really want to say what I was about to say in front of Jack, I just couldn't wait until the evening.

'I think I know what's going on,' I said, hurriedly. 'With the doors downstairs and everything.'

'I've been thinking about that, too,' Peter said. He wasn't happy – a bit grim, even.

'Can I see the doors?' Jack asked.

'Not now,' I said. 'Mummy needs to speak to Daddy.'

'And Daddy needs a cup of tea,' said Peter.

'Well, you'll have to make it yourself,' I said.

'Look,' said Peter, 'we won't have the television for a day or two. I just bought him a few DVDs – as a special treat.' He thought I was angry about him encouraging Jack's TV habit. And I was, but other things were far more important.

'I couldn't make you a cup of tea, even if I wanted to. Not unless you're there. The water's refusing to work for me.'

Jack turned to Peter. 'Is Mummy being funny?'

'I think so,' he said. 'But I'll make the tea, anyway.'

We all went into the kitchen – where Peter, with a puzzled smile, filled the kettle and clicked it on.

'One for you?' he asked.

'Please,' I said. 'Peter, it's the elements, the four elements. You know – earth, water, fire and air. Behind the first door was earth and behind the second door was water. I saw the fire on William Jonson's gravestone.'

'Now Mummy really is being funny,' said Peter, signalling to me that I was being too intense – that if I wasn't careful I might freak Jack out.

'The dirt in the larder at night, that was earth,' I said.

'Yes. You may be right,' said Peter, with a blah-blah-blah tone. 'We'll talk about this later.'

'No!' shouted Jack. 'That's boring!'

'If you want to watch any of those DVDs, you better not shout at me like that,' said Peter.

'Sorry, Dad,' said Jack.

'I think you should go outside for a bit,' I said. 'Get some fresh air. Play with something that isn't electronic, for once.'

Jack hunched his shoulders and crossed his arms.

'I'll come out and play football,' said Peter. 'When I've had my tea.'

There was a silent stand-off. Then Jack backed down. He liked football, and being out in the big garden was still a novelty. 'Okay,' he said.

'Would you like some juice?' I asked.

'No,' he said. 'I'm good.'

He slouched away.

'He's a teenager already,' said Peter.

'Please take this seriously,' I said. 'There's something very strange going on in this house. The stones that fell in Jack's room – they were earth, too. And since we opened the water door, everything changed to water-things.'

'We better not open the fire door, then,' said Peter. I gave him a look. 'Okay,' he said. 'Fine. What's this about the water not working?'

'If someone's there, the taps are fine,' I said. 'Look.'

I turned the faucet, and water came out. I shut it off.

'But if you leave the kitchen, no water. Try it.'

Peter carried his tea into the hall.

'Doing it now,' I said.

Water flowed.

'Maybe you need to be further off!' I shouted.

'I'm on the stairs,' Peter shouted.

Again, water came from the taps.

I felt very foolish. Perhaps I should lie and tell him it was as I'd said.

'Come back!' I called.

Peter came and stood in the doorway.

'That seems to have stopped,' I said. 'Perhaps because I told you about it.'

'I'm not calling you mad,' said Peter. 'But I'd just like you to think for a second about how mad what you're saying sounds. "The water is working because it heard you say something to me."'

'Not the water,' I said. 'The house.'

'And that isn't mad?'

'You said you *weren't* calling me mad.' I realized I was shouting.

'I'm not,' said Peter, trying to speak calmly.

'I am completely sane,' I shouted. 'It's this house that's mad.'

Mary started to wail. She hated raised voices – although hers was by some margin the loudest in our family.

A football bounced a couple of times in the hall and then rolled into sight. Mrs. Forster wasn't the only eavesdropper around.

'Come in,' said Peter.

Jack appeared round the door.

'I thought you'd gone outside,' I said, cradling Mary.

'Why are you shouting?' Jack asked.

'Go outside,' I said.

'I went upstairs to get my ball,' said Jack. 'It's not fair!'

'Sometimes Mummys and Daddys don't agree,' I said. 'And it's usually because the Daddys are wrong.'

'Listen and learn,' said Peter to Jack.

'You're joking,' said Jack. 'Stop it! I want you to be serious with me.'

'We will,' I said. 'We just need to talk about it first.'

'You're rubbish,' said Jack, on the point of tears – tears of anger and frustration.

'Come on, Jack Rabbit,' said Peter, and drank down the last half of his tea. He placed the mug carefully on the kitchen table. Mary had stopped wailing and started sobbing. 'I do not think you're mad,' Peter said, very quietly, leaning towards me. Then he turned to Jack, 'Right, you're Plymouth Argyll!'

'Chelsea,' said Jack.

'Raith Rovers,' said Peter.

'Chelsea,' said Jack.

'Partick Thistle,' said Peter.

They went on like this until I couldn't hear them any more.

I held Mary until she was so calm she fell asleep. Then I put her in the recliner.

When I tried to wash up the mugs, the water didn't come.

'Sucker,' I said, as if the house were saying it to me.

Chapter 19.

Straight away, I carried Mary across to the library. The dictionary entry on 'elements' had been fine, as far as it went. It had told me the basics – earth, water, air and fire. But I wanted to know more.

After half an hour, I still hadn't found anything. There wasn't even an encyclopedia.

Peter eventually sought me out, to apologize. I'd given up on the books and was cuddling Mary.

'I want to talk about it, too,' he said. 'Just not in front of Jack.'

'What's he doing now?' I asked.

'I've got him practicing free kicks,' said Peter.

'You do believe me?'

As is the way of these things, someone knocked on the front door just before he could answer.

We all went to see who it was, me carrying Mary. It turned out to be Gracie Dearie, the farmer's wife. She was wearing – wow – a bright emerald silk blouse, a matching pleated skirt, light green tights and green Converse trainers. She looked stunning, very fashion shoot, and not a little bizarre. 'Oh, hello. I've been sent to invite you to dinner,' she said. 'Welcome you to the area.'

'Thank you,' I said, immediately foreseeing problems. 'That would be lovely.' We had no babysitter, and I wouldn't want to leave Jack in the house with a stranger.

'It might be a little easier if you came here,' said Peter.

'Oh,' said Gracie, 'well, we thought that, too. But we couldn't very well say, "Can we come round to supper, please?"'

'If you bring some more of those delicious vegetables, you can,' I said.

Peter said, 'Thursday night all right?'

'I'm not sure. I think Sunday night might be better.'

It was a strange suggestion. We'd always kept Sunday evening free, so that Peter could get a good night's sleep before the week started. Peter looked at me, slightly bemused.

'How about next Monday, then?' I said.

'It's Midsummer's Eve on Sunday,' said Gracie, as if that was significant. 'Sunday would be most convenient.'

'Oh dear,' I said, then explained about our Sunday night tradition. I was starting to want to get this out of the way as quickly as possible. 'You really can't do Thursday night?' I asked.

'Of course we can,' said Gracie, reluctantly. Midsummer's Eve was clearly her desired date. 'I'll check with Matthew.'

'Eight o'clock,' I said. 'Or eight fifteen. Then Jack will be safely in bed.'

'Lovely,' Gracie said. Her eyes were twinkling as she tried to hold back the tears.

When she'd gone, Peter went out to check on Jack. Mary was falling asleep, so I thought I'd put her down for a sleep in our room. I was half way up the stairs when Mrs. Forster started hoovering. Mary woke up and started to cry. I went into the bedroom.

'Turn that thing off,' I said, loudly.

Mrs. Forster complied.

'You make too much noise,' I said. 'I'm sorry, but I don't want you in our house, cleaning all the time. The place doesn't need as much attention as you give it. We are a family. We need time on our own. Without other people around. And I don't want you starting first thing every morning.' Already Mrs. Forster was looking distraught. 'You can work from one to four p.m., three days a week. You can choose which. If we need more, we'll let you know. So, please pack up and go home. I want to try and get my daughter back to sleep.'

'I could do some dusting,' said Mrs. Forster. 'Downstairs.'

'It's our house,' I shouted, 'not yours. Now, get out!'

Mrs. Forster looked as though she had something else to say, quite a lot, but instead she very slowly pulled the plug from the socket, pressed the button to wind in the cable and carried the hoover out of the room. I went to follow her.

'I'm sorry,' I said. 'We just need time to settle in.'

'That's quite all right, Mrs. Jonson,' she said.

She looked almost ill. Her whole body was shaking as if she were about to have a fit.

'I will come back at one o'clock,' she said.

'Tomorrow,' I said.

Mrs. Forster turned and walked down the stairs. She was sobbing. It seemed, one way or the other, I was making everybody cry today.

Once I'd got her into the darkened bedroom, Mary calmed down within seconds. This made me feel even more guilty. I heard the front door open and close – a resonant bang in the echoey hall. Immediately, I felt better. I'd never been in the position of an employer. What was it like when you had to fire someone? Someone who really needed the job? Someone with a family? I didn't think I could do it.

Shaky, I went outside and told Peter what I'd done.

'It's the right thing,' he said.

'I've offended her forever,' I said. 'She'll never like me.'

'She'll respect you more, for standing up to her.'

'What happened?' asked Jack.

Peter explained.

'Hurrah!' shouted Jack. 'Ding, dong, the witch is dead!'

'Jack,' I said. 'She's not a witch.'

But I was so relieved that I burst out crying myself.

The house felt better, that evening. Peter filled a couple of pans with water, and I made bangers and mash with carrots. Already I was worrying about what I could cook for Matthew and Gracie.

After dinner, we all settled down to watch one of the films Peter had bought. Appropriately enough, it was *The Wizard of Oz*. I'd forgotten how scary it was. Jack kept saying he was fine, but whenever the flying monkeys arrived he went and stood over in the doorway – as if they might burst out of the screen, and he might have to make a run for it.

Myself, I was most affected by something else. It was the way Dorothy kept saying the word 'home' with such passion. I grew more and more uneasy. This house was the home we were giving our children. Was it the right one? Shouldn't we be bringing them up somewhere we knew was absolutely safe? But where might that be?

Mary had fallen asleep in my arms, so was easily taken upstairs and tucked up. Jack was tired, and went to bed without complaining. I tried to read him some of *Local Ghost Makes Good*, but he wasn't interested – mostly because the main character was a girl called Lizzie, but also because very little seemed to happen. We had only got as far as a scene set at the village fete before Jack told me it was boring and asked me to stop.

As his eyes fluttered and then fell asleep, I flicked quickly through the rest of the pages. Lizzie looked just like a younger version of Elizabeth from the painting – in fact, that's what I'd been expecting the whole book to be about, Elizabeth the friendly ghost making good. Little Lizzie did live in big old house that was obviously based on the New House, but the ghost turned out to be of a kindly old man – a kindly old man remarkably like Mr. Gatward. In fact, his name was Mr. Atwood.

Although they lived in the big house, Lizzie's parents, as well as being a bit nasty and never listening to her, had no money. They would have to leave the house the day after Midsummer's Day, if something didn't happen. The Dad was only interested in fixing up their old car. And the Mum did nothing but cook.

The illustrations weren't all that good. The figures were stiff and for page after page not a lot really happened. Mr. Atwood told Lizzie about some treasure that was buried under the garden of the house. There was some business to do with a sundial, and waiting for the sun to be in the right place. Finally, at noon on Midsummer Day, in the middle of her parent's farewell party, Lizzie does something clever with the sundial, unearths the casket of gold coins – which looked as if had probably been left there by a bunch of very lost pirates – and saved the day.

They all got to live happily ever after in the house, with Mr. Atwood as part of the family.

I put the book aside and went through into the bedroom.

‘Right,’ said Peter. ‘Let’s talk.’ He was sitting on the edge of the four-poster bed. I knew I must look as out of place in this house as he did.

‘I’d like a shower,’ I said. ‘Then we can talk. Can you put it on for me?’

Peter gave me a look like I was suffering from some kind of obsessive compulsive disorder – as if I was freaked out by touching things other people touched, though this was the opposite. If it was *me* that touched them, they became a problem.

‘Okay,’ he said.

I carried a towel through into the bathroom. The water was running, hot and steamy behind the shower curtain. I was relieved to see that it didn’t just shut off when I crossed the threshold.

‘Let me get in,’ I said.

I undressed more carefully than usual – folding everything up and placing it on the floor. I felt self-conscious – as if I were taking my clothes off in front of someone for the first time. Peter gave me a kiss, a bit like the one in the library. He’d seen me like this enough times before, but he still seemed to like it.

‘Vixen,’ he said – just one of our silly couple-jokes. ‘Are you okay now?’

‘Fine,’ I said, though I wanted him to stay.

He went back into the bedroom.

‘You have your ways,’ he said as he went. ‘You definitely have your ways.’

I hadn’t touched water, or water hadn’t touched me, for over twenty-four hours. I felt grunky, and wanted to wash my hair thoroughly a couple of times.

I got under the shower, which was on very full, and ran my fingers through my hair a couple of times. I was expecting that fantastic feeling of relief and release, when the jets hit you in the face and your skin starts to tingle. The showerhead made a shhhing sound. The hot water rained into the white bath then swirled around and down the plughole. That fantastic feeling wasn’t coming, though – and, after a moment, I realized my hair was still dry, completely dry. Although it was impossible, this is what was happening: I was right under a running shower but wasn’t getting wet! Not just my hair, *none* of me. My feet, too, were dry. When I looked down to check, I saw the water running past my toes, over my toes, but just not wetting them.

I gave a yelp that must have sounded quite comic.

‘Everything all right?’ Peter shouted through.

‘Give me a moment,’ I shouted back.

The plug was one of those old heavy black rubbery ones. I put it in the plughole. Then I sat down.

The water level rose, covering me up to my ankles, then my calves – covering but not touching me.

Although the water was now all around me, it was as if it was refusing to touch me.

My eyes told me the water was hot, because the bathroom mirror had steamed up, but my skin told me nothing. No heat was getting through to me. I couldn't even feel air touching me, beneath the surface of the water. It was the weirdest feeling – I suppose like being a body in a vacuum. We're so used to having the air around us that we don't even feel it.

I swished my hands through the water, like I would to make bubbles in a bubble bath for Jack. They made not even a ripple. Somehow, the water parted in front of my fingers and rejoined behind them – without being disturbed.

'Damn it!' I said.

I tried to make a big splash with the flat of my palm. Nothing happened – my hand disappeared under the smooth surface. The only thing I can compare it to is when they have lasers and smoke in a nightclub, and the lasers make a horizon that you can stick your fingers through, play with the shadows. But however hard you hit it, however much you want to, you can't move the line where the laser is.

In a way I can't really explain, I felt abandoned. It was just like when I heard my mother had died. Something had given up on me, some force for good in the universe. I started to cry, and the tears ran down my cheeks. I could feel exactly where the edges of the lines were.

Suddenly, I became very frightened. If the water could do this, what else could it do?

I screamed.

Chapter 20.

Peter came running.

'What is it?' he asked, before he was through the door.

And as soon as he came in sight of me, the water around my body got wet and the shower started to hit my head. It was like being slapped in the face.

'No!' I shrieked.

This should have been the fantastic feeling moment, but now it felt horrible – even though it was completely normal.

'What?' Peter asked.

I was in bits – weeping, shaking.

'Come on,' he said, turning off the shower. He reached under my arms and pulled me out and hugged me tightly to him. 'You're fine,' he said. He said it again and again, so I knew he wasn't sure if it was true.

'Am I?' I asked. 'Am I?' I was starting to doubt my own sanity.

Peter picked me up and carried me into the bedroom. Of course, this made me remember him picking me up on the beach in Brighton when I twisted my ankle – a holiday before the kids were born. This memory, along with thoughts of my mother, kept me sobbing for a good five minutes. Peter knew better than to ask me questions. He just held me, and waited until I'd calmed down.

This must be what it's like to be Jack, I thought. *This is what it's like then Peter's being your comforting father.*

In the end, I got my breathing under control. The sobs started to space themselves out a little more. It was so good to feel the softness of Peter's t-shirt down my side, and the tickle of his hair against my cheek. The worst thing about the not-touching water had been the sense of isolation – like I wasn't part of the physical world any more. I wanted more of Peter. I wanted these sensations to intensify so that they could protect me.

I lifted my head until we were face to face, then I kissed him. I kissed him more passionately than at any time since those first few times, after we'd started sleeping together, when I wanted to tell him how much I loved him without ever actually saying it aloud – in case he didn't feel the same way. Since then, I had wanted him often enough, and never stopped desiring him. But right now I truly needed him.

He understood. He completely understood.

'One second,' he said, and checked on Jack – then closed the door between our room and his. Mary was fast asleep in her cot.

I hurried to get under the covers as Peter toed off his socks, pulled his t-shirt over his head and pushed down his jeans.

We kissed for a few moments more, side by side, then I pulled him so he was on top.

When he entered me, I was already gushing wet. I wanted to be the water all around him, warming him, caressing him. But I also wanted to be me and in my body – I wanted to grip him as tight as I could – to run my nails down his back, to hear and feel his ragged breath in my ear, to give him pleasure.

Afterwards, we fell apart, exhausted.

I cried again, but in a completely different way.

My mouth was full of thick spit. My head was spinning with delight.

I turned towards him and told him I loved him. He looked at me with great tenderness and said he loved me.

Another moment.

'What just happened?' Peter asked.

'I should think that was pretty obvious,' I said. 'I didn't fake it.'

'No,' he said with a smile. 'Before that.'

I propped myself up on one elbow, to face him. 'If I tell you,' I said, 'you promise not to send for the men in white coats.' I was trying to keep things happy.

'Absolutely no chance of that,' he said. 'They're madder than anyone.'

As well as I could, I tried to explain. Apart from the odd *hmm* and *really*, Peter didn't say anything. Then, when I'd finished, he said, 'You have to admit, that does sound quite…'

I was waiting for the word *mad*.

'..hard to believe,' he said – getting out of jail.

'But you do believe me, don't you?'

'I believe that's what you felt.'

'Until you came in, I was completely dry. Didn't you notice that my hair wasn't wet through?'

'No,' said Peter. 'I didn't. You happened to be screaming at that moment. I thought you were being scalded.'

I waited for him to find some way of going on, going back.

'Are you afraid?' he asked. 'If what you're saying is happening really *is* happening, does that make you afraid?'

'Of course,' I said. 'It's not like anything I've experienced before. It's uncanny.'

'Do you think it's a bad idea we came to this house?'

'It isn't about what I think, Peter,' I said. 'I'm not making anything up – '

All the good feeling we'd created with the sex was evaporating, fast.

I asked him directly, looking in his blue eyes: 'What's your explanation for what I felt?'

'I don't have an explanation,' he said, and looked away. 'But you're asking me to believe something that's very difficult. It's against everything I've believed before.'

'I'm asking you to believe what I say.'

Peter was quiet for an unnerving amount of time. He had always been such a sensible, rational man. What he liked best in the world, apart from his family, were little technical computery things he could fiddle with and fix. Often, when he'd worked something out, he'd come and try to explain it to me. I'd always tried to understand what he was saying, and be interested in his work, but the language he used didn't really get through. Interface. Modulate. Sub-routine. Now it felt like I was doing something similar to him - asking him to understand a world that obeyed different rules to the ones he knew, and not just chemistry and physics. The problem was, I didn't understand those rules either. I didn't have a clue.

'I do,' he said. 'I do believe what you say. Now, what do you want to do about it? Shall we get a plumber?'

I hadn't laughed so hard at anything in years. Peter joined in, too – even though he'd been serious when he said it.

'I mean, a really good plumber,' he said.

'Out here?'

'This is probably where they've all gone,' he said. 'Retired on their millions.'

'To deal with the spooky water.'

Peter stopped laughing.

'If you think it was a mistake,' he said, 'we can always move back.'

'I'm scared,' I said, 'but I don't feel in danger. I feel like there's something I'm too much of an idiot to get.'

'You're not an idiot,' Peter said. 'You're just a bit of a freak.'

I tried to hit him, playfully, but he grabbed my wrist. It had always annoyed me that he was so much stronger than I was. Once or twice, when I'd got really angry, especially after Jack was just born, I'd tried to slap him. He'd always caught my hand in mid-air. But he'd never, ever been violent towards me.

'Let go,' I said.

He did, straight away.

Suddenly, with the excitement over, at least for the moment, I felt very tired – which, of course, was when Mary decided to wake up.

I could have fed her in the bedroom, but I needed the excuse to go downstairs. There was someone I needed to check in on.

From the hall, I turned on the lights in the dining room. Then I stepped inside, to confront Lilian.

Chapter 21.

At first, I thought someone had crept in and stolen the painting. In the place where it should have been, in the middle of the gilded frame, there was a big, blank, off-white space. But when I moved forwards, and looked from a different angle, I saw that this was because the light was reflecting off the surface of the painting more brightly than usual – because it was wet, the whole thing, glistening wet, as if someone had just pulled it out of the sea.

The water, now I could see it more clearly, appeared to be streaming from top to bottom of the painting, very smoothly, but when I looked down I saw that the parquet of the floor was totally dry. It was as if the water was being squirted out of the top of the frame and perfectly absorbed again at the bottom.

I wasn't even for a moment worried that the painting would be damaged. This wasn't normal water. This wasn't a normal painting.

Instead of afraid, I felt incredibly excited.

'Look,' I said to Mary.

Then I reached up with my forefinger to touch the surface of the canvas. It felt wet, just as I'd expected – nothing more than wet. I pulled my finger away and, without thinking, sniffed the tip. No unusual smell came to me. I touched my forefinger and thumb together. The water, which had already almost evaporated, felt no more slimy or sticky than ordinary water. Finally, I touched my finger to my tongue. No taste.

I stepped back. The sight was fascinating – like something one of those clever contemporary artists would do: take an old painting and put special-effects on it to make a scandal. Only these weren't special-effects. And I wasn't scandalized. I was delighted – childishly delighted.

Going forwards again, I put my fingers and thumb all together on the painting.

The water ran down them, a trickle on each, and then joined at my wrist into a thicker flow. This continued down to my elbow, down to my shoulder. It felt more like an animal than water – like the uncoiling tail of something definitely alive. The flow went under my t-shirt and across the top of my chest. It was exploring. I was cradling Mary with my left arm, head in the crook, feet near my hand. The water was heading towards her. It came out onto my left shoulder, and turned down. It was almost at her head.

The terror came suddenly. I wouldn't allow this to happen. I jerked my hand away from the canvas and yanked it down towards Mary, to protect her.

The tail of water, though, had dropped away the moment I broke contact. Instantly dead.

I touched my t-shirt. It was dry, apart from my sweat.

Before I went upstairs, I decided to try one more time to show Peter what was going on.

Carrying Mary into the bedroom, I said, 'No questions – just come with me.'

He gave a grunt of annoyance at being got out of bed, but did as I asked.

In bare feet, we went quietly down the stairs.

Mary, no longer distracted by strange sights, was about to start crying with hunger.

'Stop here,' I said to Peter, then carried on into the dining room. I was relieved to see the painting was still flowing with water. 'Okay,' I said, 'now come in.'

The moment he entered the room, something very strange happened. The water on Lilian didn't exactly disappear, not all in a snap, but it was like I was suddenly seeing it in two ways at once – in my way, with it still there, and in Peter's way, with it gone. And then I could only see it in Peter's way, and I knew for certain he hadn't seen it in mine.

Even though I was sure it would be totally dry, I rushed over to the painting. I could feel Peter watching me. He was judging my actions, I knew. Were they something he should be really worried about? Were they something – in his masculine way – he should *do* something about?

The canvas was very dry and a little flaky to the touch. A couple of tiny fragments of paint came off on my fingertips. They were from Lilian's dress. When I looked at them closely, they were like specks of glitter – the sort you get on the side of your hand after writing in a spangly greetings card. Mary was wailing away on my shoulder.

'What was it?' Peter asked. 'Did she move? Did she talk to you?' Exhaustion was making him exasperated.

'Not exactly,' I said.

'Because she's doing nothing now.'

'You can go to bed,' I said. 'I'll stay up to feed Mary.'

'If this room spooks you, why don't you stay in the bedroom?'

'I'll be up in quarter of an hour.'

Haunting or no haunting, Peter wasn't hanging around. He wanted all the sleep he could get.

Mary went quiet as soon as she latched on. Her tugs were strong to begin with – a little frantic, even. But having her there relaxed me. This was my baby. I wasn't completely alone. Perhaps if I had been, my reaction would have been different. As it was, I felt completely awake, and completely elated. The water on the painting coming so soon after the water in my bath told me something. It made a direct link between me and Lilian – or made the link that was already there quite explicit. The communication between us was becoming clearer. I was still some distance from knowing what she wanted to tell me. But at least now I could be certain that it was *me* she was talking to, and that she was going to have to teach me to understand her.

'Not my children,' I said, finally. 'You can do things to me, but leave my children alone, okay?'

All the time I fed Mary, I gazed at the painting. It didn't move. It didn't change. But I was looking at it in a different way. Before, it had been an interesting object, then an interesting picture of an interesting person. Now, though, it was my teacher. It was so full of details that I didn't yet understand, and perhaps never would. What was the meaning of the odd silver-looking necklace she wore, or the two beautiful rings on her little fingers, one a ruby, one a sapphire? Why did she have a small fan hanging down from a golden chain around her waist? What was the book that Lilian held in her hand, and what image was on the end of the crimson ribbon she used as a bookmark – too twisted round to make out easily? Perhaps Andrew Gatward could help me figure it out. And what did Lilian's smile mean? She looked as if she could keep a secret, but she also looked as if she'd be very willing to share everything she knew, if only the right person came along. Could that person really be me?

Before I went back upstairs, I politely wished Lilian goodnight.

Mary slept right through. Jack, however, woke at five and had too much energy to go back to sleep. I took him downstairs with him, leaving Mary and Peter to have a lie-in.

As Jack was in the room, the kitchen taps worked, so I filled the kettle and made tea. When I sipped it, though, it tasted of nothing at all. And I couldn't sense it in my mouth. It wasn't warm or hot.

I stuck my fingers into the mug, with the same result. The water in the tea was like the water in the bath.

After making sure Jack was safely in the living room, I made a more radical experiment. I reboiled the kettle, then poured fresh water out into another mug. This I held, without feeling heat, then poured over my hand, without being scalded.

Finally, I boiled the kettle again and was pouring the steaming water over my left arm when Jack rushed in.

'Mum,' he shouted, as a sharp pain dug into me.

'Run the tap!' I shouted. 'Run the tap!'

For a second, Jack didn't move. This was definitely the stupidest thing he'd ever seen me do. Then he sprinted to the sink and turned both faucets.

I shoved my hand under the flow of cold.

'Watch me,' I said. 'Watch my arm. Don't go out.'

'What happened?' Jack asked. I knew he had seen exactly what happened. He was asking a different, more difficult question.

'I did something very stupid,' I said, wincing at another wave of pain. The cold water on my arm felt both wonderful and terrible. 'Don't you ever, ever do anything like that. Do you promise?'

'I promise,' he said. He was quite pale. 'Shall I get Dad?'

Almost worse than the pain was the embarrassment. But I knew I'd have to face Peter soon – any delay would only anger him.

'Okay,' I said.

Jack went to fetch his father. As soon as he was out of the room, the water stopped cooling me, and the pain increased. I dashed into the pantry and grabbed a large plastic bottle of blue milk. I held the cool side of it against my arm, willing Jack to be quick.

He was. A few seconds later, I heard him and Peter coming downstairs – Peter asking, '..on her *own* arm?'

He came into the kitchen looking more furious than I'd ever seen him. 'Let me see,' he ordered.

I held out my arm. The skin was already beginning to bubble up into a big white blister.

'What are you using this for?' Peter asked, taking the milk bottle away from me. 'Put it under the cold tap and keep it there.'

I didn't want to explain in front of Jack my reasons for not using the tap water – that it wasn't any use when no one was there. I'd told Peter all this the night before, but he clearly wasn't thinking of that now. He was looking at a self-harmer. I didn't know what to do. I felt shocked at myself for having been so reckless around Jack. Now I was going to have to submit myself to Peter, let him take charge. If I didn't, he would feel powerless – and that was the worst thing he could feel.

'I'll call NHS Direct,' he said. 'See what they say.'

'They'll say go to hospital.'

Peter went to the phone.

'Will you be all right, Mummy?' Jack asked. I was Mummy because I was wounded.

'I'll be fine,' I said. 'I'll just have a big bandage for a few days.' We were all of us upset, though for very different reasons.

Jack was going to go and listen in on the phone call.

'Stay here,' I said. 'Please.'

Jack came and stood next to me.

'I don't want you to be hideously disfigured,' he said. I could tell hideously disfigured was a phrase he'd learned out of a comic book or from a computer game.

'I'll be fine,' I said, although I knew a scald like this was bound to leave some scar. 'The water's very cold, isn't it? You have a feel.'

Jack put his hand into the gush.

'Yes, Mummy,' he said, 'very cold.'

I had just wanted to test that he did feel it. Although I realized that, with me in the room, this might mean nothing. If Jack started to be directly affected, haunted, we would leave the house. (I was glossing over the stones. They didn't really count.) But then I saw him looking at my arm and knew that sometimes it's being indirectly affected by something that is worst of all.

Peter returned. 'They want you to go to hospital.'

'I'll drive myself,' I said. 'Take Mary along.'

'No. They say you might go into shock. We'll all come.'

It took half an hour to get ready. Peter told me to stay where I was, and I asked Jack to stay where he was. I think Peter assumed I just didn't want to be left alone, so he brought Jack's clothes down to him. Along with some green baseball boots and blue jeans, he chose a red sweatshirt that had been washed so many times it had faded to pink. Usually, Jack refused to wear it because pink was a girl's colour. I had been meaning to re-dye it, after the move. But Jack put it on now without a word of complaint. I felt very proud of him, and said, 'Come here.'

I hugged him, one handed, then whispered, 'Go and get another top.'

Peter looked at me after Jack had run off.

'Before Jack came in, I was fine,' I said. 'When it was just me in here, the water wasn't hot or cold.'

'You don't have to hurt yourself, you silly woman,' said Peter. 'You have my full attention. I'll listen to anything you want to say.'

'It's really not about that,' I said, not even sure myself exactly what I meant.

We didn't speak again until Jack returned, in camouflage, and then it was only practicalities.

I got dressed in the clothes Peter had chosen for me. Not a bad selection, I thought, before I realized that they were the next day's outfit I'd put on a chair the night before.

I wrapped my arm in a couple of damp dishcloths and, after Peter fetched a still-asleep Mary, we set off.

Chapter 22.

Peter refused to stop on the way, to let me feed Mary. 'You can do it in the waiting room,' he said. 'They always take ages.'

But I'd hardly begun to calm her down, sitting in A&E, when a nurse came to fetch me. Apart from the Jonson clan and the hospital workers, the place was empty. Mary let out a horrible wail when I pulled her off and didn't stop screeching until we were in the examining room. The nurse, who looked extremely tired, told me there was no problem me feeding my baby while she did her work.

'Accident?' she asked.

'A kettle,' I said.

'Easily done. May I take a look?'

I wondered how often people refuse. Probably mad people do. And drunk, aggressive people. Was the question even worth asking? I suppose it's polite.

'Ow,' she said.

'I'm sure you've seen worse.'

She didn't reply.

'Have you taken anything? Any painkillers?'

'No.'

'I'll give you something strong.'

I also got a bandage and a prescription for healing cream and an appointment for a check-up the following week. All the time I was with the nurse, I wondered what Peter was doing. If he told anyone I'd done this to myself, they'd probably force me to talk to a psychiatrist. They might even want me to do that straight away, worried that I might be a danger to the children as well as to myself. But when I rejoined Peter in the waiting room, he didn't seem to have moved from the chair. 'Let's get you home,' he said.

We stopped off at a 24-hour pharmacy, to get the healing cream. And I insisted on buying ten big bottles of Evian from a garage.

It was nine thirty by the time we got back to the house.

There was a note put through the front door, neatly ripped from a narrow-lined A4 pad.

Dear Mrs. Jonson,

Sorry not to catch you. I will endeavour to call again at a more convenient hour.

Yours faithfully,

Andrew Gatward

9.15am

He had written his telephone number at the bottom of the page.

I insisted on calling straight away, even though Peter wanted me to leave it.

The phone rang and rang. Perhaps Mr. Gatward wasn't back home yet, or perhaps, now he was out, he'd decided to do something else – stock up on tobacco. There was no answerphone, so I couldn't leave a message.

'I'd forgotten he was coming,' I said. 'He was so keen to look at the archives. He's waited years and years. He must have been so disappointed.'

Peter made me go into the living room, then brought me a cup of tea and some marmalade on toast. Jack, I could tell, was going to be clingy for a while. I didn't mind. I didn't mind at all.

Beneath the bandage, my arm felt a little bit better already. That was probably due to the painkiller the nurse had given me.

Around ten, the electrician came to install a TV aerial *and* a satellite dish on our roof. Peter had decided on the satellite dish without consulting me. Now, he confessed.

'As long as you can't see it from the ground,' I said. 'Imagine how common that would look. Like we were lottery winners, or something.'

'And we aren't?' Peter said.

He and the man went upstairs to try and find a way onto the roof.

I snuck across the hall and tried Mr. Gatward again.

He answered by saying the name of the village and then giving his phone number without the dialling code. I'd never heard anyone do this, outside of repeated TV programmes.

'It's Mrs. Jonson,' I said. 'I had an accident. I'm really sorry we weren't in when you came.'

We arranged for him to return straight after an early lunch. He wanted to go into great detail over this – that it would be 'merely a salad' and that 'no cooking would be engaged in'. I said that I would definitely be at home to welcome him. He said, once again, that he was sorry to hear about my accident. I really liked his old-fashionedness. You didn't meet people like him in London.

When I turned round I saw Peter standing on the gallery. 'Where's Mary?' he asked.

'Asleep. In there,' I said.

'Come and have a look at this,' Peter said.

As I went up the stairs, I asked, 'It's not more doors, is it?' I wasn't sure if I could take the house revealing any secrets right that moment – leave it till the evening.

'Not exactly,' he said.

The door into the attic was now open, above the spiral staircase.

'All the way to the top,' said Peter.

He let me go first.

The spiral staircase felt slightly wobbly as we ascended.

'Are you sure it's safe?' I asked.

'Says the woman who poured boiling water over herself,' Peter replied, with a sad chuckle.

There was a light on in the attic, quite bright. This was surprising. I had been expecting them to be fumbling around in the dusty dark with torches.

I should give the layout – the roof of the New House had four peaks or triangular pointy bits, and three gutters or whatever separating them. This divided the roof-space into four very high rooms, with a long corridor joining them West to East. Peter led me through them, one by one. The first three were empty – although the second had a skylight out of which the aerial man's feet were dangling.

'I don't want to leave Mary for long,' I said.

'It's in here,' said Peter, grabbing my hand (non-bandaged arm) and pulling me into what at first looked like another library. There were shelves full of the same kind of ivory-coloured old books as downstairs. But also, on the far wall, there were eight filing cabinets in a row.

'Looks like your friend Mr. Gatward has his work cut out,' said Peter. 'These here are the archives.'

'But why are they up here?'

'Because they're the secret archives,' whispered Peter.

'Excuse me,' said a voice behind us. It was the aerial man. 'I can take a line off one of these lights for the power. No need to turn off the mains. The aerial can go in-between the chimneys. I can put the satellite on the back of the house. You won't see nothing from the ground.'

'Great,' said Peter.

'That's a lot of books,' said the man.

'We've only just found them,' I said.

'I'm not surprised,' he said. 'They can't've used this place much. You see that lightbulb? Have a guess when it dates from?'

'It must be old,' I said, 'or you wouldn't be asking.'

'Nineteen seventy-five,' said Peter.

The aerial man looked at me. I knew he wouldn't be satisfied unless I said something definite – unless I was definitely wrong.

'Nineteen sixty-three,' I said.

'My best guess would be nineteen fifty-five,' the man said. 'That's the oldest I've ever seen, outside of a museum. And do you want to know something else?'

After a pause I said, 'Yes, please.'

'They're all of 'em like that. Not a one of 'ems new.'

'Does that make any difference to you?' I asked. 'For the work?'

'No, not at all. Just thought you'd be interested.'

'We are,' I said, hoping Peter could do enthusiasm better.

'If you was wondering whether the folks before used up here very much.'

'Obviously they didn't,' said Peter. 'Let's hope none of the bulbs blow whilst we're up here.'

‘Whilst *you’re* up here,’ I said to Peter. Then, to the man, I said, ‘I’m glad it doesn’t look too difficult.’

‘No,’ he said. ‘I’ll enjoy the view, while I’m up there. Always do. It was one of the reasons I took the job.’

I left Peter to discover the other reasons.

Mary was still asleep when I got back to her, so I needn’t have worried. Babies have an uncanny knack of sensing when there’s a real crisis, someone hurt, and going into hibernation-mode for a while. My scalding was obviously real enough for Mary. After her long feed in the hospital, she had taken herself out of circulation. I decided it might be a good idea to have a lie-down myself.

I found Jack in the library, playing Nintendo. I told him to go and see what his father had discovered in the attic. Then I carried Mary upstairs to the four-poster and laid myself down beside her.

Perhaps I *had* gone a little into shock. It wasn’t until one o’clock in the afternoon that I woke up. Mary’s squeaky grizzling noises had dragged me from the depths. I knew I’d been having some kind of complicated anxiety dream, but I couldn’t remember a thing about it. I fed Mary then went to find out what was going on, taking her with me.

‘He’s finished on the roof,’ said Peter, from the top of the spiral staircase. I’d gone in the room and shouted up to him. ‘Took his money and left. It’s all working – aerial and satellite. We’ve officially rejoined the twenty-first century. And Mr. Gatward’s still here. You’ve never seen a man so excited.’

‘Jack?’ I asked.

‘He’s here, too. We’ve had lunch, so don’t worry about that. You had a good long sleep.’

‘I needed it,’ I said.

‘How’s your arm?’ I could tell that Peter was a long way from forgiving me. He should be – I’d forgiven him far worse, hadn’t I? It was at times like this my taking him back came into play.

‘It’s fine,’ I said, and it was true. I’d been expecting the arm to sting something horrible but it just ached a little. That first dose of painkillers would have worn off by now. I didn’t think I needed any more.

‘Good afternoon, Mrs. Jonson,’ said Mr. Gatward, appearing alongside Peter. ‘This is remarkable. Unprecedented. I’ve never seen so many virgin documents.’ Virgin - interesting choice of word.

‘What are they?’ I asked.

‘Oh, I can’t even begin…’ he said. ‘There’s household accounts dating back to before the fire. Wills. Indentures.’

‘Tell her about the books,’ said Peter.

‘Amazing. Absolutely stunning,,’ he said. ‘Among the finest libraries of its kind in England.’

‘They’re magic-spell books!’ shouted Jack, also coming into view. All three of them were now standing on the rickety staircase. Jack had one of the ivory volumes in his hands and was holding it above his head, like he’d won a cup for football.

I remembered Mr. Gatward’s history book had mentioned necromancy. Was that the kind of magic Jack meant? Devil-worship?

Chapter 23.

'Abracadabra!' yelled Jack.

'What he means – ' said Mr. Gatward.

'They're all about alchemy,' said Peter.

'Most of the volumes I've looked into, that is,' Mr. Gatward said. 'But there are closely related subjects, such as astrology. I haven't had time to make more than a cursory examination.'

Jack was very keen on magic. He had watched the first two Harry Potter films round at a friend's house. When I started to get angry about this, he told me he hadn't been scared at all – not even, he insisted, by the man with a second face on the back of his head. In the weeks after this, Jack had gone off into one of his crazes. Every drawing he did at that time had a black figure with a triangular hat. The black felt-tips always ran out long before any of the others.

'They're really, really old,' said Jack.

I heard a sharp rap-rap-rap that somehow I recognized. It was the front door. Then I remembered – we had been expecting another visitor.

'Jack, it's Father Trovato, I think.'

Jack looked disappointed. Magic was obviously more exciting than Catholicism, although Catholicism was pretty exciting.

'You'll have ages to look at these,' said Peter, taking the probably-priceless volume from Jack's hands. 'Go and be friendly to Father Trovato. You can use the downstairs living room.'

Jack juddered down the stairs, two at a time.

'Be careful,' I couldn't stop myself saying.

'Make up your own mind,' called Mr. Gatward to Jack. 'About everything. Judge it for yourself. Don't take anything on trust.'

This seemed a bit odd, coming out so passionately, but I didn't question it at the time. I probably should have.

As we walked out onto the gallery, something made me whisper, 'Don't tell Father Trovato about the spell books. He might not approve.'

'Really?' asked Jack, a little disappointed. I could see he'd been looking forward to making the big announcement.

'Maybe you can say something next week.'

The sharp raps began again.

I tried to smooth Jack's hair as we crossed the hall, but he batted my hand away. 'Mu-um!' He seemed, in his excitement, to have forgotten all about what I'd done that morning. I was glad.

It was Father Trovato but it was also – although I'd never met him before – our M.P., The Right Honourable Douglas Longbone.

'We come on separate business,' said Father Trovato. 'Good afternoon. Hello, Jack. Hello, Mary.'

'Oh, so this is Jack, is it?' said Douglas Longbone, going into hearty M.P.-mode. 'Very pleased to make your acquaintance.'

Jack really didn't like it when people spoke to him as if he was an adult, but with a jokey tone. Sarcasm he liked, but irony was pretty much rubbish.

'Hi,' he said.

'And you must be Mrs. Jonson,' said Longbone. 'Really delighted to meet you.'

His handshake was firm, something he'd worked on and thought about. I suppose Masons all have to think about their handshakes more than the rest of us.

'Please come in,' I said. I really didn't want him to kiss my baby.

Jack took Father Trovato by the hand, 'We're going to sit in here,' he said, pulling him towards the living room. 'Would you like some orange juice?'

'Yes, *please*,' said Father Trovato, as if that had been *exactly* the drink he wanted.

'With ice?' asked Jack.

'Yes, thank you,' said Father Trovato.

Longbone had watched this little scene with me, taking mental notes. It was rare to meet someone as exceptionally good with people as Father Trovato.

The priest – our priest – waited without impatience in the middle of the hall. Maybe he really did want orange juice.

'My business is with your husband,' said Longbone. 'I expect you know what it's about. Is he in?'

'I'll just fetch him,' I said. 'Would you like something to drink?'

'Perhaps,' Longbone said. 'I'll wait and see if I'm invited to stay.'

I went and fetched Peter from the attic.

I was aware that Father Trovato was listening, so I didn't just shout – that would have given my location away – but climbed the spiral staircase and went into the secret library. Mr. Gatward and Peter were bent over a large handwritten book.

'We've found the catalogue,' said Gatward. 'It must have taken years.'

'It's our M.P.,' I said. 'He's back for your decision.'

'Oh God,' said Peter. 'I haven't made it.'

'You have.' I said. 'You just haven't got the guts to tell him.'

'Are you a mason?' Peter asked Mr. Gatward.

'No, no, no,' he said. 'Complete waste of time. I had quite enough of secret societies at Cambridge. In fact, I had quite enough of society of any sort.'

'Is Longbone very powerful in the area?' I asked.

'Well, I suppose so. If you want to put an extension on your house. Or stop your neighbour putting an extension on their house. He can cause some trouble, smallish trouble. But if you have something he wants, he can't risk making enemies of you. The one thing he does have is patience. He's developed that skill. He has spent quite a long time out of government. Some of his associates, however, are a little less pleasant.'

Peter said, 'Thank you,' then went to break the bad news.

I waited for a couple of minutes. Mary looked around the room curiously. This was the first time she'd been up there.

'It's very clean, isn't it?' I said.

'Hardly a speck of dust,' said Mr. Gatward. 'I assume Mrs. Forster had something to do with that.'

'I don't think she does up here,' I said. 'I've never caught her coming up.'

'But it wasn't locked,' Mr. Gatward said. 'Did Peter unlock it?'

'I suppose so,' I said.

'And the chapel is locked?'

'Yes,' I said. 'Peter has the key.'

'And the cellar, too?'

'What do you know about the cellar?'

'It's under the staircase.'

'Come on,' I said, 'you know more than that.'

'No, I don't.'

For the first time, I suspected Mr. Gatward might be lying to me. It wasn't a good feeling. But I didn't want to get into it, then. I wanted to be downstairs, where I could hear what Father Trovato was saying to my son, and where I could overhear what Peter was saying to Longbone.

I left Mr. Gatward with his archives – with *our* archives, that should be.

Chapter 24.

The Right Honourable Douglas Longbone was already gone by the time me and Mary reached the hall.

'Not a happy bunny,' said Peter. This made me laugh. Longbone did have big front teeth, and not much of a chin.

'Did you say no forever?'

'He wouldn't let me. He said he'd come back in three months, when we'd had time to settle in, acquaint ourselves with the local community, get to know how things work round here.'

'Was that a threat?'

'Yes,' Peter said. 'I think so.'

'So, you're not going to get served for ages in the local pub?'

'And we can't build that extension we so desperately need.'

'Dammit,' I said, then remembered Father Trovato. I looked through into the living room. Father Trovato was sitting on the sofa, looking back at me. I had no doubt that he'd understood what had just gone on between Peter and Longbone, even if he hadn't heard every word.

'Good idea about the pub, though,' said Peter. 'We could go at the weekend. Sunday lunch.'

'I doubt the cook's a mason,' I said.

'At least we know *he* isn't,' replied Peter, nodding towards Father Trovato – who was now laughing at something Jack had said.

'Let's see if Jack's been brainwashed yet,' I said to Mary.

'Don't joke,' said Peter. 'They had me for years.'

Father Trovato stood up when I entered the room. He looked towards the open French windows to the garden. I think he thought I was going out there. Maybe he even hoped I was.

'Is it okay if I join you?' I asked.

'Of course,' he said. 'I would like you to.'

I thought I'd try breastfeeding Mary, even though she wasn't hungry. You always learn a lot about a man when you do that right up close to them.

'Mummy,' said Jack, 'do you have a soul?'

'Oh,' I said, a bit startled, 'you're onto that already?'

Father Trovato said, 'I was asking Jack where he felt the Jack bit of him was.'

Jack pointed to his head. 'And I said here. In my brain.'

I reached under my top, undid the flap on my bra and brought Mary up to the nipple. Father Trovato did not react at all. He didn't look, and he didn't look away.

'Good answer,' I said.

'And Jack's was a good question,' said Father Trovato. 'Mrs. Jonson, do you have a soul?'

He made eye-contact and held it. I felt completely exposed. How could I answer no, in front of my son? But, then, I didn't really believe I had nothing, that when I died that would be it, me and everything about me gone, forever.

'I don't know if I'd call it a soul.'

'But it's here,' said Jack, and pointed to the side of my head. 'I can smell it,' he said, putting his nose into my ear. 'It smells of poo.'

'No, no, no,' said Father Trovato. 'Your mother's soul is not like that.'

'And what about yours?' I asked, glad to turn things around.

'Yes,' said Jack. 'Let me smell.'

Father Trovato let Jack stick his nose up close to his curly hair.

'You smell of strong stuff,' he said.

'Garlic,' said Father Trovato. 'I eat it for the blood. And, when people are in the confessional, then they know it's really me.'

'I bet they do,' I said.

Jack wanted to know was a *fessnal* was – and Trovato said that they would talk about that later, but it was a place where people went to whisper all the naughty things they'd done.

'Wow,' said Jack. 'Can I listen?'

'No,' said Father Trovato. 'But I can.'

If Jack had been fascinated before, he now became totally bewitched. I could see that he was dying to tell Father Trovato all about the spell books upstairs. It was lucky I was there, otherwise the whole thing would have been confessed.

Very gently and subtly, Father Trovato started to explain about what souls were, and how they could be healthy or unhealthy. He didn't mention God at all, and it wasn't until the very end that he mentioned Jesus. Then, from inside his bag, he produced a picture book for Jack. 'We can talk about this next time,' he said.

'Thanks,' said Jack, awestruck. He gave a friendly goodbye to the priest, then sat down on the carpet for a read.

Father Trovato's voice had lulled Mary to sleep. I put her down gently on one of the sofas.

As I showed Father Trovato to the front door, he asked, 'Mr. Gatward has begun, has he?'

'Yes,' I said.

'I saw his car, parked.'

'He came this afternoon.'

'I hope he has a head for heights,' said Father Trovato.

It took me a moment to understand. 'So you knew where the archives were.'

'I have never seen them. Mr. Jonson would have been happy to show me, but I never wanted to see them.'

'What do you know about the cellar?' I asked.

Father Trovato changed completely. I thought for a moment he was going to be sick, so suddenly green did he look – green and unnerved. 'Keep it shut,' he said, 'and keep it locked.'

'Why?' I asked.

'You will understand later. I hope we will be able to begin your instruction soon.'

'Perhaps in a while,' I said.

'It is very important,' said Father Trovato, taking my hands in his. 'More important than you know.'

We were now in the porch.

'See you on Sunday,' I said.

'Yes,' said Father Trovato. 'But, if you need me before then, you can contact me here.'

He presented me with a business card. I expected to see the word Priest beneath his name. Instead, there was just a long list of letters beside it.

As I listened to the high-pitched engine of his car driving off, I felt like rebelling. He was a brilliant teacher, but I didn't like the idea of someone so biased interfering in my son's mind. I began to wonder if we could legally challenge the whole Catholic thing in Michael Francis's will. Perhaps we needed to get Gibbons & Jump back.

'Jack,' I said, going back into the living room. He was looking through the picture book. I saw Jesus on the cross – not as gory as he might have been. 'Would you like to have a look in the cellar?' I asked, feeling mischievous.

Jack dropped the book immediately.

I fetched the cellar key from the kitchen. Jack was already waiting by the door.

'Is it smelly?' he asked.

'Not really,' I said. 'You tell me.'

I thought for a moment that we should go and get Peter. But that was just silly. There was nothing to be afraid of.

I unlocked the door and turned on the light. It seemed to me that a little sound came from below – a gasp and a shuffle. Maybe it had been a mouse, or a rat.

'Come on,' I said. I took Jack's hand, pretending that it was for his benefit, when really it was for mine.

I went down first, he was two steps behind and above me.

'Wow, it's big, isn't it?' he said.

'Very big,' I said. 'You have to promise again that you won't come down here on your own.'

'Promise,' he said, but he was looking all around him.

We were halfway down the stairs. I heard another sound, like shuffling feet. Then another sound. This one was more like a scrape from something metal.

By now, I was getting properly spooked. Jack didn't seem to have noticed either the sounds or me becoming terrified. What if something had come out from behind one of the doors? Something monstrous. But that was impossible. All of them were locked. But what if…

We were three-quarters of the way down the stairs when I heard screaming. It was Mary, and it sounded very like she'd fallen off the sofa again – even though I'd put two pillows between her and the edge.

'Come on,' I said, glad this was an excuse to get out of the cellar.

Jack took a moment to realize what I meant – expedition over.

'But Mu-um.'

'We'll come back later.'

Mary's screaming was harsher than usual. Perhaps she'd broken her arm. I grabbed Jack by the wrist, to stop him going down any further.

'Run and see she's all right,' I said.

Jack was still reluctant.

'It might be a ghost,' I said, and he was off at a sprint.

I wasn't far behind, though it took me a couple of seconds to lock the door.

'Mum!' cried Jack. 'It's a fox.'

I saw it as soon as I got in the room. Mary hadn't *fallen* off the sofa, she'd been dragged – dragged by the ankle – and now she was halfway to the French doors. The fox, quite a big one, and fitter and redder than the London sort, had her ankle in its tight jaws.

Chapter 25.

Jack ran straight towards the fox, yelling. I expected the thing to let go of Mary and run off in fright, but it just kept tugging. Mary travelled about two feet with every jerk. She was obviously too heavy for the fox to pick up and carry.

Keeping my eyes on the fox, I hurried towards the fireplace. 'Don't let it get away,' I shrieked.

I was reaching for one of the iron fire-pokers when Jack kicked the fox, hard, in the ribs – so hard that all its feet were lifted off the ground. I think I heard one of the ribs crack.

Instantly, it dropped Mary and ran diagonally, loping, out of the door. Even with what it had been doing, I hated to see it injured. Jack had clearly put a big dent in it.

Jack, my brave boy, was picking up Mary.

'She's okay, mum.'

She wasn't fine, she was screaming like I'd never heard her scream – thank God. It was such a great sound, an *alive* sound.

I'd dressed her in a towelling babygrow, which now I started to pull off – the poppers going one after the other.

'What is it?' shouted Peter from the balcony.

'It's Mary,' shouted Jack.

I pulled the babygrow off Mary's kicking legs. She'd gone blotchy pink with fear and fury.

Peter's feet banged down the zigzag stairs.

There were two rows of teeth marks, about an inch and a half apart. They were angry red but I couldn't see anywhere the skin had been broken. I checked again, squeezing the skin to see if any blood came out. What did foxes carry? Rabies? Tetanus? Who knows what else.

Peter came into the room, breathless.

'She's all right?'

'It was a fox, Dad,' said Jack, almost gleeful. 'I kicked it so it ran away. I kicked it like this – ' He demonstrated.

I was hugging Mary probably harder than the fox had bitten her. Peter came over and wanted a look – so I showed him the teeth marks. There was just a trickle of bright red blood.

'Why was she on her own?' he asked.

'We were down the cellar,' said Jack. 'Mum was showing me. Can I go again? As a reward.'

'No,' said Peter. 'Not now.'

'He wanted to see,' I said. 'I thought Mary would be fine.' Peter couldn't make me feel worse than I was already feeling.

'I'll get the first aid kit,' said Peter, and jogged through to the kitchen. He was back in moments, and disinfecting Mary's leg – causing further screams.

A figure appeared in the doorway to the garden. It was Robert Mew, the gardener.

'I heard some screaming,' he said. 'Then I saw the fox go by. It was hurt.'

'I hurt it,' said Jack.

Robert looked at the baby. He didn't cross the threshold to come into the house.

'Did it bite her?' he asked.

'Only round the leg,' I said.

'Lucky, then,' he replied. 'I did say…'

'Say what?' asked Peter.

'Robert told me not to leave Mary alone in the garden. I didn't realize the house wasn't safe, either.'

Peter said nothing, letting my words answer themselves.

'It's a nasty fox, that one,' said Robert Mew. 'Mr. Jonson wouldn't let me kill it. He liked wild animals.'

'Well, you can kill it now,' said Peter.

The gardener nodded.

'Good,' said Jack, crossing his arms and jutting out his chin.

A moment later, when he saw there was nothing more to be said, Robert Mew excused himself. 'I hope she recovers quickly,' he said. As he turned away, I noticed that he had a huge bunch of keys dangling from a chain tied to his belt. I knew that if I asked him about them now, Peter would think I wasn't taking Mary's injuries seriously enough. She was starting to calm down, a little. I could talk to Robert about his keys later.

For the second time that day, Peter called NHS Direct. And for the second time that day, we were told to go to the hospital.

I offered to take Mary by myself. But Peter wanted to come, and we certainly weren't leaving Jack with just a distracted Mr. Gatward to supervise him.

Peter locked the French doors, then went to tell Mr. Gatward what was going on.

'He hardly even looked up,' said Peter. 'Completely absorbed.'

'Perhaps he's learning a spell,' said Jack.

'Perhaps,' I said.

Mary fell asleep just as we were driving past the turn to the village.

She woke up as the nurse, a different nurse from the morning, thank goodnesss – a male nurse, took a blood sample.

'Have you seen a fox bite before?' I asked.

'Once,' he said. 'On someone's hand.'

'Did they catch anything?'

'No. Not that I know of. But I only saw them one time.'

They gave her a couple more jabs, and told us to watch her closely for fourty-eight hours. If there was anything unusual in how she seemed, we were to bring her straight back.

The whole round trip took about two-and-a-half hours – beating our record from the morning. I prayed we didn't get another chance to lower it.

Mr. Gatward came to greet us in the hall when we got back.

'I've found some remarkable things,' he said. 'How is the little one?'

'Fine,' said Peter, 'as far as they can see. Perhaps you could tell us about your discoveries tomorrow.'

'Tomorrow morning,' I said.

Mr. Gatward said, 'Of course,' and left straight away.

Mary, understandably, was a more than little unsettled. She wanted to be held the whole time – which was good because I wanted to hold her the whole time.

As we ate our small dinner of baked beans on toast (no one wanted anything heavier), Jack asked whether he could go down the cellar, as a reward for being a hero.

'Another time,' said Peter. Then said Jack could stay up a bit past his bedtime to watch TV.

'Tomorrow?' asked Jack, not distracted.

'Yes?' Peter said. 'Tomorrow.'
'Morning?' asked Jack.
Peter gave Jack a look that he couldn't misunderstand.
Jack switched the TV on.

Putting the children to bed took quite a while. Jack went off to sleep after I'd read him a couple of pages from Father Trovato's picture book. It was a Life of Jesus, quite old-fashioned, with paintings of Mary and Joseph and their donkey. I didn't mind Jack learning about all that, and it was hard to see him becoming totally Christian just because of a cartoon. Mary, though, wouldn't settle and wouldn't settle. I held her and cooed to her, but she needed to exhaust herself with crying and then get filled up with milk before she calmed down enough to close her eyes. I sang to her the same lullabies I'd once sung to Jack, before he began to prefer Beatles songs.

By the time Mary was soundly asleep, I was exhausted and not a little frustrated. Despite my resolutions not to let her out of my sight, I needed some respite. She would be perfectly safe upstairs, with the doors and windows shut.

Peter was lying on the sofa, eyes closed, when I came in. I told him straight away about the noises I'd heard in the cellar. I said I thought something was down there.

'What?' he asked. He was still furious with me – for scalding myself, for leaving Mary alone on the sofa, and most of all for believing the weird stuff I did. 'An animal?'

'I don't know,' I said.

'We'll look tomorrow,' he said.

'Why not now?' I asked. 'It won't take long.'

Peter looked at me closely. 'I'm not sure I understand you any more,' he said. 'Are you testing me?'

'I just want to see if there's anything down there.'

Without a word, he went to fetch the keys.

Chapter 26.

Very matter-of-factly, Peter unlocked the cellar door, switched on the lights and strode down the stairs. He had finished examining the place by the time I was there.

'Empty,' he said. 'And no sign of droppings.'

'Yes,' I said. But then I caught sight of something – a bright drop of water, like a raindrop or a teardrop, falling from the ceiling. It sliced down through the air, shining with a brightness that didn't seem to come from the lightbulb overhead. I didn't see it land, because of something I'd never noticed before. In the middle of the tiled floor was a drain with a thick metal grille covering it over. The water drop fell down through one of the square holes. The grille was the same grey colour as the rest of the cellar – easy to miss. The floor sloped towards it from every direction, like a very flat funnel.

'Did you see that?' I asked.

'See what?' said Peter.

I went across for a closer look at the grille. 'What's this?' I said.

I tried to lift it, and it budged a little.

'Give us a hand,' I said.

Peter joined me and together, with a bit of effort but not all that much, we lifted the grille – which was hinged – and let it fall to the side with a loud clang. A series of echoes came back from the dark hole we'd just opened up.

We both stood frozen, listening to see if Mary had been woken up. I expected a restless night, from how she'd been ever since the fox. For the moment, though, she seemed to be contentedly asleep.

There wasn't a lot of light, in the cellar, not enough to see to the bottom of the hole. But quite clearly visible were the first and second rungs of a ladder.

'Where do you think it goes?' I asked.

'Sewage pipe, probably,' said Peter. The thing didn't smell, though – or not of bad stuff. It smelt dry, woody.

'I think someone came up through there,' I said.

'What?' said Peter. 'To sit in our cellar.'

'I don't know. Perhaps they have keys to the other doors.'

'But you said the lights were off when you came in.'

'Perhaps they heard me.'

Peter looked around the whole room.

'I suppose you want us to go down there,' he said.

'We're not leaving the kids alone,' I said.

'Oh, you want me to go?'

'No,' I said, too quickly. Because really I did want him to go. Very much.

'Then you will?' he said. 'Fine. I'll get you a torch. And check on the children while I'm at it.'

He said the word children quite hurtfully.

Peter went off up the stairs, leaving me alone for the first time in the room with four doors. I think he was trying to test me – to see if I'd really go ahead with this. He knew I was scared of enclosed spaces. I don't think he expected me to be able to do it. And I didn't expect myself to, either. If he hadn't been so angry with me, he wouldn't have allowed any of this to happen.

Whilst Peter was gone, I went to the door of the water room, put my ear against it and listened. From inside, I could hear the constant gushing of the large pipe. Then I listened at the East door – the one with a door behind it, and another door behind that. I couldn't hear a sound, except my own breathing and then, when that calmed down, my heartbeat. But I did feel something. A slight draught was coming from under the door, chilly and damp.

I squatted down and held my fingers close to the narrow gap between door and floor. The air flowed between them. I could feel it twirling through.

I got down flat on the floor, and tried to look through the gap. It was far too dark. But I could smell the air of the draught, and, like the hole, it didn't smell bad. In fact, it was more like a breeze from outside.

Behind me, I heard a faint but echoey drip. I thought it had come from somewhere inside the hole.

As I was looking in that direction, I caught sight of a bright drop of water falling through the air – and down into the dark, where it made the drip sound.

Another drop followed it, and another, evenly spaced, one starting off as soon as the last had landed.

I stood up, went over to the edge of the hole. A drop fell past me, right into the centre of the black circle.

Looking up towards the ceiling, I couldn't really see where the next drop came from. There was no damp patch or area of shiny dimples. The drop just seemed to materialize in the air.

Drip, it landed. And for the next one, I held out my hand.

But the rhythm of drip and drop was broken. Nothing fell past me.

I pulled my hand away, and immediately a drop went down into the hole and gave a little drip.

Again, I put my hand out. And again no drop fell – until my hand was no longer there.

A third time, I tried to catch one of the drops.

This time, it did fall through the air. I saw it, in slow-motion. Everything in the world was slowed down.

The drop fell towards my hand, fell through my hand – right through the middle of my palm, as if I wasn't there at all.

Drip.

The footsteps on the stairs made me jump. And, when I glanced round, I was glad to see they belonged to Peter.

I couldn't speak until he'd reached the bottom of the stairs. 'That door's earth,' I said. 'That one's water. And I think this one is air.' I was pointing to the East door.

Peter came across.

'Feel,' I said, and bent down as I'd done a couple of seconds earlier. Peter came close to me and put his fingers down to the floor.

'You might be right,' he said. 'There's a cool breeze.'

'Which means this one's fire,' I said, and went across to the final door, the West door.

I put the back of one of my knuckles against it. Because I'd been scalded once already that day, I was very cautious. The metal door was just as cold as you'd expect one to be, in an unheated, underground room.

I knelt down and tried to sense whether the air around the gap beneath the door was warm. It seemed to be exactly the same temperature as the air in the rest of the cellar – apart from round the bottom of the East door.

'Robert Mew has some more keys,' I said. 'Perhaps we could ask him if we could borrow them.'

'They're our keys,' Peter said, 'not his. Let's get this over with, shall we?'

He pushed the torch into my hands.

'Okay,' I said, suddenly fearful of the dark and what I might find in it.

'Or have you changed your mind?' he asked, aggressively. And that was enough to make up my mind.

We went and stood on opposite sides of the hole. I shone the torch down as far as I could. There were another five rungs, then a floor. It looked dry. I couldn't where the drips had landed. I couldn't see any animal droppings, either. What I could see, though, was what looked like floorboards.

'Will you wait for me here?' I asked.

'I'll stand at the top of the stairs,' said Peter. 'That way I can hear Mary, if she cries.'

'Wish me luck,' I said.

I put my left foot on the first rung, my right on the second, lowered myself down.

In a couple of seconds, I was down on the floorboards – which were actually the lining of a tube-like tunnel. There were smooth planks on the curving sides and ceiling. The tunnel led off in only one direction, sloping down slightly as it went.

I shone the torch, expecting eyes to gleam back. The tunnel, all shiny wood, went on as far as I could see. It was like being inside a very long old-fashioned rowing boat.

‘You all right?’ said Peter, making me jump.

‘Yes,’ I said. ‘It’s not scary. I’m going to have a look.’

The tunnel wasn’t big enough for me to walk through upright, or even for me to shuffle along doubled over. I had to get down on hands and knees. I had to crawl.

The floor wasn’t covered with anything disgusting. It was a bit dusty, and there were lines in the dust, where the toes of someone’s shoes had dragged. Perhaps more than one person. I couldn’t tell how recently they’d been made. The marks could have been there for ages.

I stuck the torch into the front of my t-shirt, so it shone forwards, and set off along the tunnel.

Chapter 27.

The first few feet were easy. My knees slipped along the smooth boards, made even smoother by the dust.

I remembered childhood games – crawling through the narrow spaces between chairs covered over with sheets and duvets. I used to make a circle all round my bedroom, so that I didn't have to surface once.

For quite a few feet, the tunnel went smoothly on. Then, very abruptly, the boards became rough and much older-looking. Holding the torch, I examined them closely. There was a line from top to bottom where new wood met old. But what was really strange was that this seemed to happen halfway along the same long plank.

I guessed that I was now out from under the house.

The going was harder on the rougher wood. Almost immediately, I got a splinter in one of my fingers.

I slowed down, and went more carefully.

It was hard to know how long I'd been in the tunnel. I wanted to shout back to Peter, just to check he was still there, to check that Mary was all right. I felt a strong desire to turn round and go back. However, the tunnel was too narrow for that. I would have to edge out backwards.

Yes, I could do this tomorrow.

I started to reverse along the tunnel, looking between my legs to check the way.

Then I heard something unexpected – a gurgling, swishing sound. Water was in the tunnel, behind me, in the direction I was going. Perhaps it was coming from the water room. Or perhaps the drip from the ceiling had suddenly become a torrent.

I lay on my back and pointed the torch towards the wet noise.

There was water there, and it was flowing towards me, but just at the point where the new wood met the old, it stopped.

The way it looked to me, there was an invisible pane of glass, stopping the water going any further.

The tunnel there was already more than halfway full.

I hurried back until I was within touching distance of the divide. Then, aware that I might let loose a flood that would sweep me down the tunnel, possibly towards a dead end, I put my foot into the water.

I couldn't feel a thing, except where the join was. At that point I felt a strange difference that I couldn't identify - not until I'd remembered sitting in the bath. This was that feeling of having no air around your skin.

I knew that I wouldn't be able to breathe, under this water, but I needed to try. I shuffled back until my ankles, knees, hips, tummy, breasts and then shoulders were immersed. Then – leaving the torch behind – I went further, and my head was in, too.

My eyes were open, and I could see perfectly clearly. I opened my mouth, but there was no air. The strangest thing was the silence. No sounds at all, apart from those made by my body.

I had a sudden fear of drowning, so scrambled forwards again, through the divide, into the open tunnel.

I came out completely dry, of course.

Now I had no choice, I had to go on. And if the tunnel *was* a dead-end, then I'd be trapped. Perhaps if I found a place with enough room to turn round, I could return going forwards – and I would have a chance to swim back to the cellar.

I picked up the torch and put it in my t-shirt again. For a couple of slow minutes, I crawled on. The tunnel kept sloping downwards. Then, just as beneath the house, reached another metal grille above which it turned upwards at a ninety-degree angle. There was a metal ladder. I climbed it, as far as I could.

But yet another metal grille, like the other two, was over the end of the tunnel. And when I tried to lift it, it didn't move. The reason was simple – something cross-shaped was standing directly over the mouth of the hole. When I examined it with the torch, I could see that it was made of wood.

I shined the torch through the gaps in the grille, to see what I could see. There was a ceiling in the shape of an arch.

It was the chapel! The tunnel from the house came out into the chapel! I wondered who else knew about this? Father Trovato? Mr. Gatward? If I just stayed here, trapped by the water, Peter would eventually figure out where I was – with someone's help, maybe. But that might be hours away. Hours when I wouldn't be there to look after Mary and Jack.

Even as I looked around, the light from the torch seemed to fade and go more golden.

I climbed back down the ladder. There was just enough space for me to get down on my knees and bring my head down and around so that it was facing the way I'd come.

In the failing light, I scrabbled back along the tunnel, not really caring about splinters or dust.

I wanted to be back with my children, to know they were safe. If I had to swim without air for five minutes to get to them, I would.

But when I reached the divide between old wood and new, the water wasn't there. It had disappeared leaving not a drop behind.

The torch failed completely, leaving me in the dark. Finding my way wasn't difficult, though. And, when I got close to the ladder out, a faint light came down through the hole.

I climbed out of the tunnel.

'That you?' asked Peter.

'Yes,' I said.

'It goes to the chapel,' he said. 'Doesn't it?'

I was incredibly annoyed by this. Even if he'd worked it out, he could have waited until I told him.

'It does,' I said. 'I couldn't get out the other end. There was a grille with something right on top of it – something cross-shaped.'

'It's a secret chapel,' said Peter. 'Pretty obvious they needed a secret tunnel to get to it. The family were Catholics – recusants. They needed that priest's hole to hide their priest, in case anyone came looking for him. If he'd been caught, they'd all have been done for treason.'

'I know all that,' I said. 'And now we know where the tunnel goes. But I was the one to go down in there. And I was the one who almost got drowned for the trouble.'

'Was it flooded?' Peter asked.

'Flooded and then unflooded,' I said. 'You wouldn't understand.'

'Where did the water come from?'

'The house,' I said. 'Let's go to bed. I'm exhausted.' That was true, although I somehow still had the energy to be furious at the same time. The crawl down the tunnel, and the fear of drowning, had taken a lot out of me, but Peter's reaction was stoking up my anger.

I wanted to see Mary as soon as possible.

'How's your arm?' Peter asked, as we climbed the stairs. He wanted to remind me of my stupidity.

'Fine,' I said. In truth, I hadn't thought about it for several hours. There was no pain.

Mary lay a little more curled up than usual. I turned her over on her back – she didn't like that, though. A moment later and she returned to the position I'd found her. Mary hadn't slept like this – foetal – since the first couple of weeks after she was born. It disturbed me to see her showing what I could only think was fear, insecurity.

In the bathroom, after brushing my teeth, I decided to pull the bandage back and have a look at the scald beneath.

I stuck my finger in, lifted the dirty fabric and tried to see where the unhurt skin ended and the white, bloated skin began. Further and further I peeled back, and still it all looked as if nothing had happened to it. Finally, I unwound the whole bandage, and saw that my arm was good as new.

'Oh,' I said.

Peter came in without saying a word. He looked at my arm.

'Can't have been as bad as it looked,' he said.

'It's healed,' I said. 'In half a day.'

'No,' said Peter. 'It must just have gone down, like an inflammation.'

'The scalding was really bad,' I insisted. 'I thought I was going to have a scar there forever.'

'Well, you won't,' Peter said.

We went and lay down. Same bed, different houses – different universes.

Chapter 28.

At three o'clock in the morning, Mary woke and I took her downstairs for a feed and a quiet chat with Lilian.

'You don't have to scare me,' I said to the painting. This didn't feel as silly as it had done before. The lines of communication between us were clearly open. I didn't know whether Lilian was listening, but she was most definitely watching. 'If you want to tell me something, you can just tell me. Very directly. I'm paying attention now. I think I've worked out a little of what you want to tell me. You wanted me to follow the tunnel to the chapel, didn't you? And when you saw I was about to wimp out, you stopped me. You showed me where the tunnel was with the drip. The weird water means something, too. The water not touching me. I just don't understand it yet. Can't you be more direct? Can't you write? Can't you speak?'

The painting didn't speak.

'It must be difficult for you,' I said. 'I'm sorry I'm so slow. I don't know why you ever chose me? Peter might be a better bet. Maybe you'll change your mind.' Suddenly I felt panicked. 'Please don't do that – I'm really glad you chose me. It's the most interesting thing that's ever happened to me.' And the best, I thought – then added, apart from Jack and Mary. 'I'll get there in the end,' I said.

For a moment I thought I heard something out in the hall, a footstep. Could Peter have come down to get a glass of water and overheard me talking to myself? Or just decided to check I wasn't up to any more foolishness? No, he could never have made it down all those creaky stairs without me hearing him.

Mary didn't want much milk. As she was nodding off again, I undid her babygrow and took a look at her leg. The tooth marks from the fox were gone – no sign they had ever been there.

I smiled at Lilian. 'Thank you,' I said.

I could probably cut this feed out, with a couple of nights of controlled crying. Then Mary might sleep through – particularly if I started to giving a big whack of formula last thing. It might be nice for Peter to get a chance to feed her. We had all the bottles and sterilizing stuff left over from Jack.

I was thinking this, and nothing more elevated, when I walked into the hall. The place seemed brighter than usual – as if someone had turned on a light in one of the side rooms. It was only when I got to the foot of the staircase that I realized why: from top to bottom, each of the steps was covered with smooth and very shiny white ice – as if a flowing stream had been stopped by a sudden winter freeze. The wooden steps had been turned into a slope I had no chance of climbing – not with Mary in my arms. If I'd not had her, I might have been able to drag myself up, using the banisters as handholds. The message was pretty clear, though. Lilian didn't want me to go upstairs just yet. She had something else for me.

'Very impressive,' I said, and it began to snow.

The flakes didn't all start falling from the ceiling. Some materialized only an inch or two from the ground. They were huge and soft, the size of Peter's thumbs. There were thousands of them – millions maybe – extremely close together. I couldn't see the walls. The floor beneath my bare feet must have been freezing – every snowflake that landed settled – but I couldn't feel anything. And this feeling nothing, with my eyes telling me it was all frozen, was the strangest feeling of all.

Mary and me were almost instantly in the middle of a square of the purest white I'd ever seen. Or, at least, that's what I thought until I turned round, away from the staircase, and saw that the floor was clear here – a straight path back to the dining room. It wasn't that the snow wasn't settling on this, it wasn't *falling* on it. When I looked up, I could see a clear, high, empty space. It was like being inside the bottom of a transparent wall.

I walked back the way I'd come.

On either side of me, the snow was already piled up in drifts of six or seven inches.

At my first glimpse into the dining room, I really did think I was seeing a ghost. A white shape was there, human-sized, human-shaped. I stopped, terrified, and waited for it to move.

The snow around me was falling in very straight lines to the ground. There was no breeze. I tried to allow this to calm me – some hope.

The white figure was completely motionless.

I approached it slowly, fearing that it would suddenly fly towards me with a scream and a huge open mouth full of teeth. That's what would happen in one of Peter's beloved horror films.

The figure was wearing a dress – one that I recognized now, and should have recognized before.

I hurried forwards. This was Lilian, come down off the painting. Not in the same pose.

I came and stood in front of her face. I can honestly say, without any doubt, that this was the most beautiful thing I'd ever seen. It was a miraculously detailed snowman, snowwoman, impossible for even the greatest sculptor to make. (Snow, not ice, for its colour was white not grey or blue.) The lace on Lilian cuffs was there – every single detail of it. And every strand of her hair could be picked out, even a few stray ones that had escaped around her headdress. Everything was so lifelike – the face and hands so real – each eyelash, the ridges on the fingernails – that really the most amazing thing was, the statue *wasn't* moving.

I stood facing her, feeling terribly underdressed in my baggy nightclothes. Lilian was half a head shorter than me. But I felt her presence now in a different way to before, standing in front of the painting. Although she was still incredibly distant, she had come down to my level. It was easier to imagine having a conversation with her – a normal conversation, not the mad conversation we were having with my fumblings and her special effects.

The breath from my mouth went into clouds that caressed her face. Mary was gazing at her, too. I wished for Mary to remember this when she grew up – even if only as a wonderful dream.

'You were very lovely,' I said. 'And such lovely clothes.'

In Lilian's perfect hands, clasped in front of her bosom, was a small book, hardly bigger than one of her palms. I bent down and looked closer. A ribbon came out from top of it, just as in the painting, and went behind the book, just as in the painting, but because the figure was now in three dimensions I could, by moving round to the side, see what was on the end of this twisted ribbon – a tiny white carving of a phoenix surrounded by flames. It was identical to the one carved on the back of the house.

'Is this it?' I asked. 'Is this what you wanted me to see?'

There was movement around Lilian's head. At first I thought flames were forming in a halo, but then I saw it was snowflakes and that they were now falling upwards – and, as they did, her head-dress began to disappear. It looked like the snow she had been made of was going backwards in time, returning to what it had been before.

I watched as Lilian's forehead, eyes, nose, mouth all flew in long lines into the ceiling. My own eyes hurt at seeing such beauty just evaporating, and no one in the world but Mary and me would ever see it. I didn't feel… I suppose *worthy* is the word. I started to cry, very hard, and then Mary did, too.

Lilian's head was gone. The figure looked even more ghostly now. Perhaps this was Jack's headless ghost. But I couldn't see very clearly because white shapes were fluttering in front of my eyes. I tried to bat them away with my free hand. Then I realized that these were another kind of upwards-flying snowflakes – snowflakes formed out of the tears on my cheeks.

I looked upwards and my eyes cleared, as the flakes were no longer rising past them but taking straight off for the ceiling.

Another couple of vertical lines of flakes were there, to my left. I held Mary up and saw that, yes, her little tears were turning into snowflakes, too.

I laughed. This was a gift unlike any other. I didn't want to stop crying. I wanted to be able to show this magic to Peter and Jack.

For a while longer, tears kept lifting from my eyes – a mixture of joy at the beauty of this vision and sadness that was coming to an end.

The snow-Lilian was disappearing faster and faster. Only the bottom half of her was left, from the hips down.

I waited until the very end. Her feet were in tiny shoes, and then it was only the shapes of the soles of them, and then all the snow was gone.

The hall was also just as it had been before.

A little shaky, I carried Mary back to bed. Peter was there, fast asleep, but nothing he might ever dream could come close to what I'd just experienced. I felt so, so sorry for him.

Chapter 29.

Mr. Gatward arrived at nine o'clock sharp. We had been up for a couple of hours. Because we wanted to see where the tunnel came out, and because I'd promised Mr. Gatward a view around the chapel, we all set off for it together – Jack leading the way.

Hot sunlight came down onto the path in narrow beams. Mr. Gatward said, 'It's unpleasantly hot, isn't it?' Mary was in my arms, wide awake, quite content. This surprised me – she hadn't fed very well. In fact, none of us seemed to be all that hungry. Half a slice of buttered toast was enough for me. And Jack left most of his cornflakes.

As we walked round from the house, Peter was sorting through the keys, making sure he had the right one ready.

The chapel didn't seem so far away, now. If the trees hadn't been growing so thickly, it would easily have been within sight of the house – maybe fifteen or twenty yards.

I looked down at the ground, imagining the rough wooden tunnel directly beneath my feet – and myself crawling through it, full of fear, only the night before.

'Here,' said Jack, and stamped on the echoey door.

'Careful,' said Peter, 'we don't know how strong it is.'

'Oh,' said Mr. Gatward. 'I never thought I'd live to see it.'

Peter knelt down and undid the bolt. The key turned easily. Then he pulled back the door.

'I'll go first,' he said.

'Me next,' said Jack.

'No, let Mr. Gatward go,' I said.

'I can wait,' said Mr. Gatward. 'It's been more than half a century. A few seconds more don't matter.'

'I'm going to wait up here,' I said. 'With Mary.'

'How is the dear little thing doing?' asked Mr. Gatward. Mary winced a little as his dry fingers touched her face.

'The fox didn't bite very deeply,' I said. 'She's fine.'

'But what a fright,' said Mr. Gatward.

'We're down!' shouted Peter. The lights came on.

'Poor thing,' said Mr. Gatward, but I could see he was already thinking of what he might see underground.

Very carefully, he lowered himself down into the hole. With his curved spine, I wasn't at all sure that he'd be able to make it down the ladder. Everything but his straw hat slowly very gradually disappeared, and then that was gone, too.

'Morning, Mrs. Jonson,' said a rough voice, almost immediately.

I turned round and saw a dead fox hanging up by the tail, then, behind it, holding it, Robert Mew.

'Laid a trap last night. Little bugger wasn't expecting to get caught like that. Mr. Jonson used to feed it quite regular. Cost me a decent leg of chicken, but I got it.'

'Good,' I said, although the black blood around the fox's nose made me feel both sick and sad. 'You're sure it's the same one?'

'No doubt,' said Robert Mew. 'It's got a broke rib. But I'd've known it anyway. I have nicknames for them all. This one's Rommel, because I seen him in the empty cornfield that's like a desert. Desert fox, see?'

'What are the others?'

'Esmeralda, Thor, Homer, The Count and Marcel Marceau.'

'Marcel Marceau's quiet, is he?'

'Absolutely silent.'

I wasn't sure what else there was to say.

'Well done,' I said. 'What do you do with the body?'

'If you don't mind, I'll hang it up, as fair warning to the others. Not somewhere so's you'd see it, mind.'

'Fine,' I said. I knew that bloodthirsty Jack would be disappointed if he didn't get to see the dead fox.

'Jack,' I shouted into the chapel. 'Come here.'

I listened hard. All I could hear was Mr. Gatward saying, 'Wonderful.'

Jack scrabbled up the ladder.

'Wow,' he said. 'Did you shoot it?'

'Trapped it,' said Robert Mew.

He bent down to give Jack a closer look, and I saw the keychain dangling from his belt.

Jack was taking a very close interest in the fox's bloody mangled leg, where it had been snared. Earlier that morning, he'd taken a similar interest in the arm I'd scalded. He was very relieved to see that I wasn't hideously disfigured. Remembering yesterday, I remembered something else.

'Robert,' I said. 'Those keys you have. Do you know what all of them are for?'

The gardener stood up.

'To be honest, I only use about three or four of 'em. They came with the job. I don't know why I still lug them around.'

'Could you let me have the ones you don't use? Just for today. I'll give you them back.'

'Take the lot,' he said. 'As long as I can lock up this evening.'

He undid his belt with his right hand and pulled it round until the keys fell into his left.

'Can I have them?' asked Jack.

'You can hold them for a minute,' I said.

'They're very old,' Robert said. 'Probably for something in the house.'

'That's what I hope,' I said. 'Have you ever been down there?' I nodded at the door in the ground.

'Chapel?' asked Robert. 'No. I knows it's there, because of walking over it so often.'

'Why don't you have a look?' I said.

He glanced around, as if someone might see him going in.

'May I?'

'Of course.'

Robert laid the fox on a pile of leaves, treating it with respect even though he said he'd hated it. Jack immediately handed me the keys and went over for an even closer look at the dead animal.

Robert crossed himself, then went quickly and easily down the ladder. He was very athletic. The bushy beard made him look much older than he was, and so you expected him to be tentative. It was only when he was out of sight that I realized him bringing the fox to me there might not have been a total accident. Most likely, he'd been angling to get a nosey around the chapel.

With Mary resting on my shoulder, I looked through the keys one by one. There were at least four that might fit the doors to the fire and air rooms. We could try later on, when we had a minute.

Peter climbed out of the chapel.

'Jack,' he said, 'why don't you go and show Robert around?'

Jack went down straight away. He loved being an expert.

Peter came closer and whispered in my ear, 'You know you said that something was blocking your way out, up through the grille, something shaped like a cross?'

'Yes.'

'It's the bottom of the lectern. I can see it. It's down there. But…'

'What?'

'It's not covering anything. It's just over a flagstone. The grille where the tunnel comes out is next to it.'

'That means…'

We both looked towards the house.

'It does indeed mean that,' said Peter. 'Go and see for yourself. I'll hold Mary.'

Without looking as if I was interested in anything particular, I went down into the chapel.

'Mrs. Jonson,' said Mr. Gatward, his eyes blazing with energy, 'there's nothing else like this in England. It's absolutely one of a kind. The recusants usually had hidden chapels *in* their houses.'

'Really?' I said, moving towards the lectern.

'They needed to hear the mass, of course. Every day. Several times. When the houses were searched, Elizabeth's men were looking for priests but also for cups, plates, candles.'

Three feet to one side of the lectern was a metal grille. I'd been on the underside of it just the night before. I'd poked my fingers up through those holes. And, since then, someone had gone through it from here. Someone had moved the lectern out of the way, so they could climb back out.

'The Jonsons must have needed vast amounts of money to build this place. And to have done so in complete secrecy. That suggests a large self-contained recusant community – with craftsmen, an architect.'

I could see scrapes on the floor, where the wood of the lectern had left traces on the flagstones. It looked as if it had happened many times more than just the once. That might explain the sounds I'd heard going down into the cellar with Jack. Whoever it was must have a second key to the chapel. The first had come from Father Trovato. Maybe they had got the second key from him, too.

I tried lifting the lectern. It was far too heavy for me by myself.

'Robert,' I said. 'Could you just help me move this?'

Jack and Mr. Gatward came over, but I said Robert and I could handle it – and it turned out that we could.

'I think it should go in the middle,' I said. 'There.'

Together, we repositioned it, right on top of the grille. No one was getting out that way. But what if they were robbing the house, even as we were looking around here? No, the cellar was locked from the outside. They couldn't get out unless they broke the door down. I thought of the solicitors' warnings, about how valuable all the paintings were.

'Jack,' I said, 'you can stay here with the others. Mr. Gatward, could you lock up when you leave?'

'Of course. Of course,' he said. 'Though I feel I could stay here forever. I've never had such a sense of stepping right through a doorway into the past.'

Before he could say anything else, I was up the ladder and into the daylight.

'Come on,' I said to Peter, 'I've blocked off that end.'

Peter held up Mary, as if to ask what we should do with her.

'Robert,' I called down into the chapel. 'Can you come up here for a moment?'

He came up blinking, a little startled by what he'd seen.

'Can you hold Mary?' I asked. 'We need to quickly do something in the house.'

Only slightly bewildered, he took Mary in his safe arms.

'Right,' I said.

Peter and me walked until we were out of sight of the chapel, then sprinted into the hall, where I could see straight away that the lock was still on the unbroken cellar door.

I went into the kitchen with Peter. Even though we were out of earshot of the cellar, we still whispered.

‘Shouldn’t we call the police?’ I asked.

‘We will,’ said Peter. ‘When we’re sure there’s someone in there. It would be a bit stupid to get the police out just for an empty cellar.’

‘But it’s not going to be empty, is it?’ I said.

‘No,’ he said. ‘There’s two or more in there, I reckon.’

‘Really?’ I felt shaky with adrenalin.

‘Did you try moving that lectern on your own?’

‘We can’t surprise them,’ I said. ‘They’ll hear us.’

‘It doesn’t matter,’ said Peter. ‘We can keep them in there until they tell us what they’re up to.’

Quickly, Peter went into the living room and brought back two pokers from the fireplace. He gave the bigger one to me, then slid the key into the lock, turned it twice, pushed the door open and switched on the light.

Again I heard the high yelp followed by the scrabbling.

Peter marched down the stairs, ‘Right,’ he said, ‘let’s see you.’

Chapter 30.

The Right Honourable Douglas Longbone stood up from where he'd been sitting, beside Mrs. Forster, on a blue and green tartan blanket. Between them were a couple of bright torches and three plates with the remains of breakfast on them – eggshells, crusts. Mrs. Forster had some knitting. Longbone had an iPod and a copy of The *Telegraph*.

'Let me explain,' said Longbone.

'Go on,' said Peter. 'Explain.'

'Mrs. Forster was showing me – '

'Showing you what? How to break into our house?'

'Yes, in a manner of speaking. I'd heard about the secret tunnel. I asked her to show it to me. We were making a bit of a jolly out of it.'

He was trying to laugh the whole thing off.

'That's a lie,' I said. 'You're obviously here for the duration.' I pointed to Mrs. Forster's knitting, a small cardigan that looked as though it was just about Mary's size.

'First,' said Peter, 'give me the key to the chapel.'

Mrs. Forster reached for her pocket.

'Now, hang on – ' said Longbone.

'Do as I say,' said Peter, 'or I'll call the police.'

'That won't necessarily do you a huge amount of good,' said Longbone. 'In the long term.'

'Okay,' said Peter. 'I'll call the newspapers. We can keep you down here until they arrive. "MP in breaking and entering scandal" – doesn't sound too good, does it?'

Peter started to climb the stairs.

'No, no, no,' said Longbone. 'Please…'

'Why are you here?' said Peter.

Longbone looked down at Mrs. Forster. 'You tell them,' he said. He seemed to have given up.

'It's the house,' said Mrs. Forster. 'It heals you. It keeps you young. Or it stops you getting old. But you have to spend a certain amount of time here. Just coming and going doesn't work. You have to be here for hours. That's why – '

'This is what you honestly think?' said Peter

'So that's why you drove us half mad with your bloody hoovering, is it?' I said.

'Yes,' said Mrs. Forster. 'I knew that if you didn't let me come here, I'd die. I'd die very soon. When I'm away, I can feel myself aging. See what happened to Mr. Jonson.'

'So you'd prefer to spend your life cleaning, rather than be anywhere else?'

'I love this house,' said Mrs. Forster. 'I've spent the happiest hours of my life here.'

'Well, you've messed that up now, haven't you?' said Peter.

‘Why are you here?’ I asked Longbone. ‘Do you want to live longer.’

‘Of course,’ he said. ‘But mainly I don’t want to die so soon. I have two young, active children, and I have cancer. Of the lungs. I thought this might help. The chemotherapy didn’t do much. I’ll try anything – and I’ve already done homeopathy, healing prayer, you name it.’

Peter looked at the both of then, then at me – I could see he was thinking we were all as mad as each other.

‘Right,’ said Peter to me. ‘Upstairs. I’m going to lock these two down here until I’ve figured out what to do.’

‘Please don’t do that,’ Longbone said.

‘You can listen to a few tunes,’ Peter said.

Mrs. Forster stood up, pulled the large key out of her pocket and placed it in my hand.

‘It’s your decision,’ she said to me. ‘I know you believe me.’

‘It’s *our* decision,’ said Peter, ‘and if you think it’s not, you’re making an even worse mistake. Come on.’

I followed him out of the cellar. I can’t say that locking our infuriating cleaner and our smug MP down there didn’t give me some satisfaction. I mean, how many people get the chance?

We walked out of the front door, as if we thought they’d hear us if we spoke inside the house.

‘Well,’ said Peter, ‘do you believe her?’

I held out my perfect arm, badly scalded only twenty four hours before.

‘Yes,’ I said. ‘I’m certain there’s something magical about this house. I’ve seen impossible things…’

‘What things?’

I didn’t want to mention the snow and ice. ‘You know,’ I said, ‘the dirt in the middle of the night. The stones in Jack’s room.’ I could tell that Peter knew I believed there was more, but he wasn’t going to press me. Perhaps he was frightened of what he might hear – frightened of how mad I might be. ‘I think it means something that everything here is in such good condition – the floors and banisters. It’s as if it’s all new.’

‘And how exactly does this work, this healing people?’

‘I don’t know. But I think it has something to do with Elizabeth.’

Peter stood, looking down into the gravel of the drive, stirring it with the toe of his shoe.

‘I don’t believe it,’ he said. But that’s for later. What should we do about those two?’ he asked. It was a genuine question. He really wasn’t sure. I wanted to give him a hug but felt held back – Peter might think I was using comfort to try and get him to do what I wanted.

‘Let them go,’ I said. ‘They won’t be able to do it again. We have the key now.’

‘How do we know she didn’t have it copied? How do we know that every mason in the county hasn’t got a key to our home?’

'We don't,' I said. 'But we can put something over the grate in the cellar. No one's going to get in.'

Peter wasn't satisfied with this, I could tell.

'I'm going to see how the children are,' I said.

Peter went back into the house. Later, he told me that he took a camera down into the cellar. He made Longbone and Mrs. Forster hold up the *Telegraph* while he took their photos – to prove that they'd been there, on that day. This made me smile. It was as if we'd become kidnappers.

I was bringing Jack and Mary round to the front of the house when our two intruders came out the front door, Peter following behind them. Mrs. Forster was crying. Longbone was saying over his shoulder to Peter, 'Look, just consider it, all right? What have you got to lose.' He caught sight of me. 'Goodbye, Mrs. Jonson,' he said, as if we'd just played bridge together, or something. 'Goodbye, Jack, Mary.'

'What are you considering?' I asked Peter, as the two sad but also ridiculous figures walked off down the path.

'He offered me fifty thousand pounds if he could move into one of our spare rooms. And a lot more if he was alive in a year's time, and could start playing golf again. That seemed quite important.'

Just before they disappeared into the trees, Longbone turned to stare angrily back at the house. He peered up at the roof, stood on tiptoe for a moment, shook his head. Mrs. Forster kept walking, but I could see her shoulders juddering as she sobbed. Then Longbone turned and stomped away, too.

'Oh,' said Peter, 'and we'd have to take Mrs. Forster back, too. But she promises she wouldn't hoover so much.'

'The money would be useful,' I said.

'We'll talk about it later,' Peter replied.

'Can I have some money?' asked Jack.

Mr. Gatward and Robert Mew came into sight.

'I've locked it all up,' said Robert, and handed Peter the keys. 'Got to be getting along now. Thank you for the look-around.'

Before we could say anything else, he was off.

Mr. Gatward went into the house with us. He was going to go upstairs again, but I asked him to wait. Then I told Jack he could play computer games for a while. He ran straight off.

'Can we ask you a few questions?' I said to Mr. Gatward.

'Of course,' he replied.

I led him into the parlour, carrying a gently stirring Mary on my shoulder. Peter came, too.

'It's a wonderful painting, isn't it?' he said. 'I missed seeing it, when I wasn't allowed in the house. All I had were a couple of very bad black and white reproductions. And it's the colours that make it so special. Look at that hair! Just like Gloriana's. That's Queen Elizabeth the First.'

We were now all sitting round the dining table.

'Do you mind if I feed Mary?' I asked Mr. Gatward.

'No,' he said, 'I don't.' I knew he wasn't very comfortable with the idea, but he knew it would be very rude to say so.

'Why are there so many books on alchemy upstairs?' I asked, when Mary was settled and Mr. Gatward definitely unsettled.

'My theory, and it's only a theory, is that Lilian and her father were trying to make gold. From the evidence upstairs, they would have known as much as anyone in Europe about this.'

'But no one ever did,' said Peter. 'It's impossible.'

'If they had,' said Mr. Gatward, 'history would have been very different. Unless, of course, they did, and it was covered up. I'm no conspiracy theorist, however.'

Somehow, I felt he wasn't telling me everything he suspected.

'Why did they want gold?' I asked. 'Weren't they rich enough?'

'How rich is rich enough?' Mr. Gatward said. 'People always want more. But, no, my guess is they saw it as more of a spiritual quest – a way of testing how pure in heart they were. Many alchemists believed that only someone who had no material interest in gold would be able to produce it. You had to be above all worldly concerns.'

'But they were seriously Catholic, weren't they? With the priest's hole and everything. Didn't that make what they were doing dangerous? Evil?'

'That's a good question,' said Mr. Gatward. 'It's one I've thought about a lot. I've come to the conclusion that, for William and Lilian, alchemy was very closely related to the Catholic doctrine concerning the Mass – the transubstantiation of the host, the bread. This was the hottest topic of that time – the reason people were burnt at the stake. When they took the sacraments, Catholics believed that they were really eating the body and drinking the blood of Christ. Protestants thought lots of different things, but mostly that nothing physically changed in the bread and wine. But the utter transformation of matter – one thing magically becoming another – that's central to all Catholic belief. So, in a way, it's more likely Catholics would be interested in alchemy than Protestants. Because, for them, making gold from base material is little more than an amusing sideshow to the Mass itself. You can't eat gold, you see, and it doesn't get you into heaven.'

I was very aware of Lilian's golden brown eyes upon us. I wondered if she was pleased or displeased at what we were saying. Were we getting any closer? How would she let me know?

Mary had stopped feeding almost immediately. Her loss of appetite was starting to worry me. I didn't want her to have lost weight, the next time the Health Visitor came. I cradled her in my arms and felt her little fingers grabbing at my collar.

'I'm hoping,' continued Mr. Gatward, 'there will be some answers in the archives. If I can find some contemporary records, I might be able to tell you more.'

I thought about telling him to look for a tiny book that had a red ribbon bookmark with a phoenix on the end of it. But, because I felt he was holding back, I decided to hold this back from him. Before I said anything, I would have a look myself.

'Alchemy is about eternal life, too, isn't it?' Peter said.

'Yes,' said Mr. Gatward. 'Though I think that's partly a metaphor. It's about being attuned to the matter of creation. If you can make gold out of base metal, then you can probably stop your own body aging, fly, make nuclear explosions, anything you feel like. But anyone who'd succeeded would probably exist on such a high spiritual level that they wouldn't be interested in anything so trivial.' He stood up. 'If I find anything,' he said, 'I'll let you know straight away.'

I was no longer sure that he would.

When he was gone, I said to Peter, 'I have some more keys to try, downstairs.'

'Where from?'

'Robert. He says he doesn't know what half of them are for.'

I handed them over, and Peter examined them closely.

'They certainly look like they might fit.'

Mary was still awake, but she was due for a sleep. I told Peter I thought I could probably get her down in ten or fifteen minutes.

'Why don't I just try them now? On my own?'

'No,' I said. 'I need to be there.'

'It's air and fire, you reckon,' said Peter. 'Could be dangerous.'

'So, we won't tell Jack,' I said. 'Give me the keys back.'

He hesitated before handing them over.

'I just thought it might be easier,' he said.

I was back downstairs in half an hour. Mary didn't go off until she'd had a cry, a change, another unsuccessful attempt at a feed and then a winding.

Peter was sitting in the office. He had Michael Francis's photograph album out in front of him, on the desk. It was open at the last shot of Michael Francis – the last before he left for the Arctic.

'Does that man look a hundred and five?' I asked.

'I don't know,' said Peter. 'Even if it's true, it might not be good.'

'What are you thinking?'

'There might be some sort of price to pay. I mean, if Michael Francis thought he could live forever, why did he leave the house? It would be suicide, like Mrs. Forster said.'

'Perhaps it was,' I said.

'Suicide is a mortal sin,' said Peter.

I held up the keys. 'Let's go and try them.'

I half-expected someone else to be sitting down in the cellar – Matthew Maddox and Grace Dearie, perhaps – sitting on the flagstones, having a cosy picnic, when we turned on the light. Of course, it was completely empty – though there were a few toast crumbs left behind where Longbone and Mrs. Forster had been sitting.

Peter had already fetched the other sets of keys, and in a couple of minutes had unlocked the first two of the East doors – the one with the Yale lock and the dull black metal one.

We were now standing in front of the third door, which was covered in papery old leather. The keyhole was square-shaped, as were three of Robert Mew's keys.

The first was too big to fit. The second went in but just rattled uselessly around inside the lock. I crossed my fingers. One more chance.

The third fitted snugly into the hole.

Peter began to twist it. Then he stopped and said to me, 'I think you should stand further back.'

'Come on,' I said. 'No one's going to get hurt.'

Peter turned round. 'Now that's a really stupid thing to say.'

'The house doesn't want to hurt us. One day you'll understand that. Open the door. Please. I can't bear the suspense.'

Peter opened the door.

PART THREE

Chapter 31.

As Peter pushed the door inwards, a waft of lukewarm air passed over us. It smelt like the oldest thing you could imagine. Not rotten, gone-off, or even dusty. More like the soul of age.

The room itself on first glance was small, foursquare and completely empty – nothing like as interesting as the water one.

We were about to step inside when we heard a shocking slamming sound behind us.

I glanced around, expecting to see a figure. It was just the door at the top of the cellar stairs. It must have blown open and slammed against the panelling. When I looked up, I could see it swinging closed again.

'You're out now,' I muttered to myself, and to whatever spirit had just escaped.

I was about to follow Peter into the air-room when I heard approaching footfalls, coming at a run.

'Hey,' Jack shouted from the doorway. 'Hey, you promised!'

'Come on then,' I said.

He rushed down, looking around him all the time.

'Why didn't you let me join in?' he asked.

'We thought it might be dangerous,' I said. 'We were just checking it out first.'

Peter stood with the air-room behind him.

'Is it a dungeon?' Jack asked.

'Doesn't look like it. No shackles, anyway,' Peter said. 'Come and see.'

I followed Jack through the three doors.

The walls, ceiling and floor of the room were all made of bricks – very thin bricks, more like modern-day tiles placed sideways. They had been arranged in fishbone patterns. The more you looked, the more amazing it seemed. The patterns didn't repeat regularly, but they didn't seem irregular, either. There was probably some hidden logic to it, if you knew enough maths and could spend enough time studying it. Jack, however, was disappointed.

'I thought there was a skeleton,' he said.

'Let's show him the water,' I said.

Peter started to lock up the air room, which I knew was going to take a few minutes. I remembered the fox.

'I'm just going to check on Mary,' I said. 'Don't go in without me.'

'Mum,' said Jack.

'I won't be long.'

At first I thought what I could hear was Mary sobbing. I was just onto the landing, moving quite quickly, a dreadfully afraid at what I might find. But then I realized it was something else – Mary was cooing, like she did when she was very happy, like she did when I made faces at her.

I wondered whether I should go in. I knew she was okay, and if she was happy it was likely she'd go back to sleep. Seeing me would excite her too much, and possibly keep her awake.

The cooing was quite odd, though. I'd never heard her make those sorts of sounds when on her own. A few grunts of satisfaction as she digested her meal and the odd spooky giggle – that'd been about it.

I decided to try and get in and out without her catching sight of me.

When I peeked round the door, into the travel cot, Mary wasn't there.

Then I saw her, about four feet off the ground, over by the window, hovering, rocking. There was absolutely nothing to be seen around her, behind her, beneath. She was in mid-air.

My heart seemed to try to leap out and catch her.

The world was in slow-motion.

Mary was rocking, or being rocked. Mary was making cooing noises. Mary was levitating.

I started to run forwards.

Suddenly, Mary swung round until her head was towards me.

It was as if someone was holding her, and had turned to see who had come through the door. And then I realized that someone was holding her, rocking her.

I stopped dead.

'Be careful,' I said. 'Please.'

Mary bounced up and down in the air. The drop beneath her was onto parquet flooring. Her neck might break. Her skull would shatter.

I walked slowly forwards.

'Please give her to me.'

Immediately, Mary flew towards me – or that's how it seemed. The slight dip and rise in her flight showed she was being carried.

I held out my hands.

Even though she was moving quite fast, it seemed an age before Mary was close enough to reach for.

As she settled into my arms, I felt warm and fragrant air waft over me. It was a very different smell to down in the basement. It was like oranges and cinnamon and cloves and rosewater all mingled together. I knew it was Lilian's smell.

'Thank you,' I said.

For a moment, I could sense the fullness of Lilian's presence, right beside me. It was such an indescribable feeling – like what would be left of a friend if you took their physical body away but left their friendship. I loved what appeared to be an empty space, and then, with a few swift, soundless, invisible paces, I could sense that the room was again empty but for Mary and me.

Mary's eyelids were already fluttering. Although being cuddled by a ghost had woken her, she still wanted more sleep. I thought I could probably leave her safely on her own. Lilian wouldn't come back.

I settled her down in the cot. I loved her so much. My eyes were full of tears.

I hadn't even dried them when I walked straight into Mr. Gatward on the landing.

'Oh dear,' he said. 'Are you all right?'

'Yes,' I said. 'Fine.'

'That baby's not ill, is it? The fox bite…?'

'No, she's fine.'

'Good,' he said, then seemed to consider that everything must therefore be hunky-dory. 'I've made a rather exciting discovery.'

He held something out towards me – something which I didn't recognize straight away. It was very small and dark and then I saw the red ribbon dangling from the bottom of it. I reached out and lifted the ribbon up – the phoenix on the end was pulled out from beneath Mr. Gatward's thumb.

'It's Lilian's,' I said.

Mr. Gatward was completely astonished.

'But – But how did you know?'

'Because it's the one from the painting, the one she's holding.'

I was disappointed, and slightly fearful. I'd been hoping to find Lilian's book for myself, before Mr. Gatward did. But it was also amazing to see the picture, and snow statue, turn into reality.

'You're right,' he said. 'I think it's the very same one. I was just coming down to check. Shall we go and see?'

'Can I have a look?' I asked.

Mr. Gatward was reluctant to hand it over. 'Please be careful. Although it's in wonderful condition, it's still very delicate.'

I held out my hand. He placed the book in my palm. It wasn't much larger. The leather of the cover was warm and damp from Mr. Gatward's touch.

'Have you read it?' I asked.

'Only a little. I found it just a few minutes ago. It wasn't on the shelves. It was in a brown envelope in one of the filing cabinets.'

I was about to open the book when a whispered shout came from downstairs.

'Mum?!'

'What is it Jack?'

'Hurry up. You're taking ages.'

I didn't want to give the book back to Mr. Gatward. More than anything else in the house – apart from Peter and the children – I felt it belonged to me.

'Follow me,' I said to Mr. Gatward.

We went down to the cellar door.

'It might be better to stay out of here,' said Mr. Gatward, sternly. 'Until you're sure what you're dealing with.'

'Well,' I said, 'we have a better idea than we did before. We've opened three of the doors.'

'Three?' said Mr. Gatward. He seemed quite scared. 'Then close them, please.'

'Why don't you come and have a look?' I said, and went down the stairs.

Mr. Gatward's curiosity won out over his fear. I could hear him following me.

Peter was standing beside the water door, which was still shut.

'Mary okay?' he asked.

'Yes,' I said, not wanting to go into details. 'Asleep now.'

Mr. Gatward was looking all around him, talking to himself, trembling. 'Just so. Four doors. North, South, East, West.'

'Ready?' said to Peter to Jack.

'Is it really that good?' Jack asked.

Peter pulled open the door.

Part of me was expecting the water-room to have changed in some way – I don't know how. Perhaps for it to have become just another disappointing empty cell, like the air-room. Or perhaps for it still to have water in, but going in completely different directions. As it was, the waterfall-like sheet was there, just as before. And, beyond it, the pipe shot its gush of water sideways into the whirlpool.

'Great God!' said Mr. Gatward, then added, 'Excuse me.'

'Can I go in?' Jack said. 'Please can I go in? I'll put my swimming trunks on.'

'No,' I said. 'This is very dangerous. We don't know what it is.'

'No, we don't,' said Mr. Gatward. 'We certainly don't.'

'What do you think?' asked Peter. 'Impressed?'

'I've never seen anything like it,' said Mr. Gatward. 'There must be some sort of spring beneath the house. But to create that force of water pressure…'

'Can I touch it?' Jack asked.

'Yes,' Peter said. 'Just with your fingers. Don't get soaked.'

Jack put his fingertip out, into and then through the sheet of water. A thin line appeared beneath it, going down out of sight. He moved his finger slowly from side to side, and the line followed. Then he wiggled his finger faster, and the line became a wavy zigzag.

'May I?' asked Mr. Gatward.

‘Of course,’ said Peter.

The historian went and stood alongside Jack. His finger, when he put it through, made a thicker line. He followed this with more fingers, making a hole through which he could peer into the room beyond. Jack leaned over to look through, as well.

‘The tiling is Victorian, at the latest,’ said Mr. Gatward, turning round. ‘I would suspect earlier.’ He had another peek then stepped away, shaking the water from his hands.

Jack now stuck all his fingers into the water. He was getting wet down his arms. He wanted to get a better sight of the tiles.

‘Be careful,’ I said, but Jack was already toppling forwards.

Chapter 32.

Jack wouldn't have fallen in, but Mr. Gatward made a clumsy grab for him and ended up pushing him rather than catching hold. Through the curtain of water Jack went, the sheet closing behind him instantly.

The next thing I knew, my lovely boy – who's not a strong swimmer – was being swept round the room, anticlockwise.

Peter was about to jump in after him, but I held him back.

'You'll just get swept in, too,' I said.

Jack was now floating round on the far side of the room. At least he was the right way up – though I could see him spluttering. It felt like if he couldn't breathe, I couldn't breathe myself.

Jack went under the pipe on the left where the water spurted out. I thought he might bang his head and go under.

As he swept past, Peter made a grab for him.

'Your hand!' Peter shouted.

Jack heard, a little too late. Their fingers met, but couldn't catch hold.

Peter shouted in disappointment. Mr. Gatward was holding on to Peter's belt, to make sure he didn't fall in.

Jack circled round the room again. This time, he was a little closer to the middle. He was being drawn into the whirlpool. There must be a hole in the middle of the room where the water rushed out. He would never survive going down there.

This time round, Peter managed to grab Jack's left hand, but the force of the water was too much. He couldn't keep hold.

With each circuit, the chances of catching Jack grew fainter – he was further away, he was weaker.

'Both hands,' shouted Peter, himself now completely soaked. 'I need both hands! Try really hard.'

Jack's head went under for a moment. Then he spluttered back up. But he was still trying to gasp a breath as he swooshed past, and his hands were under the water.

'This time!' Peter shouted.

Jack tried really hard – reaching up as he approached. Peter grabbed one wrist, some fingers. Jack was swept onwards. Peter tensed as he tried to hold on, but it was no use.

'I'm going in,' said Peter.

'Try again,' I said.

He did. And again.

I knew it was up to me.

Jack was now so much closer to the centre of the whirlpool that he almost couldn't be reached from the door.

'Let me try,' I said.

'You're not strong enough,' said Peter.

'I'm going in,' I said, and put Lilian's book down on the cellar floor.

'Don't look at me,' I said. 'Both of you – look away.'

First, I made a test. I put my hand under the waterfall. Pulled it out. It was still dry. I hadn't felt anything.

'I can do it,' I said. 'Let me.'

'No,' said Peter.

'I'm going in,' I said. 'Keep your eyes closed.'

I stepped over Peter and jumped into the water room.

He and Mr. Gatward must have done what I said, and closed their eyes, because I went under, but didn't feel pushed around by any rush. Once I found my feet, I was able to stand up and hold my head above the surge. Jack, unconscious and all floppy, was swept towards me. I braced myself, and managed to stop him. With his body being pushed against me, it was like trying to walk through the strongest gale you've ever experienced. I couldn't do it.

I realized it was easier to go in the direction of the water.

'I'm fine,' I shouted. 'Don't look.'

Holding Jack in my arms, I allowed myself to be pushed once around the room. I had to duck to go under the pipe.

Then I shouted, 'He's here. Grab him now!'

Blindly, Peter's hands grasped out for Jack's arms. In a moment, they got a firm grip. I was able to push from the other end. Soon, we had him out. I stood there, relieved.

All of a sudden, I felt myself soaked and being swept off my feet. The water was freezing cold and a terrible force, pushing me wherever it wanted. A wave slapped into the back of my mouth. I felt myself choke, unable to breathe in. Desperately, I managed to lift my head free of the water.

'Close your eyes, you idiot,' I heard Peter shout before I was tumbled backwards, upside down

A second later, the water dropped me. I was on the slippery tiled floor of the room, unable to breathe but no longer being swirled around. I looked up and saw the white churning surface of the whirlpool.

Getting to my feet, I walked directly towards the door. And, as I did, I quickly ducked my head beneath the water. In the very centre of the room was a large black hole. If Jack or either of the men opened their eyes now, I would be sucked straight down it. That was where Jack had been heading. That is where he would have died.

I stepped over it and hurried towards the door.

'You can pull me out,' I shouted, grabbing hold of Peter's hands.

He took a firm grip and lifted me clear.

Jack was conscious, blowing water out of his nose.

We were too relieved to be angry with him or tell him off. I hugged him tight, and he let me. We were both soaked through.

Peter shut the door to the water room, locked it, then put the key in his back pocket.

'That was a stupid idea, wasn't it?' he said.

'I'm sorry I looked,' said Mr. Gatward. 'I thought you were out.'

'It's okay,' I said.

'But I don't understand,' he said. 'What did you do when we weren't looking.'

'The water doesn't touch me,' I said. 'Not when no one's looking at me. When they look, it's just the same as normal. I don't understand, either.'

'Really?' said Mr. Gatward. 'How bizarre.'

'Let's go upstairs,' I said.

Peter helped me lift a still very wobbly Jack to his feet. Then, one on either side of him, we walked him up the stairs, through the hall and into the back sitting room. Here, we laid him out on the sofa.

'Thanks, Dad,' he said, so weakly it made my husband start to cry.

'It's your mum you should be thanking,' Peter said.

I gave him the biggest hug.

'I'm sorry,' said Jack. 'I didn't mean to.'

'Don't ever do anything like that again,' I whispered.

'I promise,' he said.

Mr. Gatward quietly tiptoped out of the room. Peter went upstairs and fetched us both some towels and dry clothes.

'That was quite an adventure, wasn't it?' I said to Jack.

'You were so great, Mum,' he said. 'I thought I was going to – '

'Well, you're all right, anyway,' I said.

We sat in silence for a little while.

'Do you believe me now?' I asked Peter when he came back.

'People can do extraordinary things in the right circumstances,' he said. 'Lift cars, jump walls. People get super-strength.'

'Honestly, Peter,' I said. 'What's it going to take?'

Needing some excuse to get away, I headed upstairs to check that Mary was all right. She was fine – still sleeping. Completely oblivious to almost having lost her brother. And if we never told her, she'd never know.

Chapter 33.

It turned out that Mr. Gatward had taken himself off to the kitchen, where he'd made tea and poured out a huge glass of orange juice for Jack. I came across him, carrying the lot through into the sitting room on a painted metal tray.

'Thank you,' I said.

'I feel so awful,' he replied. 'It was me who pushed him in there. I'm so clumsy.'

'Don't worry,' I said. 'I know you were just trying to help.' Although, as I said it, the suspicion crossed my mind that Mr. Gatward might have deliberately pushed Jack in. But why? He wouldn't want him dead, would he? Just to get us out of the house? I dismissed the thought.

Jack drank his juice and we sat sipping our tea. It was such a contrast to the panic of a few minutes before.

'At least this didn't get wet,' said Mr. Gatward, and produced Lilian's book from his coat pocket. He passed the little volume to me.

'What's that?' Jack asked, at exactly the same time Mr. Gatward said, 'It's beautiful, isn't it?'

'It's a very old book,' I said. 'And, yes, it's lovely.'

'Something you found?' asked Peter.

Mr. Gatward explained about the envelope.

With a deep breath to calm my nerves, I opened the book at a random page.

Maybe not so random – the first thing I saw was an amazing drawing of a whirlpool. On the facing page, the left, were the roots of a tree against a dark background. Here were Earth and Water.

On the next page was a leaf, spinning in the Air. And on the right hand page were dozens of spiky Flames. Everything was drawn in very black ink but with very thin lines. Air and Water.

I flicked a few pages further, hoping that I might find some explanation. I could feel everyone looking at me.

There was a page of words. I brought it close to my eyes and tried to make out what it said. But the handwriting was too difficult, too old-fashioned. I couldn't tell one letter from another.

I flicked back to the whirlpool page, then turned the book round so the others could see. No one said anything – not until Jack said, 'Weird.'

'Can you read it?' I asked Mr. Gatward. 'Can you read her writing?'

'If I may,' he said, and held out his hand.

I gave him the book. He took a while to examine it closely, holding the page right up under his nose.

'Yes,' he said. 'I can read it. But it will take some time. It would be better if I were able to work at home, where I have my magnifying glass. The hand, as you'll see, is miniscule.'

I was very reluctant to let him take Lilian's book out of the house. But at least now I knew that, even if I had found it first, I would have had to go to him sooner or later. He had the skills I lacked.

'Well, let's see if it *is* the one in the painting,' I said, trying to gain a little more thinking time. I held my hand out, and Mr. Gatward – perhaps a bit slowly – passed me the book.

We all traipsed across to the parlour, where I went and stood below Lilian and then lifted the book until it was alongside the painted book.

'They're the same,' said Jack. 'She's holding that book, and she's in the past, but the book is here.'

'Yes,' I said. 'Isn't that exciting?'

'It's marvellous,' said Mr. Gatward. 'One so rarely has moments like this.'

'Or moments like down in the cellar, just now,' said Peter.

'Thankfully,' said Mr. Gatward.

'What did you know about the cellar?' I asked. 'You were pretty cagey about it before.'

'I knew about the four doors, at the four compass points, each one representing an element. That was the legend, anyway. I got a glimpse down there, once or twice, when I was a child.'

'Were any of the doors open?' I asked.

'Oh no,' he said. 'I don't think they've been opened in decades. I doubt if Michael Francis ever went down there.'

I remembered how Father Trovato, Michael Francis's spiritual guide, had warned me to stay out of the cellar.

'You're probably right,' I said. 'Especially as he put all the alchemy books up in the attic.'

'Can you do any spells yet?' Jack asked Mr. Gatward.

'Oh no,' he said. 'And I wouldn't want to, even if I could.'

'I would,' said Jack, 'I'd want to fly.'

I thought of Mary, and couldn't help laughing. Jack was probably closer to his wish than he realized. The others looked at me a bit oddly, but the moment passed.

'I think you should learn to swim properly first,' said Peter.

'And be invisible,' said Jack.

I glanced up at Lilian. I wondered where she was. This thought reminded me of Mary. And just then I heard a faint cry. I handed the book over to Mr. Gatward, deciding that I would try trusting him.

'I'll report back as soon as I can,' he said. 'Goodbye, Mrs. Jonson.'

When I got to the bedroom, Mary was blinking and stretching. I thought she was grizzly because she was hungry, but it seemed she had just woken up and was bored. After trying to feed her one last time, I changed her nappy – which was almost dry – and took her downstairs.

Peter and Jack were out in the garden, kicking a football around. It was such a male way of dealing with near-death experience.

I stood and watched them for a while. Then turned round and looked at the painted phoenix carved in stone at the back of the house. It was identical to the one on the red ribbon in Lilian's book. I cursed myself for not making a note of which page was marked that way. Surely Mr. Gatward wouldn't just pull the ribbon out and use it as an ordinary bookmark? I felt like leaving a message for him at home, but then remembered he didn't have an answerphone. Again, I'd have to trust him.

I didn't know much about what the phoenix meant – probably no more than the average person. Phoenixes were mythical birds that were reborn out of fire – 'like a phoenix rises from the ashes'. Even sports commentators used that one. The stone phoenix in front of me sat on what looked like quite a toasty little campfire of logs. It was lifting its beak to the sky and stretching its wings out to either side, just as if it had been cramped up inside an egg for a few hundred years. The two halves of the egg lay on either side of it, their zigzag edges looking like they'd fit together quite neatly. That would be one puzzle solved. There was a dome behind the phoenix that at first I'd thought was another egg, but now I realized it must be the sun shining.

'What else is there to see?' I muttered to Mary.

She gazed up at me – just as, perhaps, she'd gazed up at the ghost of Lilian.

Jack scored a goal and began celebrating over by some yellow roses.

'Unless you'd forgotten,' I said. 'We have people coming for dinner.'

'No,' said Peter. 'I hadn't forgotten.'

'I think this means a trip to the supermarket.'

'Dad,' said Jack. 'Can I stay here?'

'Not a chance,' I said.

We did the whole round-trip in about two and a half hours. I decided on a menu while we were driving there. Avocados to start with, as long as I could get ripe ones (I could). Then posh fish pie with scallops and a cheesy breadcrumb topping, peas, French beans and carrots. Then chocolate pots for pudding (not home made).

I wasn't at all hungry when we left the house. By the time we got back, though, I was starving – like I hadn't eaten in days. Mary, too, seemed to have got her appetite back. She fed once in the car park when we got there and then once again in a layby. That was the only way to stop her bawling out the car.

I had to start cooking as soon as we got home. Peter helped by peeling potatoes, and because he stayed in the kitchen I had no problems with the water. Jack – relieved that we were connected to the outside world again – was allowed to watch television. Mary watched me, from the recliner, gurgling like a little darling.

Halfway through, I had a real moment. Everything appeared to be so normal – we were just getting on with stuff. But underneath it all was something that none of us could understand. What if we *were* living in a house that would keep us alive forever, just so long as we never left the house? What would we choose to do? Jack certainly wouldn't want to stay six years-old for eternity. He already knew that most of the things he really wanted to do – drive a car, fly a plane, fire a gun – were things that only sixteen-year olds were allowed. (Most of them I'd try and stop him doing even if he were thirty-six.) And Mary's growth had slowed the first time the Health Visitor came. What if the next time Miriam Shoulder weighed her, she hadn't put anything on? And then the next time after that, too? What if Mary never put on another pound? Never started to laugh, get teeth, walk, talk? How terrible would that be – a baby who never grew up? Peter might be more tempted. He didn't like the idea of getting older, of not being able to do the things physically that he used to do. It would be reassuring to know that injuries, like my scalding, would heal themselves in a few hours. But maybe, knowing that, Peter would start to take huge risks. What was to stop him breaking every bone in his body, just so long as he did it inside the house? And then there was me. I didn't relish the idea of becoming an old woman. I didn't want to lose my remaining looks, feel by body go saggier, worry about forgetting everything from my past. But I also didn't want to watch everyone I knew and loved die off without me getting any closer to that myself. I didn't want to be that unnatural. Even with all the terrible things about it, I believed there was a reason for growing older and dying. If we didn't do that, we wouldn't be human. And I didn't want to be anything other than human.

It was strange that I wasn't having this as a conversation with Peter. But I knew that if I brought it up, he would change the subject. The house was coming between us in a hundred different ways.

Chapter 34.

Normality continued through bedtime. Jack had been exhausted by his day, physically and – though he wouldn't ever admit it – emotionally. He was asleep before I was halfway through 'Hey Jude'.

Mary, too, was tired. But I wanted to keep her awake as long as possible. That way, she might sleep through the whole dinner party.

Mr. Gatward phoned at a quarter to eight.

'I've made some discoveries,' he said. 'I can't wait to tell you. It all ties in.'

'Tomorrow,' I said. 'Nine.'

'Yes, yes,' he replied.

'Oh,' I said. 'And the ribbon – you haven't moved it, have you? It's still in the same page. That might mean something.'

'You're ahead of me, Mrs. Jonson. You think you're not, but you are. Tomorrow. All will be revealed.'

Then, at five to eight, with Mary safely asleep, there was a sharp knock at the door. Even though I hoped it was Matthew Maddox and Gracie Dearie, turned up a little early, I knew that particular rap-rap too well.

I was still putting on my make-up. It was a long time since I'd made any effort to dress up – since before Mary was born. Peter was just zipping up his trousers. The knock came again twice before Peter made it to the door.

'Father Trovato,' I heard him say. 'How can I help?'

'I would like to speak to you, and to your wife, together. It is very important.'

'Can't it wait?' Peter said. 'We have people arriving for dinner in – well, now.'

'No, it cannot wait.'

I was just about done.

'In that case, please come through,' said Peter.

I should have predicted that my husband wouldn't be able to say no to a priest.

'I will await here,' said Father Trovato, and remained standing out in the porchway.

'Mrs. Jonson,' said Father Trovato, as I came where he could see me. 'You look beautiful.'

'Thank you,' I said. 'Is there some emergency?'

'You might say that,' Father Trovato said. 'I heard about the cellar. I heard that you have been visiting it, exploring it, despite my warning. This was a serious warning I gave to you. A very serious forbidding. You do not yet know what the cellar means. It is extremely dangerous. Dangerous in ways you can't understand.'

I thought of Jack, being dragged round and round, down and down.

'How do you know we've been in the cellar?' Peter asked.

'I know you discovered some people down there. One of these people is very important, and very angry. Of course I would hear about that eventually. But my source is more immediate.'

'So it's all right for them to be there?' I said. 'But not us.'

'No,' said Father Trovato. 'It is not right for them. Absolutely not. I have attempted to speak seriously to Mrs. Forster, over many years. She will not listen. She is greedy and besotted.'

'So you heard from Longbone?' Peter said.

'Not directly,' said Father Trovato. 'From someone close to him. I have tried to talk to him, as well. But he will not accept advice or consolation.'

'He wants to live,' said Peter.

'There is life,' said Father Trovato, 'and there is life.'

'Eternal life,' said Peter.

'Yes,' said Father Trovato. 'To live for a very long time on earth means nothing if you die eternally thereafter. Mr. Longbone is merely delaying his damnation.'

'Because he's not a Catholic?' I asked.

'Because he is in a state of sin,' Father Trovato said.

This was when I heard a car approaching through the trees.

'These are our guests,' I said. 'I'm afraid you'll have to go.'

'Unless you are protected against this house,' said Father Trovato, 'you will be seduced by it, and by what it has to offer. Only the church can offer you the protection you need.'

'No,' I said. 'It's this house which protects us. You know that. And that's the problem. You're worried what else we might find out.'

'I am worried for you,' said Father Trovato, 'and for your children. I need to talk seriously to you.'

Headlights passed over us.

'I will return tomorrow morning,' said Father Trovato, stepping away towards his car. 'But you must promise to do nothing tonight.'

'What do you think we're going to do?' I called to him. 'Hold a séance?'

'There's no need for anything that elaborate,' said Father Trovato, grimly. 'As I'm sure you already know.'

Matthew and Gracie got out of their car, a brand new Mini Cooper in shiny green.

'Hello,' they said to us, very smiley. Matthew was holding a bottle of wine in each hand. Gracie looked beautiful – so young. They were oddly dressed as usual. Matthew wore a yellow silk shirt beneath a bright green suit. His shoes were orangey brown brogues. Gracie wore a yellow and green cheongsam.

'Come in,' said Peter. 'Father Trovato's just leaving.'

'Until tomorrow morning,' said Father Trovato, heaving himself down into his tiny Fiat.

'I won't ask,' said Matthew, watching him go.

'I will,' said Gracie. 'Are you very Catholic?'
'No,' I said.
'Yes,' said Peter. 'Officially, we are.'

As we went into the kitchen, Peter began to explain the circumstances of the inheritance. Our guests sat down. Peter opened the wine. I served the starters. Peter poured the wine.
'What a deal,' said Matthew, when Peter had finished.
'Are you going to stick to it?' Gracie asked.
'I think so,' said Peter. 'Jack's already under instruction. And I became a Catholic at University. With me, it's just remedial work.' He looked at me.
'I'm the most reluctant,' I said. 'But I love the house. I'd do almost anything to keep it.'
'Almost?' asked Gracie.
'It's not worth someone's life,' I said.
'Yes,' said Gracie, 'but what about their soul?'
I didn't answer.
'Are you Catholic?' Peter asked her.
'No,' she said. 'But my father was on the other side. Seriously so. I heard a lot about the Pope, growing up. None of it very complimentary.'
'No, it's not worth a soul,' I said. 'Nothing is.'
'I thought you were the one who didn't believe in all that,' said Peter.
'I don't really,' I said. 'But if Gracie's saying those are the stakes, then I'm saying that's what I think. A house is just a house – any house.'
'But this is a very special house,' said Matthew. 'I don't suppose you've had time to read Mr. Gatward's books about it.'
'Yes,' I said, 'well, most of them. I haven't managed to find *Hidden Histories*. They didn't have it in the shop, and it's out of print.'
'Oh, we've got it,' said Gracie. 'We'll lend it to you, if you'd like. We've got all his books. I think we're his biggest fans.' She laughed her tinkly laugh.
'He's really the reason we discovered the village in the first place,' Matthew continued. 'We were just passing through. We like to look at old churches and things, and when I went into the shop for a bar of chocolate, I mentioned I was interested in the church – Mrs. Willows managed to hawk me a copy of *A Kindly Place*.'
'We came back the next weekend,' picked up Gracie. 'And after that, we couldn't stay away.'
'It became something of an addiction,' Matthew said.
'We hated being in London.'
'So when the farm came on the market – '

'We weren't going to let anyone else have it,' said Gracie. 'Even though it did need a massive amount of work.'

They were quite the double act.

'Lovely avocados,' said Matthew.

'Oh, yes,' said Gracie.

Matthew and Peter started to talk about wine. Gracie asked me about how Jack and Mary were – and before I knew it, we'd finished eating and were sitting around in the downstairs drawing room having coffee. Matthew and Gracie were on one sofa, Peter and me were on another.

The food seemed to have gone down pretty well. I'd been worried they would think it all pretty boring, them being used to home produce and everything. But Matthew had come back for thirds of the fish pie, and Gracie had asked me whether the chocolate pots were Delia or Nigella. (I'd confessed they were neither, and showed her the packet.)

'It's hard to believe you've had two babies,' said Gracie. 'You look so fantastic. Do you work out?'

'Me?' I said. 'I do a lot of picking up and carrying, but I've never been to a gym in my life.'

'You surprise me,' said Matthew. 'We had a home gym built onto the farm before we moved in. Nothing fancy. Just a jogging machine and one of those workout milarkeys – with the weights and everything.'

'And the pool,' said Gracie. 'I don't know what I'd do without that. I'm in there first thing every morning, and last thing at night.'

'Not *quite* last thing,' said Matthew, flirtatiously. Then he turned to me. 'I've started to find the smell of chlorine quite a turn-on all by itself.'

Matthew's hand was on Gracie's knee already. But now it moved upwards, and I saw him give her a squeeze on the thigh. Her cheongsam, which was quite short anyway, was split all the way up to the top of her legs. I couldn't help noticing, she didn't have anything on underneath it. A quick glance at Peter was enough to confirm that he'd noticed, too. He was blushing quite fiercely.

'I could fall asleep any time, day or night,' I said.

'I don't know about falling asleep,' said Gracie. 'But going to bed…'

'Working the farm must be exhausting,' said Peter. 'You must have to get up really early.'

'Oh, we have quite a lot of help,' said Matthew. 'I like to drive the tractor around, supervise. It's really more about efficient management than anything else. That leaves me plenty of time for other things.'

'You haven't thought about having children?' I asked.

'We can't, said Gracie.

'Actually, I can't,' said Matthew. 'They've done loads of tests. Apparently the little buggers just swim round in circles – when they swim at all. It's a bit pathetic really.'

'Don't say that,' Gracie said.

'Gracie knew before she married me,' Matthew said. 'It wasn't some horrible surprise. We decided that we had other priorities.'

I was so caught up in Jack and Mary that I found it quite hard to imagine what those priorities might be. Working the land? Buying weirdly bright clothes? Coming on to other couples?

'We want to live the best lives we can,' said Gracie. 'Just in ourselves.'

'We want to try different things,' Matthew said. 'Not limit ourselves. Experience whatever's out there to be experienced.'

'There can't be all that much,' said Peter. 'Out here. Isn't it all a bit quiet?'

'Oh, you'd be surprised,' said Matthew. 'It can get quite lively, if you're up for it.'

He leaned across and kissed Gracie. They didn't snog, thank God, but it was a little more pouty and noisy than I felt comfortable with.

'The thing is,' Gracie said, 'when you're out in the country, no one overlooking your property, you have a lot more *freedom* than those people living in tiny little flats in the city – all living on top of and spying on one another.'

That was our life she was describing – a life we'd only stopped living a week ago.

'Exactly,' said Matthew. 'You can set your own rules. The law isn't going to come bothering you. In fact,' he said, 'the law is quite an interesting chap himself.'

'He's very friendly, P.C. Hollerhan,' said Gracie. 'Very amenable. And he likes a swim.' She raised her eyebrows at me, sending me quite a clear message. I didn't know where to look.

'It's getting quite late,' said Peter, coming to my rescue. 'I'm afraid we're going to be up a couple of times in the night. Mary's not been very settled since we moved in.'

'Well, it's a strange new house, isn't it?' said Gracie. She changed tack with impressive speed.

'Yes, it's funny they still call it "The New House",' said Matthew. 'I mean, look at it.'

We were sitting in front of the huge fireplace. I took the whole amazing place in once more. It would have felt much more natural for Matthew and Gracie to stay here, Lord and Lady of the Manor, and for me and Peter to get up and leave – back to our maisonette. But that wasn't how it was going to be. They were leaving, and as soon as we could possibly get rid of them. No one spoke, however. And while we were sitting there in silence, my eyes happened to fall on the fire tools – the hammer and tongs and brush. Each of them had a brass phoenix at the top. Not only that, though – the phoenixes were shaped to look like the business end of keys. Maybe the fire door would be opened by one of the fire tools.

It was all I could do not to get up there and then, go over and inspect the tool more closely.

Peter noticed that I was staring at something, and Matthew was watching too closely to miss this.

'Penny for them,' said Matthew.

'I was wondering,' I said, 'where we were going to get enough logs to fill that thing in winter.'

'Oh, I think your gardener keeps a fairly tidy stock of logs around and about the place,' Gracie said.

'You mean Robert,' I said.

'Yes, that's his name,' said Gracie. 'He's not very friendly to us, I'm afraid. We've had a few disputes concerning fences, boundary lines, overhanging trees.'

'Just about everything we could have a dispute about,' added Matthew.

'Well, I hope we'll be able to sort all of those out between us,' said Peter. 'We'd like to be good neighbours.'

'We hope you'll be a lot more than that,' said Gracie.

'Friends, then,' said Peter.

'More than that, too,' said Matthew.

It was unbearable. I stood up.

'I'm sorry,' I said. 'But I'm really exhausted. We've had a really busy week – and, like Peter says, Mary's not going to sleep through. I think I'm going to have to turn in before I fall asleep myself.'

'Of course, of course,' said Matthew, retreating immediately.

'I'm sorry we kept you up,' said Gracie. 'We should have known.'

The two of them thanked us for a lovely evening, for the lovely food and the lovely coffee. Slowly, we ushered them towards the door. They seemed to be keen on dragging the goodbyes out for as long as possible. Gracie made me promise to bring Jack round for that horse ride. Matthew was telling Peter how fascinating the carved panels on the hall ceiling were, and how he'd love to be able to come back one day and study them.

'I love that kind of thing,' he said. 'Brass rubbings.'

'You have some trouble rubbing those,' said Peter, looking the two storeys up.

'I've got a very powerful camera,' said Matthew.

'I'm sure you'll be able to come back some time,' I said. 'We'd like other people to enjoy the house. We don't want to keep it just to ourselves.'

Gracie looked as though she was about to cry. 'That's perfect,' she said. 'That's just what we… what everyone in the village has been wanting to hear.'

'How about tomorrow morning?' Matthew asked.

'I'm afraid we have Father Trovato coming back then,' said Peter. 'We'll let you know when's a good time. We're still settling in.'

'Of course,' said Matthew.

'But I'll drop a copy of *Hidden Histories* off tomorrow,' said Gracie. 'I think we have a spare.'

'Thank you,' I said.

'We're so glad you're joining the community,' said Matthew. 'You've got so much to contribute.'

And finally, finally, they were out the door – and the door was shut – and we listened to them slowly walk away.

Gracie started to say something, but Matthew immediately said, 'Wait till we're in the car.'

Gracie giggled one last time, the car doors slammed solidly and they were driving away.

Peter said, 'They did just make a pass at us, didn't they?'

'More than one,' I said. 'I think I lost count.'

'So they're the local swingers, are they?'

'Them and the local bobbie,' I said. 'P.C. Likes-a-swim.'

We couldn't help but laugh. It was so ridiculous.

'I'd heard that's what it was like in the country,' said Peter. 'Key parties and wife-swapping and everything, but… We're hardly in the door. They weren't exactly subtle, were they?'

We went into the sitting room and started turning off the lights.

'Seems like brass isn't the only thing he likes rubbing,' said Peter.

'I thought his hand wasn't going to stop,' I said. 'I thought we were going to get the full Sharon Stone.'

The last light was out.

'That was only a flash,' said Peter.

'You weren't tempted, then?' I said. 'She's very attractive.'

'She's a freak,' said Peter. 'They're both total freaks.'

'And we're not?' I said.

'Well, I'm not,' said Peter. 'I'm perfectly normal.'

The good mood between us evaporated very suddenly.

'I am not a freak,' I said. 'Don't say that.'

Peter kept quiet while we brushed our teeth and got ready for bed.

'I'm sorry,' he said, once we were tucked in and the lights out. 'I didn't mean that the way it sounded.'

'Go to sleep,' I said. 'Normal people need lots of sleep.'

I know all the advice about never letting the sun go down on an argument, but Peter needed to be taught a lesson. The cold shoulder had worked before. I hadn't let him near me for months after the affair. Even though he'd been the one in the wrong, he still held that against me. But I was so angry with him I just couldn't face any kind of intimacy.

He kissed me on the back of the head and said, 'Night night.'

I was woken by muffled screaming at I didn't know what time. It came from Jack's room, and Peter, though stirring a little in his sleep, hadn't woken up.

Chapter 35.

I got out of bed and hurried through the door – no idea what I'd find there.

The room was dark. I couldn't see any suspicious shapes, no presences.

By the time I got to him, Jack was sitting up in bed, sobbing. It took him a good couple of minutes of cuddles to calm down.

'Did I? Did I?' He kept saying, before finally coming out with it, 'Did I almost die?'

'No, no,' I said. 'Mummy and Daddy were there. We weren't going to let anything happen to you.'

'I don't want to die, Mummy,' said Jack. 'I don't want to be a dead person.'

What do you say to a child when they say this? A child like Jack who has had a genuinely terrifying experience or just a child who has woken up in the dark after a nightmare? What do you say when you're all groggy from dreams of your own, and you've never really known what the best and most comforting thing is to say? I felt lost. I wished very much I had some definite faith that I could pass on – that I could say to Jack, Jesus loves you and will look after you and make sure nothing bad happens to you. Or Allah or someone big and reassuring.

But the world was a place full of accidents. He could die, I could die, any of us could.

'You're not going to die, not for a long, long time,' I said. 'You're a fit, healthy boy. And we're here to look after you.'

'You won't die, will you?'

'I'm not planning to,' I said. 'I want to be around to watch you grow very old. We all want to be alive.'

'I was scared, Mummy,' said Jack.

'I know you were, my love. I was, too. But we're all right now, aren't we? Tucked up all safe and cosy in bed. We're all right.'

'I'm brave really,' said Jack. 'I was scared in the water, when the water was over me.'

'It was a very scary thing,' I said. 'Would you like me to sing you a song?'

Jack nodded yes.

I sang softly to him, until he'd gone to sleep. And then I went back to my own bed, leaving the door to his room open.

'Please, protect him,' I said to whomever might be listening.

Rap-rap. Rap-rap.

This time I didn't have even a moment's doubt who it was. Mary had slept right through, but I still felt exhausted as I nudged Peter.

'You'll have to let him in.'

Blearily, Peter checked his watch. 'It's half past five,' he said.

'Then tell him to go away,' I said. 'This is just rude.'

Peter started to get dressed.

'Quickly,' I said, 'or he'll wake Jack.'

Peter went downstairs in jeans and stripey pyjama top.

I heard the door open, muffled greetings, footfalls across the hall and down the passage.

Peter returned. 'He's prepared to wait,' he said. 'We've got half an hour.'

I stretched this out to an hour, taking my time in the bathroom. Mary woke up around six and I pretended to feed her for ten minutes, even though I could tell she wasn't taking anything.

We were about to go down when Jack surfaced.

'Your favourite person's here,' I said.

'Batman?' he said.

'No, Father Trovato.'

Jack ran downstairs in his pyjamas. It's great how kids can just accelerate to a hundred miles an hour from a standing start.

I went into the kitchen first and, after Peter popped in to ask where I was, made some coffee.

'Or would you prefer orange juice, Father,' I said, as I carried the tray into the living room. 'That's what Jack's having.'

'Good morning, Mrs. Jonson,' said Father Trovato. He was looking quite rumpled – not his usual sparkly-eyed self at all.

We drank the coffee while Jack asked Father Trovato about Jesus. 'When they stuck the nails in his hands, did the blood go everywhere?'

'It went everywhere in the universe,' said Father Trovato. 'Everything was touched by it.'

'Wow,' said Jack. 'It must have spurted and spurted.'

'That's not quite my meaning. But I suppose it did.'

'And what did Jesus say? Did he scream really loud?'

'Jack,' said Peter. 'It's a bit early for this.'

Father Trovato gave Peter a very stern look. 'I would say, in fact, that it is exactly the right time. I have important information for you. I think Jack may be more interested in other games. What I have to say concerns very grown-up, boring things like inheritances and strict conditions and, well, solicitors.'

'Jack can stay,' I said. 'If he gets bored, he can find something else to do.'

Father Trovato closed his eyes and seemed to be consulting with his inner voice about whether to insist on Jack leaving, and then how to begin, as Jack was staying.

'I have not slept all night,' he said, very wearily but with focus. 'I have been praying for you. Praying very hard.'

'Thank you,' said Jack.

'Praying for all of you. Because I am deeply afraid for your souls. I think you may already have lost them. It may already be too late.'

'That's not fair,' said Jack.

'No,' I said. 'It's not.'

'Let me explain. Without interruption, please,' said Father Trovato. 'You know about this house. I do not need to tell you that it is a place of strange powers.' Peter gave me a doubtful look, but kept silent. 'It heals the sick. It keeps the young from growing old and the old from dying. If you stay within the house, never leaving, you will live forever. That is, if you have someone to run your errands for you. That is, if you can bear never walking outside again. I did not find this out myself. It was something I was taught by another – by another Priest. We, the Church, have known about this house for a long time. We have watched over it. We have watched over everyone who lived here. I came to this place for a specific reason, for a specific person. I came for Michael Jonson and for his immortal soul. His father and his grandfather before him, and all their family, they had been guided by their Priests. They had not extended their lives beyond the natural term. The temptations were very great. But we persuaded them, over the years, that what was best for them was to live for most of the time away from the house. They could return, yes, to visit. They could even return to heal themselves after injury. But they could not hide here permanently in hopes of physical immortality. Peter, your own grandfather, Malcolm Jonson, left the house aged seventeen and rarely returned. Michael Jonson, however, was tempted. Up until the age of sixty, he was obedient to the conditions. But then he became frightened of dying. Terrified. He shut me out. For many, many years, he would not see my predecessor, Father Benedict. He made an alliance with Mrs. Forster. She was the one who left the house, ran the errands. He was able to hide away. A recluse. Every Sunday, I would come to offer him the sacraments. Every Sunday, year on year, he refused. Then, suddenly, he changed. He admitted me into the house. He began to talk to me. It seemed that what had brought him round was not the thought of the fate that awaited him, in the distant future, when all around the house had ceased to exist, all humanity, and he was left here for the rest of eternity with no one but Mrs. Forster for company.' I had to smile at this. 'No, it was the thought of creatures, wild creatures. He became tormented by the idea of all the parts of the world he would never see. All the wildlife that was out there. For some reason, don't ask me why, he became obsessed with the North Pole. Perhaps because it was the most inaccessible place. Perhaps because, if he stayed in the house, he would be facing another ice age sooner or later.'

Father Trovato paused, took a sip of his coffee, resumed.

'Again, it took much time, but in the end we came to an agreement. He resumed taking the sacraments, attending mass, listening to my spiritual guidance. He spent a little more time out of the house. Not enough to make any difference to his age. He remained sixty years-old until his departure. But I'm jumping a little. Michael Jonson began to accept the teachings of the Church. To seek immortality was sinful. He was in a permanent state of sin. Last year, he came to a decision. He would try to see the creatures he wished to see. He would leave the house forever. I was overjoyed. Together, we drafted his will – the will that gave you this house. Now do you understand the conditions of that will? Now do you understand why I cannot allow you to use this house in an unholy way? I had hoped to make a more gradual progress towards this – taking weeks or months. What did that matter if the decision was right in the end? The only people who are fitted to living here are ones who are obedient to outside laws. The laws of the church. So, I pray for you. I pray you make the best decision. It is for your souls.'

'Thank you, Father,' said Peter. 'We are very grateful for your interest.'

'You do not believe?' Father Trovato asked.

'In what?' Peter said. He was looking haunted, quite washed out and ill. 'In magic?'

'But you believe,' said Father Trovato, turning on me.

'I believe in the house,' I said. 'I don't know about your version of souls. You seem very happy to tell people they're going to hell, whenever it suits you. Frightening old women into giving you their last coins. Telling children to keep quiet about... You know.'

'He didn't tell me to keep quiet,' said Jack.

'Actually, Jack, he did,' I said.

'Please, Mrs. Jonson, this is inappropriate – ' Father Trovato nodded towards Jack.

'Father,' said Peter, 'perhaps – '

He was interrupted by a loud knock on the door. It was still only seven o'clock.

'You don't think it's Matthew and Gracie?' I said.

'They wouldn't come this early,' said Peter. 'She'll be swimming and he'll be – '

The knock came again, louder.

'I need to talk to you about them, also,' said Father Trovato.

Peter went into the hall and opened the door. We all looked down the passage to see who it was.

'Good morning, Mr. Jonson,' said the very tall Police officer standing in the porch. 'I am P.C. Hollerhan. Would you mind if I came in? We've had a serious complaint.'

Chapter 36.

Peter stood aside, and P.C. Hollerhan came into the hall. I wasn't going to miss out on what he said, so, with Mary in my arms, I hurried to join them. Father Trovato and Jack followed after me.

'You must be Mrs. Jonson,' said P.C. Hollerhan. 'Pleased to meet you. I'm sorry to disturb you at this time, but you seem to be up already. Father Trovato, good morning.'

'Good morning,' Father Trovato replied.

'Good morning,' said Jack, even putting on a little of Father Trovato's accent.

'Hello,' said P.C. Hollerhan, stooping a little as he spoke to Jack. He needed to. Jack couldn't have seen his face otherwise.

'There's been a "serious complaint",' Peter said to me. 'About us.'

'I heard,' I said, looking at the police officer. 'What is it?'

'You are aware, I hope, that this house has been placed on the Statutory List of Buildings of Special Architectural or Historical Interest.'

P.C. Hollerhan spread his hands out to indicate the magnificent hall. He seemed to be finding it difficult to keep his attention on us. His eyes kept turning upwards, towards the ceiling.

'You mean it's listed,' said Peter. 'Yes, we knew that.'

'Grade I, as a matter of fact,' said P.C. Hollerhan, snapped out of his reverie. 'Then you should also be aware that you are forbidden from making any alteration to the building without permission from the local planning authority. Any alteration, particularly, that detracts from the historical integrity of the building.'

'Are we under arrest?' asked Jack.

'No, no,' said P.C. Hollerhan.

'The satellite dish,' said Peter.

'Longbone,' I said. 'He's stopping us putting an extension our house.' I turned to P.C. Hollerhan. 'Is that right? He's complained.'

'We've had an anonymous complaint that you've violated the terms of your occupation of a Grade I listed building.'

'By putting up a satellite dish where no one can see it?' asked Peter.

'And a TV aerial, so I'm informed,' P.C. Hollerhan said.

'But no one can see them,' I said.

'Before I knocked on your door, I made a brief visual survey of the roof of the house,' said P.C. Hollerhan, 'and I'm afraid to say that the satellite dish is clearly visible from the drive outside the house.'

I remembered Longbone standing up on tip-toe, peering at the roof.

'Let's go and have a look,' I said.

We crunched out onto the gravel and along until we were almost round the bend. Then we all turned round.

'I can't see it,' said Jack.

'I can't either,' I said.

'The dish is plainly visible to the right of the third chimney stack from the left,' said P.C. Hollerhan.

Peter got up on tip-toe.

'Can you see it?' I asked.

Peter was a couple of inches shorter than Longbone. 'No,' he said, then did a couple of jumps. 'Wait.'

'Let me help, sir,' said P.C. Hollerhan, and caught Peter under the arms. Without too much effort, but making his point pretty clearly, he lifted Peter until he was about a foot off the ground – his eyes on the same level as the policeman's own. 'Third chimney stack from the left, sir,' he said.

'Please put me down,' said Peter. I could see that he was in some pain.

'Sir, could I ask you to confirm that the satellite dish is in plain view.'

'Yes,' said Peter. 'I can see it.'

'This is the most ridiculous thing I've ever heard,' I said. 'How tall are you? Six foot four?'

'Six foot six,' replied P.C. Hollerhan.

'And you can see it, standing here?'

'Would you like me to lift you up, too, madam?'

P.C. Hollerhan had still not put Peter down, but Peter was damned if he was going to ask again.

'No,' I said, 'but I'd be grateful if you could lift up Father Trovato, so he can confirm what you've said.'

P.C. Hollerhan dropped Peter unceremoniously, and Peter went down awkwardly, stepping out to the side and taking a while to regain his balance.

'Let's not be difficult,' said P.C. Hollerhan. 'Mr. Jonson has already confirmed the dish is visible.'

'May I see?' Father Trovato said, stepping forwards.

The policeman winced in annoyance but then crouched down, stuck his hands into the Father's armpits and heaved him with an almighty groan up to head height. 'It's there,' he said. 'Third chimney.'

'Oh, I'm sorry,' said Father Trovato. 'I forgot to put my glasses on. I can hardly see the house without them.'

P.C. Hollerhan cursed under his breath then lowered the Father to the floor a lot more carefully than Peter.

Father Trovato produced a glasses case from somewhere in his cassock. He took his time about polishing the lenses on his sleeve.

'Ready,' he said, finally.

P.C. Hollerhan heaved him back into position.

'Mmmm,' said Father Trovato. 'Third chimney from the right.'

'From the left,' grunted P.C. Hollerhan.

'I think I… Yes, I… ' said Father Trovato, drawing it out for a few moments more. 'Yes, from this height, it is definitely in sight.'

P.C. Hollerhan, sweating beneath his helmet, placed Father Trovato back on the ground.

'So,…' he said, trying to get his breath back.

'Me, too,' said Jack. 'Me, too.'

We stood back whilst P.C. Hollerhan lifted up Jack as well. Jack's keen eyes spotted the satellite dish easily.

'So, if no one else wants to see…' He looked at me. I wasn't going to risk being thrown around. 'Good. Now we're agreed on this, we would ask you to remove the offending alterations as soon as possible, or risk facing prosecution.'

'This is just vindictive,' I said. 'Are you a mason, too?'

'This is a matter of planning permission – '

'Because if you think you lot are ever getting a foot inside that house again, you're absolutely wrong,' I said. 'You can go and tell Longbone that.'

'Madam,' said P.C. Hollerhan, 'I would ask you to calm down.'

'And I would ask you to leave,' I said. 'We'll see you in court.'

'No,' said Peter. 'We will see about having the satellite dish moved so it can't be seen.'

'As soon as possible,' said P.C. Hollerhan.

'We won't be bullied,' I said.

There was a moment's stand-off. Then we all started walking back to the house.

'You're not coming back in,' I said.

'I am just going to retrieve my bicycle,' said P.C. Hollerhan. 'Then I'll be off.'

We said angry goodbyes, then watched him ride away.

He hadn't been out of sight for more than a couple of seconds before Robert Mew stepped out of the trees.

'Everything all right?' he asked.

'Fine,' shouted Peter.

'All right, then,' Robert shouted back. 'I'm around if you need me.'

'Great,' shouted Peter – and Robert disappeared back into the woods just as quickly and mysteriously as he'd appeared.

'It was good when he lifted you up,' said Jack to Father Trovato. 'I thought he wasn't going to be able to do it.'

'So, is P.C. Hollerhan a mason?' I asked Father Trovato.

'Yes,' he replied. 'He's a Junior Warden. Sir Longbone is the Master.'

'Now there's a thing,' said Peter.

'What's a mason?' Jack asked

'It's like a club for annoying men,' I said. 'Who want to annoy other people.'

Father Trovato laughed. 'Very good,' he said. 'Very good.'

In my anger at P.C. Hollerhan I'd forgotten that I'd just been getting going on Father Trovato.

Peter obviously wanted to head off any further argument. 'Father Trovato,' he said, putting his hand on the priest's shoulder, 'we will think very seriously about what you said. We will see you on Sunday morning for mass. Please don't expect us to make any big decisions by then.'

Father Trovato hesitated. He started to say something, then stopped himself. 'Yes,' he said. 'You need some time to think about it. But, please, make no more dangerous experiments.' He looked especially at me. 'Every one is in terrible danger.'

I thought about the fire tools in the living room. I wanted to experiment with them, as soon as I could get a little time on my own. I would have to think of an excuse to get Peter and the children out of the house.

'Thank you, Father,' said Peter.

Father Trovato performed his usual contortions to get into his Fiat, then drove off with a toot-toot.

'Saved by the Old Bill,' said Peter. 'Although I'd prefer it if they hadn't dumped on us quite so badly.'

'That was quite a lot to take in,' I said, trying to start a conversation. 'Wasn't it?'

Peter said, 'That's just how priests always speak. Eternal life, eternal damnation. It doesn't have to be literally true.'

'You mean you don't believe him?'

'It's not that simple,' Peter said. 'He's trying to tell us something, in his own language.'

I could see I wasn't going to get any more than that out of him.

'Okay, then, who's for breakfast?' I asked, although I wasn't all that hungry. As a family, what we needed right then was to get back to something completely everyday.

'Will the house fix me?' Jack asked, as we trooped into the kitchen. 'I mean, like it fixed your arm.'

'I don't know,' I said. 'That's what Father Trovato said. But he wasn't suggesting we hurt ourselves. That would be a very silly thing to do.'

I could see Jack watching me as I filled the kettle – I could see him remembering the sight of me pouring boiling water on myself.

Peter had taken Mary, and was doing his best to make her giggle. He wasn't really listening to what was going on around him. I decided against making Jack make another promise. Instead, I gave him a pretend stern look, which he seemed to understand. He gave an exaggerated comedy shrug and made one of his screwed up boy-faces.

We had half a bowl of cornflakes each.

'What shall we do today, then?' I asked.

'I think I'm going to have to go up on the roof and take the dish down,' said Peter. 'I'm pretty sure he meant "do it today".'

'Can I help?' Jack asked.

'You can help me carry the tools up,' said Peter. 'But you're not coming on the roof.'

'But even if I fell, the house would fix me, wouldn't it?' Jack said.

'No,' said Peter, very forcefully. 'You would die. No one said anything about bringing people back from the dead. You can help me do the preparation.'

Jack slumped on his chair. 'Prep-pation is for girls,' he said.

'Mostly,' I said, 'yes.'

Mr. Gatward arrived in his taxi just after nine.

I heard Peter calling down from the roof. I had been sitting in the parlour, looking hard at the painting of Lilian. Mary was in one of her super-bouncy moods, which meant that my lap was feeling a little pummeled. The rest of me was feeling pretty pummeled, too. What Father Trovato said had really given me pause for thought. Wasn't I being reckless? I was, as they say, dealing with forces I didn't understand.

'Mrs. Jonson,' said Mr. Gatward. He had let himself in, which annoyed me a little even though I hadn't moved to open the front door.

'Hello,' I said.

Mr. Gatward went and stood in front of Lilian. This was his big moment, I remembered – his big announcement. It would be really mean of me to spoil it for him. I gave him a bright smile, and he seemed to come to life.

'Discoveries,' he said. 'Amazing discoveries. I think we know quite a few more of Lilian's secrets.'

'Were they in her book?' I asked.

'Her book!' he said, almost dancing he was so excited. 'I think the whole *world* is in her book, somewhere or other. And other worlds, too. Heaven and hell.'

I thought for a moment about going to fetch Peter, but I had questions I couldn't ask Mr. Gatward if Peter was there.

'Tell me,' I said.

Chapter 37.

Mr. Gatward came and sat down.

'It all ties together – money, power, religion, magic. It's a story with everything. I'm sure you know quite a bit about Lilian's time already – Protestants and Catholics. Nowadays we tend to think about detailed theological questions as things that concern other people.'

'Not in this house,' I said. 'Not any more.'

'Another visit from Father Trovato?'

'How did you know?'

'Mrs. Willows told me. He always stops in there to buy mints. Anyway, when Elizabeth the First came to the throne, she wanted to end all that religious strife – or at least calm it down, so it wasn't all that people thought about. But, as time passed, and there were more and more Catholic plots against her – remember, she'd come to power after the death of her sister, Mary – as time passed, she got tougher and tougher on the Catholics. There was a whole background to this in Europe. Who we were friendly with, as a nation, and who Elizabeth the Virgin Queen might end up marrying. One of the reasons for the Armada was to get this Protestant off the throne, but that comes later. As Elizabeth started to realize that she couldn't appease the Catholics, she began to punish them for not obeying the religious laws she'd set up. This was the Act of Uniformity, 1559. I know dates can be a little abstract, but imagine that William Jonson, Lilian's father is twenty-nine. He's been married to the very young Margerye for a couple of years. Up until now, he's been at court. Mary's deeply Catholic court. But with the new queen thinking completely the opposite to Mary on every important subject, most important how you get into heaven and avoid going to hell – with a court full of possible enemies, William moves to the country and builds the Old House. He starts to have children, or he tries. In 1561, there's a stillborn boy. Then, the next year, Lilian is born. Great rejoicing, I'm sure. But life is getting harder for Catholics. The Anglican Church is established. A few years later, it becomes treason to call the Queen a heretic – which is what Catholics think. How can you not think someone's a heretic when *they* think the Pope's the Antichrist? Margerye gives Lilian two brothers, Emanuell, good Catholic name, and Peter. But Emanuell dies aged fifteen. We can only guess what impression that makes on Lilian. Remember, they hardly ever left the house and grounds. We have no records they went anywhere at all, apart from William going into London on business. Most of the life Lilian can remember, they've been in a kind of religious quarantine. They wouldn't go to the local church, of course. They have a priest, and the priest says mass for them in the house. The Old House – but that burns down in 1580. We never knew why before. Maybe now, though, we have the answer.'

'You have the answer,' I said. I'd meant it as a bit of praise, but Mr. Gatward thought I was telling him to hurry up.

'One of the things about not going to church, not being Protestant, was that you had to pay large fines – month after month – and if you didn't, they would take away a whole chunk of your property. And, of course, the Catholic Church was sending Jesuits into the country on secret missions, to convert people. Priests were being hunted. So, that's why when he built the New House, William had them make a Priests' Hole. It's also probably around this time, perhaps under cover of constructing the house, that he has the underground chapel built. This wasn't an architectural folly. This was a matter of life and death. They were living in fear of spies, hiding in their woods, reporting on them for observing Mass. Can you imagine them, crawling through the tunnel into the Chapel one or twice a day? I'm not sure if it even had an outside entrance, back then. It was probably completely underground. And they dug out a crypt, too. But I'll come back to that. The main point is, by the time Lilian is an adult, all those fines have been adding up for years. The Jonsons are supporting a huge house, a large household of loyal servants. They bring in some money from rents on their lands, but they are about to hit the wall. If they don't find money somehow, a large amount, they will be destitute. Having examined the library, I can now say with some certainty that William had been pursuing alchemical studies from the time of Lilian's birth. I'm not sure what prompted it. Perhaps the death of his first son. Many of the books upstairs have annotations in a hand I recognize as William's. I've seen it so many times before, on boring documents about land boundaries. But now it's something electrifying. He's in pursuit of the secret of all matter. The house burns down in 1580. Why weren't all the books burned with it? Surely the library is in the house. The answer is here,' he said.

With this, quite dramatically, Mr. Gatward pulled Lilian's book from his coat pocket. He clutched it in his hands, staring down at it as if it were glowing with light.

'The date 1580 occurs again and again in her notes. And she refers to it as a failed experiment. William had turned his house into a laboratory. He must have been using a pretty impressive furnace, hoping to distill or reduce the gold from whatever material he started with. Alchemists used all sorts of stuff. The furnace would heat up this mixture of everything under the sun, and then in a device called a retort, it would be cooled down. A retort was like a little dome on a stand with a long pipe coming out of the top that the liquid would run down into something else. It looked a bit like an upside-down comma, with the pointy tail bit stretched out. They would examine what they'd produced, among all the smoke and smells, and again and again they would be disappointed. No one ever made gold. Or that's what we thought. But after the failed experiment, and the burning down of the house, William starts up again. If the need for money was urgent before, it's now become all consuming. This time, though, he has something new – he has his brilliant daughter working alongside him. He has brought her up perhaps solely for this purpose. Alchemists believed that the female principle was very important. Only with a harmonious balance of male and female could transmutation, dross into gold, stand a chance. Down in the cellar of the New House, William and Lilian go to work. They analyze the failed experiment of 1580. They plan for the future. Lilian makes notes of everything in her book – I've been up all night reading it. Pretty soon, they realize they don't have enough chemical knowledge. So, Lilian is sent off around Europe. Do you remember that detail from my book? There was no explanation for it at the time – why a daughter should go, rather than a son. But the sons weren't up to it. Only Lilian knew which books to seek out, which authorities to consult. In 1584, Lilian returns. How excited they must have been. William marks his pride, I believe, by commissioning the fine portrait of Lilian behind you. This is Lilian as a woman of wisdom and science. They are on the verge of the greatest breakthrough, and of securing their family's future forever. In her hand, Lilian holds the key to all of this – her spell book. And then, quite suddenly, William himself dies. Lilian records it here, devastated, but then she goes on. We must assume she goes on, because after 1590 there is no record of her. She just disappears. But…' said Mr. Gatward. He was so excited, he was weeping. 'But the house is saved. The fines are paid. Lilian's family is able to continue their secret faith. They are able to expand their holdings of land. All that rubbish that I've spent my life fussing about. This field bought in 1597, this one in 1600. And I'd always assumed it was because Lilian's brother Peter was doing quite well for himself, managing the estate. Instead, it's a miracle. A small West Sussex family discovers the greatest secret of the universe, the mystery of the ages, *and they don't tell anyone*.'

Mr. Gatward took Lilian's book and hugged it to his chest.

I gave Mr. Gatward a few minutes to gather himself together. He seemed quite exhausted, his eyes twinkling with tears.

'But they told *someone*,' I said gently. 'They told their Priest.'

'I'm not so sure,' Mr. Gatward said. 'The church tended to disapprove of alchemy.'

'It still does,' I said, and began explaining to Mr. Gatward a little of what Father Trovato had told me.

'All this time?' he said.

I heard some crunching footfalls on the gravel, then there was a knock at the door.

When I answered, Mary on my shoulder, it was Gracie Dearie. This time she was dressed in a bright orange tracksuit with white trim and bright orange trainers. She was quite out of breath and her forehead was dripping with sweat. It was another hot sunny day.

'Brought you this,' she said. It was a copy of *Hidden Histories*. 'We marked some bits.' I could see that pink Post-Its were sticking out from pages here and there.

'Thank you,' I said.

'Thank you,' Gracie replied. 'For last night. Sorry if we were a bit –' She took another breath. 'Forward.'

Mr. Gatward came into the hall.

'Hello, Gracie,' he said.

'Oh,' she said, quite shocked. 'You're here.'

'I've been helping Mrs. Jonson with some papers,' he said.

Gracie looked down, and I saw she was looking at Lilian's book which Mr. Gatward was still clutching.

'How beautiful,' she said. 'Can I have a little look?'

'No,' said Mr. Gatward, quite sharply.

'I'm afraid now isn't a very good time,' I said. 'Perhaps when you come round with Matthew to look at the ceiling.'

'Oh, can't I even have just a little peak?' Gracie said, flirtatiously.

'We're in the middle of something,' Mr. Gatward said. He sounded quite waspish. 'You've always been too impatient. Both of you.'

'Another time,' I said.

'Fine,' said Gracie, though I could tell she was desperate to get her hands on the book. 'See you soon. Thanks again for dinner.'

She ran off. I watched her tight bottom bob off round the corner.

She was just out of sight when a voice from above said, 'Well done.'

'Haven't you finished yet?' I asked.

'No,' Peter said. 'I think I've found somewhere else I can put it, a bit further back and lower down.'

'Where's Jack?' I asked.

'He's up here, too,' said Peter. 'But he's perfectly fine. He's just got his head stuck out through the roof. I've told him if he comes an inch further, he'll be banished downstairs forever.'

'Be careful,' I said.

'Found anything interesting, Mr. Gatward?' Peter asked.

'Oh yes,' Mr. Gatward replied. 'You could say that.'

We went back into the house, into the kitchen, and I made Mr. Gatward a cup of tea.

'They are a strange couple,' he said. 'Matthew and Gracie. We had high hopes for them, in the village.'

'They said last night that they were your greatest fans,' I said.

'Really?' said Mr. Gatward. 'How odd! They've hardly even spoken to me. Not after the first couple of weeks. I think that's the first word I've said to Gracie in, oh, two years.'

'Didn't they want to ask you about your books?'

'I think they came round for tea. They wanted me to sign their books. The first time that's ever happened, I can tell you – because the books are all signed anyway. All the ones Mrs. Willows sells, and no one else sells any. So they wanted me to sign books that were already signed.'

'What did you do?'

'I signed them, but in a different colour pen. And then I answered their questions. They were a little disappointed to find out I didn't know anything more than I'd put in the book. They were particularly interested in this place.'

'They still are,' I said. 'Very.'

For quite a few minutes, neither of us said anything. Then he spoke, and as he did so he picked up the copy of his book.

'*Hidden Histories*? I didn't know a tenth of it! No local historian has ever discovered anything like this,' he said.

It was time for my questions.

'What do you think happened to Lilian?' I asked. 'How could she just disappear?'

'The last entry suggests she was making experiments all the time. I suspect she may have died in one of them, and that the family kept it quiet to avoid drawing attention to themselves. Her body was probably secretly interred in the crypt. Have you ever been in the crypt?'

'No,' I said. I remembered the tunnel continuing beyond the upwards entrance through the grille to the chapel. If I'd know there were dead bodies in there, I would have fled back to the house even faster.

'Now might be a good time to check,' Mr. Gatward said. 'That would solve the mystery once and for all.'

'But the real mystery is what she did, isn't it? How she made gold?'

'There's no chemical formula, I'm afraid. The crucial words in the book are "harmonious conjunction". It was a coming together of different elements – earth, water, air, fire – in ascending order of energy. But also male and female, sun and moon, young and old. Alchemy took everything for power and was able to transmute anything.'

'Alchemy is also about eternal life,' I said. 'And that's a power of the house – at least, that's what Father Trovato said. So, if Lilian succeeded, why didn't she live forever?'

'I don't know,' said Mr. Gatward. 'Maybe she did. Maybe that's what her disappearance meant. There's a lot of very mystical writing in her book which I can't pretend to understand. "I am become earth," she writes. "I am become water, aire and fire also."'

And snow, I thought.

'Do you think Lilian might have become a ghost?'

'What? *Local Ghost Makes Really Good*? That seems a bit simple, after all she'd learnt. I think perhaps she became a power.'

I nodded. That was an explanation.

Mary didn't seem to be hungry, but I tried to feed her. Mr. Gatward leafed through *Hidden Histories*, chuckling to himself occasionally.

'Here,' he said, 'I ask the question as to why good Catholics such as William, Emmanuel and Margerye were buried in the Protestant graveyard in the village? And today, right now this minute, we can find out if they really were. After almost five hundred years.'

'Mary looks like she could do with a sleep,' I said. 'If you can wait.'

'Of course I can wait.'

In truth, Mary wasn't all that tired. But with the curtains drawn, and after about half a dozen lullabies, I got her to doze. I felt a little wary about leaving her alone again – I'd been doing that too much. Lilian would watch over her, though. The house was the safest place in the world for her, I was convinced of that.

Even so, I went into the attic to tell Peter. Jack was there, just as he'd said, right at the top of the ladder. I whispered up to him, so as not to give him a big shock.

'Tell Dad I've put Mary down for a nap. I'm going with Mr. Gatward to the chapel.'

'Can I come?' asked Jack.

'Not this time,' I said. 'Aren't you having fun here?"

'It's a bit boring, after the first bit,' said Jack.

'I'd like you to check on Mary. Can you do that?'

'Yes, mum.'

'Be careful on the ladder.'

'Yes, mum. I promise.'

Chapter 38.

The keys were hanging up on the brass hook in the kitchen. I took all three bunches – Mrs. Forster's, Robert Mew's and Father Trovato's – just in case we came across any more locks. At the last minute, I remembered to grab a torch.

Mr. Gatward seemed particularly light on his feet, as we walked under the trees. Perhaps it was the excitement, or perhaps it was all the time he'd been spending in our healing house.

The trapdoor to the chapel wasn't that heavy, and I was able to pull it back by myself. I clicked on the torch and we carefully made our way down the wooden steps..

'I don't like dead bodies,' I said.

'If there's anything there, it'll be a skeleton by now.' said Mr. Gatward. 'In any case, the Elizabethans – particularly the Catholics – preferred to inter their dead. We may find some fine funerary art.'

I wasn't sure that *skeletons* sounded all that much less scary than *dead bodies*.

The chapel smelled of the incense Father Trovato swung around during the mass.

Together, Mr. Gatward and me managed to inch the lectern off metal the grille. He needed a couple of minutes to recover after this.

'They knew how to make things, back then,' he said. 'Built to last. Not like now.'

I cast the beam of the torch over the wooden panels on either side of the pews. None of them had any carvings on – there wasn't a phoenix in sight.

'I'm ready,' said Mr. Gatward.

I led the way. I knew the first part would be fine, just down into the rough tunnel again.

'There's no room to turn round,' I said. 'So make sure you're facing in the right direction.'

'Which direction?' Mr. Gatward asked. 'Sorry, I'm not very good on things like that.'

'Copy me,' I said.

At the bottom of the ladder, I went down onto hands and knees, then crawled forwards – away from where I'd been before.

The torch almost immediately picked out a circular wooden door. It looked bizarre, like something out of the *Lord of the Rings*. There was a lock, of course.

I waited until Mr. Gatward was right behind me. This was reassuring – another person – but it meant I couldn't make a quick exit if there was a rat or something worse.

When I tried to put the first likely key into the lock, I found that the circular door just swung open.

It swung closed almost straight away, with a little thud.

‘In we go,’ said Mr. Gatward. ‘I haven’t felt this excited since I was a boy.’

‘What about last night?’ I said.

‘That was a book,’ he said. ‘This is a tomb.’

It wasn’t a good word to hear echoing under the ground. I pushed the circular door open with one hand and kept the torch firmly gripped in the other.

At first I thought the small, low, stony space was empty. But that was only because the beam of the torch was shining straight ahead. When I got a little further forward, I began to see things to either side – raggy, bony, skully things.

I gave a yelp, as if I’d just jumped into very cold water. It sounded high and a bit ridiculous. It also made Mr. Gatward flinch away.

‘They’re here,’ I said.

After a moment’s pause to tell myself to stop being silly, I crawled into the middle of the crypt. There were shelves on three of the walls, and on each of them a corpse was laid out.

Mr. Gatward’s ragged breathing seemed to fill the whole room, and to give it that huge expanding-contracting feeling that you get when you’re about to faint.

Unlike the house, the crypt was dusty and cobwebby. The palms of my hands and knees of my jeans were getting dirty.

The skulls looked quite small and not really threatening. Of course, I imagined them picking themselves up and flying towards me, empty mouths open. But then they didn’t, and I began to see them for what they were – dead things.

‘You’re right,’ said Mr. Gatward. ‘Do you mind if I have the torch?’ I did, but I managed to unclench my fist enough to hand it over.

‘I think this one is Emanuell.’ The light hit the body to our left. It was smaller than the others. About Jack’s size. ‘It’s definitely the body of a boy of the right age. This one…’ The light flashed round to our right, ‘is a woman. Look at her grave clothes. And her hair.’ The shiny silver strands seemed out of place. They looked much newer than everything around them. ‘So that’s probably Margerye. Which would make this…’ The torch beam landed on the skeleton right in front of us, ‘Meet William Jonson.’

Even though we’d been talking about them so much, what they did and what they believed, there had still been a gap between me thinking of them as people in history and me thinking of them as people who’d really lived, had bodies, died. This made it all seem so specific. Like us, they’d been in one place and one time. Like us, they’d done lots of things to escape that.

Mr. Gatward moved in for a closer look, leaving me in the half-dark.

‘Hang on,’ I said, and went to his side.

Along the edge of the shelf was some writing, carved into the stone. I was going to point it out to Mr. Gatward, but he'd already spotted it. 'Let me read it,' he said. 'Ah yes. "Et expecto resurrectionem mortuorum." That's, "And we look for the resurrection of the dead." Nicene Creed. The house rules for good Catholics. Well, you wait on, William. We won't disturb you again, I hope.'

We paused for a minute. I don't know if Mr. Gatward was praying, but his eyes were closed.

It was only when we'd turned around, ready to crawl out again, that we saw the writing on the floor.

'My God,' said Mr. Gatward, 'it's her.'

The letters were upside down, so we had to move to where we'd come in to be able to read them. 'ELIZABET IONSON.' And then below that, 'ET VITAM VENTURI SAECULI'.

'What does it mean?' I asked.

Mr. Gatward sounded choked as he translated. '"And the life of the world to come," he said. 'It's the next line. After the one about resurrection over there.'

We looked at the floor beneath our feet. The words weren't carved in stone. What we were standing on looked more like the flat outside of a ceramic pot – a jelly mould from Victorian times, or something of that sort. The light from the torch wasn't great for colours, but it looked a rich, golden kind of brown. This took up about the space you would dig for a grave.

'It is her?' I asked. 'She can't be buried here.'

'I don't know,' said Mr. Gatward. 'I've never seen anything like it. It looks like a Table Stone – the kind they have in churchyards. But I've never seen one like this. It's been fired in one huge piece.'

I had been right that it looked like pottery, but that didn't help with the huge disappointment.

'So this is her gravestone?' I asked. 'Her body's under here?'

'I don't know. We'd have to see if we can lift it up.'

'No,' I said. 'I'm not doing that.'

Mr. Gatward wanted to see if I'd change my mind.

'Why is hers different from theirs,' I asked. 'Why isn't she just out on a shelf, wrapped in some bandages.'

'I have no idea,' said Mr. Gatward. 'Maybe because she was different. I don't know.'

He seemed to have shrunk a little.

'Shall we go?' he said, and handed the torch back to me.

'One second,' I said.

Mr. Gatward stood in silence whilst I did something I didn't really understand myself. I cleared my mind and tested to see if I could feel Lilian's presence in the crypt. If her body had been buried beneath the floor, it would be a different place, it would give off different sensations. I was working my instinct rather than anything I believed in my conscious mind. I reached out to Lilian. But rather than feel her here, I felt something else – it was like the opposite of Lilian. I don't mean that she was good and it felt evil. Nothing like that. More that this was precisely the space where Lilian wasn't.

'I'm ready now,' I said.

Mr. Gatward went first, leaving me to pull the circular door shut behind us.

Chapter 39.

'Even so,' said Mr. Gatward, as we climbed into the chapel. 'Even so, it's terribly exciting.'

'Oh yes,' I said, trying to sound enthusiastic.

'No one in almost five hundred years has known the things we've known.'

'No,' I said.

We had stopped in the middle of the aisle. Mr. Gatward was looking around him. I gave him the torch, and he began to pick out particular details.

'That's how history is. You think you've found a solution, but you've only found another mystery.'

'Yes,' I said, as the beam of light hit the painting above the altar. It was Jesus on the cross.

'And this one's easy enough to solve. We lift the lid, and she's either there or she's not.'

'I don't want to disturb it,' I said. 'I think we shouldn't.'

Mr. Gatward turned the torch on my face. 'My dear, but then we'll never know. We'll never be certain.'

'You just said, we'd only find another mystery.'

'Maybe we will,' he said. 'The mystery of when she died, who buried her, why she was interred rather than – as you said – simply laid in the crypt. Perhaps her body was disfigured by an accident. Perhaps they had no body, so created her a fitting gravestone – one that had been fired in great heat.'

'Whatever it is,' I said, 'we're not disturbing it.'

'Mrs. Jonson!' cried Mr. Gatward, shining the torch on the grille in the floor. 'It would be a matter of moments. A team of strong men. A few crowbars.'

'I'm sorry,' I said. 'If you try to force me to do something I don't want to, we'll only end up falling out.'

Mr. Gatward put his hand to his mouth.

'I'm going for a walk,' he said in a high voice, then turned on his heel and scurried up the steps and out of the chapel.

I knew that he'd rushed away to calm his emotions, to stop himself getting thrown out.

When I came into sight of the front of the house, someone shouted my name.

It was Peter. He was standing on one of our kitchen chairs, just at the spot where P.C. Hollerhan had lifted him up.

'I think that's sorted,' he said. 'Come and have a look. Can't see it at all.'

I went straight to him.

'Be careful,' I said. 'What if a car comes?'

Peter climbed down off the chair. I handed him the keys then took his place.

'The signal seems to be fine, even though it's lower down.' he said. 'I've been using Jack to go up and down to the TV, reporting back. He got more and more excited.'

'Where is he now?' I asked. 'He's meant to be looking after Mary.'

'I thought you'd be pleased,' said Peter. 'I'm doing this for all of us.'

'How long have you been out here?'

'Only about five minutes.'

It was another marker of the growing distance between us – I couldn't care less about anything on television. My life was full of things that made TV programmes completely not worth watching.

'I am pleased,' I said, faking it. 'I'm going to check on Mary.'

As soon as I walked through the door of the house, I shouted, 'Jack! Jack!'

He didn't reply.

I hurried up the stairs, turned right and straight into our bedroom. Mary was there, absolutely fine, still sleeping.

'Mum!' shouted Jack. 'Come quick.'

He didn't sound like he was scared or in pain. I closed the bedroom door and called, 'Where are you?'

'I'm in the attic, Mum. Quickly.'

Across the upstairs living room I went, then up the spiral staircase.

There was a thump on the ceiling, and immediately I heard Jack say, 'Oh no.'

I got about halfway up the stairs before Jack shouted. 'Wait. Wait.'

There was another thump. It sounded like Jack was stamping his foot.

'Don't come in!'

I stopped. Jack had that kind of voice people get, when they shout to you to stop you coming into a room where they're wrapping up a present for you.

'What is it, Jack?'

Another thump, louder than the two before. Then Jack gave a grrr of frustration.

'But I wanted to *show* you,' he said. 'And it's not *working*.'

'Can I come up now?' I asked.

'I suppose so,' he said.

As I came up into the room, Jack was standing a couple of rungs up the ladder out onto the roof. I was glad to see the skylight at the top was safely shut.

Jack jumped and landed, making the thump.

Then he ran across to me and said excitedly. 'Mum, I was flying! I was flying across the room from over there to over there.'

He pointed to the ladder and then to a spot about five or six feet nearer to where I was.

'Like this,' he said, and ran back to where he'd been where I came in.

Another thump, but Jack followed it by going on tiptoe and pretending to fly across the room.

'I was about this high,' said Jack, his hand marking a level about two feet off the floor. 'It was brilliant. I was almost steering.'

'What happened?' I asked.

'Dad kept asking me to go down and look at the TV, to see if the picture was there. I tried to jump as far off the bottom as the record was, which was there.' He pointed to the floor, close to the ladder. 'Every time, I broke the record more and more. I was going really really far and not touching the ground. I was flying.'

I believed him, even though I didn't want to. I knew I believed him because I was already feeling jealous.

'What did it feel like?' I asked.

'Like I wanted it to,' said Jack. 'It felt creamy.'

'Try again,' I said.

Jack went back to the ladder. He was about to jump when I heard Peter come to the top of the stairs in the hall.

'He's fine, isn't he?' Peter said loudly.

'He's fine,' I said, just as Jack jumped.

'I told you he was fine,' said Peter, just as Jack didn't thump down as he should have done but floated sideways towards me.

'Look! Look!' he shouted. His arms were out to either side, wavering, as if we were trying to keep balance.

'What's he doing?' asked Peter.

Jack was halfway across from the ladder and still not touching the floor. His face was beaming with pride.

'He's – ' I didn't want to say flying but I didn't know what else to say. 'He's just showing me something,' I said.

'So, everything's fine, isn't it?' Peter said.

'It's all fine,' I said, just as Jack flew into my arms.

'I can fly!' whispered Jack. 'Daddy doesn't know. I want to surprise him when I can do it really well.'

'I'm going to have a look at the TV,' said Peter.

I tried to calm Jack down, but there was no chance. He'd just done the impossible – and fulfilled one of his life's dreams.

'You have to be very careful,' I said. 'I don't want you to get hurt.'

'But, Mum, when I'm really good at it, I can fly everywhere. I won't even need to go in the car.'

'I think, probably, that it will only work in the house. Please promise me you won't go too high.'

It was such a ridiculous thing to be saying.

'I promise,' said Jack. 'Can I do it again?'

‘One more time,’ I said.

But it didn’t work again, although Jack tried and tried.

‘Maybe after you’ve had a break,’ I said. ‘I think we need to do something very normal. How about you come with me to the shop? You can have whatever you want.’

Bribing kids isn’t good, I know. But sometimes there’s nothing else.

‘Okay,’ said Jack.

Mary was already stirring when I went to check on her again.

It took me about ten minutes to get ready. We left Peter happily reunited with his two hundred channels. I did ask him if he wanted to join us, but I think he was quite happy where he was.

I got a bit of a shock when I opened the door as Mr. Gatward was standing in the porch.

‘I wasn’t sure if I could come in,’ he said.

‘Of course you can,’ I said.

‘I am sorry about what I said. It’s entirely your decision how we proceed.’

‘I know it is,’ I said. ‘That’s why it’s okay.’

‘I’d like to have a serious look at the family papers today,’ said Mr. Gatward. ‘Start to find some supporting evidence for the improvement in the family finances, after 1580.’

Chapter 40.

Jack helped me push Mary's buggy along. All he wanted to talk about was flying. 'Then I'll teach Jameel,' he said. 'And then we can have fights in the sky like jet fighters. If we can fly, we can be superheroes.'

Talk of superheroes always made me think of Carpet Superheroes – and Jack had done a lot of talking about superheroes round about the worst time. This time, I smiled to myself. Carpet Superheroes woman couldn't *fly*, could she?

'Jack,' I said, 'you can tell Jameel about flying, but please don't talk about it with Dad. He doesn't believe in it, and it'll only make him annoyed. Okay?'

'Okay,' said Jack, who wasn't listening.

After this, I let him run on ahead, zooming and imagining. 'Stay off the road,' I shouted. I was still preoccupied with what we'd found or maybe not found in the crypt. It wasn't possible that Lilian had died like any other woman, then been buried in some secret ceremony. I hadn't paused in the house, like I had standing on Lilian's grave, but I knew that her presence was much stronger in the house than anywhere around the chapel. In fact, her presence seemed to run out just about where the smooth wood turned to rough in the secret tunnel. The house was where she was alive.

Mary enjoyed the trip out. She was looking all around her, taking in the hedgerows bright with flowers and loud with birdsong. I remembered that this was the sort of thing we'd been looking for, when we decided to move to the country. In London, she'd have been gazing at wheelie bins, litter and graffiti. It was another bright, summer day but the air felt close, as if a storm wasn't far off. I wished I could enjoy the sunshine without being preoccupied with other things.

When we got to the common, the two boys we'd seen before – the older one and the ginger one – were out there playing football.

'Why don't you go and say hello?' I asked. 'I'll get you something and bring it over.'

'No,' said Jack, suddenly wanting to hide in my armpit.

'They look very friendly,' I said.

Jack had a quick glance around me.

'No,' he said.

I wasn't sure if the village shop would still be open, but it was before twelve and Mrs. Willows was there behind the counter.

I said hello then turned to Jack. 'So, what would you like?

'Beer,' he said

Mrs. Willows laughed, a little nervously.

'He means ginger beer,' I said. 'Don't you?'

'No, beer beer,' said Jack.

'If you mess around, Jack, you won't have anything.'

'Alright then, ginger beer,' said Jack, as if it was a punishment.

'Please,' I said.

'Please,' he said, as me.

I picked a couple of cans out of the fridge and took them up to pay for them.

'You didn't come all the way just for these, did you?' asked Mrs. Willows.

This was annoying – it made any question I might casually ask seem less than casual.

'Oh, we were just out for a walk,' I said.

'You told me I could have anything,' said Jack.

'Break the bank,' I said.

Mrs. Willows took the money and gave me my change.

'I did have one question,' I said, deciding that I might as well be honest. 'Do you remember selling a copy of Mr. Gatward's book to Matthew and Gracie Dearie, when they first came here?'

'No,' she said. 'I don't remember their first visit.'

She was inviting a follow-up.

'You remember their second visit, then?'

'How could I forget it?' Mrs. Willows said. 'They walked in, told me they were buying the farm, then took every copy of *Hidden Histories* that we had in.'

'What, two or three?'

'Thirty-three,' said Mrs. Willows.

I must have looked satisfyingly amazed, because she said, 'I know, that was my reaction. They told me that they wanted to send it out to all their friends, instead of the usual, boring change of address card. I remember Mr. Gatward wasn't very pleased when I told him. He wanted other people to be able to buy it.'

'Oh,' I said. It seemed that neither Matthew and Gracie nor Mr. Gatward had been entirely honest about what had happened.

'Why are you interested, my dear?'

Jack had wandered away, and was closely examining some superheroes on the label of a tin of spaghetti hoops.

I explained that we'd had Matthew and Gracie round for dinner, and they'd mentioned how they first discovered the village.

'You were checking out their story, were you?' Mrs. Willows said. 'Seeing if I would back it up?'

'Well,' I said, 'they seem unusually interested in our house. I wondered if that really had all come from reading Mr. Gatward's books.'

Mrs. Willows leant towards me. 'You catch on fast, I can see. I wouldn't trust a single word they said. They pretend to farm the land, but I've heard they have produce delivered and then pass it off as their own. Everything about the pair of them's fake.'

'And the way they dress,' I said.

'They're like cartoons,' said Mrs. Willows. 'What she wears hurts my eyes, sometimes.'

I described their outfits from the night before.

'Typical,' said Mrs. Willows. 'Though I suppose she has got the legs for it, hasn't she?'

'They are very friendly, though,' I said.

'They don't do anything for other people,' said Mrs. Willows. 'Not a thing. That's what I've got against them. They're selfish.'

'I hope you won't think that about us,' I said.

'I heard about your unwelcome visitors,' said Mrs. Willows. 'In the cellar. I think you acted quite fairly. Myself, I would have prosecuted. That's trespass pure and simple.'

'Mum,' said Jack. 'Can I open my beer? It's going warm.'

'Not in here,' I said, visions of a sugary shook-up explosion in my head. Just then, Mary gave a loud grizzle.

'Another time,' I said to Mrs. Willows. 'Have a good weekend.'

'We won't be seeing you in church tomorrow?' she asked.

'No,' I said, then almost said, We have our own church. But Mrs. Willows probably knew that already. 'No, I'm afraid not.'

'I'll see you next week, then,' said Mrs. Willows. She certainly knew how to blow hot and cold.

We sat on the bench opposite the shop to drink our ginger beers. I managed to feed Mary at the same time.

Jack finished his drink in about ten seconds, burped, then looked turned around to watch the boys.

After a couple of minutes, he started climbing up and jumping off the bench, seeing if he could fly. I think he thought if he could start flying, that would impress the boys and break the ice.

Their kickabout got closer and closer to us. In the end, one of them miscued a shot, and it ended up rolling to my feet.

'Well, I'm not going to return it,' I said.

Jack was all shy when he picked up the ball, but then he gave it a punt over their heads and suddenly turned into a different boy.

'Can I go, Mum?'

'What have I been telling you?'

He sprinted away and was soon racing round the common with the best of them.

I sat there having what should have been a lovely time with Mary. Thoughts of Peter kept getting in the way, though. Because he didn't believe what I told him about the house, he was living in a different place. It was almost like we were living apart. After his affair with Carpet Superheroes Woman, we had talked once or twice about him moving out. To me, that had seemed to be dodging the issue. Either we loved each other and could live together or we couldn't. Now, though, I started to think that a separation might not have been a bad idea. It would have allowed us to have a definite reunion, after I'd worked through my emotions. In some ways, I'd tried to gloss the whole thing over – not really allowing myself to be as angry as I was. (Hard to do with the children around needing loving, happy Mummy and Daddy.) This meant that every time I got angry with Peter now, it wasn't just some minor thing about him doing something wrong or annoying. I brought all my pain into it, wham, just to give it some expression. This wasn't good for me and it wasn't anything like fair on him. Officially, I was supposed to have forgiven him for his mistake. But I was starting to see that really I had stored the whole thing up, as resentment. If I revisited the past too intensely, I risked splitting us apart. Peter seemed to be hiding at the moment – emotionally hiding. All this stuff about the TV. I knew he was being male and practical, solving problems, showing me how competent he was. He didn't understand that there were other kinds of knowledge that had become much more important. He needed to show that he still knew who I was.

Chapter 41.

Jack had been playing with the boys for fifteen minutes when I heard a familiar yell.

I looked over and saw that he was on the ground, clutching his left elbow.

I knew he'd hate it if I rushed over, all concerned – that would make him look bad – so I waited.

He picked himself up while the other two stood around looking a bit ashamed of themselves.

'Okay?' I shouted, without being able to stop myself.

Jack was inspecting his elbow very closely. Then I saw him grimace, take hold of something between his fingertips and give it a pull.

He'd obviously taken off a layer or two of skin.

'I'm all right,' I heard him say to the older boy, the one who'd probably knocked him over.

They went back to playing, although I could see that Jack's elbow was red with blood.

About five minutes later a woman about my age came out of the cottage next to Mr. Gatward's and shouted across the road, 'Lunch!'

I stood up began to walk over, thinking I should introduce myself, but the woman turned away back to the house without spotting me.

Jack, a little out of breath, ran back to me.

'Let me have a look,' I said.

He turned his arm round. There was a nasty scrape about the size of my thumb. It was fairly clean.

'How was that?' I asked.

'Fine,' Jack said.

'What are they called?'

'Don't know,' he said.

'You're hopeless,' I said.

'No,' said Jack, 'I won.'

As we walked past the boys' cottage, I tried to sneak a glimpse in through the windows. There were net curtains up, and all I could see were a few ornaments outlined along the windowsill. The garden was beautiful, though – hollyhocks shooting off all over the place like pink and white rockets.

'I'm sure we'll bump into them again,' I said.

Jack didn't seem to mind at all that he hadn't properly introduced himself.

Maybe it was for the best, I thought, that they hadn't suddenly become best friends. The way things were at the moment, inviting them over to the house might not be the greatest idea.

When we got back, I handed Mary over to her father and made us all a ploughman's lunch.

'Can you go and call Mr. Gatward?' I asked Jack, then whispered, 'And no sneaky flying, okay?'

Jack nodded, tore his eyes from the TV and headed up to the attic.

'What was that?' Peter asked.

'Jack's learning to fly,' I said.

'Oh,' said Peter, still mostly absorbed in what he was watching, which involved fast-moving cars. 'Right.'

I needed to say something.

'Can you take them out this afternoon? I need a bit of a break.'

'Sure,' said Peter. 'We can go for a drive. Explore the area.'

Mr. Gatward was a little subdued as he ate his cheese and pickle sandwich. 'I have confirmed what we thought,' he said to me. 'Subsequent to 1580, the Jonsons made several important acquisitions of land from neighbouring estates. Prior to then, they had been selling.'

'So, what next?' I asked.

'I think I need to work some more on Lilian's book.'

'Where is it?' I asked.

Mr. Gatward patted the breast pocket of his jacket. 'Very close to my heart,' he said.

'I think I'd like to look at it this afternoon,' I said. 'Would that be all right?'

'Of course,' said Mr. Gatward, and pulled it out straight away. I could see that he had been chastened by our argument in the crypt. He didn't want to risk being banished from the house again.

I picked the book off the table and placed it carefully on top of some cookery books on the shelf – I didn't want Jack to get it sticky with orange juice, not after almost five hundred years of being kept unsticky.

'You can have it back when I'm finished,' I said.

'Thank you,' said Mr. Gatward.

It was a relief to get through something uninterrupted, for once. We weren't all that hungry – the house, I had by now guessed, was having that effect on us – but we picked at the food on our plates.

After coffee, Mr. Gatward went back to the attic and I helped Peter get Mary ready for their trip out.

As soon as they were off, I went and checked on Mr. Gatward. He had made himself comfortable with a table and chair. Only one document was out in front of him.

'I put everything back where I find it,' he said.

'I'm sorry about this morning,' I said. 'I will think about having the stone lifted. But, for the moment, I want to leave things as they are. I don't like the idea of digging her up.'

'I thought you believed she wasn't there.'

‘No one likes being proved wrong,’ I said.

There was a moment’s silence.

‘I am making major discoveries all the time,’ said Mr. Gatward. ‘But they seem quite small stuff compared to what we’ve already found out.’

I patted him on the shoulder and said, ‘I’m sure there’s more to come.’

There was.

Chapter 42.

On the way downstairs I popped into the upstairs living room and collected the fire tools. These, I left outside the cellar door. Then I went and fetched all the keys from the kitchen. Finally, I carried everything down into the cellar – including Lilian's book – and locked the door behind me.

For quite a few moments, I just sat at the bottom of the stairs. I didn't have any doubts I was doing the right thing – I had dismissed Father Trovato's warnings as soon as he had given them. My trust was in Lilian and the house.

One by one, I opened the doors for which we had keys – the Earth door in the South, the Water door in the North and the Air Door in the East. Each of them gave me a different emotion. I remembered the thrill of the root touching my neck, the terror that Jack might drown, and the disappointment at the sight of the dull bricks. Then I turned my attention to the final door, the Fire door in the West. Very carefully, I tried inserting the phoenix tops of each of the fire tools into the keyhole and turning them both ways.

None of them worked. I wasn't surprised. It would have been much too easy a solution to the puzzle. Really, I had just wanted to get them out of the way, as a possibility.

Next, I sat down beside the grille that led to the underground chapel and flicked through the pages of Lilian's spell book.

There was a lot of writing, which I was frustrated I couldn't understand. Sometimes the sentences included drawings that looked like suns, moons, buttons, diamonds and pendulums. Lilian had beautiful handwriting – so flowing and without mistakes. There were a few dates 1577, 1579.

Finally, I was ready. I opened the page marked by the red ribbon.

I had seen it before, or at first I thought I had, because it was the page with the dark ink drawings of the rooty earth and the whirlpool of water. But there was a difference to these pictures, which it took me a second to work out – each image was speckled with stars.

I quickly flicked through the book, trying to find the original drawings, but there *weren't* any original drawings. These ones I was looking at now were those I'd seen before – without stars, I was sure, because I would have remembered that. Somehow, the stars had come out since then.

I thought for a second of going upstairs to show Mr. Gatward, but something else grabbed my attention immediately. Out of the corner of my eye, even as I looked back at the Earth drawing, I could see the open Earth door – and the hairy white roots tunneling through the soil like lightning. Amazed, I looked up at the real thing then down at the picture again. They were the same – exactly the same. Hundreds of years after Lilian had drawn the lines of the roots, they still followed exactly the same tracks. They hadn't grown or shrunk or been pulled out. They started bottom left, then went diagonally right, splitting once, then twice into a shape like a bull's horns.

Breathless with excitement, I carried the book over to the door. The stars on the page started to glow as I came nearer. And this was when I noticed something I felt stupid I hadn't spotted before: the roots were growing up rather than down. That was why one of them had fallen far enough out to stroke me on the back of the neck. If they had been growing normally, it would have just dangled there a couple of inches from the soil.

I felt a sudden whoosh of vertigo. If these roots were upside down, then either there was a tree beyond this door growing downwards or else in some bizarre way this small part of the house was upside down.

It was a beautiful but also quite horrifying picture – a tree whose leaves burrowed but whose roots waved in the air.

I held the book up to my eyes and squinted at the glowing stars. Their light was like red coals in a fireplace. They picked out places where the white roots changed direction or forked in two.

There were stars shining faintly on the opposite page, too – stars which looked a little woozy, as if their light was coming from under the water.

I carried the book over to the Water door, the underwater stars getting brighter every moment.

But the sheer curtain of falling water was in my way. It would be difficult to check that the patterns in the whoosh and swoosh of the whirlpool were the same without getting the book wet.

I looked hard at the page, trying to memorize how the water swirled around. I also looked at the stars, how they were placed. They looked like a great lopsided V with a necklace of seven pearls at the right end. Then I walked back to the grille and put the book down safely down in the middle. It wouldn't fit through any of the holes.

Back at the Water door, I stuck my head through the falling sheet and stared at the image from the page brought to brilliant, churning life. Every eddy and splash and bubble seemed to have come from those old lines of ink. What an artist Lilian had been, on top of everything else.

Of course, although the water was hitting me, I wasn't getting wet.

I flashed back to seeing Jack's mouth going under the surface, him not being able to breathe.

It would be difficult, but I knew I needed to check something. I got down on my hands and knees and stuck my head under the water. It was no good, with all the bubbles I couldn't see any distance at all. I stood up again – and swore.

After a deep breath, for bravery, I jumped into the Water room.

I landed badly and thought for a moment that I'd sprained my ankle. I hadn't been able to see my feet to judge the distance to the floor. A few flexes, though, told me I was all right for the moment. The untouching water swished around me. Best to do what I was here for and get out.

I took a proper deep breath, ducked down under the surface and then dropped to my hands and knees.

I found the first of the stars almost straight away. I had practically been standing on it. Another was to the left of this, and another, and another. A whole chain of stars leading in almost a straight line until they turned abruptly right and headed away, slightly more zigzag. It was the V-shape.

The stars were made of small black five-pointed tiles, neatly inlaid into the white.

After another big breath, I went back down and crawled towards the hole in the centre of the room. There weren't any stars beyond this, just white tiles.

I did something I hadn't done before – looked straight down into the hole. And there I saw something beyond amazing – stars. Real stars. I knew right away they couldn't be a painting because they were twinkling.

Keeping my hands on either side of the hole, I stuck my head down into it as far as I could go –

– and somehow, by some miracle, stuck my hair up into fresh, cold, salty air.

I looked all around me, shocked. I was in the middle of a wide, calm, empty sea. And above me was a black sky full of the most heartbreakingly clear stars.

This water, unlike the water in the house, seemed to support me like real water, although it still didn't wet me. I floated there, wherever there was.

I don't know a lot about astronomy. If it was right in front of me, I could pick you out the Big Dipper and maybe Orion's Belt. What I was looking for, though, was the V-shape that was drawn in the book and tiled into the floor.

I turned around and around. But it was only when I'd almost given up and just let myself float there that I spotted it – directly overhead. It was the wrong way round, though. Upside down. I was the wrong way round.

In trying to turn, I lost my grip on the slippy tiles, and found myself floating up into the sea.

If I got washed away here, I knew I'd never be able find my way back to the hole into the house.

I stuck my legs out to the side, toes stiff, and managed to keep my grip on the real world.

I looked again at the V, this time with its sharp point downwards. And it was still the wrong way round – it was back to front. The little pearl necklace of stars was on the top left and the zigzag shot off to the right.

I took one last look at the beauty of the sky, one deep breath of that salty air, then I brought my knees up to my chin, paddled with my hands and pulled myself back into the Water room.

For just a few seconds, I lay on my back, looking up at the turbulent surface. I felt too overwhelmed to move. But then my lungs started to hurt.

I stood up, found where the door was, walked over to it and hauled myself out into the cellar.

Chapter 43.

'Thank you,' I said. 'Thank you so much.'

My head was spinning with all the new dimensions opening up in it. Through the Earth door, the house was upside down in the earth. Through the Water door was another universe pressing right up against ours – where day was night, where land was sea, where everything was back to front. And through the Air door was… It couldn't just be a cube of bricks.

After a few minutes recovery time, I went back to Lilian's book and checked once more.

The star maps on both the Earth and Water pages were exact copies of those in the roots and the tiles. Or maybe that was the wrong way round. Maybe the book had come first and the roots and tiles had been created afterwards.

I turned the page – to where Air stood opposite Fire. The stars on the Air page were a little hazy, like stars seen through a veil of cloud. They made a shape like a dead-end corridor.

Wary of being disappointed, but knowing that I was being greedy in asking for any more wonders, I carried the book up to the threshold of the Air room.

In the centre of the stars was the leaf I had seen the first time Mr. Gatward showed me Lilian's spell book. As I looked closer, though, I saw that it might be other things, too – a pentagram or a kite or even a human figure. It had five definite points that seemed to be sketchily joined.

I looked up at the tightly laid bricks of the room, the foursquare corners. I breathed in the stale air.

Again, I placed the book safely back on the grille, although I wasn't afraid of it getting soaked as it might've been in the Water room.

I had decided to walk into the middle of the Air room and ask for Lilian's help. But I took one step inside and fell over – or more like I fell down and down, without actually hitting anything or being sure I was falling.

The brick floor was collapsing – moving further away from me as I fell towards it.

I was also falling forwards, though.

Falling meaning flying.

The room was opening up all around me – the bricks flying soundlessly back until the eight square corners of the room disappeared into the smooth inner surface of a sphere.

I touched down on the floor of the huge room, expecting to jar against the bricks, but they cushioned my landing and then gently pushed me back into the air. They were like the softest, springiest bouncy castle ever.

I didn't feel weightless. I knew I still weighed the same as when I'd entered the room – more's the pity. But my weight didn't matter any more. The air was supporting me.

I could use my thoughts to climb through it, float through it – just as Jack had done.

For the first few minutes, I was all over the place. I bounced off the walls and ceiling, which bounced me back. Soon, though, I managed to get a little control. I pushed with my arms and kicked with my legs until I was right in the middle of the room.

It was only now, looking down beneath me, that I realized quite how huge the sphere was. The space had opened out until it was probably as high as the hall.

I made a circuit of the room, looking for the stars. And there they were, hanging in the air. They only looked like the star map when you got close to the door and saw them from the correct angle. I had to experiment for a while before I found that out. But with every passing moment, I grew better and better at flying. It wasn't something I needed to learn, more like something I had always been able to do but had become a little rusty at. I suppose we spend so much time flying in our dreams – or at least I do – that we're actually pretty good at it. I felt amazing, like I'd always wanted to feel. I'd come home to this skill.

I made my way to the very middle of the sphere and hung there motionless. Then, for a laugh, I stretched until I was lying flat. The air was the most comfortable mattress you could imagine. I closed my eyes and rested there.

The most unpromising-looking room had turned out to be the most exciting of all. What was I always telling Jack? Don't judge things on first impressions, give them a chance.

Was I going to be able to tell him that I could fly, too? Probably not. It would annoy him, and he'd also want to come down here with me. I didn't want to share this. Unless… I thought about Mary. How she had giggled when Lilian held her up in the air of our bedroom. It would be wonderful to have my baby with me. What games we could play! Then, wisely, I dismissed the idea as too dangerous. She might fall. Look how far down it was. But the door was locked, and Lilian wouldn't let her come to any harm. She'd catch her.

After a couple of spins and a forward roll that made me feel a little sick, I made my way to the door.

The room seemed to sense that I was leaving as it began to collapse back into its foursquare form as I moved away from the centre.

The marvellous patterns in the brickwork. Now I understood them. As the walls contracted, the bricks slid silently into place. The room was the most amazing 3-D puzzle.

It was back to how it had been before. Only now, I could see there were a few places where the bricks had little holes in them. These were the remains of the star map.

I fetched the book and checked they were the same, making that long dead-end shape – they were.

Placing the book back on the grille for the final time, I went round the doors, closing them one by one – first Earth, then Water.

I was just about to close the Air door when I heard a flicking sound. I immediately thought it might be the tail of a rat, coming up through the grille. When I turned around, I saw Lilian's book was now open on its back, and the pages were being fluttered this way and that – as if someone had left it on a windowsill and it was being read by the wind.

This wasn't the wind, though. I knew it was Lilian, reunited with her work of all those years ago.

I watched as the pages were opened, pressed down for a while then flicked away from. This was Lilian's quicksilver personality, jumping from one thing to the next, brilliant, impatient. Not like me at all. I wondered again why she had chosen me.

As I watched, the red ribbon was slowly drawn out of the book. It dangled in the air from two points, about waist height. Then it started to turn in on itself, becoming a circle, looping around itself at the top, pulling away until the circle became smaller and smaller. I could see that a simple knot was being tied into it. Another knot followed, circle and closing circle, and then a third and final knot. They were all in a line at one end of the ribbon.

The book on the grille had finally stopped fluttering. It was wide open at the page showing Air and Fire. This was Lilian where placed the knotted ribbon. Then, to make her point even clearer, the book snapped shut – and I felt the room empty of anyone but myself.

Wow.

Chapter 44.

Something made me want to get out of the cellar quite quickly. I wanted to think about what had happened, but somewhere else – out in the garden, maybe.

Before that, though, I took a close look at the keyhole in the Fire door. I seemed to have run out of keys I could try in it. The shape of the hole was unusual. Perhaps because I'd started to think about things being upside down and back to front, I recognized it. It was a wavy flame, very thin, starting around a circle and extending downwards. That would make for a very unusual key. Certainly not like any of those I'd seen in the house.

I stepped back to look at the whole door. It was made of very smooth dark wood, very plain and undecorated, apart from a large oblong shape right in the middle of the top half. Here, the wood was cut in by about an inch. It looked like a window, but not one you could see anything through.

I carried the fire tools up to the top of the stairs, making a bit of a racket as did. Then I brought up the keys and the book.

For one second, I thought I might have been locked in – I didn't know who by. But the key turned in the door, and I swayed out into the hall, arms full of stuff.

Mr. Gatward come out of the kitchen holding a cup and saucer.

'I couldn't find you anywhere,' he said. 'I'm afraid I helped myself.'

Did I believe him? Or had he suspected that I'd gone down to the cellar and waited for me there all this time?

'Oh, that's fine,' I said. I couldn't have looked much more guilty. 'I'll join you in a minute.'

I handed over Lilian's book to him – one less thing to carry. He seemed relieved to get it back.

'What are these knots?' he asked.

'I put them there to help me remember something,' I said.

'You should be careful with a ribbon this old,' he replied, but didn't say anything more.

After putting the fire tools back by the fireplace, I went downstairs to join Mr. Gatward.

'Find anything out?' I asked.

'Yes,' he said, very cool. 'Did you?'

'Not really,' I said. 'I was trying to open the last door. But what I thought was the key didn't work.'

'Maybe it's something more complicated than just a key,' Mr. Gatward said. 'Everything upstairs seems to be coming out far too neatly.'

'What do you mean?' I asked.

'The family's fortunes turned, after the success of Lilian's experiments. But the accounts suggest they were covering this up. Which is just what you'd expect.'

'Why are you interested in this?' I said. 'Surely there's more interesting things to be looking into.'

'Well,' said Mr. Gatward, holding up Lilian's book, 'the most interesting is this – and you deprived me of it.' He seemed to be joking.

Swiftly, I took the book back from him, and opened it at the page for the Earth and Water drawings – but the stars had faded completely away, as if they'd never been there.

'Yes?' asked Mr. Gatward.

I knew I could roughly remember the shapes of the star maps, even if they weren't in front of me. I already had a suspicion of what they were.

'Tell me what you think these drawings mean,' I said.

I wasn't expecting to hear anything useful. But Mr. Gatward began by saying, 'The four elements, as discovered by the Greeks. The philosopher Aristotle included a fifth one – aether. He said the stars were too imperishable to be made out of water, earth, air or even fire. Pretty advanced thinking.' I thought of the stars I had just seen. It was hard not to believe they were made of something purer than anything we encountered on earth. 'Four elements,' continued Mr. Gatward, 'one room for each. Alchemy was about bringing everything into play at once. These rooms were part of whatever machine they used to produce gold. Perhaps they just needed a supply of each element. The doors would be open. The whatever-it-was right in the middle. Of the elements, the most crucial was fire. Alchemists used fire constantly. And as time went on, they got better at heating things up. Even though no one discovered the philosopher's stone – or we thought they didn't – a lot of genuine discoveries were made. William Jonson was no doubt messing around with his forge when he burned the house down.'

Whilst Mr. Gatward talked, I helped myself to tea. It was slightly stewed, but I needed something strong.

'What about the stars?' I asked. 'You said before there were lots of astrology books in the attic.'

'Almost as many as there are alchemy books.'

'Are there any links between the two?'

'Oh, the whole Elizabethan world-view was of interlinked and overlapping forces. That's why alchemy became so complicated, taking people years to become adept at even the basics. If, for your experiment, everything has to be right – including the stars – then you might have to wait years for things to align.'

'And some of the star signs are fire signs, aren't they? And Pisces is water…' I was remembering all those horoscopes I'd read, over the years.

'Follow me,' said Mr. Gatward.

He led me through into the living room.

'Turn the lights on,' he said, as he moved across to the tapestry curtains and started to pull them shut.

I did as he asked – remembering, even as he turned around to face me, that the curtains were decorated with the twelve signs of the zodiac.

'Here we are,' he said. 'Have a look.'

I came closer. There was Sagittarius with his curved bow, looking like he was about to shoot an arrow into Scorpio's tail. There was Leo with his bum uncomfortably close to Virgo's head.

The figures were made of gold thread that glimmered as I moved towards it. The whole tapestry was a sky map.

'It's the Northern sky,' said Mr. Gatward. 'I think. What you'd see north of the equator.'

I picked out a few more star signs I knew. Gemini, the twins toppling down onto Cancer, the crab.

'Now,' said Mr. Gatward, 'here's the magic. Go and turn the lights off.'

I flicked the switches.

'And close the door,' said Mr. Gatward.

I pushed it shut, then turned around. It was magic – the stars were shining in my living room. Through small holes in the tapestry, the sun shone from outside.

'Whoa,' I said.

'It's a masterpiece,' said Mr. Gatward. 'There's nothing else like it in the world. Not that I know of. Not in this form.'

I was hardly listening to him. Almost straight away I had picked out the shapes of the star maps.

Easiest to spot was the V-shape, which was near the top, upside down. What had that been? I needed to turn the lights back on to check, but I wanted to take in the marvel of it.

'If you asked me,' said Mr. Gatward, 'I'd say this is something Lilian designed. She may even have helped make it, too. Perhaps this is what they were doing, confined to the house for all those years.'

Yet again I had one of those moments when I couldn't believe that this house, these things, were owned by Peter and me. I was starting to understand better why we had been allowed to take them over – the Catholicism, Father Trovato, and the agreement he wanted from us. But all these riches, which we couldn't sell, seemed to come from another world.

I was now close enough to stick my little finger into one of the holes. Mr. Gatward stood to the side, a couple of beams of light landing on his face and making strange shapes there.

'But why are you suddenly interested in astrology?' he asked. 'Is that what you found out, down in the cellar?'

'Mr. Gatward,' I said, turning to look at him. 'What are you really after?'

‘Glory,’ he said, soon enough. ‘Historical glory. If I can publish something about this, with full documentation, it will be a sensation. You will allow me to write it up, won’t you?’

‘This full documentation,’ I said. ‘That would include knowing where Lilian’s remains were.’

‘I could probably work around that,’ Mr. Gatward said. ‘But I can’t deny, it would be very useful.’

‘And there’s nothing else?’ I asked.

‘Isn’t that enough?’ he asked. Did I believe him? I wasn’t sure.

‘Not enough for some people,’ I said.

‘Oh, I’d want to live long enough to see the work published,’ he said. ‘But I’m not after any other kind of immortality.’

His even mentioning the word made me suspicious of him all over again.

‘Thank you for showing me this,’ I said. ‘How did you know about it?’

‘It’s in the inventory,’ he replied. ‘I saw the constellations, the holes and worked the rest out for myself.’

‘But you’ve never seen it before?’ I asked.

‘Closed, yes,’ he said. ‘But not in it’s full splendour.’

We stood back to admire it – a whole bright universe.

‘They were so clever, weren’t they?’ I said.

‘They were marvellous,’ said Mr. Gatward. ‘That’s why I love them so much.’

Just then, I heard Jack coming through the front door. His shout of ‘Mu-um!’ was unmistakable – as was Mary’s wailing, which I could also hear.

Mr. Gatward pulled the curtains back into place while I went through to give Jack a hug.

‘Did you have a nice time?’ I asked.

‘Yes,’ he said. ‘Can I have some juice?’

‘Sorry,’ said Peter, holding Mary out towards me. ‘She just started crying. I think she’s hungry.’

‘I bet you are,’ I said to the little love.

Mr. Gatward came through and said hello.

‘Did you have a lie down?’ Peter asked.

‘A bit of one,’ I said.

Chapter 45.

Jack had decided that he wanted to be a professional footballer, so he needed to do training. Peter played with him in the garden, and I sat on the bench cuddling Mary, watching and shouting encouragement.

I tried to concentrate on just what was in front of me – us, being a family – but the stone phoenix carved into the wall was there above their heads.

Eventually, Peter came over to have a sit down, leaving Jack to kick around by himself.

'He's good,' Peter said.

'He made some friends this morning,' I said. 'Well, almost.'

I told him about the boys on the green.

'It's a start,' said Peter. 'I'm sure he'll see them again.'

We were so similar in what we said and thought.

'Yes,' I said. 'I saw where they live.'

'That how he scraped his elbow?' Peter asked. 'Sliding tackle?'

'Yes,' I said.

'I was thinking,' Peter said. 'Why don't we all go to the pub this evening? Just have a quiet drink.'

'That would be lovely,' I said.

I looked at Peter. I felt sorry for him – all the things I was seeing and doing and he was missing out on. I decided I should try to include him, not by telling him but by showing him. The Water room was out of the question, but perhaps the stars would come out in Lilian's book. Then I remembered that Mr. Gatward was expecting to take the home with him tonight. That left the Air room, but if water touched me, when Peter was watching, then air too would probably do something – stop supporting me or not lift me up in the first place.

'Do you remember anything more?' I asked. 'From your first visit here? The very old man?'

'I've been thinking about that,' Peter said, as Jack celebrated scoring a goal. 'I get the feeling my father brought me. I don't remember rain or cold, so I think it was summer, like this. I remember cake in the garden. And I remember that I didn't just see a stone phoenix, I saw a metal one as well, shiny brass – but it was smaller. I think they kept it in a cupboard.' Peter's eyes were closed now. 'I remember being lifted up. The old man held me by the hand and then lifted me up.'

'We'll have to check the cupboards, then,' I said.

'I wish it had been my father who lifted me up,' Peter was becoming sad. 'I don't have enough memories of him like that.'

'Why do you think they were showing you the phoenix?'

'I don't know. Perhaps I'd spotted the one out here. Perhaps they thought I wouldn't be interested in anything else.'

'So you didn't go in the cellar?'

'No, I'm pretty sure I didn't.'

'Let's have a look in the hall, see if we can spot a phoenix there.'

'My eyes were better then,' said Peter. 'But I remember seeing it close up.'

He looked away from me. There was so much more we needed to talk about, to sort out.

'Hey, you see that bird over there on the wall,' shouted Peter to Jack. 'That's a phoenix. Do you think you can help us find another one?'

'I don't see it, either,' said Peter. 'What about you, Jack?'

We were all – even Mary – lying in a cross shape on the parquet floor of the hall, looking up at the ceiling. She was on top of a blanket, so she didn't bang her head.

'What about that one?' Jack asked, and pointed. 'That's got birds on it.'

We all squinted towards where he was pointing.

'That's a coat of arms,' said Peter.

'Is it a shield like knights had?' Jack asked.

'Yes, exactly,' said Peter. 'It showed who they were – who their parents were. But it was a kind of code. Those birds probably mean Jonson or another family name.'

'Is phoenix for us?' Jack asked. 'Is that our bird?'

'Probably,' said Peter. 'If we could find it.'

I turned myself around on the slippy floor, to look at the ceiling from another angle. I'd always thought the carved panels were arranged randomly among the plain ones. But now, in a flash, I realized that they were dotted about like stars. That might mean nothing. Perhaps I was starting to see hidden meanings where there were none.

I looked again. The carved panels were in clusters of two or three. If they had been just random, they would have been spread out more. The shape they made was like a headless man running along, two hunched arms and a very long trailing leg. But then, when I turned my head so it was lined up with the front door, feet towards the living room, I saw another shape – a bow. This was Sagittarius, just like in the curtain.

I really wanted a closer look – and then something unnerving happened. I felt myself start to lift off the floor. Not much, only a millimetre or two, but my desire to have a better look at the ceiling was making me fly. Could I stop myself?

Chapter 46.

I'd thought that the Air room might be the only place I'd be able to fly. That way I could keep it under control. But if Jack could fly in the attic, why couldn't I fly in the hall? Or anywhere else in the house?

I sat up, and concentrated hard on being heavy (not hard), and was glad to feel my bum bump solidly onto the floor.

I didn't want Jack to be disappointed, so I said, 'I know where we can find some more phoenixes.'

Peter and Jack followed me upstairs, where I showed them the fire tools. I worried for a moment that Peter would have the same thought I'd had, and would want to try them out as keys.

'Oh, yes,' he said.

'Do you remember these, from when you were a boy?' I asked.

'No,' he said.

Jack had picked the poker up and was about to start swordfighting with it, a little too close to Mary's eye for my liking. Peter swiftly disarmed him. 'Look at this,' he said, holding the phoenix end up for Jack on inspect.

'Why is its bottom on fire?' Jack asked.

I explained about how a phoenix lived and died and was reborn.

'I want an egg like that,' said Jack. 'Then I can have a phoenix as a pet.'

'A bit difficult to house train,' said Peter.

I thought of William Jonson burning down the house. They couldn't have had a phoenix as a pet, could they? With all the other wonders I'd seen, I wouldn't put it past them. It would have come in handy for heating up their furnace.

'We still going out to the pub tonight?' Peter asked.

'As long we don't stay out late,' I said.

Peter gave me a significant look.

'Yes, I can drive,' I said.

'I can drive,' said Jack. 'I can drive and I can fly.'

He leapt into the air. I thought just for a second that he was going to take off and glide across the room, whooping, but he landed normally.

'I *can* fly,' he said. 'I can.'

'I have something else to show you,' I said. This time, they followed me to the downstairs living room – where I repeated Mr. Gatward's performance.

Peter and Jack weren't quite as wowed as I had been, but it gave me the chance to check that – yes – the constellation mapped on the hall ceiling was Sagittarius.

It was also – because it wasn't the V or the dead-end corridor or the bull-horned shape – probably the one the stars in Lilian's book had picked out on the Fire page.

In my wonder at Lilian's sky tapestry, I had completely forgotten to get Mr. Gatward to answer my question. Which of the star signs were matched with which of the elements?

If Sagittarius was the only one left, then Sagittarius must mean fire. I turned the lights off and on a couple more times. Earth was Virgo the virgin, Water was Pisces the two fishes – as I'd known already, and Air was Gemini the twin boys.

'I think that's enough,' said Peter.

'There's never enough,' I said. 'Not here.' I was marvelling at the way everything in the house had significance. And I was sure I wasn't even picking up on a tenth of it. The whole place was like a code – a code that, with Mr. Gatward's help, I was starting to crack. One thing in one part linked up with another in another part. If you understood the meaning here, it led you to another puzzle there. You didn't have to be worried, though, because you knew that the solution was always going to be somewhere in the house. It was all of a piece. Because the place had been burnt down, they had been able to start again, and rebuild it as a place where *this* time alchemy would work. Everything we could see was for that purpose.

'The house is a code,' I said to Peter.

'Right,' he said. The lights were out. He pointed right at some of the holes that made up Sagittarius. 'Dot dot dot.'

The kids hadn't had a bath for a few days, so I put Peter in charge of getting them decent. I knew we'd be on show for the whole village in the pub, and I wanted to make a good impression.

While they were occupied, I went upstairs to see how Mr. Gatward was getting on.

As usual, he was sitting at the table with just a single book in front of him.

I peered over his shoulder. The book was on astrology. I could tell because Mr. Gatward had it open at a page showing Sagittarius. Even after everything else, this was a little spooky. The book wasn't old – from the 1950s or 60s. Probably something Mr. Jonson had bought when he wasn't speaking to Father Trovato, when he was making his own investigations into the house. I wondered if Lilian had ever appeared to him. I didn't like to think so.

Mr. Gatward gave a jump as I touched his shoulder. He hadn't heard me.

'Mrs. Jonson,' he said, rather quickly. 'I was just mugging up. I realized I hadn't answered your question – what you asked before I showed you the tapestry. The truth is, I'm afraid I didn't know. I always thought astrology a load of mumbo-jumbo, so I never paid much attention to it.'

'What have you found out?' I said.

‘The signs of the zodiac, as you said, are divided up so they tally with the elements. Sagittarius – ’

‘Is fire,’ I said.

‘Oh,’ said Mr. Gatward, ‘so you’re ahead of me again.’

‘I don’t know many others,’ I said. ‘Pisces.’

‘Look at this,’ said Mr. Gatward, and turned back a few pages. There was a chart. Across the top were the words Cardinal, Fixed and Mutable. ‘There are twelve star signs and four elements – and four into twelve goes three times. So the star signs are divided into three groups.’ Mr. Gatward continued his explanation, but I’d already seen what I needed: the four constellations mapped in Lilian’s book – Virgo, Pisces, Gemini and Sagittarius – were all what’s called Mutable.

‘Does Mutable mean they are weaker than the others?’ I said, pointing at the word on the page.

‘Um,’ said Mr. Gatward, unsettled at being interrupted. ‘I think it means they work by affecting other star signs. Mutable meaning able to change. Not the dominant force. They’re not the thing that will make you one kind of person or another.’

‘Cardinal is the dominant force,’ I said.

‘Yes,’ said Mr. Gatward. ‘But for an alchemist, you see, mutability was everything. If a thing was one thing, and they knew it couldn’t be changed into another, or help change something into another thing, then it wouldn’t have interested them.’

‘I suppose not,’ I said, looking again at the four star signs beneath the word Mutable.

And then I realized. The place to look for the key to the fire door was where the fourth star sign was – Sagittarius – on the ceiling of the hall.

Normally, this would have meant tons of scaffolding and thousands of pounds of cost. But I’d already had a glimpse of myself flying in the hall. If I could get a little more time alone, perhaps I could find something up there – something on or hidden behind one of the panels.

The very thought of it gave me vertigo, and I had to hold on tight to the edge of the table.

‘Oh dear,’ I said, thinking I was going to be sick.

‘Are you all right, Mrs. Jonson?’ Mr. Gatward stood up and allowed me to sit down on the chair.

‘I think it’s all starting to catch up with me,’ I said.

‘I must admit,’ said Mr. Gatward, ‘I’m feeling quite exhausted myself. If you don’t mind, I’ll come back tomorrow morning.’

I thought about saying no. Mr. Gatward could have a day off to recharge his batteries. But I knew that he’d be disappointed if I didn’t let him keep going.

‘We have mass first thing,’ I said. ‘So, we’ll be up.’

'Nine o'clock sharp, then,' said Mr. Gatward. 'Though I'd like to take this home for a little bedtime reading.' He pulled Lilian's book up so it was poking out of his breast pocket.

'Please, be careful with it,' I said.

'You know I would guard it with my life,' Mr. Gatward said, very chivalrously.

He picked up the astrology book from the desk and slotted it back into its place on the shelf.

Seeing I wasn't about to move, Mr. Gatward said, 'I'll just go and call the taxi.'

I grabbed a couple of minute's rest, my head turned sideways and pillowed by my crossed arms laid out on the desk.

I'd had enough for one day. A trip to the pub was just what I needed. No cooking. A half of cider then an early night.

I could hear Jack's shouts from the bathroom.

My children were safe and happy. I could just doze off for a few…

Chapter 47.

At first, I thought I was being strangled.

I couldn't breathe.

Someone had snuck up behind me and grabbed my throat.

But when I turned round, the room was empty – and still I couldn't breathe.

Perhaps I'd swallowed my tongue. How could that have happened?

I stuck my tongue out. It was where it should be.

I felt my heart start to beat faster.

Fast as I could, I ran towards the spiral staircase.

Peter would save me. Peter would know what to do.

As soon as I got down into the living room, I felt the air around me.

I took a deep breath and sobbed with relief.

But a second breath wouldn't come. My mouth was open and air seemed to be going into my lungs. I wasn't breathing, though.

Again, I rushed down the stairs, around and around – feeling like I was about to faint with dizziness.

When my foot touched the carpet, I was able to snatch another breath. Only one.

Across the room I went and out onto the landing.

A deep breath here.

I rushed into the bedroom, expecting to be able to breathe in again. But it didn't happen. I wasn't allowed.

I bashed on the bathroom door.

'Can't breathe,' I hissed. 'No air.'

I'd never had an asthma attack.

Peter pulled Mary out of the bath, rushed through into the bedroom and placed her on the bed.

Then he started asking me questions.

'Have you swallowed anything?'

I shook my head. The world was going blurry.

'It might be a panic attack,' he said. 'You need a bag. Come with me.'

He grabbed my hand and pulled me out through the bedroom and onto the landing.

I was about to faint. I knew it.

The last thing I could do was grab hold of Peter, so I didn't fall over.

I was going to suffocate, going to die, and I didn't know why.

The last thing I saw was Mary, through the open doorway, kicking her little legs in the air.

I woke up, with a huge gasp, on the floor of the hall.

Peter was in the kitchen. I could hear him saying, 'Bag! Bag!'

I opened my eyes.

Mr. Gatward was by my side, holding my hand.
'She's awake!' he shouted.
Another huge breath of beautiful air into my lungs.
Everything I could see was starry with tears.
'Oh God,' said Peter. He came out carrying with a plastic shopping bag from the supermarket. 'Oh thank God.'
There was a toot-toot from outside.
'I'll tell them to wait,' said Mr. Gatward.
Peter lifted me up into his arms and gently held me.
'You're breathing,' he said.
'I'm breathing,' I said.
He hugged me tight.
'Is Mummy okay?' Jack asked, from the top of the stairs.
'I'm okay,' I gasped, then tried to smile.
'Watch your sister,' said Peter. 'Mum's fine now.'
'Just let me lie here for a minute,' I said.
I closed my eyes and breathed and breathed. Then I looked up again, and saw Peter, and behind him Sagittarius mapped out on the ceiling.
This hadn't been a panic attack. I hadn't felt less panicked in weeks. It was something else –
I had been forced downstairs. The moment I tried give up on my investigation, to take some rest, the air had been sucked from the room. Or, like the water, the air had been there but I hadn't been allowed to touch it. Lilian was forcing me onwards. As if there as no time to spare. No time at all.
This was terrifying.
Mr. Gatward came back in.
'How is she?' he asked.
'I'm fine,' I said, but I wasn't.
I fainted, and when I woke up I was in the four-poster bed – Peter sitting anxiously beside me.
'What time is it?' I asked.
'Don't worry about that,' my husband said. 'The kids are asleep.'
'What time is it?'
'Half past eleven,' he said, and I can't remember anything else about that day.

I really did feel fine the next morning when Jack came in and woke me – as if the whole airless thing hadn't happened.
Jack wanted to watch TV, so I went downstairs with him and turned it on.
I say downstairs, but Jack didn't touch a one of them – he flew straight out into the middle of the hall, at least ten metres off the floor.
'Jack,' I whispered. 'Come back here now.'
Reluctantly, he dropped down at the bottom of the stairs.

I hustled him through into the living room, then went down on one knee to look him in the eye. 'You have to be very careful,' I said. 'If your father sees you, you'll come crashing to the ground. I don't want you to get hurt.'

'But I will get fixed,' Jack said. 'So I am safe.'

'What if you don't get fixed?' I sad. 'What if it doesn't work?'

Jack thought about this with a big frown on his face.

'Why can't Dad see?'

'I don't know,' I said. 'I wish I did.'

'Watch this,' Jack said, and started to whizz in circles around the room. 'I'm Superman.'

'Very good,' I said. 'Now stop flying, and sit on the sofa.'

But I had to laugh at what a weird thing this was to find myself saying.

Jack was still hovering when there was a knock at the door. I thought for a second it was Father Trovato, but today was Saturday, and he came earlier than this.

On the doorstep were Matthew and Gracie. He was in his tweedy farmer's outfit. She was wearing the wifey equivalent.

'Good morning,' they said. 'May we come in?'

'We're not really up yet,' I said. 'What is it?'

'Look,' said Matthew, 'Jeane… This is a little difficult to explain. I know you know about the house – what a special place it is. But I don't think you realize what a special time this is.'

'Midsummer's Eve,' said Gracie. 'Tomorrow is Midsummer's Eve.'

'Yes,' said Matthew, clearly annoyed with her for interrupting. 'And as the turning point of the year, it's a very important day.'

'And night,' said Gracie.

'Please shut up,' said Matthew to her. She did. 'I will be direct – we need to be in your house for Midsummer's Eve. We want to perform certain rituals. We are prepared to pay…' He then named an amount of money I couldn't believe.

'No,' I said.

He doubled the sum of money.

'This is our house,' I said. 'And you freaks are never coming in it again.'

'Oh yes we fucking well are,' said Matthew.

'Bitch,' said Gracie.

Matthew was about to raise his hands against me when I saw a green figure over his shoulder.

'Leave them,' said Robert Mew. 'Leave them now.'

Matthew and Gracie turned around to face him.

'Ah,' Matthew said, 'the protector.'

'The lady of the house has asked you to leave,' said Robert. 'Please go.'

Matthew walked up to Robert. Matthew was a couple of inches taller. 'I could kill you,' he said. 'Maybe I will.'

Matthew made a grab for Robert's throat – and, in a blur of movement, Robert stepped aside and, before I knew it, had Matthew in an armlock.

'You will go,' Robert said. 'And you will not come back.'

'We will go,' said Gracie.

Robert released Matthew, and we watched as they got into their car and drove away.

'Thank you,' I said.

'It's all right,' Robert replied. 'Nothing.'

'You really are our protector,' I said. 'You shouldn't be working at this time.'

'Ah,' said Robert, already walking away into the trees. 'If you won't let me have that second man…'

'You can,' I said. 'You can bring your son.'

'Thank you,' called Robert, and then passed out of sight.

Chapter 48.

When he got up, I didn't tell Peter about Matthew and Gracie. I knew if I did, he wouldn't leave the house, and I very much needed to be on my own.

After Peter had had a few sips of tea and woken up a bit, I told I was thinking about weaning Mary. 'We will need to get some formula,' I said. 'They don't have any in the shop.'

'Can't they order some?' Peter asked.

'I thought you could take Jack to the supermarket,' I said. 'This morning.'

Peter looked at me a little suspiciously.

'This afternoon,' he said. 'I need to know you're all right.'

'I am,' I said. 'If you do it this morning, you can feed her her lunch.'

'I'll go this afternoon,' Peter said. I could tell there was no changing his mind.

Matthew and Gracie's visit made me realize I still hadn't looked at their copy of *Hidden Histories*. I went upstairs and quickly got dressed. The time on Peter's watch was well past nine.

Past nine, and Mr. Gatward hadn't come. He had always been so punctual that I found this a bit worrying.

Today I was planning to get him to talk me through what Lilian had written in her book. I was sure there would be some hint about how I should go on – something about fire.

I took *Hidden Histories* with me into the parlor and eagerly began to read.

The pink Post-It notes, when I went through them, were on the pages relating to the New House. I read what was written beside them. At first there was little I didn't already know. There was a bit more about Lilian's trip abroad. She had gone to Louvain, Paris, Venice, Rome. The ambassadors in those places had sent reports back about her. She met many of the most important alchemists of her time. The most interesting bit was this: 'One of these, a young French Catholic nobleman named Paul de Joyeuse, became her close companion. They journeyed together through France and Spain. Paul was a brilliant and handsome young man, almost exactly the same age as Elizabeth. They were rumoured to have been wedded in a secret ceremony, although no evidence of this has ever been found. It does seem likely, though, from reports by local government agents watching the Jonson family that Paul de Joyeuse paid Elizabeth a return visit some time in 1588.'

It was ten o'clock when I finished, and Mr. Gatward still hadn't arrived.

I phoned his number – and no-one answered.

'He must be on his way,' Peter said.

'Perhaps he's had a fall,' I said. 'I should go and see if he's all right.'

'I'll go,' said Peter.

I thought about this for a moment, but I realized I needed to deal with this myself. The visit from Matthew and Gracie had given me a real sense of urgency.

'I won't be long,' I said.

I ignored the speed limit, driving to the village. The day was bright and blustery. I jerked to a halt outside Mr. Gatward's cottage then went straight up to the door.

I knocked loudly, several times. I called to him through the letterbox. Defeated, I turned to look around.

The two boys were flying a kite on the common. It was very windy. The weather was turning. Their kite was high up. How much less exciting than really flying, I thought as I started towards them.

'Hello,' said a voice behind me. 'Can I help you?'

The door to the cottage next door to Mr. Gatward's was open. A man about my age with short red hair was standing in it.

'Good morning,' I said, and explained who I was and who I was looking for.

'Haven't seen him, I'm afraid.'

'Do you normally?' I asked. 'I think he might have had a fall.'

'He made a bit of a racket in the middle of the night,' said the man. 'Nothing since then.'

A woman appeared behind the man.

'I'm Sarah,' she said. 'And this is Teddy.' We shook hands. Her perfume – Poison, I think – was very strong. Teddy still wasn't cracking a smile.

'I saw your boy playing with Archie and Harold yesterday,' she said. 'I hope they weren't too rough.'

'Oh no,' I said, then told her I'd been expecting Mr. Gatward, and that I was worried something had happened to him.

'I'll get the key,' said Sarah. 'He doesn't usually lock it, though.'

She was again out in a moment.

Sarah led me round the side of the house and into Mr. Gatward's back garden. She unlocked the conservatory door and we went in the house. 'Andrew!' she shouted.

The books in the back room were in a real mess. We had to climb over them to get through.

'Oh dear,' said Sarah. 'This doesn't look good.'

'It was late, was it?' I asked. 'The disturbance you heard last night?'

'It woke me up,' Sarah said. 'We usually go to bed around half eleven. Oh, look.'

One room might have been an accident – they might just have toppled over – but the front room was the same.

'He must have been burgled,' said Sarah.

We went upstairs. His bedroom was empty – a wardrobe, a chest of drawers, a single bed, an alarm clock. A glass tumbler had been knocked over and was lying on the floor. The carpet didn't look damp. The brown duvet was pushed back, as if someone had just got out.

'That's scary,' said Sarah.

I picked the glass up and put it back on the bedside table. This room didn't have a book in it. At least he gave himself some time off, I thought. Then I remembered how Mr. Gatward always was at the desk in the attic – one book at a time. And hadn't he referred to Lilian's book as 'bedtime reading'?

I checked around but Lilian's book wasn't there.

A quick look into a neat little bathroom, and we were done.

'Shall we call the police?' Sarah asked.

'Let's just make sure,' I said. 'Mr. Gatward booked a cab for nine.'

'That'll be Mike,' Sarah said.

We locked up the back door and hurried round to Sarah's house again. I stood with her in their very low ceilinged country kitchen as she phoned Mike. She had his number up on a corkboard – a grubby card with a picture of a taxi. Anytime Cars, they were called.

'He says he came at nine but Andrew wasn't here,' said Sarah. 'He waited ten minutes, tried the shop, then left.'

'Thank you,' I said. I thought I might want to speak to Mike myself. 'Can I take his number?' I asked.

Sarah copied it down on the back of a brown envelope.

'Thanks,' I said, shoving it in my back pocket. 'I think you should call the police now. Let's hope it turns out all right.'

'I'm sure it will,' said Sarah, though she didn't look convinced.

As I drove back, I tried to think what might have happened to Mr. Gatward. I suspected Matthew and Gracie might have something to do with it – they were the only people I could think of who were obsessively interested in both our house and in the village historian. If they felt Midsummer's Eve was such an important time, perhaps they had been forced to take action. After all, Gracie had seen Mr. Gatward holding Lilian's book.

I remembered seeing something about this in *Hidden Histories* – just after the bit about Lilian and Paul de Joyeuse. It hadn't seemed important before I knew Mr. Gatward had gone missing.

A few raindrops fell onto the windscreen as I turned through the gates and down the drive. The shadows of the trees all around me felt darker than usual.

The other possibility I had to consider was that Mr. Gatward had just taken the book and made a run for it. You didn't know how anyone would react if they discovered the secret of eternal life. Maybe he'd disappeared, intending to set up his own experiment somewhere. That didn't seem very likely, however. He knew he'd be missed at nine o'clock sharp but hadn't made any excuse. One phonecall would have bought him a couple of days. And why would he make a mess of his own house?

Mr. Gatward had said he'd guard Lilian's book with his life. Maybe that's just what he was doing.

It was around eleven o'clock when I hurried back into the hall. Things were just as I'd left them. Peter handed Mary over to me, but I knew there was no point trying a feed – she wouldn't be hungry. Instead, I told Peter I needed to see if Mr. Gatward had left any clue to his disappearance – then I took Mary and the copy of *Hidden Histories* up into the attic library.

It didn't take me a second to find the passage about Lilian's notebook. Mr. Gatward was writing about the portrait in the parlor. He mentioned her beauty, then spoke of how intelligent she looked.

I could hear his voice on the page. I did hope he was safe.

Mr. Gatward ended his description by saying, 'If only she could open up her notebook to us, if only we could turn those long hidden pages, what secrets of Elizabeth's alchemical life might be revealed!'

I felt so stupid. I had *seen* what Mr. Gatward had longed for, and I hadn't been able to understand any of it.

Well, that wasn't exactly true. I had worked some things out. And Mr. Gatward was always insisting I was ahead of him, and that I understood more than I knew. But what did I understand? I understood that I had to open the door of the fire room, and in order to do that I needed a key shaped like a flame. If this was hidden behind a fire sign – Sagittarius – it was probably in the roof of the hall. Midsummer's Eve was important. I needed to get the door open before then. Perhaps I could persuade Peter to go now.

I headed downstairs, only to face another interruption. It was P.C. Holler an. There can't have been that much crime in the village, not that he was going to bother investigating.

'Mrs. Jonson,' said P.C. Hollerhan, then started to ask me a lot of questions about why I thought Mr. Gatward was missing. Without mentioning Lilian's book, I told P.C. Hollerhan most of the basics – my arrangement to see Mr. Gatward at nine.

'On a Saturday?' the policeman asked.

'He didn't want to stop his research,' I said. 'He was very excited by what he'd discovered.'

'And that was…?'

'Something about land acquisition in 1581,' I said.

P.C. Hollerhan looked at his boots, which weren't as shiny as they should have been.

'I'm impressed by your concern for Mr. Gatward, but I'm afraid we can't deal with this as missing persons until twenty-four hours have passed.'

'What if he's been kidnapped?' I blurted out.

'Why would anyone want to kidnap Mr. Gatward?' P.C. Hollerhan asked.

I thought about mentioning Matthew and Gracie, but I knew that would get me into trouble. P.C. Hollerhan wasn't going to risk losing out on his swims, and extras.

'I'm not sure,' I said. 'Perhaps it was a burglary that went wrong.'

'If Mr. Gatward hasn't turned up by the middle of tomorrow, we'll take it seriously. But I'm sure he'll be back. He probably just forgot your appointment.' P.C. Hollerhan smiled. 'I'm glad to see you've taken down the offending item.' It took me a moment to realize he meant the satellite dish.

'Well,' I said, 'we take the law quite seriously.'

'I'm glad to hear it,' P.C. Hollerhan replied.

And that was all the help we were going to get from him.

Chapter 49.

Peter finally loaded Jack into the car around one o'clock. As he was strapping himself in to the front seat, I noticed the wound on Jack's elbow – it was nearly healed.

'Look at that,' I said to Peter.

But Peter wouldn't admit it was unusual.

'You're a tough one, aren't you?' he said to Jack.

'Nobody heals that fast,' I said. But he just wouldn't listen.

'You sure you don't want me to take Mary, too?' Peter asked.

'No,' I said, 'if she's outside the house, she'll just get hungry.'

He seemed reluctant to leave. Jack was sitting in the passenger seat, fiddling with the volume on the radio.

I went back inside with Mary, listening to the sound of the engine driving off.

I looked up at the hall ceiling. Should I go up there now? What if Peter forgot something and came back? That would be the end of me. I could phone in an hour, check he was at the supermarket, then take half an hour to explore.

For the moment, I went into the kitchen and fetched the keys for the cellar and the Air door. Those were the only ones I needed, so I left the others behind – a bad mistake.

'You're going to enjoy this,' I said to Mary.

I took her down into the cellar, carefully locking the door after us. Even if Peter came back, he couldn't suddenly interrupt.

When I opened the Air door, the room looked its usual boring self.

I placed Mary on the floor, just outside the door, then stepped onto the bricks – which fell away beneath me, and rose above me, and expanded further and faster than before.

I was left hanging there as the room expanded until it was a vast sphere the size of… I don't know what. I'd never seen an open space that big – not even Tate Modern.

'Smaller,' I said, scared. 'Much, much smaller.'

Straight away the room began to contract. It went back to how it had been the first time.

'Smaller,' I said.

Obligingly, it made itself a space about the size of the upstairs living room.

'Thank you,' I said, and went to pick Mary up.

I knew she would fly with me, that she'd be able to fly all by herself, but I still felt terribly nervy when I first took her up into the air with me. What if she weighed me down? What if we fell together?

But it was as I'd hoped it would be – and before I knew it, Mary was floating along side me, giggling her head off. Her laughter echoed off the hard brick walls. She kicked her legs and waved her arms. This was the best fun ever. I knew she'd love it. She was so unbelievably loud – that can be the only explanation as to why I didn't hear them come in upstairs, didn't hear them try the cellar door.

I tried to stop. After five minutes I took Mary out of the room, which closed up behind us. But she started to bawl.

'Five minutes more,' I said. 'Just five.'

The room returned to the sensible size it had been. I kept hold of Mary. Ten feet off the ground. Laughing, laughing – both of us. Her hand in my hand, thank God.

That's how we were when the grille clanged back and Peter's head stuck up out of the hole. I saw the back of his head.

'Don't look round,' I shouted, starting to grab Mary. 'Don't look!'

But he did – he did.

The room didn't contract gradually as it had before. It snapped back to usual size before I'd even started to fall.

I had been lying flat, Mary out to my left.

As I started to fall – as Peter began to shout 'Mary!' – I started to pull Mary towards me.

I remember her face. The terror in her face. I don't think it was the falling scared her, I think it was the walls suddenly coming in so close.

We were only five feet off the floor, but it was a hard brick floor.

I yanked Mary by the arm, pulling her closer.

Peter was a growing blur to the side of what I could see.

Mary was almost on my chest.

I felt the floor smack against the back of my head. It was like being hit by cricket bat.

I felt my teeth crack.

I felt a heavy shape land on my chest.

I felt nothing more.

Chapter 50.

I woke up in a noisy, blue place that turned out to be the hospital.

A woman nearby was having a loud phone conversation.

'You're all right,' said Peter, who was by my side. 'You're going to be all right.'

'Mary?'

'She's okay.'

'Okay?' I tried to lift my head. I realized that it felt weird, soft.

'Don't move. Mary's here. Mary's fine.'

I tried to turn my head. Everything felt stiff. It wasn't painful, though. Mary was in a cot to my left side. She was in clothes I didn't recognize. Jack sat next to her. He smiled at me, then rushed across to give me a hug.

'I'm sorry, Mummy,' he said. 'It's my fault.'

'No, it's not,' I said. Quite sure it wasn't, whatever he meant.

'Be careful,' said Peter. 'She's a bit fragile. Watch out for the tubes.'

'I thought you were dead,' said Jack. 'I thought you'd died because of me.'

I held him for a few minutes as he cried.

'I'm okay,' I said. 'Daddy says I'm okay.'

'But you've got a broken skull,' said Jack.

'A what?' I said, trying to sit up – not a wise response.

'Calm down,' said Peter. 'Just rest for a minute.'

Jack kissed me on the forehead.

'Don't die,' he said.

'Tell me now,' I said to Peter.

'You landed on the back of your head. I've seen an x-ray. You were very lucky. You had severe concussion. Your skull broke in three places. They've pinned it back together.

I put my hands up to my head. The softness was a bandage of some sort. It felt foamy behind my head.

Then I panicked. I kicked my legs and lifted my bottom, just to make sure I wasn't paralyzed.

'Keep still,' said Peter, and grabbed my wrists to hold me down. 'You'll pull it out.'

There was a thin tube coming out of my left arm, up to a clear bag.

'What else?' I asked.

'There was some swelling,' Peter said. 'Some bleeding. They think that's going to be okay. They're going to keep an eye on it.'

'The brain's like a squishy in a box,' said Jack. 'It squishes around.'

'Your brain had quite a hard squish,' said Peter. 'It's badly bruised. They need to keep you under observation for a while.'

'Is Mary really all right?' I asked.

'She has a pulled elbow,' Peter said. 'That's all.'

'She has nurse elbow,' Jack said.

'Oh, my baby,' I said. 'Oh, I'm sorry.'

'It's fine,' said Peter. 'Shouldn't be any long lasting damage.'

'We have to get back to the house,' I said. 'If we go back to the house, there won't be any damage at all. The house will fix us.'

'You're not going anywhere,' said Peter.

'What day is it?' I asked, in a sudden panic.

'It's Sunday afternoon,' said Peter. 'About one o'clock. You've been out for almost twenty-four hours.'

I closed my eyes. It was Midsummer's Eve. Was I strong enough for what was ahead? I needed to get back to the house.

'You just appeared,' I said.

'Jack wanted to tell me about flying,' said Peter, 'as we drove to the supermarket.'

'I wanted to make Dad *believe*.'

'He gave so many details – like you telling him not to fly above a certain height. That rang true. But then he kept going on about it. I thought he needed to be taught a lesson – shown you weren't flying all round the house the moment we went out. Forget Mary's formula, I thought, we could get that any time.'

'What did you think you'd find, when you came back?'

'I don't know,' said Peter. 'I thought you'd be up to something secret. And when we arrived home, we couldn't find you. Then Jack heard Mary laughing in the cellar. When I tried the door, it was locked from the inside – and when I looked for the keys, they were gone. But the key to the chapel was still there. That's what gave me the idea of sneaking up on you. I thought I'd see if you'd really gone mad. Part of me was convinced you'd lost it. I took the key and told Jack to come with me. He helped me move the lectern. Then he fetched a torch, because I'd forgotten to bring one. You should have seen him. He was so excited at going down the tunnel.'

'It was spooky,' said Jack.

'But I insisted on going first. And the next thing I know, I'm poking my head out in the cellar, and I hear someone shout and look round to see who it is. And you know the rest.'

'I don't,' I said.

I was starting to feel very woozy, but I wanted to hear what Peter had to say, so I didn't mention it.

'You were out cold. Mary was screaming her head off. It was the two things together that made me really freak out. You'd never have slept through it normally, if she were making that racket. Jack stayed with you and held your hand. I carried Mary upstairs and called an ambulance.'

'We had a ride in the ambulance,' said Jack. 'With the lights on and everything.'

'They brought us here,' said Peter. 'Then they took you off, and there was just a lot of tests and waiting. When they kicked us out last night, they gave us the details of some B&Bs. We're staying in one now. It's not bad.'

Peter was putting a brave face on it, and I loved him for this.

'Father Trovato is here,' said Jack. 'But he didn't have breakfast at the breakfast place.'

'Why is he here?' I asked.

'I called him,' said Jack. 'You know, the last rites.'

'He was going to do that?'

Peter looked very awkward. He was against a background of blue curtains. Every now and then, I heard the woman's voice as she talked into her phone.

'He did it already,' he said. 'We weren't sure if you were going to make it. I asked him to. It was me.'

Only then did it hit me what I'd put them through.

'I'm sorry,' I said.

'It's okay,' said Peter. 'You're going to be fine. As soon as you're released, we can go back to the house and you can heal up there. Father Trovato says that's fine.'

'Where is he?' I asked.

'Just taking a walk,' said Peter. 'When you started to wake up, I asked him to go out. I didn't want him to be the first thing you saw. Jack can go and find him.'

'No,' I said. 'I want to be with you.'

All these things I'd gone through without even being awake. I closed my eyes. I thought I was going to be sick. Then I felt how hungry I was.

'I'm starving,' I said, my eyes still closed.

'We can get you something from the shop.'

'I got a magazine with a gun,' said Jack.

'I think I need to rest,' I said.

'That's good,' said Peter. 'We should call the doctor. They wanted to know when you woke up.'

Jack pressed the button for the nurse. I listened as Peter told her to tell the doctor I'd woken up.

I drifted off until I heard a voice saying my name. The doctor was a woman with long blonde hair tied back. She shone a light in my eyes and asked me if I could see with one eye shut, then the other.

'Very good,' she said. 'If you notice anything unusual, please tell someone straight away.'

I started to laugh, hysterically. Peter and Jack joined in, too.

The doctor looked a bit confused, then smiled.

'Private joke,' Peter managed to say.

Chapter 51.

I slept for an hour or so.

This time Father Trovato was there when I woke up.

'Hello,' I said.

'I'm glad you are alive,' he said. 'You must do what the doctors say.'

I was waiting for the sermon – dangerous experiments – but he didn't say anything else.

Mary was awake, too. Peter was sitting in the other visitor's chair, feeding her from a bottle.

I teared up. This wasn't how I'd planned to wean Mary.

I remembered something.

'Mr. Gatward?' I asked. 'Is he all right?'

'Mr. Gatward is still missing,' said Father Trovato. 'It is worrying. The police are now taking it seriously.

Just then a nurse came in with a little tub of pink syrup for me to drink.

'A little top-up,' she said.

I didn't want to drink it – I didn't want to be put to sleep again, but she watched me until I'd swallowed it.

'You've been on some strong stuff,' said Peter. 'I think it was morphine.'

'Oh, that's what it is,' I said. I had been wondering why things seemed so distant.

Father Trovato stood up. 'You must do what the doctors tell you,' he said.

I wasn't sorry to see him go, partly because I needed a pee.

They had put a catheter in, but I wanted them to take it out. I wanted to be able to move around.

Peter called the nurse back. She said that I had to stay where I was.

I used the catheter, which felt bizarre.

The pink syrup knocked me straight out.

The next time I woke up, Peter and Jack were holding my hands.

'Visiting time's over,' Peter said. 'We'll be back in the morning. Look after yourself.'

Jack gave me a kiss on the lips, so delicately. They get so rowdy at his age that you forget how gentle they can be.

'I love you, Mum,' he said.

Mary was on Peter's chest in the Babybjorn, but he bent down so I could stroke the side of her face.

'How's her arm?'

'Fine,' he said. 'She's on painkillers, too.'

'What time is it?' I asked.

'Eight o'clock,' Peter said. 'We'll be back at ten. Say goodbye to Mary.'

A nurse came round and pulled our curtains back. I was in a ward with five other women. It was the one in the bed next to me who had been on her phone. She was about twenty-five, mixed race, hair extensions and false nails. Seeing her, I felt like I was back in South London.

'Margie,' she said, introducing herself. 'Acute appendicitis.'

What was I going to say? Flying accident?

'I had a bang on the head,' I said.

'He seems nice enough,' said Margie. 'But when they're drunk…'

'No,' I said. 'I fell onto a brick floor.'

'I believe you,' Margie said. 'Thousands wouldn't.'

Her phone began to buzz and she took the call.

I wondered where my clothes were.

Carefully, I pulled myself into a sitting position. This made me feel very dizzy for a couple of minutes. When I'd recovered, I looked around me. There was a small bedside unit with a blue door on the front. I hooked my toe through the handle and tried to open it. Margie caught what I was doing and signalled that she'd help. I mouthed, 'Okay.'

I slid down from the bed, onto my feet. That didn't feel too bad. Bending down, though, seemed to bring a whole wave of blood into my head. I thought I was going to black out. But I braced myself until it passed. Then I pulled open the door. My clothes were there, neatly folded up. Luckily, my jeans were on top. I reached for them and managed to get them up onto the bed before the next lot of dizziness hit me.

The brown envelope with Mike the cab driver's number on it was still there, in the back pocket.

This made me think about Mr. Gatward again. Where was he? What was happening to him?

Margie said goodbye and flipped her phone shut. 'You should have waited,' she said. 'I would have helped you.'

'I bet you're not supposed to get out of bed, either.'

'No, I'm going to have a whole week, feet up on the sofa, watching TV,' Margie said. 'How great is that?'

'Can I borrow your phone?' I asked.

'No problem,' she said.

She was about to throw it but I said, 'Wait.'

Pulling the drip behind me, I was able to make it over to her bedside. I needed a bit of a rest when I got there, though. I felt very exposed in the hospital gown – and I was exposed, up the back.

'Bloody thing,' she said, passing me the phone. 'I hate it.'

I said, 'I'm going home.'

'You don't look very well,' she said. 'I think you should probably stay here.'

'I'm calling a taxi,' I said. 'Where are we? Where's the main entrance?'

'Lift's at the end of the corridor. Two floors down and it's right in front of you.'

I dialled the number, digit by digit, having to go back again and again as I got them wrong. My fingers felt terribly fumbly.

'Anytime cars. Mike speaking.'

'I need a car as soon as possible,' I said.

'I can't do you for half an hour,' said Mike. 'I'm on my way back from town.'

I told him where I was, and where I wanted to go.

'Heard they had an ambulance there today,' he said. 'Are you all right?'

'I'm okay,' I said. 'They've just discharged me.' Margie frowned at me, then ticked me off with one of her false nailed fingers.

'Okay,' Mike said. 'I'll turn round and be there in… twenty minutes.'

I gave the phone back to Margie. 'Thanks,' I said.

'Don't worry,' she said. 'I understand. I'll cover for you. You get away from him while you've got the chance.'

I swayed back over to my own bed, got the rest of my clothes out of the cabinet then set off down the ward.

'Where's the loo?' I asked Margie.

'First on the right,' she said.

The cubicle wasn't occupied.

First of all I had to remove needle from my arm. It was taped down in a few places.

I washed my hands as well as I could, then peeled the tape back and pulled the needle out. It bled for a while as I pushed down onto it with a wodge of loo paper.

I needed to tie a knot in the tube to stop the clear liquid coming out.

Someone knocked on the door.

'Busy,' I said.

Next was the catheter. I sat down on the loo and took a deep breath, then blew all the air out. It wasn't as painful as having Jack, but I wouldn't recommend it. I managed not to cry out.

Luckily, I'd been wearing a long sleeve top, so I was able to cover my arm.

It was only now that I looked in the mirror. There were bandages all over the top and back of my head.

'What are you doing?' I asked myself.

But I knew the answer.

I washed my face and then put on my clothes. I tried shoving the catheter into the tampon disposal box, but it wouldn't fit.

Instead, I balled it up inside the gown and stuck it under my top. I put the drip up my sleeve, as if it were still in me. Then I walked back to the bed as steadily as I could.

I put the gown and catheter in the cabinet and hid the drip stand behind the blue curtain.

'I'm off,' I said.

'If they ask,' said Margie, 'I'll say you went to the loo.'

Then I had a thought.

'Do you have any cigarettes?' I asked.

Her handbag was on her bedside cabinet, and from it she produced a soft pack and a lighter.

'Thanks,' I said.

'You're far better off without him,' said Margie. 'Go, girl.'

I made it to the lift and pressed the button. When it arrived, there was a doctor inside but he didn't even look at me.

The walk to the entrance seemed to go on forever. I held the cigarettes up in front of my chest, like an ID pass. But nobody challenged me, and I made it out into the cooler air of the carpark.

There was a smoker's shelter next to where a load of bikes could be locked up to frames. I couldn't think of the right word.

I went and stood there, then lit a cigarette. I had no idea what the time was, or how long it had taken me to get ready.

The nurse who had brought me the pink stuff came out of the front door and walked towards me. She was chatting to another young woman. I turned away, then realized the back of my head was probably more noticeable than the front. I turned to face them but with my eyes down, blowing out smoke.

They walked past.

Mike's cab arrived about five nervy minutes later.

He got out and was looking around when I walked slowly up to him.

'You don't look too well,' he said.

'I'll be fine once I get home,' I said.

Chapter 52.

The longer the journey took, the worse I felt. I sat in the back, falling asleep and waking up. The painkillers seemed to be wearing off.

When Mike turned a sharp corner, I banged my head against the window – which startled me.

The vision in my right eye had started to get blurry. When I closed the other eye, I couldn't see very much.

I had decided to go back alone, rather than try to take Mary with me. Too many times already I'd put her at risk. And I wished Peter could have come to help me, but he was looking after Jack. He couldn't have done anything anyway, apart from stop me doing what I needed to do. This was the end – this was between Lilian and me.

'Are you sure you're all right?' Mike asked, once or twice.

'It's worse that it looks,' I said. 'I'm just tired.'

But a huge headache had started, worse than the worst migraine.

I lost consciousness again.

When I woke up the last time, as we were passing the road into the village, I realized that I'd lost all vision in my right eye.

The cab's headlights lit up the trunks of the trees as we passed them. I looked behind us but couldn't see anything because the road was so dark.

The house was dark, too.

I hadn't even thought about how I was going to get in.

'Look,' I said to Mike, 'can I pay you tomorrow? I don't have any money.'

'Place looks empty,' he said. 'Are you sure someone's here?'

I was too fuzzy to think of excuses. 'Yes,' I said.

Even though I knew it would be locked, I went up to the front door.

Mike was watching me closely.

I put my hand on the knob and heard a click as the lock drew back. I turned the handle and the door opened.

'Okay,' said Mike. 'You can pay me another time.'

'I'm sorry,' I said.

The pain in my head was worse even than when I cracked it open. I was squinting, though I didn't want to.

I closed the door behind me and held onto the knob as I listened to Mike drive away.

Then I slumped to the floor for I don't know how long.

The next time I opened my eyes, I felt a little better. My vision was the same, but I didn't feel so dizzy.

I stood up and then lifted myself off the ground – flew.

Flying's a lot easier than walking, when you know how.

Silently, I glided up to the landing.

The house was very quiet and dark. I didn't want to turn any lights on.

I quickly checked each room, making sure the place was empty.

I knew I didn't have all that long. They would discover pretty quickly I had run away from the hospital. Margie's excuses wouldn't deceive them. She would probably tell them I'd called a cab.

Back in the hall, I began to examine the ceiling up close. I couldn't see anything, though. I needed a torch.

Once I'd fetched one from the kitchen, things were a little better. I scanned from one side to another. Where to start?

I decided to inspect each of the panels, one by one – the panels with carvings on.

My headache was slowly clearing.

I started in the far right hand corner.

About five minutes had passed, and I'd examined about that many panels, when I heard the smashing of glass.

I turned off the torch.

There were voices, coming from downstairs. A male voice and a female voice.

I flew down to the doorway into the passage and peeked through.

The tapestry curtains parted, and I saw Matthew step in, followed by Gracie. He was wearing a dark tracksuit but with three white lines up the sides of his legs and arms. Gracie was in something very tight, a black leotard perhaps. She had her hair tucked under a small peaked cap.

They headed straight towards me.

I panicked, flew straight up and almost hit my head again on the ceiling.

As they came into the room below me, I zipped across to the landing – towards the main bedroom.

Matthew went into the kitchen. 'All clear,' he said.

'Upstairs,' said Gracie.

In the bedroom, I thought about climbing onto the top of the four poster, before realising there was a much better place to hide.

I risked shining the torch on the wooden panelling, trying to remember where Mrs. Forster had shown us the secret catch.

Matthew and Gracie's footfalls had reached the top of the stairs.

I felt the priest's hole door open, jumped inside and – just as the bedroom door started to open – pulled it shut after me.

'Clear,' said Matthew.

For a moment, the light from his torch seeped through the gaps between the panels.

I heard the door to Jack's room open.

'No one in here,' said Gracie.

'Let me just check,' said Matthew. He went off for a few moments.

Gracie's torch came closer and closer. I heard her fingernails scratching against the wood.

'Where are you?' she asked.

I could hear her breathing, right up close.

Matthew came back.

'I've found the library,' he said, sounding incredibly excited. 'It's got everything – Mary the Hebrew, The Emerald Tablet. Everything.'

'I'm trying to find the priest's hole,' Gracie said.

'We'll have time for that later,' said Matthew. 'They say she'll be in hospital for weeks.'

The torch turned away.

'We'll have all the time in the world,' said Gracie.

'But we haven't got any time this evening,' Matthew said. 'It's… quarter to eleven. That gives us an hour and a quarter.'

'We don't need that long,' said Gracie. 'We don't need more than an hour.'

I heard the smack of a kiss.

'Look at this bed,' said Matthew.

'It seems a shame not to,' said Gracie.

I listened to the sounds they started to make. Gracie made loud groan almost as soon as Matthew began touching her.

'Oh God,' she moaned. 'That feels so good.'

I heard the whole thing – every last grunt.

Chapter 53.

'What's that?' Matthew asked, soon afterwards.

That's when I heard the sirens and the engines.

One of them banged out through the door, then hurried back in. 'It's the bloody police,' he said.

'What are they doing here?' Gracie asked.

There was a lot of scrabbling and swearing as they hurried to put their clothes back on.

They padded out of the room.

I heard the front door open and Peter call my name.

I needed to get out of the priest's hole. I didn't have long.

With the torch on, I found the catch – it was a lot easier to see on the inside.

I hauled myself out of the priest's hole and shut it behind me.

Loud footsteps were coming up the stairs. Boots.

I couldn't think of anywhere better to hide, so I flew up on top of the four-poster. It was quite high up, leaving only a small gap between the top of the bed and the ceiling.

Someone rushed in and turned on the light.

'Where are you?' said Peter, his voice quite desperate.

He went through into Jack's room and the bathroom. Then he paused for a moment.

He found the priest's hole much quicker than I had. But, of course, it was empty.

'Damn,' he said.

'Found anyone?' I heard P.C. Hollerhan say.

'No,' said Jack.

'Sarge!' shouted a voice from the hall. 'Sarge, there's a broken window here!'

Everyone rushed off to see.

Then I heard more shouting and a woman shrieking, 'Get off me! Get off me!'

I moved to be closer to the door.

Gracie and Matthew were brought into the hall, where the lights were all on.

'Where were they?'

'Up the chimney, Sarge. They were trying to climb out, I think.'

'Good work. Have you searched the rest of the house?'

'Still looking, Sarge.'

'Carry on.'

'We were just trying to help,' said Gracie. 'We heard something was wrong.'

'What did you hear?' asked the voice of the Sergeant.

'We'd like to speak to our lawyer,' said Matthew. 'Before we say anything else.'

'Fine,' said the Sergeant. 'Hollerhan, read them their rights and then put them in the car.'

'Yes, sir.'

I wanted to shout out, 'Search their house!' But I kept quiet.

The police continued their search.

I went back inside the priest's hole and waited there.

I heard them searching our house from top to bottom. They shouted their progress. 'No one in the cellar!'

'Have you tried every room?'

'There's one we can't get into. No key. The others are a bit bloody weird.'

After about half an hour, during which people came and went from the room, once with a dog that sniffed around and barked, the house started to go quiet. Cars were driving away.

I heard something. It was Peter was calling my name again.

I hovered down and risked opening the hatch.

'I know you're here,' Peter shouted. He was in the hall. 'I know you're hiding somewhere.' I crossed to the door. 'I hope you're right.' I peered through the crack where the door opened.' I hope you know what you're doing.' I could see Peter's outline, standing in the middle of the hall. 'I love you.'

He went out and locked the door behind him.

Chapter 54.

I waited until all the cars had driven away. I waited until the house had been quiet for a good ten minutes.

I'd flown down from above the bed and was about to walk into the hall when I heard a loud creak. It seemed they'd left at least one person behind.

I learned who it was soon enough. P.C. Hollerhan's voice echoed loudly through the hall as he said, 'Hello, Sir Douglas. It's Richard. I'm in the house.' He explained to the person at the other end what had happened. 'Yes, I know,' he said. 'She may be away for several days. They've left me to watch over the place. I thought you might like to come and keep me company.' There was a very short pause. 'All right, I'll expect you in ten.'

The footsteps seemed to come closer as P.C. Hollerhan walked across the landing.

Again, I waited – back in the priest's hole but with the hatch open – I waited until I heard the footsteps creaking away, and then, a few minutes later, the unmistakable sound echoing up through the house: the click of our kettle as it reached the boil.

Sir Douglas Longbone must have raced over. He arrived just in time for a nice hot cup of tea. P.C. Hollerhan met him at the door.

'Thank you for this,' said Longbone.

They went into the kitchen.

I flew out into the hall. A light was spilling sideways out of the kitchen but the hall was still in darkness.

I landed on the opposite side, near the door to the dining room. From here I thought I would be just about invisible.

P.C. Hollerhan had made himself very much at home. Not only had he brewed up but also he'd also cracked open a new pack of digestives.

The policeman and the M.P. sat down and started to chat. They seemed quite settled, which was both good and bad for me. I could explore the hall roof but if I made a sound or they suddenly decided to go on patrol, I would splat straight down onto the floor. The area up by the ceiling was very dark, though – as long as he didn't turn the lights on, I was probably okay.

But the darkness worked against me in another way. I could hardly see anything. My hands ran over smooth panels and intricate carvings that I wished I'd had more time, and light, to appreciate. I searched for catches around the edges. I tried pushing the panels to see if they lifted up. Nothing worked.

Even if it had been broad daylight, and I'd been able to make as much noise as I wanted, it would have taken me a couple of hours to check the whole ceiling out. Without all that, I needed to do something else – I needed to read the code of the house. I pictured what I'd seen, lying on the floor directly below me – the constellation of Sagittarius, picked out in wood. And then, on top of this, I thought of the image of the centaur with the bow and arrow from the tapestry. Where was the most important point? What did your eye look at without you even thinking about it?

The answer seemed to be in the question. It was Sagittarius's eye – it was the fieriest part of him, glinting as he took steady aim.

I crossed to what I thought was roughly the right area. P.C. Hollerhan gave a laugh from the kitchen. There were no carvings where I was looking. The panels were all equally smooth.

That's what I thought, but I was wrong. Because one, when I ran my fingers across it, felt as rough as sandpaper. It didn't look any different, but in this feeble light that mean almost nothing.

I tried pushing the panel up. That didn't work. I tried feeling around the edges. No catch there. What else was there I could do?

I remembered the bricks in the Air room. How they'd expanded and contracted when I'd asked them. Perhaps I'd come to the end of the line. Perhaps I just needed to ask Lilian directly what to do?

'Lilian, please,' I whispered as quietly as I could. 'I don't know what to do.'

Nothing happened.

'If you want me to help, you'll have to help me.'

I thought this was it. I was faint, exhausted. I'd ruined my family. I didn't know enough to solve these puzzles on my own.

'I don't know what you want me to do,' I said. 'I give up. I don't want any more of your secrets. I don't care about them. I just want my family back to how it was.'

Perhaps those were the magic words.

I felt something happen to the air around me. It began to stir. It began to swirl. The vast room was silent but it was far from still.

Chapter 55.

I moved back onto the landing – a safer place – and watched as the air in the room began to twirl round and round. There wasn't very much dust, but what there was began to glitter as a swaying column of twisting air began to climb up from the floor.

P.C. Hollerhan and Longbone would see – surely – they would come out to find out what was happening. But they didn't seem to have moved, and now the whirling tornado – that's what it seemed to be – had almost reached the roof of the hall.

This wasn't a beautiful sight, like the ice statue of Lilian, and it wasn't terrifying, like the whirlpool drowning Jack. This was something else. This was a practical vision. It was telling me what I needed to know, right now. It was showing me what to do. And because of that, it was the most fantastic, welcome sight I could have seen.

The top of the air-spout reached the rough panel. It began to intensify, narrowing down and spinning faster and faster against the plain surface.

I couldn't tell what was happening until the whole panel, in one instant, seemed to collapse.

The tornado spilled dark particles out to either side.

I flew forwards and reached out to grab some of them. They were hard, sharp. I felt them scratching against my fingers.

The panel hadn't been sandpaper at all, it had been made of very tightly packed sand! This now spilled out on all sides of the spout, like melted chocolate from a chocolate fountain. It would surely rain down on the floor, alerting Hollerhan and Longbone.

I should have become used to marvellous things. The sand never touched the ground. The sand never reached the ground. Instead, it was sucked into the tornado and carried back up the twisting column. It went into the oblong hole where the sand panel had been, and then it was gone. Pretty soon the tornado was gone, too. It didn't die out, just seemed to pop sideways in all directions when its work was done.

As quickly as I could, I felt my way across to the dark hole that had been left behind.

When I stuck my hand inside, into the dark, the space looked strangely familiar. It was just like the priest's hole, but raised so high off the floor no one could ever have reached it. Not unless they could fly. I managed to heave myself inside, keeping a few inches above the tops of the ceiling panels, though I felt fairly certain they would support me.

I couldn't see anything. I had to turn my torch on, if only for a second. The double click resounded through the hall. The light flashed on and off, but I saw something I knew I'd been expecting – another phoenix.

Below me, I heard Hollerhan and Longbone hurry out into the hall. 'What did you hear?' Hollerhan asked.

'Some kind of scratching,' said Longbone.

Hollerhan turned his powerful torch on and scanned the room with its beam. I moved back, away from the hole. The light flashed past, then returned.

'I can't remember that gap,' said Hollerhan.

'Was it there when you arrived?' Longbone asked.

'I don't think so,' said Hollerhan. 'You'd think I would've noticed it.'

I heard their footsteps getting slightly louder as they came and stood directly below me. The beam of Hollerhan's torch got brighter as it lit up the gap. I forced myself further and further back into the corner.

Then I heard the two of them coming up the stairs. 'What's directly above here?' Longbone said. 'It must be part of the attic, mustn't it?'

The torch shone in from a new, sideways angle.

Then I heard Hollerhan and Longbone going into the upstairs living room and then clanking up the spiral staircase.

Now was my chance.

I grabbed hold of the phoenix and tugged.

In an instant, the panel floor had dropped away from beneath me and I was falling down.

I had tumbled ten feet at least before I realized I was being dragged down by the weight of the bird. It was so heavy it must have been solid brass.

Fear shot through me – the memory of the awful crack as my head hit the stone floor of the Air room.

I slowed us up, and we landed right in the middle of the hall – totally exposed to view.

A glance upwards showed me the four wooden panels that had opened like a trap door – they were now folding back into place, leaving only the one hole.

The phoenix was attached to a piece of hard, dark wood. It had a heavy handle, dangling from its beak. And suddenly I realized what it was – a doorknocker – and then just as suddenly I realized which door I must knock on.

Chapter 56.

When I went into the kitchen, the keys weren't hanging from the brass hook.

I thought Peter had taken them away, or one of the policemen, but then I saw all of them lined up in a row on the table, in between the mugs and the biscuit crumbs: the original front door key, Mrs. Forster's keys, Robert Mew's, Father Trovato's keys to the chapel. They were like the story so far, and if I took two of the four away P.C. Hollerhan was bound to notice. They were probably coming back right now. Their mugs were only half empty.

A glance at the clock showed me it was seven minutes to midnight. I didn't have a choice – this might be my only chance to see what was behind the Fire door – I grabbed the two bunches I needed.

I heard heavy footsteps coming down the spiral staircase as I swooped across to the cellar door. I had the keys scrunched tight, to try and stop them from jingling, but the door-knocker came loose and gave a loud clack-clack.

'Hey,' shouted one of the men. 'What was that?'

P.C. Hollerhan and Longbone started to run.

I couldn't stop the cellar key from grinding as it turned in the lock. The door came open as Hollerhan banged out onto the landing, Longbone's lighter footsteps doing their best to keep up.

I pulled the door open and swung it shut behind me. I dropped the keys once before getting the right one into the lock. I was making so much noise. I tried to grab the keys dangling down but I lost my grip on the door-knocker.

Never in my life have I heard anything as loud as that brass bird sliding down the stairs. It went fast but bumped and rapped sharply every time it hit a step. No way Hollerhan and Longbone wouldn't know exactly where I was now.

I locked the door just before the handle started to turn.

'Mrs. Jonson,' Hollerhan said. 'Mrs. Jonson.'

I ran down the stairs and began unlocking doors – still careful to do them in order: Earth, Water and then all three Air doors.

All the time, Hollerhan and Longbone, speaking over one another, were trying to persuade me to open up.

In each room, the stars were clearly visible – glowing like points of flame.

I heard Hollerhan get on his radio and inform someone that I'd been found and that I'd locked myself in the cellar.

'You're not very well, Mrs. Jonson,' said Longbone. 'You've had a very serious bump on the head. You don't know what you're doing.'

I did.

'They'll be back in five,' said Hollerhan.

'Break the door down,' said Longbone. 'Do it now.'

I heard Hollerhan take a few steps back. I wasn't about to let them stop me, though. The final piece of the puzzle was about to be set in place.

As Hollerhan slammed against the cellar door, I heaved the brass phoenix up and eased its wooden backing onto the Fire door. The wooden panel fitted perfectly into the wooden hole. It had been hundreds of years since these two pieces of wood had touched, but they reunited as snugly as if the carpenter had just laid them aside. I felt the weight being taken off my hands as the door healed itself up.

There was a splintering sound from upstairs. Hollerhan would be through, probably next time he slammed his shoulder against the door.

I also heard a lot of sirens approaching the house. They couldn't all have arrived so quickly unless they'd been hiding nearby. Hollerhan would soon have help breaking the door down.

I wished I'd had time to think about everything that had brought me to this point. I wish I could say I appreciated what I was about to do. But I didn't – I just grabbed hold of that brass phoenix and hammered like hell.

I knew something very strange was happening the moment the first clap sounded. At first I thought it was the space behind the door, echoing. But then I realized that Hollerhan and Longbone had gone completely silent. No further smash on the cellar door came.

Ever since I started on this, I'd been looking for keys – keys to open doors. I hadn't realized that there was no key for the final door – or no key that I could get hold of. This door could never be opened from the outside. Instead, I just needed to find the right way to knock on the door and ask to come in. Because the key – I heard it now – scraping into the lock – this key was on the *inside*.

The door began to open and I saw the fierce light starting to glow around its edges.

I stepped back and the door swung all the way open, showing me the way into the Fire room.

PART FOUR

Chapter 57.

It was vast, so big I couldn't see the edges. Was this the hell that Father Trovato had promised me if I kept on with my dangerous experiments? The flames that licked the doorframe and blazed up inside the first feet of the room gave off no heat. Like the water, like the air, they didn't touch me. Surely, if it was hell and I'd been lured here by some devil, I would be starting to burn?

I looked into the blazing room, knowing that I would have to step inside – knowing that once again I would have to put my whole trust in Lilian and in the house.

In the very heart of the fire – I could see it clearly – there stood a figure. I thought for one mad moment that it must be my husband, and that he must be burning to death. But the figure stood there, quite calm, quite still, completely unaffected by the furnace-like blaze surrounding them. I could see them through the open doorway that, for some reason, wasn't burning. The fire did not come that far.

Perhaps I should be clearer. This was not a figure made of flames. This was the outline of a figure where the bright flames left a darker gap. And the gap went all the way to the bricks of the far wall. It was almost as if there were a person-shaped tunnel running through the whole infernal room, from front to back. And there was nothing there to burn, I was sure. This room of our house was totally empty. It was the air itself that seemed to be on fire.

The light from the burning room scorched into the backs of my eyes. How long before the fire spread? How long before our beautiful old wooden dreamhouse was razed to the ground? But still I didn't turn and run. Still I stared into the light.

I knew this figure. With every passing second, I was surer of that.

I knew her, and I knew she had a message for me.

As I watched, she put her left hand out and beckoned me towards her. Of course she was left-handed! – I'd known that all along.

It was madness but I felt certain that she wouldn't let me come to harm. It was a while since I had started to trust her. But did I trust her enough to trust her with my life?

Of course I hesitated. Nobody wants want to die like this. Nobody wants to be burnt alive. What I was about to do was against all reason.

Reason, though, was something I had given up on or which had given up on me quite some time before.

I nodded to her.

The figure beckoned me again.

I moved forwards, to the edge of the flames.

I could see her better now. My eyes seemed to be getting used to the bright light. Was that a smile I could make out among the flames?

With a final thought for my husband, my children, I stepped over the threshold – into the heart of the burning room.

Lilian was there, her shape, and we met in the middle of the inferno. It wasn't hell, though – I had been right about that.

As she turned around to face me, I saw that she was smiling. Then she looked down, and I saw she had something in her hands. It was her book. I saw the ribbon dangling down beneath it. But the ribbon wasn't red and the book wasn't leather, they were both shining molten gold.

Lilian held the book out to me, offering it. Even though I had been protected from the burning all around me, I felt sure I would feel a terrible heat from the book. But I took it in my hands, and as her fiery fingers through brushed against mine I did feel something like a heat – a fire running me. I was being given courage for what was to come. This was Lilian's gift to me. I looked into Lilian's golden eyes and thanked her, again and again. More than anything, I wanted her to speak. I had been pursuing her so intensely, and if she didn't speak now I would never know what her voice sounded like.

Silently, Lilian put her hand on mine and gently got me to open the book where the page was marked.

Chapter 58.

I saw that the ribbon was now knotted with four knots.

This brought a lump to my throat – I had solved the puzzle of each of the doors. Lilian was saying she was pleased with me.

I looked into the bright pages of the book, where on the left hand page I could see a picture picked out in dark lines. It was something I recognized immediately – it was a plan of the house – but it was more than that. What it looked like most of all was an architect's plan, all thin ghostly lines showing where floors meet walls and walls meet ceilings. But even though it was on the page, it was in three dimensions – you could see through and around it. On the bottom of the right hand page was something that was slightly harder to recognize, because I'd never seen it from the outside – the underground chapel. I should have known that straight away because linking the two were a couple of parallel lines that sloped gently down the page. This was the tunnel.

I looked up at Lilian, hoping now would be the moment she spoke. Perhaps she was about to explain how her experiment had worked. All she did, though, was place her thin finger on the picture. She wanted me to look at the cellar, at the space exactly in the middle of all the doors. I saw that Lilian herself was now standing there and that I was beside her and that what was around us – in reality, if you can call it that – was no longer the house but the picture of the house in her book.

Lilian motioned for me to move away from her. I still had the book in my hands, the action in front of me repeating itself on the page. I was holding it but I could see us in it.

As I backed away towards the stairs, I watched Lilian turn once in each direction – Earth, Water, Air, Fire. She then raised her hands and pointed towards the sky that, through the empty roof, I could see was bright with all the constellations on the tapestry. There, too, were the sun and moon. It wasn't a real sky. It was everything in the sky all at once.

Finally, Lilian brought her hands down and put them on her belly. And I could see inside her, too – I could see that there was a small child in her womb. It was far too tiny for me to be able to tell whether it was a boy or a girl, but I knew it must be a boy. That was the only explanation – another thing had to be in balance, as well as all these other forces – female and male.

I glanced quickly down at the book and saw that I'd been right, for there were now two figures standing where Lilian had been, and one of them was her and the other was a fine-looking young man. They looked like Adam and Eve. Was this her visitor, Paul de Joyeuse? Was he the baby's father? And was the child conceived simply as an accident or as part of their whole experiment? There wasn't time to think anything through. My head was spinning from all I'd seen already.

When I looked back at Lilian, I was seeing her from the outside. But that wasn't such a good word any more. Inside and outside were combining. In a huge rush, out from all four doors, vast jets of force hit Lilian, one after the other.

The first, from the Earth door, was like the root of a tree, but growing faster than any root had ever done. The one from the Water door was like the jet from the pipe in the Water room but a thousand times stronger. From the Air door came a tornado that twisted faster than the eye could see and snaked slowly from side to side. Finally, from the Fire room, a jet of flame shot out so terrifyingly vast that I thought it would simply blow Lilian away. But she stood in the middle, absorbing all these incredible forces into her body. Then, down from every one of the stars, came beams of pure light. And these she accepted too. This went on for one minute, another. But what did time mean any more?

Lilian made a gesture with her hand, very definite, and everything stopped all at once, everything disappeared. Everything obeyed her.

Lilian was alone, floating in dark space. I looked at the book. The page was blank. Then the stars came out above Lilian, the earth appeared beneath her feet.

She looked at me, and smiled, and nodded. I saw her lips move. 'Goodbye,' she said.

And then, where before I'd seen the baby in her womb, I saw another shape begin to glow – I immediately recognized it as an egg. And the egg cracked, and out from the crack emerged the bright golden winged shape of a phoenix. It stretched its wings for a moment, shook itself loose. Then it took flight.

And with this Lilian's body exploded like the big bang, but it didn't scatter. It stopped in space, in every direction.

I held the book up to protect my eyes, and on the page which had been empty a moment before I saw the house forming again, being created from the inside. This time, though, the lines it was made out of were sparkling gold – every one of them.

I closed the book.

I understood. Lilian had shown me what had happened the first time – when her alchemy had succeeded, and she had become both gold and immortal – immortal because gold. And she had gone into the fabric of the house and become one with it. She was it's glistering essence, in every board and brick and panel.

Then it was over. I was back in the fire room, which was still burning brightly. But I was on my own. The small gold book, with its dangling ribbon, still glowing molten hot, was cool in my hands.

I felt deeply upset that I would never see Lilian again. I started to weep – and my tears, when they hit the cover of the book, hissed and turned to steam.

Chapter 59.

I walked out of the Fire room, expecting something to happen. I thought the book might instantly become hot and I would be horribly burnt by it.

And something did happen – the flames of the room came out with me. It was as if I was coated in them, aflame but not aflame. I was like a match head, but I wasn't being burnt away.

I walked over to the grille and to the bottom of the stairs. I climbed the stairs and unlocked the cellar door.

The way was blocked. P.C. Hollerhan was standing there.

'All right, then,' I said, 'arrest me.' But he was motionless. He looked alive and dead at the same time. He had a watch on his wrist. I looked at it, and saw that it was exactly midnight and that the second hand was trembling but not moving.

I pushed against him, and he fell backwards to the floor. Longbone was there a few paces away, speaking into the mobile phone. There were some other figures, too, over by the door.

I walked across to them, leaving a trail of flames behind me.

More policemen were there, frozen whilst running in. Mike the taxi driver was with them. And behind came Jack, sprinting, and next to him Peter carrying Mary. Bringing up the rear, I was glad to see, was Mr. Gatward.

The front door was open. I could see more figures out there, all statue-like.

I thought for one instant that something moved, but it must have been the light from the flames glinting against a shiny surface.

I was standing in the middle of the hall. My flames lit up the ceiling with its carvings, they reflected up off the shiny parquet.

And pretty soon my halo of flames began to do their job – they spread out – all Mrs. Forster's compulsive waxing and polishing and making flammable which she never understood, now it was finally paying off. The wood caught fire. The fire spread from where I stood at the centre of the circle. Soon it was climbing the walls, attacking the panels. But the people in the room weren't harmed – I knew they wouldn't be.

I stood between Jack and Peter and Mary, watching the flames caressing but not touching them.

I walked into the dining room. I wanted to see the painting that had started everything. Lilian was there, just as usual – pale, beautiful – but her hands were empty. She had given her spell book to me. I held it in my hands.

Around me, this room caught fire, too. The table and chairs, the curtains and all the other paintings. The Canaletto. The Constable. I stayed just as cool while the house began to burn.

I don't know how long it lasted, the whole thing – it could have been an hour, it could have been a day – I wandered through the house from top to bottom, sometimes walking, sometimes floating, saying goodbye to it, carrying the fire which it needed.

I visited the library in the attic, running my hands along the spines of the books and watching them burst into flame. I lay down on the four-poster bed until it was a cage of dripping brightness. I wrapped myself in the tapestry curtains, turning the heavens into an inferno. I saw Jack's Gameboy become a black, bubbling, smoking mess. I saw Mary's muslins smouldering in a pile on the chest of drawers. And then I pushed past P.C. Hollerhan – completely unhurt by what was going on around him – and went back down into the cellar. Because the walls were stone, there were fewer flames here. The ceiling was burning away though, collapsing to either side, and I could see up one storey, then two. And as the wood burnt, what had been sealed up within it for all those hundreds of years came running out, cascading down the walls, dripping from the roofs – the gold – the gold that both was and wasn't Lilian – Lilian's phoenix-body – what Lilian had turned herself into in that one alchemical moment.

I stood on the grille and watched as snakes of molten gold flowed down the sloping floor and into the hole, down into the sloping tunnel. They ran quickly, these white hot rivers, as if more than gravity was pulling them, as if they knew where they wanted to go. Thin trickles down the stone walls met other trickles as they were tugged down into the hole.

The doors to each of the four rooms had burned away, and the rooms stood empty, their vast forces exhausted.

When I raised my eyes, I saw that the frame of the house was almost completely gone. I could see the shape of P.C. Hollerhan, motionless, ridiculous, outlined against the night sky.

The final few dribbles of gold ran down beneath my feet.

I held up my hand and watched the last of the flames retreating along my arm until all that was left was a gentle blue halo around my fingers, holding Lilian's golden book, and then with a flourish of scarlet this went out, too.

The book suddenly felt heavier, very real.

I climbed the stone stairs.

The beautiful house was gone – all that it had left behind was ash, black ash.

I touched my head. I'd completely forgotten my injury. My head felt different. I didn't feel like the dark was coming down on me any more.

As I stepped over the threshold and out of the house, the night wind hit my face and ruffled my hair. There was a clap of thunder and torrential rain began to fall. Beneath my feet, the gravel was already running with muddy water. Time had started again, I could feel it.

Behind me, I could hear my name being called by voices I didn't recognize and voices I did. Around me were police cars parked with their blue lights flashing and all their doors wide open.

I walked a little way along into the trees and then turned around to look at what I knew would be, had to be there – the new house, perfect in every detail, just as it had been before and yet, in a way that only I would ever understand, completely different.

Chapter 60.

Making sure I could find the place again easily, I buried the golden book at the foot of one of the tall trees. It was the biggest tree – the tree directly in front of the door of the house.

I marked the place with a stone then, just to be sure, paced out the distance to the front door. Twenty steps.

Then I walked inside and gave everyone there the fright of their lives.

Jack rushed to give me a hug. Peter put his free arm around me, careful not to crush Mary.

'Yes,' I said, in answer to their repeated question. 'I'm fine.'

'How?' said P.C. Hollerhan, completely bemused. 'But you were down in the cellar.'

'No,' I said. 'I wasn't.'

Hollerhan wanted to arrest me, I think, but he didn't know quite what for.

'I was the one kept prisoner,' said Mr. Gatward.

'But you're all right?' I asked.

'A bit shaken up,' he said. 'And pretty sore all over. But I'm fine, generally.'

'Oh, thank goodness,' I said.

'However, I think I need to speak to this man,' said Mr. Gatward, and went quickly over to the Police Sergeant.

Longbone – who was hanging around in the shadows – left pretty fast, after I asked what he was doing there in our house.

After Mr. Gatward had spoken to him, the Police Sergeant went to have a quiet word with P.C. Hollerhan – who was then escorted to one of the cars. They put him in the back.

Peter wanted to return to the hospital as quickly as he could, but I insisted on doing one thing.

I went into the kitchen and turned both taps on.

They worked.

I washed my hands, and they got wet. I washed my face.

I filled a glass with water and drank it down in one. It tasted wonderfully normal.

They kept me in hospital under observation for twenty-four hours.

My next brain scan showed a recovery that one consultant called 'remarkable' and the other 'miraculous'. They asked if they could do some more tests, perhaps write a paper about me. I said I'd be happy to do anything that helped medical science, but that I doubted they would learn much from me that was useful.

Mary's arm was put in a little sling that annoyed her. We were told to be very careful how we picked her up.

The woman from Social Services came to see me in the morning. She said she understood this had been an accident – she had read the paramedics' reports – but that we were having too many accidents for her liking. If we had any more, she would have to start looking for what she called 'contributory factors'. So, we wouldn't be able to keep any alcohol in the house for a while.

On the Tuesday, Peter drove us back in the car. The rainstorm had cleared itself away. The weather was sunny again. Peter hadn't asked me what had happened. He was waiting for me to bring it all out. Jack wasn't so coy.

'Why did you really escape from the hospital? Were they sticking too many needles into you?'

'Something like that,' I said.

They told me their side of the story. After he dropped me off at the house, Mike had immediately called the police. He was sure I was in no fit state to have been discharged from the hospital. The police checked with the hospital, who were alarmed that I'd escaped. They contacted Peter, to see if he had helped me. Peter insisted that they take him and the children straight to the house. He told them there were hiding places only he knew about. So, Jack got another ride with lights on and sirens wailing.

When they couldn't find me, they started to search the woods – though all they found there was Robert Mew.

So, P.C. Hollerhan was left in the house to hide out and listen for any sound of me – which was when he called Longbone and put the kettle on. Everyone else drove only as far as the main road, where they waited anxiously for word of me. After a while, Mr. Gatward appeared, walking along the road. But there wasn't time to find out what had happened to him. This was just when Hollerhan radioed for backup, because he'd found me and had me cornered, or so he claimed – and the whole convoy raced off in a long line up the drive.

'We'd heard you'd locked yourself in the cellar,' said Peter. 'And then you appeared out of nowhere.'

'Not quite nowhere,' I said.

I was so glad to get back to the house. This time, walking in to that familiar warm wood-polish smell, was the first time it really felt like home.

It also felt different – more fragile, less permanent. I knew that its powers had gone. But this would have to be proved by our regained appetites, and the fact that our little cuts and scrapes took the usual time to heal. We had to hope there wouldn't be anything worse than small injuries, just as we'd always hoped.

Jack was really disappointed he wasn't able to fly, like before.

'What if I never do it again?' he said.

'At least you did do it,' I said. 'That's more than most people.'
He was glum for a while then said, 'I probably just need to practice more.'
'No jumping off anything high,' I said. 'Promise?'
'I promise,' he said.

I'd completely forgotten that I'd arranged for Miriam Shoulder the Health Visitor to come on the Tuesday – hardly surprising. She'd been before we were back, not found us, and put a card through the door. I called straight away and rearranged her visit for the following morning.

Peter wanted me to go to bed but all I really wanted to do was sit on the bench in the garden and watch the day pass – the sundial on the back wall of the house, telling its always-slightly-wrong time.
Jack had decided he wanted to be goalkeeper, so he had Peter taking endless penalties against the hedge.
I watched them all afternoon, feeding Mary whenever she got hungry, as happy as I've ever been before or since.
It was all so normal – just a family being together in their garden – but I appreciated it so much more than I would have done, in other circumstances. In its own way, this was as magical as anything – Jack diving to left and right, wanting to know I'd seen. Mary looking happily around at everything she could see. Peter encouraging Jack, checking on me and Mary, just generally being Dad. This was the everyday alchemy we made ourselves. Time turned into gold.

Chapter 61.

I let Peter give Mary the last feed of the day, formula from a bottle. It grieved me to see Mary sucking so happily on that plastic thing which wasn't me. Weaning certainly hadn't gone quite as planned – but Peter was beaming down at her as she hungrily sucked. I knew I probably should have let him do this a bit earlier. What was I going to do with the freed up time? Read a book?

When the children were in bed, I took Peter with me down to the cellar. The door didn't seem splintered at all from P.C. Hollerhan's attack. It must have been the last thing in the house to repair itself. The window that Matthew and Gracie smashed had stayed broken – perhaps because a Policeman had been standing keeping an eye on it the whole time. With Peter beside me, I opened the doors onto the four dull empty rooms that were now there – even the Water room was dry boxy brickwork, like the Air room used to be. The phoenix brass knocker was on the door to the fire room, shining brightly. Peter looked surprised to see it there, but said nothing – not for a while.

Step by step, I took him through what I had seen and then what I had done. We went up into the house, and I showed him exactly where I had walked when they had all been stood still as statues. Then he followed me into the cellar again. I described the rain of gold that had run around me and into the tunnel. I told him everything I could remember of what I'd seen and what I'd felt. I didn't want there to be any more secrets between us.

Peter kept very quiet all the way through. Sometimes he would ask me a question, usually about what I thought it all meant.

I had to explain to him several things Mr. Gatward had explained to me – for example, about what a retort was, and how it collected all the gold together when the house burnt down and the gold flowed out of the base material.

'When the first house burnt down, in 1580, that wasn't an accident. It was an experiment – a trial run. It didn't work, but maybe it gave them an idea how to go on. Remember about the base material, that's important.'

'I see,' said Peter, he was still staring at the door knocker.

'What is it?' I said.

'This,' Peter said, walking over and lifting the clapper. I thought for a moment he was going to knock, and wake the children, or something else. 'You know I said I remembered seeing another phoenix – being lifted up to look at it? And you thought it was a carving on the ceiling. Well, I think this is it. I think what my great uncle showed me was this.'

'But that's impossible,' I said.

'Only if you don't believe people can fly,' Peter replied with a smile. 'I've always told myself that what I remembered was being lifted up. Because what it felt like was something completely different – something much more scary. What I actually remember is flying high up to the ceiling, with an old man holding me tightly by the hand and telling me not to be afraid. But I think the whole thing was so terrifying that I never wanted to think about it, or anything I couldn't explain, ever again.'

'You flew!' I said, and gave him the biggest hug.

'I did, and long time before the rest of you lot,' he said.

'I have a little more to say,' I said. 'But it may not top your major revelation.'

'Come on,' said Peter. 'I'm sure it will.'

Taking Peter by the hand, I led him until we were both standing in front of Lilian's portrait. When I returned to the house, I'd half expected to find her changed. Particularly, I thought her book would have disappeared, and she would be holding something else – perhaps a phoenix. But there she still was, exactly the same.

'The base material was Lilian,' I said. 'Lilian's body. She changed into the gold, just like the bread transforms into Jesus's body in the Mass. That's what the other alchemists didn't understand. That was her secret.'

'Not any more,' said Peter.

'It's very scientific and religious,' I said. 'As well as being very magical.'

When I'd finished he just looked at me and said, 'You're pretty magical yourself, you know.'

'No,' I said, 'I'm just ordinary.'

We stood there for a while, then he took me in his arms. I felt his warmth and love all around me, in a way it hadn't been since the affair. He was completely back with me.

'You don't regret making the decision you made?' Peter asked. 'We could all have lived a hundred years.'

'Being nagged to death by Father Trovato,' I said. I thought about it for a moment. 'Of course, it would be good to know we'd all be healthy. But, no. I want to grow old with you – and that involves the growing old bit.'

'Here?' he asked. 'In the house? Not back in London.'

'Of course here,' I said. 'I want us to live here the rest of our lives.'

'Fine,' said Peter. 'But the local M.P. hates us and Father Trovato's still going to nag us.'

'I think that when he realizes this house has changed, he might start to lose interest in us. We won't be such special cases anymore.'

'Because, you know, I'm happy to go back to the flat, if you ever want to change your mind.'

'I won't,' I said. 'This is the place for us.'

‘And money?’ Peter said. ‘It’s going to be… interesting.’
‘We’ll scrape through, somehow,’ I said. ‘We always have.’
‘Maybe we’ll have to sell the lawnmower,’ Peter said.

Chapter 62.

As before, Miriam Shoulder came. She was very concerned about the pulled elbow, but I assured her the doctors had said Mary would make a full recovery – just so long as we were careful with her. She was also disappointed that when she came to weigh her Mary had only put on a couple of ounces.

'I'm sure that'll change,' I said. 'She's been eating almost non-stop the last couple of days. Like she's making up for lost time.'

'That's good,' the Health Visitor said. 'But I'd still like to keep an eye on her.'

We arranged for her to come back the following Tuesday. I could hardly blame her for wanting to keep an eye on Mary.

But what if Mary had gone for weeks and then months without putting on an ounce?

The first thing I'd have had to do in keeping us all alive forever would have been ban people like her from coming in the house.

What a palaver it would have been. And how terrible for Mary to be stuck at one stage. All the Jonsons before us must have sent their children away, so they could grow up.

I'd been very worried about Mr. Gatward, and wasn't going to feel happy until I'd seen him for myself, and heard his own account of what had happened to him.

So, Peter arranged for Mr. Gatward to come around the next morning.

It had taken him a bit longer to recover from his ordeal than it had me. He told Peter and me from the start what had happened to him. Because we knew it wasn't going to be suitable, we'd sent Jack off to play in the garden. He was excited because I'd arranged for him to go and play with Archie and Harold, later that afternoon.

'I wasn't really asleep, more like on and off dozing, when I heard someone coming up the stairs. Of course, it was very frightening. But when I saw it was Gracie Dearie, I was strangely reassured. You see, I'd never taken that pair all that seriously. Everything about them was so exaggerated as to be comic. Well, they certainly weren't comic this time. They were dressed head to toe in black. And they were very clear what they were after – Lilian's book and its contents. They asked me where it was. Politely at first. I wouldn't tell them. I'd given you my promise that I would guard it with my life, so when it wasn't in my jacket pocket I put it in a little hiding place I have under a rickety floorboard. That's where I keep my pension money. They searched around and made a bit of a mess. When they couldn't find it, they started to become a very threatening. I tried to escape at one point, and they put a sock in my mouth to stop me shouting. Luckily, it was a clean one. And they tied my hands behind my back. Tightly. I knew they'd planned this because they had brought some rope along specially. It was bright yellow.'

Mr. Gatward seemed to be quite enjoying telling his story. I was glad to see he wasn't too traumatized.

'Well, when it became clear they weren't going to find the book, and I wasn't going to tell them, they decided to take me somewhere they could be a bit more persuasive. By this time they had changed completely. Matthew had twisted my arm behind my back. We'd had a bit of a struggle in the bedroom, knocking this and that over. They hustled me into the back of their very quiet car. It was about three o'clock – no one about. Once we got to their house, they handcuffed me to their bed. They've got quite a little torture chamber there, I can tell you. I'm a bit embarrassed to say, really. It wasn't too uncomfortable for the first hour, then I felt the blood cutting off from my arms. In the end they agreed just to have me cuffed by the one leg.'

'Still,' I said, 'poor you.'

‘They kept asking me where the book was, but I simply wouldn’t tell them. Gracie was the worst. She threatened to do all sorts of things to me. She even went and fetched a whole lot of knives and peelers and things from the kitchen. And Matthew started discussing the most painful way to harm me. They got quite, what should I say? – this excited them, sexually. They disappeared several times. And, when they came back, Matthew seemed to have calmed down. He kept saying they really didn’t want to hurt me at all. He said they would let me go as soon as I told them where to find the book. Gracie got very angry with him, at one point. She said time was running out. Apparently they believed they were coming up to the one moment in the year when the alchemical experiment might work – Midsummer’s Eve – the turning point of the whole year. Sunday turning into Monday, too. I could appreciate the logic of that, even when handcuffed to a bed. They knew a lot more about alchemy than they’d let on before. I’m pretty sure they had been touring round, looking for historical references to alchemists. When they came across *Hidden Histories*, I’d put enough into it that they felt they were onto something. They didn’t want anyone else to find out about it, either. That’s why they bought up all the remaining copies. They didn’t send them out to their friends at all. They had them in a big pile in the corner of their bedroom.’

No wonder they’d been able to lend me a copy.

‘They asked me lots of specific questions about what I’d found in the archives. They promised me eternal life if I would just help them achieve it themselves. I think this was their thing – as they didn’t have any material worries, they’d decided to live as long as they possibly could. This led them to believe a lot of very strange things.’

I remembered their odd conversation with Peter and me, when they came round for dinner – how they’d wanted to talk about the soul and what it was worth. I told Mr. Gatward what they’d said, and also that they’d told us they couldn’t have children.

'No other kind of immortality, you see. And anyone looking for eternal life is going to end up interested in alchemy sooner or later. Gracie kept on at me, but I could see although she was holding a knife to my throat she didn't really want to cut me. Then Matthew went back to the house and had another search, more thorough this time. They kept me all Saturday. When they heard the ambulance coming to your house, they got very excited. And when they found out you'd gone off to hospital, and Peter and the children had gone with you, they could hardly contain themselves. They started planning their break-in there and then, despite not having the book. It was bizarre – as if I was no longer in the room. They thought just by being in the house when Midsummer's Eve began, they would learn something – the big secret. Apparently, when the police caught them, they managed to speak to P.C. Hollerhan alone. He hurried straight round to release me, but told me not to tell anyone about it. Then he just left me there, outside the door, and drove off again. So, of course, I made my way to your house. I wasn't going to let him get away with that. Not likely. They're all as bad as each other, that bunch.'

'Well, we're very glad you didn't come to any harm,' I said. 'And I've got some good news for you. I've changed my mind about Lilian's grave. I would like to open it up.'

'Oh, thank you,' said Mr. Gatward. 'Thank you. Though I swear, I was never going to mention it ever again.'

He seemed anxious.

'I'm afraid I have a terrible confession for you. I don't know how to say this.'

'I think I already know,' I said.

'When I finally got back home and opened up my hidey-hole…' Mr. Gatward looked at his hands that were clenched together.

'It was gone, wasn't it?' I said.

'I swear,' said Mr. Gatward, 'Matthew and Gracie don't have it. They'd never be able to keep quiet.'

'I know they don't,' I said. 'I have it – but it's a little different now. Come on.'

Peter called Jack in from the garden where he'd been playing. I carried Mary and we all trooped out the front door.

I paced out the distance – twenty steps – to the biggest tree, and lifted the rock and began to dig. I dug deeper than I remembered burying the golden book.

'I don't understand,' I said.

Because the book wasn't there.

Chapter 63.

'Excuse me,' said a familiar voice. It was Robert Mew. 'If I could just speak to you in private for a moment.'

He meant me, so I went with him a little way further into the wood – just far enough that the others couldn't see or hear.

'I thought it best to keep it safe,' he said, and held Lilian's book out to me. I didn't take it yet, though.

I looked into his brown eyes.

'I don't understand,' I said. 'How did you know where it was?'

Robert's whole stance had changed. He stood up very straight, looking noble. 'Father Trovato and his kind aren't the only ones who have watched over this house. We have watched, too, but for different reasons. We have watched from the woods.'

'Who is we?' I asked.

'That I can't tell you,' he said. 'Friends. Protectors.'

'I still don't understand how you found the book.'

'When I heard about your accident, I decided to keep a twenty-four hour watch on the house. I knew people would try to get in, if it was empty. I saw you return. I saw Matthew and Gracie breaking in through the back window. I don't know how many times I've caught them trespassing before.'

'Why didn't you do anything?' I said. 'I could've done with a bit of help.'

'You had all the help you needed,' said Robert with a smile. 'If I had interfered, it wouldn't have happened the way it did – the way it *had* to happen. We knew you would outwit all of them, church and state, scholars and servants, politicians and sorcerers. Powers spiritual and temporal, powers emotional and intellectual, powers obedient and disobedient – you defeated them, every one. You were pure in heart. We had faith in you. When I saw the house burning down, I knew it had been accomplished, after all these years. I watched with great joy, thinking of those who had gone before me.'

'You saw it?' I asked.

'We all saw it,' said Robert, and the trees around him seemed to murmur their agreement.

I had to ask him the question. 'Why me?'

'Because you hadn't known of it. Because you didn't desire it. And because you could reject it.'

'But I'm just nobody.'

He smiled and said, 'The right person doesn't always know that's who they are. Perhaps, in some cases, that's exactly why they are the right person.'

And now he placed Lilian's book in my hands. 'Let's go and return this to its rightful owner, shall we?'

Chapter 64.

Everyone was amazed to see the book and how it had been transformed. Jack wanted to hold it, and I let him.

'It's so heavy,' he said.

'It's pure gold,' said Robert.

Mr. Gatward when he held it was hardly less boyish in his delight than Jack. He pointed out the ribbon with its added knot. 'Four now,' he said. 'That must be significant.'

'It is,' I said. 'I'll tell you one day.'

Peter held the book for less time than the others. 'What can I say?' he said, looking at me. 'I'm sorry. I'm sorry I didn't believe you. I do now. I believe.'

Even Mary wanted to get her free, non-sling hand on the bright shining thing. It was too heavy for her to hold, but I sat down with her at the foot of the tall tree and she had it in her lap until she got tired of it and became fascinated with my left thumb – this took about a minute.

Meanwhile, I asked Jack to go and fetch the key to the chapel, and not to forget a couple of torches.

When he brought all this back, we all walked though the trees until we came to the door into the earth.

Peter undid the lock and we made our way down the steps and then gathered around the grille.

'Are you sure you want Mary down there?' Peter asked.

'Are there dead people?' Jack asked.

'Yes,' I said. 'Very dead. But they're nothing to be afraid of. And, yes, I do want Mary down there.'

I passed Mary to Peter and he went carefully down. The rest of us followed, one by one – descending the ladder, crawling the short length of tunnel, passing through the round door and coming out into the low crypt. William and the others were there, exactly as they had been. Still awaiting the resurrection.

'Wow,' said Jack, more fascinated than scared. 'Real skeletons.' Death was something he was going to have to learn about. I'd made quite certain of that.

We gathered around Lilian's grave. 'I don't know whether we'll be able to manage,' said Mr. Gatward. 'It looks very heavy.'

'I think you'll be surprised,' said Robert. 'It's just a lid.'

I reread the words of the Latin inscription – 'And the life of the world to come'.

'How do you know?' Mr. Gatward said. 'You haven't lifted it off before, have you?'

'No,' said Robert. 'Of course not. But I have reliable information about how it was made.' He wouldn't say anything more than that.

We placed the torches on the dusty floor, where they could shine some light across what we were about to do.

Peter gave Mary back to me. She seemed quite unconcerned about where she was.

Together, Peter, Robert, Mr. Gatward and Jack, one on each corner, slid their fingers around the edges of the long, flat coffin shape. Together, they lifted the lid (just as Robert had said) off what looked like a patch of dull black sand.

'Nothing there,' said Mr. Gatward.

But something was glinting in the torchlight – just one tiny sparkle of gold. And the black sand looked very familiar to me.

'It's for you to do this,' said Robert to me.

I bent down, Mary held to my chest, put the book down on the floor and brushed away at the golden speck.

It grew and grew as the black sand was swept aside – swept aside so easily – and in a moment it was recognizable as a fingernail and then, with a little more brushing, a long slender finger.

'Help me,' I said.

The others knelt down, and together, with our bare hands, we dug away and dug away until there she lay – Lilian, exactly as in the portrait in the house, exactly as when she was a snow-statue, exactly as she had stood before me in the fire. The detail of the gold was exquisite. Every tiny thread of her lace was there in filigree.

I looked back up the tunnel, to where the molten gold had flowed down out of the house, flowed into the cast that had been awaiting it all that time.

'So beautiful,' said Robert. 'I hadn't expected her to be quite so beautiful.'

'How much is it worth?' Jack asked.

'It's priceless,' said Mr. Gatward. 'Utterly priceless.' Then he apologised and started to cry one final time.

'It doesn't matter what it's worth,' said Peter. 'We're never going to sell it. We're never even going to tell anyone it's here.'

'No,' I said, and glanced at Mr. Gatward, who nodded his agreement. This part of the glory wasn't going to be made public. He had plenty enough of the stuff as it was.

Lilian lay there, exactly as in the picture, all but for one thing. I passed Mary over to Peter, then picked up the golden book from the floor, brushed the dust off.

Very carefully, I slid it until it was held securely in Lilian's hands. Back where it belonged.

'Bravo,' said Mr. Gatward.

'It is done,' said Robert Mew.

'Goodbye,' I said.

Then I stood up and took Mary again. I felt Peter put his arm around me and gently pull Jack so he was snug against us. I ran my fingers through Jack's hair, like I love to, and he let me do it. He was looking down at the golden lady shining in her dark grave. Mary was looking at her, too.

I wondered if Mary would ever dream of this, this vision, when she grew up.

The End

Afterword

Hello,

thank you so much for reading *Lilian's Spell Book*. I know reading time is hard to find, and to read a whole novel is - these twittering days - an act of generosity. So, thank you.

The main thing I'd like to do in this Afterword is ask your opinion: What did you think about the story? What do you think could be better about the story?

I'll tell you why - I'm a writer who has been lucky enough to have published a few books. But *Lilian's Spell Book* has (to put it bluntly) not gone down well with publishers.

Yes, I'm talking rejection emails.

Almost without exception, they've said that they like the first half, but that the second half isn't *scary* enough.

They also weren't sure about all the breastfeeding and mothering stuff that goes on.

So, what they wanted - I think - was a more straightforwardly terrifying ghost story, with a more straightforwardly likeable heroine.

But that wasn't ever what I was trying to write. *Lilian's Spell Book* is supposed to be about wonder and about comfort rather than about shocks and worse shocks. *Lilian's Spell Book* is supposed to be about about the everyday meeting the miraculous and finding they have quite a lot in common.

I was happy with the book when I finished it. (It's the only book of mine that's made me start crying, when I finished the last sentence.)

And so first of all I tried it out on Wattpad, where it went down pretty well. And now I've put it up here on Kindle, rather than stuck it in the bottom drawer, to see how it is received. To see if there are readers - such as you - who like it, as it is. To see if you agree with what the publishers said, when they said no.

Which means that what I'd like to ask you is, do you agree? Did you want more scares? Did you find the second half of the book disappointing? Did the build-up to the end feel underwhelming? Did Jeane, Peter, Jack, or any of the characters annoy you?

In essence: What would you have me change about *Lilian's Spell Book*, if I was going to rewrite it?

Be honest.

I'll take every comment seriously.

Best wishes,

Toby Litt
London
July 2017

t.litt@bbk.ac.uk

Other books by Toby Litt –

Adventures in Capitalism
Beatniks
Corpsing
deadkidsongs
Exhibitionism
Finding Myself
Ghost Story
HOSPITAL
I play the drums in a band called okay
Journey into Space
King Death
Life-Like (Seagull Books)
Notes for a Young Gentleman (Seagull Books)

Mutants: Selected Essays (Seagull Books)
Wrestliana (Galley Beggar Press)

https://tobylitt.wordpress.com/books

27042256R00155

Printed in Great Britain
by Amazon

Other books by Toby Litt –

Adventures in Capitalism
Beatniks
Corpsing
deadkidsongs
Exhibitionism
Finding Myself
Ghost Story
HOSPITAL
I play the drums in a band called okay
Journey into Space
King Death
Life-Like (Seagull Books)
Notes for a Young Gentleman (Seagull Books)

Mutants: Selected Essays (Seagull Books)
Wrestliana (Galley Beggar Press)

https://tobylitt.wordpress.com/books

27042256R00155

Printed in Great Britain
by Amazon